PRINCES OF ASH

ROYALS OF FORSYTH U

ANGEL LAWSON

SAMANTHA RUE

FOREWORD

Queens!

If you're still here, I feel like this forward note may not be necessary, but just in case you've stumbled in here from social media or a well-intentioned recommendation from a friend, and you're not sure what's going on, here's a catch up.

As always, we ask friends and family to by pass this series unless dark romance is your jam. If it *IS* your jam, we can talk about it but not over Thanksgiving dinner. If it *isn't* then we need to pretend like this doesn't exist. Discussing contractual relationships, forced breeding, c*ck warming, and everything else in these books isn't something we want to talk about while passing the gravy boat.

You know where we do love to talk about it? In our Facebook group Monarch's, our discord, both where you can also find book-specific spoiler groups and chats. Make sure you join!

For the rest of you degenerates, Princes of Ash follows similar content warnings.

- Breeding/Preg Kink
- Non/dub
- Insertion/inflation

- Medical kink
- Edging/withholding
- C*ck-Warming
- A little bit of guy-on-guy stuff
- Mentions of miscarriage/Preg complications
- Bullying/Hazing
- Forced bed-sharing
- Murder, Maiming, Non-sexy whipping, Stalking
- Also, if you're sensitive to issues surrounding torture, prior non-graphic childhood sexual abuse, drug addiction and use, degradation, public humiliation/exposure, physical abuse/punishment, and misogyny, you may want to sit this one out.

I think that about covers it. We're so excited to share this one with you. Just a reminder to check out our exclusive Royals of Forsyth U website for bonus content and links to our store!

—Samgel

FORSYTH READING ORDER TIMELINE

BeForsyth

-The Backstory

The Lords Prologue from the heroes point-of-view.

Where to get it: Included in Lady of Forsyth, available on Amazon

Lords Era

-Lords of Pain

-Lords of Wrath

-Lords of Mercy

-Saint Nick

Lavinia and Nick during Christmas

Where to get it: Bonus content on forsythu.com

Dukes Era

-Dukes of Ruin

-Archduke of Mayhem

Aprils Fools bonus content from Archie's point-of-view

Where to get it: Bonus content on forsythu.com

-Dukes of Madness

-Dukes of Peril

-Madam of Mayhem
Aprils Fools bonus content of Mrs. Crane and the Dukes
Where to get it: Bonus content on forsythu.com

Princes Era

-Princes of Chaos
-Princes of Ash
-Princes of Legacy (2024)
-Lady of Forsyth
Bonus HEA content written for the Lords Kickstarter.
Where to get it: Available on Amazon

Barons Era

-Lords Outtake
Bonus HEA content.
Where to get it: Included in Lady of Forsyth, available on Amazon

HOUSE COMPASS

NORTH SIDE
COUNTS
ΚΝΤ
EX-KING: LIONEL LUCIA (SUPER DEAD)
CHILDREN: LAVINIA (DAUGHTER)
PLEDGES: CASH "MONEY" MALLIS (DEALER)
WEST END
DUKES
ΔΚΣ
KING: SY PERILINI
DUKES: NICK BRUIN, REMY MADDOX
QUEEN/DUCHESS: LAVINIA LUCIA
ARCHDUKE: CAT.
DKS MEMBERS: BALLSACK, KAZ
STAFF: MAMA B (MANAGER)
PAULY (MEDIC/TRAINER)
CUTSLUTS: LAURA
FAMILY: TIMOTHY MADDOX (DAD),
SARAH (MOM), MANNY PERILINI (DAD),
DAVIS BRUIN (DAD)
LOCATIONS:
THE GYM (TRAINING/FIGHTS)
ROYAL INK (OLD ROYAL GAZETTE)
BARONS
ΒΡΝ
KING: TIMOTHY MADDOX
BARONESS: REGINA THORN
CHILDREN: REMY MADDOX (SON)
OLD BLOODLINE:
CLIVE KAYES (EX-KING, DEAD)
WHITAKER KAYES (GRANDSON)
LOCATIONS: CRYPT
EAST END
PRINCES
ΨΝΖ
KING: RUFUS ASHBY
PRINCES: PACE ASHBY,
LAGAN "LEX" ASHBY,
WICKER ASHBY/KAYES
PRINCESS: VERITY SINCLAIRE
STAFF: STELLA (HANDMAIDEN)
DANNER (SERVANT)
THAD (SECURITY)
FAMILY: EFFIE (BIRD)
CHARLIE (BASTION SECURITY IT)
MIRANDA & MICHAEL (DEAD)
PNZ MEMBERS: TOMMY WRIGHT,
RORY LIVINGSTON,
JASON HARKER (DEAD)
LOCATIONS:
THE PURPLE PALACE
THE GENTLEMEN'S CHAMBER (STRIP CLUB)
GOLDEN ROW (FRAT HOUSING)
BASTION SECURITY
THE GILDED ROSE
SOUTH SIDE
LORDS
ΛΔΖ
KING: KILLIAN PAYNE
LORDS: TRISTIAN MERCER,
DIMITRI RATHBONE
QUEEN/LADY: STORY AUSTIN
FAMILY: DANIEL PAYNE (DAD/FORMER KING/DEAD AF)
STAFF: AUGUSTINE (MANAGER)
MRS. CRANE (MADAM/BMF)
LOCATIONS: THE AVENUE (MAIN INNER CITY STRIP)

1

Verity

I FEEL like an intruder in my own skin as I'm led up the aisle.

It can't be the dress, all white and sparkling, because it's not so unlike the one I wore my first night in this palace. It's older, though. That much I'm sure of. The touch of age has softened and yellowed the lace that frames my décolletage. Its long silk train drags behind me as if this were a wedding, and why shouldn't it be? After all, three men dressed in their finest tuxedos are waiting for me across the room, their heads bowed as each step brings me closer to them.

We're unequivocally bound.

And then there's the man pressing my hand firmly into the crook of his arm, guiding me with pride.

Rufus Ashby.

My father.

He could be the source of this feeling—this sense that I don't belong in my own body—but I know he's not. It's not the weight of the tiara on my head, nor the PNZ members' gazes following me as they stand erect, hands clasped behind their backs. It's not the cloying scent of roses. It's not even the sight of the throne ahead, the memory of all the pain I've felt in this room, and the dread that there's more to come.

I know exactly what it is.

It's the strange, tainted life growing inside me.

I'd block it all out if I could—the stares of the frat. The weight of Ashby's hand pushing on my knuckles. The curling sensation of sickness as I grow closer to the three men standing before the throne. However, I can't possibly do it. I feel every gaze, every inch that brings me closer to them, as acutely as a thousand pinpricks. Or worse, the feel of them inside of me, making deposit after deposit of sperm.

It isn't until we reach them—Wicker, Lex, and Pace—that I notice how stony their faces are. Perfectly composed, heads lowered in a supplication that I know can't be real.

I fight the urge to spit in their faces.

Ashby turns as soon as we reach them, spinning me to face the room. A sea of somber faces stares back at us, and I swallow back bile at the memory of what they all did to me, not even a whole week ago. They all wait for him to speak, which isn't a surprise. Ashby does seem to love having a captive audience, and he's the King. If anyone thinks the coronation might be about the Princess, then they're proven wrong the instant he steps forward.

"To create is to reign," he eventually speaks, lifting his chin.

"To create is to reign," the men in the room repeat.

Candlelight sharpens Ashby's features, and I shudder to think how much of them might be reflected in my own. He's my father. As absurd as the statement was, I have no doubt in its truth.

"That's the saying, isn't it?" His blue eyes scan the room, lips curved into a satisfied grin. "I've dreamed of this day. I won't deny it. To stand here with my blood," he lifts a hand, gesturing to me, "and my spirit," he turns to gesture to the Princes next. "And, most importantly, the heir they've made for me. For *us*."

I stand, frozen with disgust, as he places a palm on my belly, not even meeting my gaze.

He actually appears misty-eyed as he addresses the room. "Today, *I* reign. Not with fear. Not with influence. But with blood and spirit. This isn't just a coronation—it's a promise met. Renewal and hope, but most of all, legacy."

He turns to me next, finally looking into my eyes as he takes my hand.

"Do you understand the covenants of your position?" he asks.

Despite how my belly roils, I nod.

He traps me in his stare, wide and fervent. "You will nourish the child that blossoms within your womb."

I nod. "As you command."

"You will serve it before anyone else—even your Princes."

"Even their King?" The words escape my mouth without my bidding, but I can't find it in myself to regret them, even as his stare turns hard and flinty.

"I assure you," he says, voice low, "your King and the well-being of his heir are as one."

His heir. I hear the word loud and clear, and that roiling sickness in my belly hardens to stone. I realize that's what I'll need to endure what's coming.

Hatred.

"I understand," I say, hiding my doubt. It's been less than forty-eight hours since the Valentine's party—since I revealed the pregnancy—and I haven't been able to worry about much beyond this moment. My coronation.

"Danner," Ashby says, holding my stare. "I'll anoint our Princess as her Princes recite her covenants."

My eyes scan the room furtively, preparing myself for whatever new hell they're going to put me through. That's the difference between the girl I used to be and the woman I am now. It fascinates me as Danner steps from the shadows, passing a vial to Ashby. It's familiar, similar to the one that was filled with the blood taken from me on the throne. Similar, but not the same. This one has a red ruby on the stopper.

"You shall be anointed with the blood of the greatest princess of them all. *My* princess. The mother of my first heir, Michael." He unstops the vial, tipping it into his open hand. "May her blood bless your womb as you carry on my greatest gift: my name."

I see now how womanhood is gained in Forsyth. It's not about age or biology or losing one's virginity.

It's about pain.

And not just pain, I ponder as Ashby coats his palm in the ancient, red-tinged oil, but the constant endurance of it. It's about a man pushing his slick palm to my belly and knowing to anticipate a sting.

"My sons," he says, "declare the covenants."

"The Princess shall conduct herself with the grace of a mother," comes Lex's voice, flat and toneless.

Pace's mechanical words come next. "The Princess shall not profane her body to the influence of other men."

There's a tense pause, and then Wicker's cutting hiss. "The Princess shall thank her Princes for their successful seed."

Lex adds, "The Princess shall be protected at all times."

On and on it goes, their resentful voices ringing out behind me. Ashby's palm remains pressed to my belly as we listen, but there's no warmth in his touch. My eyes scan the room—Pace says something about the Princess' required examinations—and the muscles in my shoulders tighten.

I already know these covenants. Stella and I read them back-to-front before I even decided to reveal the pregnancy. And we didn't just read—we weeded through them to find the sinister subtext underneath.

A Princess' time in the palace is split into two markable phases: attempting to make a baby and actually carrying one. Plenty of Princesses have walked these palace halls, but she doesn't reign until she's created life.

Despite searching for hours, we couldn't find anything about a third phase of a Princess after she gives birth.

"The Princess shall agree to these covenants wholly, explicitly, and without reservation." Wicker is the one who finishes, and when Ashby raises an expectant brow, I do just as they ask.

Wholly, explicitly, and without reservation. "I swear to abide by the covenants."

If he's surprised by the easy agreement, Ashby doesn't show it. He merely pulls his hand back, revealing a sickening sight. The belly of my dress is stained with a red handprint. "She reigns," he says, turning to smirk at the crowd.

"She reigns," they all echo, in varying degrees of boredom and excitement.

Leaning down, he pitches his voice lower, something only meant for me to hear. "This next part is one of my favorites."

My muscles coil tight.

"I've given a lot of Princesses away on their coronation nights, but this one is special," he says louder for the others to hear. "This is more than just symbolic. Tonight, I'm giving my daughter to my sons." Behind him, a PNZ member makes a low, amused snort, and Ashby tenses. Twisting his head, he searches for the source, snapping, "You will not pervert this glorious event."

It's a struggle to restrain my own scoff.

Every part of being a Princess is rooted in perversion.

Composing himself, Ashby finally steps aside, gesturing to the space in front of me. "Come."

Behind me, I hear their resistant, shuffling feet, and then they're standing before me, the three of them—Wicker to my right, Lex to my left, and Pace in the middle. My Princes are perfectly poised, hands clasped behind their backs, gazes locked to some vague point over my shoulders. Some of Pace's small, loose twists fall in his eyes, but he doesn't flick them away. The muscle at the base of Wicker's jaw is knotted tight, his blue eyes somehow both empty and full of fire. And Lex might as well be a mannequin, stiff and motionless, his pale jaw dotted with an uncharacteristic shadow of stubble. Bitter hate boils under the surface.

Good.

"Kneel for her," Ashby suddenly commands.

Before I can snap my shocked gaze to his, Wicker loses his straight posture, exploding, "Fuck that!"

Ashby's nostrils flare wide. "Kneel!"

Wicker glares at his father, and for a moment, it's as if they're blood, too. The swirling fury in their blue eyes, blonde hair gleaming in the candlelight, expressions obstinate and full of rage. But some part of me knows they couldn't ever be truly related. Ashby is too bright—too icy and stiff and obvious. Wicker glares back at him, not with ice but with a knife's gleaming edge. There's a wicked violence in his nature that's too Baron'esque to be anything else, and when Ashby glances at Lex, I see that darkness transform into bitter defeat.

The part where Wicker grits his teeth and slowly drops to his knees?

That's the part Ashby has instilled in him. Defeated compliance.

And I savor it.

The sight of Wicker below me, the sound of Lex and Pace following suit, the way they all look lined up in front of me in submission...

It's as close to feeling intoxicated as I can get.

"Welcome your creation," Ashby growls.

Pace moves first, pitching forward to press his mouth to the red handprint on my stomach. He lingers for only the barest moment, and from my vantage, I can see the flutter of his dark eyelashes before he pulls back, lips painted red. Wicker is next, that knot at the back of his jaw pulsing as he springs forward. I flinch as much at the hatred in his eyes as I do the sudden movement, the hard bounce of his lips barely brushing my dress. If he notices, he doesn't care, immediately snapping back to his position.

He looks almost as sick as I feel.

Lex is last to bend toward me, slowly, but when he does, his amber eyes rise to mine, trapping me in their fiery heat as his lips press to my belly. His stare is the most complicated. There's menace, yes. Anger. Distrust. The threat of violence. But there's also a strange sense of connection, as if this hatred and hurt we feel has bound us in some inevitable way.

There's an unmistakable tension that grows in the room at my lack of reaction, and Danner, who's been standing off to the side, clears his throat and leans in.

"You must bestow them with your grace now, Princess."

I cut my eyes to him. "My... grace?"

"A touch, a kiss." Danner glances at them—the Princes—and then back at me. There's a plea in his eyes. "A physical sign of affection will seal the union."

Of course. If this is a wedding, then there must be a kiss.

I follow his gaze to them, idly wondering, "And if I don't?" I know Ashby hears the question because the same fury sparks in his eyes that was once meant for Wicker.

It's purely rhetorical.

I've never once been under the impression that I had a choice in this.

"Girl," Ashby hisses, leaning close to my ear to whisper, "you may be pregnant, and you may be my biological child, but I still wield a power you do not want to test."

The cutting voice in my ear... it's the voice of the man in the video who gave his son lashings for failing to make enough deposits. A mixture of fear and revulsion shudders down my spine. My Princes are still on their knees, and I step forward, towering over the three of them to bestow my grace.

Grace. The word churns in my mind. An undeserved favor that cannot be earned, only given. At this moment, I understand the meaning behind it. These men—*these rapists*—they do not have my forgiveness. Nor my respect. But as my Princes, as the potential father of the heir, I can give them my grace.

I step to the right, looming over Wicker's broad shoulders, fascinated by the loose lock of golden hair curling in front of his eye. I loathe how handsome he is, how everything about his face is perfectly symmetrical, the product of generations of excellent breeding. It's also a big part of what makes him powerful. The deceit of it.

Running my finger under his sharp chin, I tip his face up to mine, watching as his piercing blue eyes glare daggers at my mouth. I bend at the waist, brushing my lips over his. It's just what Danner wanted: an intimate caress. His lips are stained with the metallic taste of old blood, but my kiss is so gentle and coaxing that I can feel his breath go shallow against my mouth.

All it takes is a sweep of my tongue.

His jaw yields instantly, lips parting to taste me back. He's so easy, so fucking bound to his weakness that a sound even escapes him, throaty and full of desperate grit.

But before he can surge up, I bite down—*hard*—puncturing his bottom lip.

Wicker jerks back, hissing as his eyes bore into mine with some mixture of shock, arousal, and rage. "Bitch!" he spits, wiping his mouth with the back of his hand. Fresh blood smears across his snarled lips.

Moving a few steps to my left, I stop in front of Pace next. His expression is cold—resentful of being on his knees. In his mind, that's my place, a position of submissiveness. Perfect for a *pet*.

But not here. Not when I'm being honored for the gift in my womb. Running my fingers down his cheek, I admire the sharp bone there as his black eyes watch me. The hollow beneath it. The cut of his jaw. The way his throat moves with a casual swallow as I touch the bob of his Adam's apple.

He doesn't even flinch when my fingers close around the column of his throat. If anything, he just tips his head back, a challenge in his eyes as my thumb digs into the pulse. It's incendiary, the frustration and anger that mixes inside my chest as I bend down to push my lips against his, fingers tightening. But he doesn't give me what I want. There's no whimper or wheeze, no sign it's affecting him at all.

There's just his mouth pinching mine into a slow, slick liplock.

When I pull back, I'm hoping to see the loss of breath in his eyes, but the closest sign of weakness I get is another swallow against the tightening vise of my palm.

When I step away, finally letting him go, my hand twinges.

Lex is somehow the easiest and most difficult. He waits for me with a hard gaze, eyes locking into mine. I only hesitate for a moment before reaching out. My fingers smooth back his hair, nails dragging along his scalp until they meet the tight band that holds it all in place.

He grunts as I yank it free.

The long strands cascade around his face, brushing his cheeks and shoulders as he glares at me from beneath the wild mane. *This* is the man I know. Lagan. Not the sterile man who toys with me on his examination table, but this feral, untamed, relentless animal that fucks me with abandon.

That's the man I choose to give my grace to.

I do it with a fist in the back of his hair, twining it around my wrist and wrenching his head back. His eyes are tight, but I know it's not from the pain. It's from the way I descend, never closing my own eyes as our lips meet.

I watch the coldness in his stare grow as I kiss him. Lex doesn't kiss me back. His lips don't move at all, actually. He just watches me, rigid and coiled, mouth pressed into a tight, unhappy line as if he's simply waiting for it to be over.

Maybe this whole coronation thing isn't so bad after all.

I release him, hoping the pull is painful, and nod at Danner, signaling I'm finished.

"Pace," Ashby says when I resume my position beside him. "You wanted to do this part."

I discover then why Pace is in the middle. It's him who reaches into his pocket, extracting a small golden box. My pulse quickens at the sight when he pries it open, revealing a ring. It's lying on a bed of purple velvet, shaped like a crown. Much like the tiara I'm wearing, it sparkles with gold and diamonds. Unlike the tiara, this ring is new. Every successful Princess gets one—the *real* golden ticket to East End. I stare at it, this piece of metal and rock, and I can't contain it.

A low, grim laugh escapes my throat.

This is it? This is what every Princess endures pain and torture to get? Her coronation, the ring, three gorgeous men kneeling before her, and not even a vague promise as to her own future?

It's a joke, is what it is.

Behind Pace, Lex and Wicker watch me like I'm one step away from losing my mind. I may just be, and the sensation of Pace reaching out to take my hand doesn't make it any better.

His touch isn't like his father's or Lex's. Where they're cold, Pace is a roaring fire, his skin hot enough to singe me as he plucks the ring from its bed of velvet. His dark eyes hold mine, too. That might be the worst part—the sly, malicious quirk of his mouth as he lifts my third finger, threading the ring onto it.

But just as he twists it, a tight sensation tugging at the skin, the door at the back of the room flies open. The sound is loud enough to snap the breathless tension in the room, making me—and everyone else—jump.

"Don't you fucking dare take this any further."

All eyes move to the disturbance: a slim, commanding silhouette glaring down the aisle at us.

Fucking hell.

It's my mother.

SHE DIDN'T COME ALONE. Sy, Nick, and Remy are a hulking, furious force that storms into the room behind her. My insides clench up so tightly at the sight of them that it's a struggle to even remain standing. Each of their gazes seek me out, pinning me with that frantic Bruin intensity, but none so intense as my mother's.

This wasn't supposed to happen.

I was supposed to have time before I faced them and the reality of what they've seen- that video of the cleansing—a detailed montage of my own destruction.

Shame isn't a strong enough word for the emotion that tugs me under. It's despair, hopelessness, and disgrace, all mingling into the hard pit of my stomach currently occupied by a fetus.

Coolly adjusting his shirt cuff, Ashby greets, "Libby," and my shocked gaze whips to him. It's a name I've only heard once or twice in conjunction with my mother and never by anyone who wasn't a close confidant. "Sorry, you missed the ceremony, it was really quite beaut—"

His words are cut off when my mother, dressed in tight spandex pants cuffed with leopard print and a low-cut matching shirt, strides up to the King and slaps him across the cheek.

I hear a gasp, then realize it came from me.

"You rat fucking bastard," she seethes.

Hardly looking fazed, Ashby tilts his head at Danner. "Prepare the conference room." He then chuckles, rubs his jaw, and adds, "I always forget just how cliché your West End temperament can be."

My mother lunges, and that's what draws the Princes out of their shocked lull. Pace grabs her around her upper body, wrenching her back. "Hands off, jailbird," Nick growls, grabbing Pace by the shoulder and spinning him around. Faster than I doubt anyone could react, he has his pistol drawn, barrel pressed to Pace's temple.

Ashby gestures to Nick. "Point proven."

My mother goes for him again, but this time, Sy is there, trying to pull her back to the invisible line that separates East and West. Unfortunately for him, she came wearing her signature spiked heels, and all it takes is one tactical stomp to have him roaring in surprise.

"What the fuck, Mama B!" he shouts, hopping on one foot.

Meanwhile, Remy marches straight up the aisle toward me, eyes bouncing around, and *fuck*. There's already been enough blood involved with this ceremony. The last thing I want is more, especially if it's theirs, and judging from all the PNZ members springing to their feet, that's exactly how this will go down.

"Stop!" I shout, holding up my hands, probably looking like a lunatic in this blood-stained dress. Okay, there's no probably. "Nick, put the goddamn gun down." His blue eyes flick to mine, narrowing, and I wonder for a second if I even have any right. Maybe they saw that video and are done with me. Maybe I'm not worth making peace over anymore. Maybe I'm damaged goods.

But suddenly, he huffs, relaxing his elbow and dropping the barrel.

Strangely enough, I actually feel I have more sway with the dark-eyed man currently snarling at my mother. "And Pace, don't you ever fucking touch my mother again!"

A shadow crosses the doorway—Danner returning. "The conference room is ready," he says in that quiet, stoic voice, as though nothing is out of place.

Ashby, unshaken as always, makes a sweeping gesture toward the door. "So let's begin the negotiations, shall we?"

IN THE QUIET of the conference room, my mother avoids my gaze. I'm pregnant, carrying her first grandchild, and she can't even make eye contact. The Dukes are bad enough, but my face feels bloodless at the notion she's seen the video of my ruin.

That idea from before of being a stranger in my own skin is something I embrace now. Let this thing inside of me have the churning shame of it while I hide in a dark corner.

"Thank you, Killian, for being here on such short notice," Ashby says from the seat at one end of the table. "Normally, we have the Baron King witness such things between our houses, but he was unavailable."

Killian Payne sits at the other end, an aggrieved expression on his face. I don't blame him. Who wants to get involved in this shit-show? My mother and Sy sit on opposite sides of the table from me, but Remy, Nick, and all three of my Princes have been left outside in the hallway, under strict instruction to keep it civil. Dimitri Rathbone is the peacemaker. God help us all.

While we waited for Killian to arrive, I had time to change, having Stella help me out of the heavy lace and into something less bloody and symbolic. Now, I'm withering under the weight of the tension.

"It's unfortunate that you had to interrupt our ceremony this evening with such a dramatic entrance," Ashby starts, gesturing to Danner in the corner. He's holding a stack of folders in his hands. "It's as if you didn't trust me to carry out these negotiations as planned."

"We didn't." Sy stares at him, and there's a sharpness to his gaze that I'm not used to seeing. "You shouldn't have made her sign anything before this meeting."

Danner walks around the table, passing a folder to each of us while Ashby continues. "I've already taken the liberty—" a pause while Ashby smirks at my mother, "pardon the term—of writing up the next phase of our agreement. I'm sure you'll understand that it must adhere to the principles of the Princess' previously agreed upon covenants."

"You've got to be fucking kidding me," Sy grinds out. "This is a negotiation, Ashby, which means both parties give and take." There's a second where Sy's gaze flicks to me; blink, and you'd miss it, and I shrink back into my seat.

"I don't see how much leverage you have, Perilini. The Princess is carrying my heir, which, by extension, rightfully makes her my property."

"Like fucking hell," Mom snaps, eyes flaring.

Ashby ignores the outburst. "The covenant has been signed and sealed." He looks down at the table. "Maybe it's best if Killian reads over the proposals—an unbiased participant."

Killian sighs, and I get the feeling he'd throttle Ashby with his bare, heavily tattooed hands if he had the chance, but he flips open the folder and begins reading instead. "The Princess will continue to visit West End, one day a week, under supervision, for the duration of her pregnancy. She will live in the safety of the palace with her Princes and will continue her education at the university to the best of her ability and health. East End will provide all healthcare and emotional support needed during this time. Yadda yadda, at any point, if the strain of these things poses a risk to the child, all activities will cease." He takes a breath and looks up at my mother. "Liberty Sinclaire may attend one doctor visit, host a baby shower, and will receive notice at the time of birth. Verity Sinclaire and child will be available for visitation three days post birth."

"You've lost your fucking mind." My mother's voice is clear and unwavering.

All eyes move to her. Ashby leans back in his seat. "Libby, do you care to expound?"

"I'll expound my heel into your testicles, you fucking snake." She presses her palms onto the table, scowling. "I raised this girl for twenty goddamn years. You have no place in her life. You're a sperm donor, *at best*. I'll be damned if I'm going to let you dictate my place in her life or vice versa!"

He laughs without a trace of humor, looking toward Sy. "Let me know when we're really ready to negotiate because I don't think that you—"

My mother snaps, "No, *you* don't think. You don't need to because here's what's going to happen." She bears down, eyes sparking with threat. "*My* daughter moves home with us—her real family. She'll return here for doctor appointments—*supervised*—and return to West End immediately. Any union with your Princes will be dissolved. I will have full access to my daughter and her child as she wishes." Her final words emerge through gritted teeth. "And when the child is born, we will retain custody."

Sy leans back, massive arms crossed over his chest. "Sorry, you didn't think you were negotiating with me, did you?" He nods toward my mother. "Because she's the one you have to convince. I'm just here to put pen to paper."

The tightness of futility twisting in my chest isn't unlike being bickered over like the last piece of meat at the family dinner table. "I signed the covenants. I did it this morning, by choice," I say, finally speaking up. My mother's eyes snap to mine for the first time, flaring. Lower, I admit, "We both know coming home isn't an option for me, Mama." The words are obviously half empty, and Sy must hear that. It's not all a lie. I did sign the covenants, by choice, at the silent dining room table as Ashby sat across from me. Maybe that's what made it so easy—the lack of pain and humiliation in it. For the first time in my life, I felt like an adult.

I'm not stupid. It was clearly a tactic. Ashby wanted me to feel that way, empowered and independent instead of trapped and hopeless.

But the parts that made it easier are a lot harder to swallow. The Dukes and my mother know what the Princes did to me, and there's no walking away now. Not with their baby inside of me.

"Verity," Sy says, pitching closer over the table. "You don't have to keep this up. Not after what they did to you."

My face falls, but before I can form a response, Killian agrees, "You have something they want. That gives you leverage, Verity."

Ashby's next words emerge pointedly. "I don't think we need the West and the South coaching our Princess."

Sy's eyes roll, but it's Killian who snaps, "She deserves to know her status in that seat."

"It's okay," I cut in, offering Killian a flat, dull smile. "I know the play here. With all due respect, Killian, you don't have all the information. I know what I'm doing."

My mother thrusts a finger at me. "Now you listen to me, missy."

Finally, I burst, "Listen? You want me to listen? I might if you ever said anything!" My mother's mouth snaps shut, lips pursed into a tight, angry line. "When were you going to tell me that Ashby is my father, Mama? Because you should have told me back when you were grooming me to be a rival Royal. You should have told me the instant you discovered he chose me as Princess. You should have told me *something*!" Shaking my head, I release a tight, bitter laugh. "I can't believe you'd let me go into this so ignorant and unprepared."

"Let you?" she shrieks. "Short of tying your ass up and dragging it back to the gym, I did everything I could to stop you from doing this."

"Everything but tell me the truth."

Her eyes widen. "I was protecting you!"

"You were *storing* me. If not for Duchess, then for something else."

From beside me comes Ashby's low chuckle. "You did raise a sharp one, Libby, I'll give you that."

Her furious gaze whips to him. "Call me that one more time, and I'm going to come over this table and feed you your teeth, you smug son of a bitch."

He shrugs. "You did have twenty years. Surely, the girl realizes you've been keeping this secret as a sort of currency."

I did realize it, but hearing the words said aloud still stings, all the more when she meets my gaze, saying with certainty, "She realizes that you only wanted her when she became useful to you, and one day she'll realize that I was right to give her those twenty years."

"Ms. Sinclaire," Killian warns my mother. "No one can appreciate the complexity of family drama quite like I can. Trust me. But let's stay on topic here. We need a compromise."

She drops back into her seat, eyes narrowed. "Well, it sure as fuck isn't going to come from me. I'm not leaving this shit palace without my daughter."

Ashby takes a moment to look between them, that serene grin never leaving his lips. "Danner, hand me that remote control."

Danner moves silently across the room and returns with a remote. A moment later, a massive television slides up and out of the floor. "I was hoping it wouldn't come to this," he sighs, pressing a button, and a still photo pops up. My stomach sinks like a boulder. I recognize the image immediately, even though it only reveals my face. My makeup is smeared, and my hair is a mess.

This is moments after all three of my Princes raped me on the ceremonial table. Moments before the Royal Cleansing, when every member of PNZ coated me with their cum. This is the moment they broke me. Maybe it's even the moment they sealed my fate here, their seed finally taking hold.

Maybe the child growing inside me was created in the midst of that.

The thought alone makes my stomach churn, but worse than that is Sy's grimace as he pointedly averts his gaze. Wordlessly, I spring from my seat, knees smarting when I slam down on the floor to wretch into the trash bin in the corner. My back heaves, the flexing muscles painful as I lose whatever was left of the morning's post-contract breakfast.

I hear chair legs scrape against the floor, but only one of the people in the room reaches me.

"There, there," Ashby says, his hand giving my shoulder a pat. "I'll need to have Lex make you some shakes for that morning sickness."

Shuddering, I flinch away from his touch, scrambling to my feet. "Turn it off. Please, just... turn it off."

"Turn what off?" When I turn, my mother is regarding the image on the screen with a drawn face. "What is it I'm looking at?"

I freeze, looking at Sy, and he gives me a small shake of his head, eyes sliding away.

It hits me then.

Lex really was bluffing during our dance the other night.

She hasn't seen it.

Ashby's eyes flick to mine, the threat unspoken. If we don't get them to agree to his proposal, he'll show it. "Please," I whisper, too desperate to feel ashamed of the way my voice cracks. "Please don't show her. I did it—I signed the covenant."

My mother's whole body is rigid as she growls out, "What did they do to you?"

Ashby pulls out my chair for me, casually explaining, "There was an unfortunate incident a few weeks ago. We learned that Verity has been engaging in a campaign of espionage with your Duchess, Lavinia Lucia."

"That's a gross exaggeration," Sy says, eyes sliding from Ashby to me. A silent understanding passes between us. "Girls like to gossip. It was locker room talk that you've blown entirely out of proportion."

Panic builds in my chest as I numbly take my seat, the fear of revealing the truth about the Monarchs worse than them seeing the video. The video of the cleansing makes me look bad, but the betrayal that led to it? Well, it affects more than me.

"Verity revealed classified and sensitive information about assets in my Kingdom to Lucia during an unapproved visit to West End." His voice raises a notch. "Her misguided loyalty to the West End put my Kingdom at risk, and because of those actions, she was punished accordingly." He nods to the screen and holds up the remote. "That punishment was recorded and is currently on a server waiting to be released to all of Forsyth. If you give me my demands, I won't release it. If you refuse, it will be delivered before your next breath." His lips turn up at one corner. "My Pace is incredibly gifted in this area, you understand."

Sy curses under his breath, and when our eyes meet, his are filled with both pity and annoyance. "First, let me assure you that I was unaware of any unapproved visitation, and that's been handled with my Queen. Second—"

"*Your* Pace?" My mother's slow, mangled laugh fills the room. Her eyes are full of a pain I can't quite understand, but it's hidden beneath a wrath that's so West End I get overcome by a wave of homesickness. "Is that what you tell him, Rufus? I wonder how loyal those *gifted* boys will be to you when they find out where he came from."

Ashby pauses with his hand poised over the paper, eyes locking on hers. "You overestimate your credibility."

"And you underestimate how much currency I've collected." Her head tilts, and she rests her elbow on the arm of her chair. Her sharp red nails gleam from the overhead light. My mother isn't just smart. She's a survivor. She's also fucking terrifying. "You're not the only one with leverage, King Prick. Now that you've revealed to the world that Verity's our daughter, I have no reason to keep your other secrets. Including ones that could threaten the house of cards this gaudy castle was built on."

Sy, Killian, and I exchange a look. None of us are privy to whatever this leverage might be.

There's a long moment where they just stare at one another, Ashby stiff and unblinking. That unsettling half-grin is still frozen on his face, but I detect something uncharacteristic in his gaze.

Apprehension.

"You can have a week out of every month," Ashby concedes, breaking her stare to open the folder.

My jaw drops, but I'm quick to compose myself. Quicker than Sy, at least, whose forehead is puckered up in confused shock. I wasn't expecting to be able to go home ever again—not after everything.

I see the moment it clicks for my mother that she has him by the balls. "You just had her for nearly two months. I want that time back." Her nails tap on the table. "I want her in West End every other month, in fact."

Ashby doesn't even look up from what he's jotting down to scoff. "That's a demand so absurd, it borders on humorous, Liberty."

"Two words, honey." My mother leans over the table, catching his gaze. "Dungeon twins."

Ashby drops his pen, head whipping upward to gape at her.

Mother inspects her nails. "As far as currency goes, that's a nice golden bar."

Huffing, Killian taps his fingertips on the table. "What's it going to be, Ashby?"

"Give me a moment!" he snaps, making me jump. Sy sees this, looks between Ashby and my mother, and straightens.

"That's a fair deal, Ashby." Sy nods. "One month here, one month there."

Ashby looks at him, openly seething. "It's anything but fair. This is *my* heir. I won't have it at the mercy of your West End mongrels."

Killian straightens, too, obviously sensing some hope. "You can take precautions. Send a Prince with her."

"No," Sy says, the tone brooking no argument. "You can send someone with her, but it can't be a Royal."

"Danner," I suggest, perking up at the prospect. An entire month back home without Ashby or any of the Princes breathing down my neck. Suddenly, I'm curling my hands into fists to hide their shaking.

"I need Danner here." There's a vein in Ashby's forehead that's protruding oddly, and I realize why.

He's going to *agree*.

What the fuck does 'dungeon twins' mean?

"We'll send her handmaid," he says, picking up his pen. The muscles in his face are taut as if he's gnashing his teeth.

My mother chimes in, "We want someone with her when she's here, too. One of my boys."

"Ballsack," Sy decides, nodding. "He's a good kid, strong fighter. And you've had him in your dungeon before. He'll behave himself."

Ashby's fingers flex around the pen. "Fine," he grits out. "One month, then she returns here," his gaze flicks to Sy, "and the Dukes give us an arms shipment of our choice."

"We can accommodate that," he says, eyeing my mother for approval. "She can return here for medical care. We all trust you have the baby's best interest at heart."

Ashby's glower rises to Sy. "I've waited twenty years for this. I assure you, I'll spare no expense."

Around me, the negotiations continue—stipulations like how I'll be required to fulfill my duties on campus and all fraternity-related events. I can barely believe it. This morning, I signed my life away—for the second time—and now my mother's gained me a morsel of it back.

When the next nine months are finally hashed out, Killian runs a palm through his hair and clears his throat. "So everyone is in agreement?"

Everyone, that is, except me.

But I've known, for a long time now, no one cares about what I want.

I'm just a pawn in a larger game.

A vessel to carry an heir.

2

Lex

Tick... tick...tick...

It's the only sound out here, emerging from an ornate clock at the end of the hall. Seems appropriate considering that, right now, the palace hall may as well be a minefield. Nick Bruin made the smart decision to leave the minute the Lords arrived, announcing he would head back to West End to keep an eye on the Duchess. Pace grunted and offered to escort him out.

I haven't heard gunshots yet.

Probably as close to optimistic as this can get.

I don't expect Pace to return. Not with Dimitri Rathbone standing in front of the conference room door, arms crossed over his chest like some kind of emo prison guard. He idly toys with the piercing on his lip, clearly preferring to be anywhere else. I watch him with my face pinched in disgust, holding back a comment about the high risk of infection that comes with piercings near the mouth.

I'm not sure if he's here to keep us out of the meeting or to make sure we don't kill each other, but I have a strong suspicion it was determined we need a babysitter.

The quiet isn't new. The palace has been quiet since Valentine's Day. Even Wicker. Although, considering our covenants changed the moment Verity revealed the positive pregnancy test, he's probably been jacking his dick raw. Our bodies are no longer a temple, and our seed isn't valuable anymore. It's still locked down—can't risk having a second pregnancy out there—but the chains around our dicks have been loosened, as the ropes around our necks have tightened.

Pace has been the most silent. Even for me, he's hard to read. It's not anger—not exactly. It's almost like he's just waiting for the next punishment or conflict. It's like he's busy preparing something in his head, and he doesn't have space for anything else. Last night, I caught him fixated on the video feed of her bedroom, idly skating his lower knuckles over his tense lips, over and over.

I'm some unfortunate mixture of both of them.

There's the preparation, of course, rearranging my head for this next part of Father's game. There are even absurd amounts of masturbation, standing in my shower every morning with my palm around my dick, thinking of red hair and plump tits, stroking my returned hardness until I grunt out a mediocre release.

Mostly, though, there's this sick feeling in the pit of my stomach that I can't shake.

I think it might be misery.

Across the hall, Wicker flops into an armchair, running a hand through his hair. He shifts uncomfortably, tugging at the bow tie around his neck. Even disheveled, lip swollen from the Princess' kiss, and with a red dot of blood marring his white collar, it all looks intentional, like he walked off a photoshoot.

Unlike her, we didn't have the opportunity to change after the Dukes burst in, and the dichotomy of our formal wear, compared to Maddox and Rathbone in street clothes, feels like another line in the sand between all of our houses.

Remington Maddox is pacing, but it's not the nervous kind. He's bored out of his mind, moving from painting to painting. "Fucking cherubs," he mutters under his breath. "Way too much blue for this place." He slowly walks down the hallway, studying a still life of a basket of roses. He pulls a face.

Since we both attend the addiction support group on campus, he's the Duke I'm most familiar with. I'm used to his quirky habits—the way he can't stop moving, how he's content to talk and have no one answer, and the long, dreamy pauses when he speaks. I can't decide if he fried his brain on Scratch or if there's something deeper going on with his behavior. I've heard rumors about mental illness, which tracks, but I'm a scientist. I don't trade on rumors. What I'd give to look in this fucker's medical records.

Pausing in front of a large, contemporary painting, he lifts his finger to the frame, asking, "Fuck me, is this a Richter?"

"Jesus, don't touch the art, you mutt," Wicker snaps. "And, of course it's a Richter. Father isn't usually one for contemporaries, but even he couldn't resist the appeal of adding a modern master to his collection."

"My old man's been trying to track one of these down for years. What he wouldn't give to slap one of these up in a clean, sterile hotel lobby," Remy smirks, eyes sliding to Wicker. "Even came close at an auction two years ago, but he was outbid at the last second."

"We know," I say, offering him a cold smile. "Who do you think outbid him?"

Remy takes this in with a delighted snort. "Being outplayed by the King of East End. And he calls me the family embarrassment." I'd be disappointed by his amusement—so hard to get a rise out of this one—but I don't expect any different.

If there's one thing the Royals have in spades, it's daddy issues.

"So," he says, turning to a flat space in the wall and leaning back. He crosses his long legs in the front, black leather boots sticking out from under his baggy jeans with his shirt unbuttoned halfway down his chest, revealing a swath of tats. I watch, unable to look away from his frenetic energy, as he pulls a marker from his pocket. "What's it like knowing you knocked up your sister?"

"She's not our blood sister, dumbass," I snap, but regret it the instant I see the grin toying on his mouth. Remy may be all tattoos and scars, but he comes from money—old money that's probably stained with blood—and he's not stupid. "It probably feels a little like finding out DKS has been harboring an Ashby bloodline for decades."

"That's the difference between the Dukes and Princes," he says, pulling off the marker cap with his teeth. "We're not obsessed with bloodline and lineage in West End. We pick winners." He nods at Rathbone. "Same with them. The Lords don't need blood to reign."

Wicker looks up at Rath, his mouth tugging into a sharp grin. "Well, just the blood that comes from popping cherries. I saw you and the Lady in the Pit. That was some high-class fuckwork, Rashbone."

"Shut your mouth, Ashby." Rath's fist curls, and he gives Wick a long look that suggests he'd like to shut it for him. Instead, he rolls his eyes, sighing. "How long is all of this going to take?"

"As long as it takes for two opposing Forsyth factions to sort out possession of a pregnant Royal woman," I say, without a trace of irony. I'm aware that outside of Forsyth, things don't work like this, but our town is built on the seeds of corruption, crime, power, and loyalty. We were raised in this world; my brothers and I were raised for *this moment,* seemingly more than we even knew. One of us impregnated Father's secret biological daughter.

Jesus. The implications are more extensive than any of us can comprehend. We're in uncharted territory.

Rath leans his head closer to Remy, watching my brother and me curiously. "So, whose pampered little swimmer do you think hit the mark?" He gestures down the hall and then between us. "Tweedle-Dee, Tweedle-Dumb, or Tweedle-Dick?"

"I bet it's him." Remy jerks his chin at me. "He interns a lot. Medical shit, right? Fifty bucks says that one made it." His lip curls up distastefully as he stares me up and down. "Not a speck of purple on this guy. Probably jizzed into a test tube."

I force myself not to stiffen, but only just. If that bitch told them about my deposits...

Hot rage boils beneath my skin, but before I can do more than square my shoulders, Rathbone nods at Wicker. "My money's on the golden boy. I doubt he can go ten minutes without humping the nearest available hole."

Wicker's better at composure than me. He lifts his arms, casually lacing his fingers behind his head. "The flirting looks a little desperate, Rathbone. Your Lady not satisfying you? If you want a spin on my cock, all you gotta do is ask. I can lower my standards for a charitable deed."

Rath sneers back. "Oh, you're a little too busy disappointing your family to bother with disappointing me."

"Christ," Remy mutters. "Can't she just be... what's it called? Self-impregnating?"

I scoff. "Hermaphroditic, you idiot."

"And trust me," Wicker adds, smirking, "we've pumped your little mutt bitch with so much cum, it's probably running through her veins."

Well, that does it.

Remy's eyes harden, and he pushes off the wall, the muscles in his shoulders flexing. "You better start watching your tongue, Ashby, or someone might feel inclined to take it from you."

"Oh, now you want my tongue?" Wicker parts his lips, licking them lasciviously.

"Wick," I warn. It wouldn't be the first time my brother's antagonistic flirting has gotten him into a scrap. Annoyed, I ask Remy, "And what do you care what we do to her? It's not like she was ever yours."

"Yeah, we popped her cherry on our own dicks." Wicker makes an obnoxious popping sound with his lips. "It was bloody, but deliciously tight." Suddenly, it hits me what Wicker is doing. He's trying to see how much the Dukes know—how much Verity has divulged to them. She lost her hymen on the throne—all Princesses do.

If the Dukes knew that, they'd never let us live it down.

But to my surprise, Remy doesn't call out the lie.

He does, however, stalk forward, stopping right in front of Wicker's seated form. "Maybe West End's tired of seeing its girls used as Royal fodder."

Wicker chuckles up at him, tipping his head back. "Then maybe West End should do a better job of protecting them."

"That's the thing about *our* girls, you see. They're red and purple, born to fight." Remy leans over, slamming his palms on the armrests. "All we gotta do is give them the weapons."

Wicker spreads out, looking entirely unconcerned by the display. "Load her up all you want, Maddox, because she's got our baby inside her." His mouth tips up into an icy grin. "She's our bitch for life."

Remy rears up, fists clenching.

Rath tsks. "Boys, boys, boys." The silver blade of the knife in his hand gleams as he waves it. "Don't make me turn this hostile negotiation around." Rath twirls the knife skillfully. "I'm here to prevent a murder or avenge one. Your choice."

Remy twists to glance at him, nose flaring in frustration. "Come on," he sighs. "Just a little murder?"

Rath gives him a stern look. "You've got murder at home, Maddox. You didn't even finish the last one." He quirks an eyebrow. "Cash Mallis is still alive, after all."

I snort without meaning to, the sound snapping back inside at the sudden rattle of the knob behind Rath.

The double doors swing open, a stone-faced Danner stepping aside to allow Killian to exit first. "Thank you for your service today, King," Danner says, voice a hoarse whisper.

With a tight grimace on his face, Killian simply nods at Rath, and they fall into step, taking the long hallway to the main foyer.

Perilini comes out next, face pulled into a tired frown. Remy straightens and looks over his head, eyes pinging. "Everything okay?"

"We'll discuss it at home." He follows the Lords out without a glance spared at me or Wick.

Verity steps out next, and I rip my eyes away. That's the hard part. Just looking at her is enough to cause an avalanche of infuriatingly overwhelming *want*. It's like all those months of being unable to get my dick hard have rushed in on a tidal wave. Even worse? The memory of her bitter lips on mine a couple of hours ago, the way it made my cock swell, the sight of her green eyes as she pulled my hair...

It's nothing compared to the knowledge of what's happening in her womb.

Her mother exits right behind her, sidling up to Verity with a dark scowl. It's impossible not to see the similarities. Her mother's hair is darker, but still a lush, vibrant red. They share the same mouths, and both have a faint spattering of freckles over the bridge of their noses. Not to mention the ball-breaking attitude.

But for the first time, I see the ridge of her brow, the fairness of her complexion, and her eyes. Bottle-glass green. I don't need to glance down the hallway to confirm what I already know. I've seen the portrait so many times that even without any talent, I could probably reproduce it with enough paint.

She has Michael Ashby's eyes.

I feel like a goddamn fool for not noticing the line of genetics. Being adopted, you get used to not looking like anyone in the family. There are no pieces to put in place. No matching eye color. No comparative body shape. In a way, it's freeing. Pace's dark complexion never mattered any more than Wicker's sharp cheekbones. The bonds that tie us together—that make us brothers—are forged in nurture, not nature. In our household, that revolves around shared experiences, not DNA sequencing.

But still, there's a tightness in my chest that feels dangerously close to jealousy when I look at Verity standing next to Father. She's the one thing we could never be.

His blood.

"Ashby," Mama B says, sliding him a vicious look. "It's been a displeasure doing business with you."

Father gets that look on his face that's never fun to see, lax and sleazy. "Come now, Libby, you know that's not true." He grins. "We've had a couple of pleasurable moments, don't you think?"

Wicker coughs, and for a second, I think he may actually gag at the implication of a sexual relationship between Father and Liberty Sinclaire. Verity also looks queasy, but that could be the pregnancy hormones. Still, it's impossible not to look at the two of them without considering the intimacy of their relationship. A *secret* relationship.

The three of us spent last night doing the math.

Before becoming Princes, there were no parameters on who we fucked—as long as we wore a condom. But we still mainly stuck to East Side pussy because it'd been drilled into us that good breeding was the most important thing to practice. We knew only to place our seed where it would be nourished by someone worthy.

Liberty Sinclaire is not worthy.

Yet... Father chose her. He had unprotected sex with her. He created a child with her. His child is now carrying one of our children.

It's fucking depraved.

Without wanting to, my gaze darts to Verity. I hate how my body reacts to her, the thud of my heart in my chest, and the rush of blood to my cock. It's a biological nuisance. She's the only woman who's gotten me hard and kept me that way through completion in months.

That doesn't make it any easier to swallow.

Mama B takes her daughter's hand and leans in close. "Remember what King Payne said, okay, baby? You have power here. If someone hurts you," she glances directly at me, "you can stab them."

You can fucking try.

At Verity's stiff nod, her mother sighs, dropping her hand. "I'll see you tomorrow."

The sense that things aren't exactly kosher between the two of them distracts me for a moment. And a glance at Wicker suggests that the cut of Mama B's neckline distracts him.

I kick out, catching his ankle.

He jerks upright, brows knitting together. "Tomorrow? What happens tomorrow?"

"Tomorrow," Mama B says, leveling an unimpressed stare at

Wicker, "my little girl is coming home where she can be protected and pampered by men who know how to take care of a woman."

With the final jab thrown, Mama B strides out, her pointed heels clacking against the hardwoods.

FROM MY CORNER in the pitch-black room, I wait.

There are very few places in this palace where someone can sit with their thoughts and know they're not being watched by someone or another. One of them is the solarium out back. The other is the exam room in the basement, where I'm currently occupying my usual stool, arms folded, eyes fixed on the pane of the glass in the door.

It's how I see her blurry silhouette approaching from the hallway.

She's four minutes late.

The sound of the knob turning shatters the silence, and then she's pushing through. There's a moment of apprehension—this place is usually lit up like an operating room—before she shuffles her way inside. I hear more than see her feeling the wall beside the door for the light switch.

When she finds it, the room explodes with quick, buzzing fluorescent light, and then she spins, her eyes snapping to mine.

"Holy fucking—!" Gasping, she clutches her chest, eyes wide. When I just stare at her, unblinking, she visibly forces the frightened tension in her spine to abate. "You—you startled me."

I bite down on the wad of gum I've been chewing for the last thirty-four minutes. Nicotine. It's as close to a stimulant as I can get at this hour. "Undress."

Verity freezes. She's wearing a deep blue, soft-looking sweater and dark-wash jeans. If she thinks her dress code as a Princess was strict before, she's about to discover my father's—*her* father's, *fuck*—standards rise exponentially once fertilization has occurred.

She shrinks back, and even though her chin rises in a show of bluster, I see her green eyes flick to the exam table. "What for? There won't be any more deposits."

My jaw works around the piece of gum, the flavor of it faint now. "You think I wanted you naked before because it got my dick hard?"

The words are spoken low and harsh, and it makes her eyes tighten. "So you just want to humiliate me," she decides, teeth clenched. "Again."

"You think a lot of yourself." My eyes narrow as I speak to her like a child. "I need to examine your body. Pregnancy doesn't just happen in your uterus."

She hugs her middle, hunched and nervous, but readjusts her arms instantly as if she's crossing them to look tough. "I want to know what's about to happen."

Her eyes dip down to my attire. I still haven't made it up to my room, but I've shucked my jacket, bow tie, and waistcoat in an untidy attempt to get comfortable. My tuxedo shirt is untucked and unbuttoned, revealing the tight undershirt beneath, and though I'm still in the dark pants, my dress shoes are abandoned by the door, with nothing but black socks to cover my feet. My hair, which I'd spent ten minutes getting up into a smooth ponytail earlier tonight, is now in a loose, haphazard state.

Because of her.

"Let's get something straight." I stand, satisfied by the way she skitters back, eyes tracking me sharply. "You betrayed us. You stabbed my brother in the back, and then you humiliated me in front of the entire frat."

Her arms drop, eyes flashing in fury. "You're going to talk to *me* about being humili—"

I'm in front of her in a blink, towering over her startled form. "I'm talking now," I hiss, watching as she stumbles back two steps. "You fucked us over. Make no mistake, Princess, you're the enemy. And the things we do to enemies? Well…"

We stare at one another for a long beat, our crimes laid out. There are no secrets in this house. Everything is recorded, documented, filed, and leveraged. There's an irony here. I'd been so judgmental about Verity betraying West End by aligning herself with the East. Turns out, she's more loyal than I ever expected. She's not a traitor.

She was playing us the whole time. I kept telling her she didn't know me, but I was the one that had no fucking clue what was going on with her—outside of labs and physical exams. And even then, I'd failed by not catching on to the fact she was pregnant first.

I reach over her shoulder for the lab coat hanging on the back of the door. She flinches so hard she bangs against it, blinking as I step away, threading my arms through the sleeves. "Fortunately for you, the moment you step into this room under my medical care, you're safe."

She releases a gnarled chuckle. "I'm supposed to believe that?" Her eyes are tired, and the black eye makeup she put on hours ago is all smudged and smeared. Her hair is still up in the fancy style from the ceremony, but wisps of red curl by her face. I don't feel sorry for her—not one fucking iota—but I don't see Verity standing before me. I can't. I see a patient.

She, on the other hand, sees a monster.

"Princes have a job," I explain, sauntering to the sink. "More like a fight, really. Your problem is that you think West End has some monopoly on winning. As a Prince, there are a lot of ways for me to lose, but only one way for me to win, and that's to deliver a healthy newborn in approximately eight months. So, it's like I said," I gather my hair back, tying it up, "when you're in here, you're safe."

I can hear her chewing on her bottom lip. "It's that easy for you? Shutting your emotions on and off?"

"I'm a doctor," I say, shoving my sleeves up my forearms, "or will be. In this room, I deal in science. Not emotions."

There's a short pause, and then, "There were a few times our deposits felt emotional to me."

I pump the soap in my hand, trying not to remember the last time we were in here. The slick, fevered kisses. The way her hand felt on my cock.

Below my belt, my dick stirs to life.

Slamming my fist down on the faucet handle, I insist, "That was about creating a conducive environment for conception. In this house, we use our skills for the betterment of our family, and right now, that means your pregnancy is priority number one. Believe that or don't. I don't need you to trust me." I turn to look at her. "I just need you to obey me."

Someone like Wicker might think this is the wrong word to use. *Obey*. Verity's eyes flash indignantly; I know that's the last thing she wants to do. Because she doesn't trust me. Can't, really. If she weren't pregnant, I'd make it my mission to destroy her.

"Fine," she relents, stepping out of her shoes. It's not because she has no other choice—although that's true. It's because she trusts we both have the same endgame.

She thinks a Princess can win, too.

Scrubbing my hands, I hear Verity unzipping her jeans and the soft shift of fabric as she removes her clothes, but I pull two latex gloves from the box and tug them on before turning to face her. In the last two months, she's lost any sense of modesty when she's here. This is my domain, and similar to how she is while with Pace, her behavior modifies. I can see it in the growth of her pubic hair. His demand.

In my examination room, I demand compliance.

I assess her body, taking in her nudity and how her hands clench at her sides. Her pale skin pebbles from the chill of the underground room. There's no evidence of her pregnancy yet. Her stomach and breasts have yet to swell, but that doesn't stop my gaze from lingering on her tits, because my cock hasn't gotten the message about her betrayal. I use every ounce of willpower to maintain control. There's no other option. The video she showed of me at the Valentine's Day party? That was a personal attack. My brothers don't come off in a good light. They look like submissive pawns to my father's terror, but me?

The entire room watched me down on my knees while my father flogged me like an animal.

I hate Verity Sinclaire.

But the woman in front of me, all female, ripe, and fertilized...

My body wants her on a primal, biological level that doesn't comprehend things like deception. It just *wants*. Wants to invade her. Wants to grab her soft hips. Wants to keep breeding her.

Gruffly, I say, "Get on the table," and tear my gaze from her body. The paper covering the hard, padded surface crinkles as I methodically pick through the supplies I'll need for the appointment: blood withdrawal, speculum, ultrasound gel. I place them all on the cart beside the ultrasound equipment and turn.

She's on the table as directed, but there's a wariness in her eyes.

Wordlessly, I place my phone beside us, hitting the button to record.

"Today, we'll start our prenatal examinations." I step closer and turn on the lamp that hangs over the bed. "I'll withdraw blood to check for hCG levels and perform a full-body exam. Along with a transvaginal ultrasound, we should be able to get a better timeline to approximate conception." A laugh bubbles in her chest, and she does nothing to hide it. I pause. "Something funny?"

Her soft tits bounce as she adjusts. "That you think you can pinpoint which one of you is the father is absolutely hysterical."

"I'm not trying to determine paternity—not yet. We need to have a baseline so we can assess your progress. Confirm the fetus' growth to make sure he's healthy."

"He?" She rolls her eyes, the muscles in her thighs tensing as her legs squeeze together. "Of course, you think it's a 'he.'"

I scoff. "You'd prefer a female enter this gene pool? Look how it's worked out for you. Chances are, this one couldn't be kept a secret for twenty years." I grab the rubber tubing. "Arm."

She sticks it out, and I wrap the tubing around her bicep. Her nipples are peaked, hard and tight. Her tits are a nice size, and a thought bobs up to the surface of my mind unwillingly.

I wonder how big they'll get when she hits the second trimester.

Or—I swallow—when she's nursing?

I take two vials of blood and cap the ends, writing her details on the sticker on the side. "It's early. Most doctors wouldn't even test you yet, but I've been monitoring you closely enough. We're looking for a hCG range of five to four-twenty." I place the tubes in the refrigerator and come back to the table. "Put your legs up," I instruct, adjusting the light. "I'm going to check your cervix before the ultrasound."

There's another beat of hesitation; her muscles tense as she stares straight up at the ceiling. "What does that mean?" Her voice is high and tight, and my hand clenches around the speculum.

"I'm going to examine you," I say like it isn't obvious. "It's not like we haven't done this before."

She squirms, knees pressed together. "Are you going to..."

Impatiently, I snap, "What?"

"Are you going to make it hurt?"

Fuck, but I could.

I could strap her down again. Spread her so wide that the tendons in her thighs strain. Dig my fingers into the soft give of her womanly hips and spear my cock right through her. I could fuck her hard and fast and dirty—the way I've wanted to for two goddamn months.

But that's part of what got me into this mess.

Giving in.

Letting go.

"No more than it should," is my answer, even though it's a physical pang to give it. When I tap her knee, she relents, and although the motions are stilted and unsure, she places each heel in the stirrups, giving me full dominion over what's between them.

Her pussy is the sweetest thing.

It's all pink and tight, her lips parted for me like a perverse invitation.

It's nothing I haven't seen before. I've been knuckle-deep in this cunt a dozen times, probably. This is the first time I've felt the sudden rush of blood to my cock, though. In the amount of time it takes me to slick two fingers and slide them inside, it's fucking throbbing.

I fix my stare on a cluster of three freckles on her inner thigh as I go through the motions. That's what they have to be. Detached mechanics. If she caught one inkling of the fact my body is back to working condition, that it wants her bad enough to be sitting on this stool with a raging erection, she could use it against me.

She *could*.

It's the hard truth I face as I get up to turn out the lights, wheeling the monitor closer and readying the transducer.

As I'm applying the gel, she says, "You were bluffing." When I glance up, she's watching me back, fingers lacing and unlacing anxiously on her abdomen. "You never sent that video to my mother."

"And do you that favor?" I ask, giving her a dry smile as I insert the transducer.

Her palms drop to the table, fingers digging into the thin paper. "Favor? How would that have been—"

Pointedly, I flick on the monitor, adjusting the wand. "All you Forsyth chicks are so naive. You think Princesses are kept in line with gifts and wealth and luxury. You think he controls you by giving you what you want." Smiling bitterly, I turn to the image on the screen, the static blobs shifting. "But that's not how he does it, you see. He does it by threatening you with things you don't want. Things that horrify you so much, you'd give anything—*anything*..." I snatch the words back before they can emerge, thoughts of my brothers swirling around in my head.

Pace's empty eyes when he closes himself into his room. The flash of dread on Wicker's face when he has a particularly unseemly job. The way they've both become so good at hiding it...

I shake out of it more slowly than I like, setting my jaw. "He knows how badly you don't want your mother to see that video. He owns you now. Why would I ever take that privilege away from you, Verity?"

There's a click from her throat when she swallows. "How the hell is that a privilege?"

"The privilege of being an Ashby," I say, the words bitter. "Welcome to the family."

My focus shifts back to the screen. Rath was right before. I interned for an obstetrics clinic over the summer, another form of Ashby privilege that put me into positions other pre-med students couldn't have imagined. I've been wondering if this is why. How long has Father planned for this? Did he get me that position so I'd be prepared to deliver what's possibly my own child?

Either way, I'm fluent in the technology—no expense spared—and I nudge the transducer when I see a speck form in the area. "You'll feel a little pressure," I say, pushing it against her cervix.

Verity cranes her neck as she peers at the screen. "Is that... it?"

It.

I point to the screen, ignoring how suddenly heavy my limbs feel. "Right there." I circle around the dark spot. "That's the embryonic fluid."

Her mouth parts in awe. "It looks like the eye of a hurricane."

"Kind of." I fall silent at the confirmation of it all. Seeing and hearing it are different from reading lab results. There's a baby in here. A baby me or one of my brothers made. There's something shocking about working so hard for something and finally experiencing it coming to fruition.

Creation.

Some part of one of us found some part of Verity Sinclaire, and together, they're in the process of making a human being.

But then, over the hum of the electronics, our eyes meet, and the chest-numbing awe at seeing the creation come to life extinguishes in the space of a heartbeat. Until the fetus comes to term, it comes with the attachment of this woman—this betrayer—whom I can't trust with the smallest of things.

Much less the Ashby heir.

3

erity

STELLA HELPS me dry off after my bath, combing out my hair. "I'll spend the morning packing your things so they're ready when it's time to go."

I look up, catching her eye in the mirror. "I'm sorry you have to come with me."

"I'm not," she says, chipper as always. The gown she helps me into isn't one I've worn before—lush and satin-feeling. "Getting out of this haunted house for a few weeks sounds like a vacation to me. Plus, you'll need me more than ever now that you're pregnant."

I look down, noticing how the gown clings to my flat belly. "It'll only be my second month. I don't see how things are going to change much."

"Maybe not at first," Stella says, arching an eyebrow, "but things can change quickly. Today, it's morning sickness. Tomorrow, it could be mood swings! I've been listening to a lot of podcasts for expectant mothers, and apparently, even in the first eight weeks, you can look forward to any number of symptoms, from heartburn to crippling fatigue!" She says this with a big, toothy grin, as if that's something she's excited about. I've been around Stella long enough to understand that the sunny disposition is just how she deals with unseemly topics.

My eyes narrow. "You've been listening to podcasts?"

"Oh, yes." She spritzes me with something that smells like roses. *Always roses.* "Never let it be said that Stella St. James takes her job anything less than seriously. I'm prepared for anything, just wait and see." She spins to look at me, wide-eyed. "Are you cold in that? Or hungry? I can have the kitchen staff whip you something up. I've cross-referenced the approved foods list with things that are supposed to settle your stomach. Fair warning, there's a lot of green stuff."

"I'm not hungry," I say, even as my stomach growls. The mere thought of putting anything into it makes me feel unsteady.

I have one more night left in this place before I can go home to West End.

I think about it when I slip into bed minutes later, the scent of roses thick in my nostrils. There's a smell to West End, like old metal and asphalt, that I might actually be anticipating. God, the sounds, too. The palace is always so quiet and tense, but West End is louder, full of life, and as I nod off to the sight of my bedroom's heavy velvet drapes, I imagine steel, wood, and the deep peals of youthful laughter ringing off the old brick of downtown.

I'm not sure how long I've been asleep when something familiar tickles at the back of my awareness. It's hard at first to understand what it is. Not a scent exactly, but there is a taste, bitter and fleshy. In that unconsciously primal way, two halves of my mind split in different directions, one seeking it while the other shrinks back. There's pleasure in it but also pain, and when I move my tongue to either chase it or rid myself of it, I realize why.

"That's right, Rosi," comes a deep, gruff whisper. The mattress rocks beneath my shoulders. "Suck for me."

My eyes blink open, forehead knitted together in panicked confusion. I try to pull in a breath, but it emerges as a gasp, the back of my throat confusingly full. I struggle to lift my arms from the quicksand of slumber, hands grasping wildly as my vision sharpens on the figure straddling my chest, pinning me down.

"Calm down," he hisses. There's a tug on my scalp, his fingers wound into a hard fist around my hair. "Bite down, and I'll make you regret it. Loosen that jaw, beautiful." I strain to peer up into his eyes, but it's too dark. All I can make out is the sway of his hair as he rocks into my mouth. It makes me gag, and the grip on my hair tightens. "Finally awake, huh?" Pace's low chuckle turns my stomach to stone. "I was wondering if you would. My cock's been in your mouth for almost an hour."

I can feel it, too, the ache at the hinge of my jaw drawing a soft, pained sound. Warm fingers graze along my throat, lifting my chin. Sticky heat coats my lips, followed by the loss of air.

There's little else to feel beyond the hard poke of Pace's erect cock as it slams into the back of my throat, his balls pressed against my mouth. I gasp, desperate for air, but inhale hair and flesh. He's on top of me, knees straddling my head. My arms are trapped beneath his legs, and I claw at them, but they're as thick and sturdy as the trunk of a tree.

My cries are muffled, covered by his grunts as his cock thrusts in and out.

I inhale through my nose, fighting off a gag. I'm used to Pace and even Wicker using my mouth to get ready to make a deposit, but the pointed, shallow drive of his hips tells me to brace myself.

Because with Pace, it's never easy.

The vibration of my cry makes him shudder. "Fuck," he groans, tipping his head back. The light from the fireplace finds the angles of his face, illuminating the edge of a cheekbone. His lips are parted as he pants out quiet, mindless words. "Fuck, I've been waiting for this. Not like the others. Not just weeks. *Years*, Rosi. Wanna come down your tight throat."

I push my hips off the bed as if that could help me escape the intrusion. But I know it can't. Pace doesn't want a blowjob. He wants his cock warmed, drawn to the edge over and over again. It's a test of wills—his or mine, I'm never sure. I didn't see it at first. I just thought he was the creepy fucker that stalked me freshman year. But it's so much clearer now. People think Wicker is the manipulative one, but they're wrong. Pace is the one who makes this happen.

In the groggy web of half-wakefulness, an instinct kicks in. It's new and frightening, the way I adjust to the knowledge that this is my last night here, and I just need to get through it.

One more night.

If I can satisfy Pace, then it'll be over for a whole month.

I flatten my tongue down the ridge of his cock and give him a firm suck. In response, he slams a palm against the headboard, spitting a curse. The hand tangled in my hair tips my head up for a thrust, the taste of him salty and thick.

"You should have seen their faces when we watched you on that video with Lucia," he says, running his other hand down the length of my hair. He may as well be playing with a doll. "They didn't even see it coming. For a second there, they really bought into this whole Princess thing. Wanted it. Wanted *you*. We finally see you now, though." Head tilting, he pitches his next words like a curious question. "You know that, right? I've never hidden the fact that I watch you, have I? That you're constantly monitored? Yet, for some reason, you refused to believe how far my reach extends." He leans forward, and the movement pushes his cock deeper down my throat. "You can't hide from me, Rosi. There are no limits to what I see. None."

I try to shake my head—the thought is as repellant as the baby being Wicker's or Lex's—but he holds me still, emitting a rough sound. His fingers twisting in my hair is the second signal that he's close, then the tightening of his jaw. His thrusts grow erratic, painfully rocking in my mouth. I think about all those times he came inside me, pumping far longer than either Wicker or Lex.

He's going to fucking drown me.

He pops off like a rocket, the surge thick and warm on the root of my tongue. I can barely breathe from the size of him, and this only makes it worse. I choke, inhaling through my nose in an attempt not to suffocate.

"Swallow, swallow," he's saying, half coaching me through it and half lost in his own ecstasy, eyes lazy slits as his brow knits up. I try, working my throat around the flood, because I know how fast I need to get it down to keep up with the sheer volume of it, slick and bitter.

But just when I think I've got it under control, another stream follows.

Panic claws at my lungs, eyes wide as I stare up at him.

The way he caresses my cheek is contrastingly tender. "Just a little more," he whispers. "I know it's your first time." Thumb moving to my chin, he holds my jaw open even when self-preservation tries to clamp it shut. He pumps in, catching a wayward stream from the corner of my mouth. Sighing, he pushes it back through my lips alongside his pulsing cock. "That'a girl. Take it all."

I shudder, the cum thick and unsettling as it hits my churning stomach.

He finishes with a slow, rolling growl, his cock giving one last twitch as he feeds me the last surge.

The second he slips from my mouth, I sputter, wrenching my head to the side to gasp in lungfuls of air. I barely feel him climbing off and flopping to the bed beside me because I'm too busy curling over the side of the mattress, coughing, feeling the fluid rising back up.

"Anything that comes back up, you'll swallow it back," he says. "Understand?"

I close my eyes and take a deep breath, willing my stomach to settle.

I stay like that for minutes, not moving again until I'm sure that nothing is coming back up. Reaching over, I flick on the giant wall sconce, daring to look beside me.

Pace hasn't left.

He's stretched out in the middle of the massive bed with his hands propped behind his neck. His dark eyes are so heavy, they're almost closed, one corner of his lips tipped up into a satisfied expression. He's kicked up a knee, emphasizing the curve of the spent cock flopped beside his hip. With the jewels adorning the headboard above him, it might be the most like a Prince Pace has ever looked—lascivious and spoiled. On his face is the ease of a man who just dumped a gallon of cum down his enemy's throat.

"Get out." My demand is hoarse and full of tight anger.

"And break the covenants?" His chest jerks with a dry chuckle. "I think not."

Looking down, I realize for the first time my gown has been pulled off and abandoned on the floor beside me. "I know the covenants," I snap, rushing to cover myself with the sheet. "And what you just did isn't one of them. I'll tell Ashby that you—"

"Fucked your mouth?" Pace shrugs. "Go ahead. Your womb is protected, but your throat is fair game. Also," his eyes finally slide to mine, "you know *your* covenants. The Princes' covenants say at least one of us has to sleep with you every night you're in this palace." He flexes a leg, the cut of his body intimidatingly masculine. "I volunteered."

"Why?" The question is curt, instinctual, even though it's obvious. He wanted one more night to punish me for betraying them.

"The same reason I volunteered to give you the ring," he says, dark eyes dropping to my mouth. "My brothers have given up on having a real Princess. They think there's no hope for you. But, Rosi..." His long arm shoots out, capturing me despite my attempt to flinch away from it. He pulls me forcibly against his side, the sheet sliding away. "Oh, I think you're coming along just fine. That move you made on Valentine's Day? That's the part of me I've been leaving inside you, hoping it'd grow. I'm thinking that's literal, too." He reaches down to flatten a palm to my belly, lips brushing my ear as he whispers, "This baby inside you? I bet I'm the one who put it there."

I struggle against his hold. "You don't know that."

"Nah, but I feel it." He cups my breast with a wide palm and exhales, like a man content. "I feel how much you're mine now." His words are evil, but his hands are gentle as he strokes my hair with one hand, his fingers idly circling my nipple with the other. His eyes rove my body as he shucks the sheets lower, revealing the part of me he wants most. "When I came in here and undressed you tonight, I was thinking how much I'd miss saving my cum for you." His fingers dip between my thighs, stroking, and even though I fasten my legs together, I know he feels the shameful slickness that's been building. Inhaling as if he can smell it, he suddenly wrenches me to my side, spooning in behind me. "I told you, didn't I? Every drop of me is meant for you. A little thing like pregnancy shouldn't get in the way of a promise."

I could thrash and fight as he slots his cock up to my entrance, pushing in, but I don't.

One more night.

Just one more night.

His voice is sleepy and deep, tickling my ear when he says, "You may be leaving here tomorrow, but you'll be taking East End with you. In the baby growing in your belly," he splays his hand over my stomach, "and every last drop of me that just ran down your throat."

I HAVEN'T BEEN ALONE with Wicker since that day in the solarium. I still remember the way he looked, drawn and full of exhaustion, the setting sun pushing a warm glow through his blonde hair.

Most of all, I remember the way I felt watching him.

Beautiful doesn't even begin to describe Wicker. I know I should be used to his face by now, but the perfect symmetry of his eyes framed by the sharp planes of his cheekbones is always startling. Like he's part alien combined with an ethereal angel—both lacking the grace of humanity. Whitaker Kayes wasn't made for human consumption, which is why I'm pretty sure he doesn't know how to truly act civilized.

It's hard taking him in all at once, especially in a closed space like the back of the car. Even worse when we're alone. I mean, how crazy is it that I'd rather feel the palpable anger rolling off Lex, or the quiet tension that Pace wields like a knife, than sit here with a petulant god.

Stella sits in the front next to Rory, the frat member who was unlucky enough to have chauffeur duty this week. She's unnaturally quiet, probably scared out of her wits to say something that'll sabotage the exchange.

Me and her both.

I still remember the sound Rory made when he ejaculated on me.

"I never took you for the kind of chick who'd run home to mommy," Wicker says, fastidiously picking a piece of lint off his shirt, "but here we are."

I know I shouldn't answer, and I suck on my teeth for a full thirty seconds before replying. "I'm not running home. I'm *going* home. There's a difference."

He looks out the window, and just like that day in the solarium, the rising sun finds him, rays clinging to the sharpness of his smirk. "Is there? Because I don't see the other Royal women living apart from their men. There's probably even some Countess out there curled up in whatever hovel North Side has holed up in." He snorts. "The point being, the other frats are a unit. Even if there are cracks under the surface—and I assure you there are—no one on the outside sees it."

Ah, there it is. "So that's what this is about," I realize, staring out my own window. "Presentation. You're afraid the other frats will judge you for me not living at the palace."

I feel his stare on my cheek, burning like a laser. "Don't you?"

My laughter is short and wry. "I judge you for a lot of things, Whitaker Ashby. Raping me repeatedly, for instance. Treating everyone like your underlings. Your massive ego. The way you sit back and watch your father abuse your brothers—" Suddenly, his hand clamps around my throat, the move so swift and violent that I snap back in rigid shock.

Those perfect blue eyes stare back at me, simmering with hatred. "You don't get to comment on that," he growls, squeezing. "*Ever*."

"Princess?" comes Stella's nervous voice.

I flick my eyes to hers, managing a minute shake of my head. She turns back to the road, hands wringing in her lap, but even though I know she wants to, Stella doesn't intervene.

In the rearview, I see Rory pressing his mouth in a tight, grim line. He doesn't even glance back at us.

I hold Wicker's stare, filled with cold, steely fury. "I'm not afraid of you." My own stare is daring him to leave a mark on me. I almost want him to lose control. For him to be the one going home to Daddy with the news he's snuffed out the life of his daughter and grandchild.

But if I was dead, I wouldn't be able to see it.

His lips pull back into a sneer. "You are such a bitch."

"Yeah, well, at least I'm not a whore."

The car slows, coming to a stop, snapping us out of our standoff. Wicker's nostrils flare with a thin restraint, but he releases me with a small shove, slumping back into his seat. Rory hops out, and I swallow, trying to settle my racing heartbeat.

By the time he opens the back door, I think I may look composed.

"After you, Princess," Wicker says, voice back to its lazy tone.

Rory offers me his hand, and I pause, glancing toward it and then back to him. It's the same hand that stroked his cock as he stood over me, and sometimes I wonder about it. This is the same boy who was so upset that his sister had gone missing. How can someone care about one girl while abusing another?

He shifts, feet shuffling as he waits for me to take his hand.

I step out of the car myself, edging around him.

Standing next to Stella, I smooth my skirt and assess where we are. There are invisible lines all over Forsyth, borders that define the parameters of each frat. There's no way the men who originally came up with a common social system would have known it'd devolve into this.

A black SUV is parked across this barrier, and Nick Bruin leans against the side of the car. He's in a tight black T-shirt that reveals the dark ink that marks his skin. His arms are crossed over his chest, his legs stretched out and crossed at the ankle. Ballsack stands a foot away, hands shoved in his pockets, his eyes trained on our car.

"Rory, grab the luggage," Wicker says, watching Nick. Ignoring my wince, he throws an arm over my shoulder and draws me against his hard side. "Remember, you may live with them, but you belong to us."

I'm not expecting it when his hand captures my chin, wrenching my face up to his. I'm expecting the ensuing kiss even less. Wicker licks out, parting my lips so expertly that it's startling—as if my body has fallen traitorously in sync with his.

It's a hard kiss, full of teeth and a strength that I can't even hope to match. I clutch the collar of his shirt in a fist and ride it out, desperate to ignore the way he's palming my backside, making my skirt ride up.

"Jesus, Ashby," Nick says, pushing off the car, "stop dry-humping her and check the product so we can get the fuck out of here."

Wicker bodily pushes me away, like *I'm* the one who was kissing *him*. "I will as soon as you bring what you owe me."

Ballsack emerges from the back of the SUV carrying a crate in his hands—I'm assuming the guns Ashby requested at the negotiation. Wicker and Nick eye one another and nod. I'm pushed across the 'line' while Ballsack and Rory make a trade, the guns for the luggage.

"Is this all?" Wicker asks, following Rory around the back of the vehicle. He rests the crate on the tailgate and wedges off the lid.

"That's just a sample of what we have to offer," Nick says, eyeing my throat with a scrutiny that suggests Wicker may have left fingerprints. "Tell your brothers to test those out and make an order, and we'll deliver the rest at the next drop-off."

Wicker inspects the contents, reaching in and pulling out a revolver. I've never seen Wicker hold a weapon before, and it's strange seeing those slim fingers, used to expertly play music and make passes across the ice, gripping the handle as confidently as the bow of his cello or the neck of his hockey stick.

Our eyes meet, and I feel the memory of his fingers on my throat, a strange twist of heat in my chest.

"We'll be in touch," he says, placing the gun back in the crate. He brushes off his hands. "See you on campus, Princess."

"Get in the car, Ver," Nick says as Rory slams the trunk. He glances at Stella. "You, too."

I climb in the front seat while Stella and Ballsack get in the back. Once I'm inside, I release a long exhale. That went faster than I was expecting, and I'm grateful, so relieved that my muscles go lax all at once.

For the first time in weeks, I feel like I can breathe.

"Everything go okay after we left yesterday?" Nick cuts his eyes to me. "I mean, no one took anything out on you for us showing up like that? Because, look, we tried, but Mama B found out about the ceremony and lost her shit. There was no stopping her."

"No." I spin the crown ring around my finger. I don't know if it's just the newness of it or the sparkly metal, but I can't keep my eyes off it. It's like the minute they put it on my finger, I felt different.

Owned.

"The palace was operating as normal."

I catch Stella's eye in the side mirror. We'd discussed before leaving that I would adhere to the covenants. Neither of us would or *could* reveal a word about the inner workings of East End. I'm taking Pace at his word. He's watching.

We take a turn that goes away from both the tower and the gym, down toward the old industrial area that's seen a bit of revitalization over the last few years.

We pass a few shops, including the boutique where Remy buys all of his fantastic boots. The coffee shop next door is new, as is the indie bookstore. I take in all the changes, and Nick pulls up in front of an old building. It's four stories with a faded brick façade. Across the top, you can still read the muted painted words, *The Royal Gazette*.

"Are we running a job?" I ask, peering out the window. If Pace or the others find out Nick took me somewhere dangerous, this whole thing is going to blow up fast.

"Nope. Turns out Saul had secrets." He rolls his eyes as if this wasn't a surprise at all. He turns off the ignition. By the time Stella and I are on the sidewalk, Ballsack already has our luggage out of the back.

"And this building was one of them?" I ask, trying to follow.

"When Sy became King, everything transferred into his name." He pulls out a big metal key and shoves it into the lock. "And I mean *everything*. Bank accounts, insurance settlements, his university pension, but what no one knew Saul was doing was collecting property like he was Daniel Fucking Payne." The tall door unlatches with a loud click, then creaks open. "Since Saul had no heirs, at least that we know of," he gives me a meaningful look, "he specified in his will that his entire estate go to his successor."

"Holy shit," I say, processing what that means. The Bruin-Perilini boys grew up modestly. Sure, they had a house and a supportive family, but when their parents walked away from being Dukes, they lost all of their connections. Not just in West End but all of Forsyth. "So Sy owns all of this."

"Yep. The whole block." He jerks his chin at Ballsack. "Keep an eye on the door."

Ballsack nods. "You got it."

There's a staircase, but I'm relieved when Nick walks over to an elevator and stabs the up button. The doors open, and Nick grabs both of our suitcases and carries them in.

Once inside, he presses the button for the fourth floor. I grip the handrail as the elevator starts to rise. "Last night, after the negotiations, we had to have a long talk about where you were going to stay during your time in West End. You sure as hell can't live in the tower. It's too small; besides the three bedrooms, there's only the loft. Plus," he winks at Stella, "I don't think you and your handmaiden want to see Remy's junk every morning."

Stella blushes, and I wrinkle my nose. Remy's good-looking and everything, but I've had enough dicks in my face over the last few months to last a lifetime.

"Mama B wanted you to come back to her place," he continues, "but Lavinia asked Sy to reconsider."

I feel an unexpected sense of relief just hearing that. "Wow, seriously?"

"She figured you needed a space of your own." He shifts, looking at me head-on. I'm not afraid of Nick, but he's intimidating as hell. The face tattoo and the intensity in his eyes just enhances his attractiveness in a weird way. "Even I can admit that being a Royal woman isn't easy. We put Lavinia through hell." His gaze drops to my belly. "I imagine you've earned the right to a little privacy."

The bell chimes, followed by the door opening. We step directly into a wide, expansive space. It's mid-renovation, but the bones are visible. An open kitchen to the right, and a large living room in the middle. Huge windows look out over three sides, including one massive view toward the river. On the walls, there are some framed bits of yellowing paper, which looking closer, I realize are article clippings.

Gruesome articles.

"Yeah," Nick says, jerking his chin at the wall, "Lavinia goes apeshit over all these old newspapers we've been digging up."

I grimace at a front page spread declaring *Forsyth Carver Slays Another*. Below it, I begin reading about some psycho who terrorized the campus a few decades back, but when footsteps echo in another part of the space, I look up to see Lavinia emerging from a hallway.

"You're here!" She rushes over and pulls me into a hug. "God, I've been so worried those little pricks would pull something at the last minute."

"Things have been a little tense, but I think everyone needed a little space." I pull back and take in my friend. It's so good to see her. "Thank you for setting this up."

"Of course. After..." The thought trails off, and her forehead creases. Whatever she was going to say is changed to, "We had to keep you safe."

She saw the video. So did Nick and the guys. I know that, and they probably see me differently now, but everything that happened to me in the palace is part of me. I own that.

I give her a tight smile, because, again, there's no guarantee that I'm not being watched, and walk over to the window. The sunlight streams through, and I feel warmth on my face. "This place is amazing."

"Apparently, Saul had big plans for this building," Nick says, slinging his arm around Lavinia's shoulder. She pushes up on her toes and presses a kiss against the tattoo of her lips on his throat. "For the whole district. Apartments, condos, lofts, offices, retail..." He looks around the cavernous space. "He started here on the top floor. It's already fitted with plumbing and electrical—enough for a working kitchen and bathroom."

"Was he going to move in?" As far as I knew, Saul had a penthouse near campus, but it makes sense he'd have other places. Daniel Payne had the Hideaway. Ashby has his club.

"Oh no. This was his hidey-hole for whatever purebred sugar baby he had lined up at the time. A glass case to keep them in." He looks down at Lav. "Little Bird fell for the place, and we decided to finish the renovation and move in after graduation. You can stay here in the meantime."

It's definitely unconventional, but he's right. Staying at the tower isn't an option, and the more I think about it, neither is going back home with my mother. This place is bright and airy—I can see why Lavinia likes it. I like it too—it's the opposite of the palace.

Nick turns to face me, grinning while spreading his arms wide. "Welcome home."

4

Pace

"It doesn't even make sense," Wicker says as we step out of the car into the university lot. He slams his door particularly hard, earning an annoyed glance from Lex.

"The covenants aren't there to make sense," Lex insists, snapping his fingers in front of Wicker's face. "They're there to keep us all in line."

Wick blinks, tearing his eyes from the smooth legs of a passing senior. "You know he fucked around on his Princess." He punctuates this by jabbing a finger into Lex's sternum.

Lex smacks it away. "Yeah, we've done the math. He got Liberty Sinclaire pregnant two years after Michael was born. And look how that turned out."

"Here's some more math: the fidelity covenant was added sixteen years ago," I pitch in, adjusting my bag. "She's probably the reason he made it."

We make our way toward the courtyard, trying to ignore all the glances. In no universe would the Princes arrive on campus without their Princess the week following a pregnancy announcement, and that's spectacle enough.

But some of these people have seen the video.

The video of Lex.

Being whipped.

"Fucking bitch," Lex mutters, giving a group of curious freshmen the stink eye. "Should have broadcast her cleansing to the whole metro area."

Image is something Lex and Wicker have always placed a lot of importance on. Maybe it's because I spent time in the system before becoming an Ashby, but it never really meant much to me. At least, not in the same way.

I step in front, comfortable confronting the gawking head-on. People never look at me for too long; rumors of my stint in the Forsyth Penitentiary are still close enough to the surface of the gossip mill. My brothers would shy away from *that* image. I harness it.

A girl from my languages class hastily passes, ducking her head.

"Fine," Wicker grits out, still fuming about the fidelity covenant, "we can't risk getting someone pregnant. That, I get. What I *don't* get," his eyes fixed on Forsyth University's leading track star, Malcolm Tran, "is why the *fuck* I can't fool around with other guys. It's, like... fucking heteronormative whatever."

Lex snorts. "We also can't risk passing an STD to the Princess, idiot."

Wicker's lip curls up. "As if I'm ever putting my dick in that again. Been there, done—" But his gaze drifts upward, words fluttering away as he comes to an abrupt stop. Lex and I follow his gaze.

Lex huffs. "Shit. It's Monday."

Yes, it is.

And Verity Sinclaire is at her spot in the courtyard, collecting her Royal favors.

A line of PNZ members approaches her, one by one. Some of them are wielding our house's signature white roses, but others have come bearing sparkly, wrapped gift boxes. Probably jewelry. Gadgets. Shiny trinkets.

Baby clothes.

From the first glance, there's a tug in my gut that I can't even begin to ignore. It was one thing to be at the coronation, kissing her stomach. It was another to find her sleeping that night, peeling off that gown and seeing the flat plane of her belly. Still, it's another thing altogether to stand here amidst a crowd that understands what's inside her.

I release a long, ragged breath. "The fuck is she wearing?"

"For the next four weeks," Lex says, looking away, "she's West End."

She's wearing the uniform, too.

From her canvas high-tops and ripped-up, black leggings, to the tight red shirt, her cleavage on full display, Verity looks every inch the cutslut she was raised to be. No pristine white. No pearls. No gold or purple.

Red and black.

Without tearing my eyes from her, I ask Wicker, "You were saying?"

I don't even have to look to know his dick is getting hard.

Mine sure as fuck is.

"Whatever," he says, feigning a flippancy I almost buy. But then, with just as much conviction, he adds, "She'd have to beg me to fuck her."

Lex swings an arm over his shoulders, leading him away. "Good luck with that."

I don't follow them, though. I stand there and watch her, the way she accepts box after bundle, stone-faced, not even meeting their gazes. There's always been something about Verity, since that first time I saw her online. It's not just that she's pretty. It's not even that she's transformed from pretty to hot.

It's this *softness*.

Even dressed in her West End armor, she exudes vulnerability. Accepting a box from Matt Kramus, she shrinks into herself even as her shoulders square. It's the fascinating duality of it. How can someone be so weak, yet so tough? How can the girl who looked my brother in his murderous eyes, playing that video for the frat on Valentine's Day, be the same watery-eyed girl who took my cock in her throat last night?

Lex would sink into her softness.

Wicker would seek out the toughness.

But I want it all.

I want the way her eyes find mine, and I want the way she flinches at the knowledge I'm watching. I want the way her shoulders curl inward protectively, but I also want the heat of her glare.

I move to the end of the line.

It's been a long time since I paid Royal favor to a Princess. The whole ritual of it always felt unseemly to me. Transactional, like we're paying a hooker to perform for our house. If I had my choice, it'd be the Duchess or Baroness—women who adorn their Royal men because they want to, not because of the prestige of the position.

But I think I'm beginning to understand because when I finally make it to the front of the line, approaching my Princess with a sly, vicious smirk, it's with the knowledge she has no choice.

A Princess must *always* accept her gifts.

I grab her chin. "Open."

Her eyes flare with anger at the demand, flitting from side to side as if she's considering rebelling. Her cheeks flex with a restrained grimace, which is how I know she won't. Too public for such a spectacle, especially since she's West End right now. She wouldn't want to jeopardize our fragile peace, would she?

Sighing, she points her gaze to a vague point over my shoulder and parts her lips.

I wrench her face up, gathering saliva in my mouth.

Then, I spit onto her tongue.

She shudders when I clamp her mouth shut, waiting for the bob of her throat as she dutifully swallows me down.

"For my beautiful Princess." Trailing a fingertip down her neck, I graze the valley of her cleavage, and then lower, resting my hand on her belly. Leaning in, I whisper, "May she reign."

~

East End is known for the golden row—the blocks of townhouses the frat lives in—and the Purple Palace. But this is the side of East End I know best. It's wedged up against the north, past the luxury boutiques and mansions, and embodies Father's kingdom better than anything else. The buildings are modern, clean, and nondescript, some having no signage at all.

I park Wicker's flashy sports car in the alley out back, stepping out into the cold rain. Raising my hood, I march up to the door, *Bastion Security* etched into the glass, and jab the buzzer. While I wait, I look over my shoulder, scanning the area. That gnawing vigilance is still in the back of my mind, even months after my release from prison, but I don't mind it.

It's how I know Father is watching me.

The only true point of surveillance is a camera built into a decorative lamp post across the street. I've watched it enough to know the dome isn't sealed correctly, so whenever it rains, condensation builds up inside it, making the picture little more than a blurred smudge.

Right now, the rain is pelting the dark pavement, but I don't know how much longer the weather will hold. I've been waiting for this downpour for a week. Impatiently, I slam my hand into the buzzer again. And again. And again.

Finally, I see a figure stumbling down the hall, his thin mustache twitching into a frown. He's wearing his signature loud Hawaiian shirt, this one an obnoxious neon green, and a pair of basketball shorts. There's half a burrito clutched in his left hand.

Charlie's a pasty nerd nearing his late thirties, but unless someone saw his atrocious facial hair and male-pattern baldness, they wouldn't know it. The guy is infamous for being a sleazeball around the frat, always acting like he's one of the guys.

He pauses when he sees me but quickly recovers, unlatching the door.

"Well, this is an unexpected—" He grunts in surprise when I slip in, pushing past him.

"I need some eyes in West End," I say, making a beeline for the room in the back. Charlie releases baffled sputters as he follows behind me, his socked feet slapping against the floor.

"Eyes in West End? Shouldn't I be asking you for that?"

Stepping into Charlie's tech room, I grimace at the smell of armpit and microwave food, before glancing around at the monitors. A cycling feed of the golden row is up on the main display, which doesn't come as a surprise. The others show various views of businesses around Forsyth. It's nothing I don't already have access to.

"Cut the shit," I say, turning to level him with a look. "I've seen the alley's security event feed, so I know you're working with Nick Bruin."

"Wh-what?" Charlie gives an impersonation of innocence that doesn't even approach convincing. He doesn't even stop chewing his burrito. "I'm not—I'd *never*—"

Pressed for time, I stress, "Yes, you would, and if I actually gave a flying fuck about you trading intel for pictures of his abs," Charlie's mouth snaps closed, "then your ass would currently be occupying the Barons' crypt. Lucky for you, the Princes have an interest in cultivating your—" I sneer, "—connections."

After a long, tense beat, Charlie chuckles, dropping into a leather desk chair. "That's overstating it a bit. He was looking for something that didn't have anything to do with East End. Something about the Lucia chick's sister. I figured, what's the harm in a little spank bank material?"

I caught it on archive footage I've been going through since the tournament. This same dark alley on a night a few months back, days before my release from prison. If I'd been here, I would have caught it in real-time, Nick Bruin and his Duchess waltzing right up to Bastion Security and snagging some footage from a local pharmacy.

Luckily for everyone involved, I *wasn't* here.

I would have shut that shit down instantly.

"First of all, that's not your decision to make. Second of all," my eye twitches as Charlie turns his back to me, wolfing down the last of the burrito, "I don't have time for your pussy pretense. Bruin's also contracted you for surveillance on the downtown strip recently. You know it, I know it. Don't embarrass yourself."

Wiping his hand on his shirt, he speaks around a mouthful of tortilla and beef. "Look, no offense. I think you do great work, Pace. Hell, I probably taught you most of it. But the thing is," he turns to give me a shrug, "the Dukes are scarier than you."

I fist my hands in my pockets, jaw tight. "You think so?"

Charlie swivels side to side in his seat, not a care in the world. "Also, that Nick Bruin is a snack. Granted, straighter than dry spaghetti. I'm just trying to boil him a bit. This isn't some Royal flip I'm doing. Personally, I prefer East End dick." He stops the swivel, twisting to meet my gaze. "But, you know... the Princes are not without leverage. Your brother—"

"Isn't a part of this," I snap. "And the next time you suggest he should be whored out for the benefit of you *doing your job*, you're not going to have one."

Stupidly, Charlie doesn't look intimidated, clucking his tongue as he turns back to the screen. "This is about the Princess, I assume?" He shakes his head. "It's a no-go, anyway. The Dukes have got your walking tribute to a creampie locked down like Fort Knox. She's a little jewel in their cap, isn't she? You Royals must be shitting yourselves. They've got the Lucia heir *and* the Ashby heir in West End. I mean, it's obviously not about the Sinclaire girl. I've seen her around. She's not even their best gutter slut." His slimy laugh makes my spine go rigid.

Unblinking, my head tilts. "What did you just say?"

"No, no, I get it, I get it," Charlie rushes out, grabbing the mouse to navigate through a nest of folders on the monitor. "Big tits, nice hips. Not my thing, obviously, but fuck me, that footage of the Royal Cleansing?" Clicking a file, his eyes roll back dramatically as it brings up the recording.

On the screen, Verity's dead eyes look ahead as a long ribbon of Tommy Wright's cum lands on her collarbone.

Charlie groans. "So much premium Forsyth cock in that video, I haven't jerked off this much in *years*. It's a shame you didn't gag her, though." He frowns, leaning back in the chair as he clicks on another timestamp. This one is Rory Livingston, face screwed up as he comes. "All that crying really wilts my dick, so I always have to mute it."

"Hm." I take my hands from my pocket.

If Charlie hadn't put his back to me, he'd probably understand what's coming. As it is, he barely has time to flinch in confusion when I grab a thick fistful of his hair, shoving the barrel of a gun into the middle of the hand currently resting on the mouse.

A deafening crack resounds when I pull the trigger.

Charlie gasps, snatching his hand back, and for a comical moment, he just stares at the ragged, bleeding hole there, eyes full of wide shock.

Then, he opens his mouth and screams.

I yank his head back before he can bolt away. "Clearly, we're having a little miscommunication. I'm not your thirteen-year-old intern anymore, Charlie. I'm your boss. I'm your president. I'm motherfucking god as far as you're concerned, so you'd better start praying."

"You shot me!" He even looks at me when he says this, grasping his wrist so hard, he's shaking. Blood gushes down his pasty forearm. "Pace, you shot me!"

"See, this is the worst part about maiming people," I say, waving the gun menacingly. "They always think they have to tell you about it. Why is that?" Not giving him time to answer, I give his hair another hard yank. "To clarify, I'm not asking you to flip on the Dukes. I'm telling you. Get me a camera in that fucking newspaper building by tomorrow night, or I'll gut you, balls to throat."

I shove him forward as I release him, ignoring the agonized sound he's screeching through gnashed teeth. While he processes this information, I approach the server cabinet, yanking out hard drive after hard drive, until the image of Verity on the blood-spattered screen goes black.

Then, I take them all to the next room to power up the metal shredder.

Charlie stumbles in five minutes later, pale as a sheet and still clutching his mangled, bloody hand. "You can't—there's pivotal information on those!" he says as I feed another drive into the shredder. It's loud, the tumblers cranking away as they tear through the disks.

I toss the last drive in. "I have off-site backups. Probably because you only taught me a fraction of what I know."

When I turn to him, I can tell he's seeing me in a different light. There's spite—an unmistakable glare—and also a lot of pain, which is expected. But there's something else, too.

Right now, I'm scarier than Nick Bruin.

"I'd never get a camera into that building," Charlie grits as I pull the gun back out, racking the slide. "I mean, not *that* building! You've gotta understand, they're—they're making that place into their home. I'm not the only guy they've contracted. I'd be caught. But," he rushes out, holding his hand aloft, "there's another place. Across the street. It's—it might get your eyes through some windows."

I pause, thinking. "That'll do." Charlie's posture sinks in relief, until I add, "For now."

He whimpers as he grips his wrist "For now?"

"Until you can find me something closer." Passing him on my way out, I pause only to make one thing known. "Verity Sinclaire is the best woman in Forsyth. Wanna know why?" He flinches as I lean in, my stare hard. "Because she's mine."

Charlie cuts it close.

I spend the whole day impatient and jittery. I can catch glimpses of her on the campus footage, but it's not enough. I have backdoors into her SMS and email, so I know when she orders a coffee. I know when she makes an appointment with her advisor. I know when she adds grapes to her shopping list.

But I can't fucking *see* her.

West End is an ancient, crumbling maze of low-tech bullshit. This wasn't a problem back in the day when I was watching her as a cute little freshman. But now, I'm a Prince. There's no hope of me crossing the boundaries to watch her myself.

The notification arrives with only five minutes to spare.

Charlie: Would have gotten this to you sooner, except there seems to be an issue with my mouse hand.

His next message is an IP address with login credentials. Not wasting any time, I plug it into the RTSP address format and bring up the streams.

Streams.

Plural.

I'm not as disappointed as I expected to be.

Each camera is looking right into a window. Three of them are black, but two of them are illuminated. One is obviously a kitchen, the bigger one the main living space. The tension in my back slowly unwinds as I see her silhouette passing between them, a mug clutched in her hand. She's wearing a bulky sweater. Must be cold in there. Her hair is pulled up, a couple of tendrils swaying loose around her temples.

Leaning back in my seat, I watch.

"*Please, god, no.*" Behind me, Effie loudly preens her feathers. "*Please, god. Please, no.*"

I slide her an exasperated look. "That's the last time I let you watch anything from the dungeon archives." I had to transcribe a video for a contract this morning. It was tedious enough hearing all the 'Please, god's in person. Now I have to hear it third-hand.

She pecks at the bar of her cage. "*Pretty bird?*"

"Yes," I agree, reaching back to let her out. Effie immediately jumps to my desk, her little head bouncing back and forth as she watches the screen with me. Verity is on a sofa, legs curled beneath her, a textbook open in her lap.

Effie's voice softens. "*Gentle, gentle.*"

I stroke distracted fingers along her back. "Yeah, that's our girl."

A hot frisson runs down my spine just hearing myself say it. That's what Verity is now. I look at her stomach and feel my cock begin to swell. My baby is in there, taking root. All this time, I thought the best way of having a girl might be locking her up in my dungeon, or having her on her knees, my cock nestled in her warm mouth. None of it compares to the knowledge that a part of me is inside of her.

Possessing her.

Of course, it could be Wicker's or Lex's, but it wouldn't matter. There's no way the three of us didn't make that baby together, imbuing our Princess with the essence of us. That's something my brothers don't understand yet. I can see it in them. The bitterness. The anger. The misery. They still think this is a punishment, something we're enduring.

But for me, nothing has ever felt more right.

Or more mine.

She eats a bowl of cereal at nine and goes to the bathroom shortly after. Then, into the bedroom at ten. She probably doesn't even realize her dresser mirror is placed in an unfortunate location, where someone looking through her window can glimpse half a tit when she dresses for bed.

I get frustrated and tense when she turns out the light, but then a blue glow appears, illuminating her face as she settles into bed.

The laptop.

Instantly, I pull up the screen mirroring program, feeling more of those electric zings as I watch her cursor move on my screen. It's better than having her here with me, this knowledge that I'm getting her unfiltered, without reservation.

She opens her email first, sending a document titled *Geopolitical Structures of North Asia* to her poli-sci professor.

"A little light reading for us before bed," I say to Effie, downloading the file.

Next, she does some searches on morning sickness. Apparently, there are a million different 'cures', and each personal account would swear on their fetus that *theirs* actually works. I watch her expression on the screen, nose wrinkling with every disgusting recipe.

There's a moment where the cursor pauses over the search bar.

Then, she begins typing in the text box.

"Forsyth abortion providers."

I jolt from my seat, startling Effie into a flapping fit, but before I can grab my phone and send Verity a text, she begins backspacing.

On the screen, a tendril of her hair flutters with a sigh.

"Maternity jeans."

Slowly, I set my phone back down, sinking back into my seat. "You're goddamn right."

Effie squawks. "*Please, god, no.*"

I don't even realize how long I've been watching her until a knock sounds at my door. I jolt again, this time fumbling to pull up the feed of the hallway. If Father finds out about these cameras...

But when the door swings open, it's just Lex, shirtless and mildly disgruntled. "It's after midnight. Are you going to—" His words cut off when he sees the screen.

Immediately, he shuts the door behind him. "Is that...?"

Releasing a breath, I sink back into my seat. "Yeah. It's her."

Lex steps closer, zeroing in on her face. "How the fuck are you watching her right now?" He cuts his eyes to me. "If you crossed into Perilini's territory—"

"Give me some credit." I reach down to adjust my cock, which I now realize has gone from semi-hard to full-on boner. "I've got friends in low places."

Lex's gaze tracks my hand, eyes narrowing. "Why are you even bothering? Personally, I'm glad to be rid of her for a month."

There's a tinge of betrayal in his voice that makes my shoulders tense. "We have to make sure she's not organizing against us," I offer, trying to make it casual.

Lex can sense how weak that argument is. "Let her. So long as we get a baby in eight months, we win." Straightening, he nods to Effie.

"Put her away and come to bed. We have that job tomorrow, and you still have to show up at practice. You and Wicker need to rest."

Shrugging, I turn to put Effie back into her cage. "Then I guess you don't want to hear about the coffee she had today."

As expected, the room grows tense with a sudden silence.

"Excuse me?"

When I turn back, Lex is glaring daggers at Verity's image on the screen. "A large Americano. Enough caffeine to wake the dead, am I right?"

The knot at the back of Lex's jaw twitches. "She knows that's not allowed."

"Not in East End," I remind him. "But she's in West End now, and how would we know if she fudged the rules a bit, huh?"

I can see the moment he breaks, nose flaring with a curt huff. "I want a nightly report," he grinds out, eyes never leaving the screen. "Anything she eats, drinks, or comes into contact with. If it's going into her body, I want to know about it."

"Done," I say, already pulling up a spreadsheet. Verity Sinclaire might not like belonging to me.

But she's about to find out that belonging to Lex is so much worse.

5

erity

"WHY DO they call it morning sickness if you feel awful all the time?" I'm on my knees in front of the toilet, neck coated in a sheen of sweat. I haven't been on my knees this long since Pace made me suck him off under the table during the PNZ meeting that one time. "And what's the point of the prenatal vitamins if I'm just going to barf them up?"

"Poor thing," Stella says, laying a cool cloth over my neck. "Are you sure you don't want—"

"I *want* to die," I snap. Nothing I've eaten in the last forty-eight hours has stayed down. Not crackers. Not bread. Not the chocolate donut Remy brought me in an attempt to make me feel better. Which… it did make me feel better until it rushed back up. "But not here. A little help?"

Stella's slim arms come around my waist, helping me get on my feet.

"Bed?" she asks, angling me back to the bedroom.

"No." I shake my head. "Couch."

The entire bedroom suite at the loft is new, and it should be comfortable, but as much as I hate to admit it, the mattress on the massive Princess bed in my room at the palace was way more comfortable. I only lived there for a couple of months, but I've somehow grown disturbingly familiar with the plush sea of silks. The mattress here feels too small, and the pillows too firm. I've spent the last three nights tossing and turning, cursed with a twinge in my neck.

The oversized couch in the living room is a different story. I could spend days here under the chenille blanket Lavinia brought me. Leaning back on the soft pillows, I close my eyes and struggle against another wave of nausea. "I think if I just sit here and not move... I'll be okay."

Stella wrings her hands as she watches me, but I catch the way her eyes flick over her shoulder. She's been incredibly attentive, even more so than she was in East End, and that's saying a lot. But I can tell she has somewhere she'd rather be. Unlike at the Purple Palace, the Dukes allow her freedom here in West End. But no matter how many times I tell her she can go, she refuses.

"I'll just be in the kitchen," she says.

My eyes flutter open. "Thank you, Stella. I'm sorry I'm being such a bitch."

"You're not being a bitch!" she answers a little too quickly. "You're creating a life, and that's hard work."

"Maybe, but you're a lifesaver." They're all lifesavers: the Dukes, Lavinia, Stella, even my mother. I can't imagine how hellacious it would be to go through this in the chilly tension of the palace.

I keep my eyes shut and try to keep the nausea at bay while Stella quietly moves around the kitchen. I've been to campus every day, fulfilling my duty as Princess and attending classes. I refuse to let this situation stop me from getting my degree. Plenty of other women have managed to survive a pregnancy and go to college. I'm determined to be one of them.

"Try this," Stella says, and I open my eyes to see her approaching with a cup, steam wisping off the top. "It may help."

Glancing skeptically at the contents—tea, *gross*—I take a sip, tasting the sharp edge of ginger. I wait for the instantaneous urge to puke, but after a moment, it seems like it isn't going to come. I wrap my palms around the mug, warming one before using it to massage my own neck. "Where did you get this?"

Her eyes dart over to the big box on the counter. "Well... you see..."

"Seriously?" Sneering, I sniff the drink with a little more suspicion. "I thought I told you I don't want anything from him."

"My god, you can be stubborn!" It doesn't happen often, but sometimes Stella gets these flashes of steely resolve, and right now, she's propping her hands on her hips, mouth pressed into a tense line. "You haven't been able to keep anything down all day, and I'm not going to leave here until I'm sure you're alright." She marches over to the box, removes a package, and aggressively inspects it. "Prince Lex sent all kinds of things that may help. These are ginger candies, which will help settle your stomach. If you won't take them for yourself, then at least try it for me?"

I deflate at the pleading look in her eyes.

The box from the palace was delivered to the gym yesterday. By the time Ballsack dropped it off, it had been completely rummaged through and thoroughly checked for anything compromising, like bugs or recording devices.

Fucking hell, I think after taking a few more sips. The tea isn't just the first thing I've been able to keep down today, but my nausea actually abates. Groaning in defeat, I hold out my hand. "Let me see that candy."

Stella's face lights up.

If I thought my life would get easier away from the palace, I was wrong. The nausea and exhaustion are one thing, but the way people here handle me makes me wonder if coming back was such a good idea. The Dukes still treat me the same, but sometimes they'll suddenly avert their eyes, and my face will grow aflame with the possibility they're remembering what they saw on that video of the Royal Cleansing.

The cutsluts are different. I used to be a sister to them, but now I'm just a visitor. Lavinia isn't allowed to be alone with me anymore, one of her Dukes always hovering nearby whenever she visits. There's zero hope of a meeting with Story. And though Stella is never more than a text away from flitting through the doorway, I feel more like a job to her than a friend. My mother would welcome me with open arms, but I'm still furious at her, so I take Sy's cop-out with this living arrangement and hole up here.

The old newspaper press is full of open, cavernous rooms. It's never very quiet, with old pipes knocking and radiators hissing. Everything here is hard and cold. In the short time I lived at the palace, I grew accustomed to the odd rhythms of the house. The creepy secret passageways. The hush. The lushness of everything.

I would never admit it aloud, but I miss my solarium.

My solarium?

When did it become mine?

I keep waiting for Wicker to walk in and demand I bend over a table or for Effie's squawk about Wicker's balls. More than once, I've woken with a start, confused by sleep, thinking Lagan is standing at the end of the bed, feral and wild.

Pace told me I'd been conditioned, and he isn't wrong. I feel restless, caught between two lives, and due to this godforsaken pregnancy, I can't even enjoy finally being back home.

Possibly because it isn't.

Home, that is.

But if this isn't home—and the palace sure as hell isn't, either—then where is it?

Stella drops a few of the candies in my hand, and I pop one in my mouth, freezing as I suck the flavor from it. *Son of a bitch*. They're delicious. Pulling the blanket up toward my chin, I wonder, "What else is in there? Any more candy?"

"Let's see," she picks through the box. "A journal that you're supposed to write in every day. There's a fetal heart monitor. I guess you attach that to your belly? Oh, a pack of nausea wristbands!" She immediately slips one on her wrist. "That may come in handy. Also, there are three pregnancy books, lavender bath beads, and," she lifts a container, beaming, "more vitamins."

I cut my hand over my throat. "Absolutely not. I'm done with those. I think they're part of what's making me sick."

Stella's face falls. "Are you sure? Prince Lex is a pretty smart guy, so if he thinks you need—"

I roll my eyes. "There are people all over the world without access to this stuff, and they have healthy babies every day. Missing a few pills isn't going to hurt me or the baby." I glare at the bottle. "Starving to death might."

She nods, packing everything back in the box. "Oh. He sent something else, too." There's a pause, and then her cheery, "Aww!"

"What?" I sit up, feeling much better.

She holds up a U-shaped neck pillow covered in silk that matches my bedding back at the palace. "He wants you to be comfy."

My lip curls in distaste. "He didn't seem to care much about my discomfort while putting me into this situation."

"Well, he does now," Stella says, more of that obstinance shining through when she tosses me the pillow. I catch it clumsily, fingers fumbling against the silk. "And just because he's terrible and you hate him isn't any reason to make yourself suffer harder."

Pursing my lips, I inspect the pillow. "You're probably right."

"I'm definitely right," Stella corrects, admiring the band on her wrist. "Do you think—"

"It's all yours."

She gives a delighted grin, saying, "It's my first Fury tonight! Are you going?"

My own smile plummets. "No." Even if my stomach remains settled and I could handle being treated like rival Royalty from the others in the gym, chances are almost certain Ashby will be there. "Hm. Isn't Ballsy fighting tonight?"

Stella bites her lip, but I still see the responding smile threatening to break through. "I think so. Is he any good?"

Restraining a grin, I answer, “He’s West End, so probably. You should go and check it out. Friday Night Fury is always lots of fun.”

“But not for you?”

My nose wrinkles. “Not like it used to be.”

Stella understands things better than people give her credit for. She gives me a solemn nod. “Family is about more than DNA and zip codes. Eventually, they’ll remember that.”

Her statement isn’t as comforting as it should be. When I decided to become Princess, I always knew I’d have the Dukes and West End to lean on because they *were* my family. But learning the truth about Ashby being my father...that changes things, even if it shouldn’t. There are too many secrets. Too many unknowns. One of those unknowns includes who exactly is the father of the baby I’m carrying.

It’s something I try to push out of my mind because what does it matter? They’ll all claim it as theirs, but the more layers that are uncovered—generations of lies and deceit, I wonder more than ever: what the hell have I gotten myself into?

Ballsack wins his fight.

I know this because Stella spends the whole weekend gushing about it, which somehow necessitates a complete recounting of just how much his muscles rippled when he took out a ‘scrawny’ Beta Rho.

By the time Monday rolls around, I’m grateful for the excuse to get out, even if it means standing like a statue for my weekly ‘favors’ from PNZ. It’s the beginning of my third week in West End, and with every gift I take, I can hear the clock ticking in the back of my mind. In less than two weeks, I’ll be traded back to the Ashbys, and the gnawing unease in the pit of my stomach grows more turbulent with each day that brings me closer.

I spend my poli-sci class sucking doggedly on the candies, and when I rush to my stats class—a required math elective—I come to a sudden stop at the scent of ginger in the air. I’ve recently discovered that the professor is an ex-Prince, which is both horrifying and convenient. In the last couple of weeks, I've caught him staring at my belly with a wistful expression, only snapping out of it when I cover my midsection with my bag. But he gives me liberties the other students lack, and I find a new one waiting for me.

"For you, Princess," he says, gesturing to the table by the door. On it sits a steaming electric kettle, paper cups, a bowl of fresh ginger, and teabags.

If I turn to make myself a cup, it's mostly just to stop him from staring.

I think about it during the lecture, wondering who's responsible. Stella is a possibility, but it's far more likely that it was Lex himself. The thought sits uneasily on my tongue as I sip the tea down. On a day like today, any attention from my Princes is suspicious.

At the end of class, I don't wait until the room has emptied before slinging my bag over a shoulder and pushing to my feet, snagging up my cup. I walk with the pulsing throng of students down the hallway, feeling their heat against me.

Hopefully, Lex doesn't realize just how useful this tea is.

A skinny LDZ member I recognize from my Life Painting class bumps into me. Or, well, that's how it seems—especially to any eyes watching from a camera. I gasp, the tea splashing all down my front, and the LDZ guy whips around, an apology on his lips.

Until he realizes who I am.

His mouth pulls up with a mean snicker. "Check it out. The Princess' tits are already leaking."

Around him, other people join in the laughter, hot rage grasping my diaphragm as I chuck the cup into a nearby bin. Warmth rises to my cheeks, and I make a show of searching around me for an escape. As planned, however, I find it right beside me.

The door to the women's restroom.

I shove through it, the sound of their jeers still audible even when the door slams shut. I don't give myself time to dwell on it, though. That's what the frat members—all of them, each house—fail to understand. They're pawns in this game just as much as I am. We're all serving our Royalty in one way or another. The difference between me and them is that I know it.

I scan beneath the stalls, and when I'm sure it's clear, duck into the one at the end of the row, knowing no one else would ever use it. Its reputation for having a peephole somewhere in the tiles generally keeps people away.

Working quickly, I pull out my ancient MP3 player and find the track I'm looking for, hoping the audio is good enough to reach any prying ears. The moment I hit the play button, my soft sniffles fill the room. In about three minutes, they'll transform to sobbing, then five minutes later, back down into strained hiccups. This will eventually evolve into the sound of wet, awful retching. Oh yes, I'm an absolute mess in here. This is definitely not a stall to be approached by the feeble of spirit.

I have twenty minutes altogether.

Wasting no time, I run my fingers along the tile, searching. It's amusing to think people believe there's a peep hole in this stall, as if any man in Forsyth could ever be so restrained as to only *look*.

There isn't a peephole.

There's a whole-ass access door.

It pops open silently, allowing me to heave the tiled panel to rest against the other side of the stall. Dusting my hands off, I bend down to peer inside, pulling a face: darkness and spiderwebs. There's nothing for it, though. We've been meticulously planning this meeting for two weeks, and this might be the only chance I get.

Bracing myself with a long inhale, I push a foot inside the hole, crouch, and duck inside.

It's not my first time in this dusty hollow between the women's toilet and the main utility access room. I did a bit of a dry run last Wednesday to verify its usefulness, so I know the general location of the next access door.

Holding my breath, I push the panel outward.

Even though we've timed it to be certain no workers would be present in this part of the building, I still peer out warily before wriggling into the room. Once I'm sure I'm alone, I place the panel back into the wall and make a swift beeline for the door at the back of the dim room.

Then, I take the staircase down.

The irony of finding secret passageways and basements isn't lost on me as I descend. I suppose you can take the Princess out of the palace, but you can't take the palace out of the Princess.

My target is barely a dozen meters from the bottom of the steps, a large metal door bearing a sign that warns, "*Staff only. Keep out.*"

The boiler room.

Checking once more behind me, I yank it open, disappearing inside. It's loud in here, the boiler machinery thrumming like a heartbeat, but worse than that, it's sweltering. The moment I enter, a brunette head of hair whips around, wide eyes meeting mine.

"You made it!" Story's face spreads into a smile, but I can see the nervousness in her jitters. "And right on time, too. No problems?"

I drop my bag, unzipping my jacket. "All went as planned. If Pace has the restroom bugged, all he can hear is my crying and puking." I scowl as I gather my hair up, the heat already making sweat bead on my skin. "I bet he jacks off to it."

Before Story can react, the door opens again, making us both skitter to the edge of the room. It's just Lavinia though, nose wrinkling as she meets us. "Fuck, it's like a sauna in here."

"Which is bad for any tech equipment," I explain, gesturing to the boiler. "And too loud to bother with any mics." The idea is solid. Pace and the other Princes—even Ashby himself—have no reason to surveil the boiler room in the college's basement. It's the safest place to meet the Monarchs. I know that. I'm the one who came up with it.

Still, my blood rushes with anxiety, adrenaline making my teeth chatter even through the heat radiating in the room.

If we get caught again...

Lavinia immediately begins taking off her sweater. "God, I feel like Freddy Kreuger is about to bust up in here. So we need a new plan, right? Since the Princes are apparently fine with spying in other territories. *Ugh.*"

Story fans herself, grimacing. "Yeah, I guess we overestimated their loyalty to the Royal boundaries."

"Nowhere is safe," I agree, glancing nervously at the door.

"I never got to say, but," Lavinia begins, deflating. "What happened to you that night... I never should have pushed you for information—"

"No." I shut that down instantly. This is the first time Lavinia and I have had a *real* chance to speak. We're not allowed to be alone together anymore. The Dukes seem content to push some boundaries of their agreement with Ashby, but never that one. "I'm the one who took the risk of going to the gym. I should've known better."

"You should have taken the escape route Stella offered you," Lavinia rambles. "We had it all organized. Ballsy's cousin was going to drive you up to Northridge where Marcus' sister was waiting to—"

"Get West End and South Side mixed up in a Royal war. No, thanks," I say. "Plus, you think Ashby would let his *blood* heir go that easily? He'd track me to the ends of the earth."

"I know," Lavinia admits. "There's a reason I didn't run when the Dukes first took me as Duchess. My father would have tracked me down. Kings don't let go of their daughters easily—even if they don't see our value."

Story mutters, "Well, we didn't know Verity was his daughter back then."

"There's no point in talking about this. I accepted that there is no way out of this the day I took the pregnancy test." I take a deep breath of the warm, humid air. "All I can do now is use it to our advantage."

"Our advantage?" Lavinia asks, wiping a drop of sweat off her cheek.

"I've been thinking about it between bouts of vomiting and rage," I explain. "I still have access in East End—more so now than ever before."

"Ver..." Story sighs, twisting the cuff on her wrist. "It's too dangerous now. If we want to take down the Princes—"

"They're not really the ones we want to take down," I snap. "Look, you guys, these three? They're not like the Lords or the Dukes. They didn't climb their way to the top because they wanted the position. They were made Princes against their will because they're weapons." They both listen intently, which makes me feel less foolish. "Powerful weapons, yes, but in the end, it's *him*. Don't you see?"

"You mean King Ashby?" Lavinia asks.

"If East End has a sickness," I nod, "then you can consider him patient zero."

"So how do we take down a King," Story asks, looking from Lavinia to me, "who's also your father?"

Lavinia raises her hand. "Some of us have a little experience in this area. Want me to see if any explosives are buried under the palace?"

God, I'd laugh if it was funny, but this place is a hellscape. "This is my fight. I wish I could say I still follow the original dream, but the truth is, I don't. I'm doing this because, in less than eight months, I'm having his grandchild. And one of his weapons is going to be the father." This. This is what runs through my head at night when I can't sleep. "That's not a Royalship that ends once we graduate. This is life."

Understanding, Lavinia adds, "It's survival."

Story raises her chin. "Then let us help. What's the plan?"

"The Princes are his weapons, but they're not loyal. Not really." I pull at the front of my shirt, seeking air. "Ashby controls them with an iron fist. There's no room for rebelliousness, but there are cracks. I've seen them."

I think back to the recording of Lex getting whipped. The way the others fell into line. How they're programmed to accept abuse from their vile father. But each has shown me small moments where I know they hate the hold he has over them.

Story's eyes brighten, revealing a glimmer of hope. "You think you can turn them."

I snort. "Not even remotely."

"Then we take them out," Lavinia says matter-of-factly. "What's their strength in East End? Their last name? Because you're the real deal."

I shake my head. "No, it's not that. It's not money, influence, or name allegiance that makes the Princes powerful."

It's yet another way they're different from the Lords and Dukes. The Princes don't think of East End as theirs. It's an obligation. A duty.

No, their power is entirely internal.

I stop short, realizing. "It's their bond. They love each other. They're the only people in this world they're loyal to. It's how Ashby manipulates them, by leveraging their fear for one another. It's why they stay and fight. It's their weakness."

"So if you broke their bond..." Lavinia says, forehead creasing in thought.

I smirk, the pieces of a plan falling into place. "I break East End."

6

erity

I GIVE a little time for the hallways to clear before stepping out of the bathroom. Walking across campus has turned into a landmine—like an invisible ripple in The Force. Everyone senses it, even if they aren't a part of it. The PNZ frat boys stumble over themselves the minute I'm in their presence, while the DKS boys glare protectively at anyone who crosses my path. The Lords clearly want to keep a distance from the shit-show, and the Barons couldn't care less about any of it.

This is driven home when I stumble upon the demoness herself, Regina Thorn, the current Baroness. Of course, the problem isn't necessarily Regina, who's leaning against a pillar beside the elevator.

It's the two Barons currently sucking on either side of her neck.

I snap back around the corner with a grimace, shuffling my feet as I consider taking the stairs up to the studio. But my muscles are sore, and I do enough stair climbing at the Dukes' loft. Reluctantly, I take another peek hoping they'll be moving along soon. The last thing I need is for someone in PNZ to see me in proximity to the Royals of yet another rival house.

Unfortunately, Regina looks as though she doesn't have a care in the world.

Her head is tipped back, eyes fluttering as one of the Barons—Liam, I think—nibbles at her ear. On her other side, her second Baron is palming her bare thigh, lifting her skirt. The motion tugs at something within me, the sight of his hands on her flesh like that, so possessive and familiar. It's like...

Like they're *real* lovers.

Liam whispers something into her ear that makes her bite down on her bottom lip, and when he reaches up to grope at her breast, she releases a low, agonized groan.

Both Barons chuckle distractedly, their hands all over her, pulling and squeezing and stroking.

For a moment, I get the strangest vision of being in her place.

Not with the Barons.

With the Princes.

Certainly, Wicker would be the one with his fingers trailing up my inner thigh, dipping beneath my skirt. Pace would be the one teasing my nipple through my top, whispering in my ear about the dirty things he'd be doing to me if we weren't in public. Only, maybe that'd actually be Lex, memories of his quiet, deep voice teasing me to orgasm down in the palace's exam room ringing in my mind.

It takes me a long moment to shake out of this... fantasy? Only that's not quite the right word. Envy, perhaps. Their soft intensity is what I always thought being a house girl would entail, with the passion, pleasure, and intimacy.

But I never got that.

As I watch them, I imagine the expression on my face must be much like my stats professor when he stares at my belly. The Barons are creeps, but they love their Baroness. They caress her, hold her, devour her.

And when my eyes drift from the Baron's hand upwards, suddenly catching Regina's eye, her expression must be what mine is like when I'm gawked at by ex-Princes: sour, offended, and full of irritation.

Since I'm not in the mood for whatever bullshit she's ready to dish out, I turn and head for the staircase. The door is heavy, and when I enter the stairwell, it's quiet and secluded. Still, I climb a full flight before allowing myself to take a breath, trying to shake off this sudden electricity beneath my skin. My heart is racing, saliva pooling in my mouth, and between my thighs...

Slam.

I jolt at the sound of the heavy door below closing, fretting that a Baron has followed me. Sy had sat me down my first night back in West End and warned me that a true Princess—one who wears the Princes' ring and bears their child—is in more danger than any other Royal woman.

Worried, I begin climbing, but the sound of rapid footsteps behind me makes me push harder, faster, my calves burning as I rush to outrun the intruder.

I've just reached the next floor, panting, hand extended for the doorknob, when a hand slams against the surface. My shocked yelp is owed just as much to the force as it is to the large, masculine form boxing me in from behind.

A low, gruff voice speaks into my ear. "You're not using the heart monitor."

I gasp, turning to meet amber eyes. "Lex! Jesus, you scared me!"

If I *were* wearing the heart monitor, he'd know the panicked gallop of my pulse because Lex's face is stony with anger. For a moment, I'm convinced he knows about the meeting in the boiler room, and every cell of my being is preparing for the punishment.

His tense jaw clicks around his gritted words. "I left instructions."

I twist the knob, but his palm still holds the door shut. "Seriously?" I growl, giving it a futile tug. "You get one examination with me a month. No more, no less. I'm not strapping on some device just to feed your obsessive need for control over my body."

He pushes me into the door, his body a brick wall against my back. "You seem confused," he hisses into the side of my head. "Just because you get to spend three weeks in the gutter doesn't mean your body doesn't belong to us."

My nostrils flare. "Let me go."

"Not until you obey."

Unbidden, his words from my last night in the palace float back to me.

"I don't need you to trust me. I just need you to obey me."

Jaw clenched, I insist, "I've been obeying."

He grabs my shoulder and spins me around, pushing me into the hard surface. It's only then that I catch full sight of his incensed face. "Is that what you call gulping down metric fucktons of caffeine? Because I'm pretty sure my specific instructions were to never drink coffee."

Caffeine?

He doesn't know about the meeting, I realize.

The relief is short-lived as my jaw drops. "How do you know about that?" I've been so careful about getting coffee these past couple of weeks, not even buying it myself but instead having it delivered like some illicit, criminal thing.

"We know everything." Lex scoffs, eyes dipping down to my chest. "The same way I know you're horny right now. You broadcast it like a billboard."

"What?!" I gape at him, hot anger rising to the surface of my skin. "Am not!"

Mechanically, he begins listing off, "You're flushed. Sweaty. Rapid pulse. Dilated pupils. Plus," he reaches between us to flick me, "your nipples could cut glass." Sputtering, I slap his hand away, but he goes on. "Pregnancy hormones, Princess. They're going to do a lot more than make you salivate over watching while the Baroness gets finger-banged in the corridor, so listen the fuck up." He punctuates this by gripping my chin, forcing my eyes to his. "You need everything I send you, up to *and including* the vitamins I had made specifically for you at the compound pharmacy. They contain folic acid, iodine, and vitamins D, C, A, E, and F, which stands for *fucking take them*, or else."

I gnash my teeth against his grip. "Since you know everything already, you should be aware that the pills make me nauseous. I can barely keep anything down."

His thumb digs into my cheek, eyes hardening. "I don't care. You find a way to keep them down because, in seven months, the baby that comes out of that toxic waste dump you call a body had better be so goddamn healthy, he defies science."

"Why do you care?" I snap, planting my palms on his shoulders and shoving him. "You couldn't even fuck me right. It sure as hell isn't yours."

Lex almost stumbles but quickly corrects, grip tightening, and I see the words land as the barbs they were meant to be. His eyes flash hot, and he jerks me close, sneering, "It's not yours, either. The sooner you realize that, the better it'll be for all of us."

Swallowing, I look between his amber eyes, remembering all too clearly the same eyes glaring back at me during the Royal Cleansing. Wishing so badly they wouldn't, my eyes begin welling. "You're the biggest bastard I've ever known," I say, clamping down on the urge to cry, scream, or hit. "I hate you so fucking much, I could—"

I don't actually see it coming.

One second, I'm consumed with the need to hurt him, and the next, his mouth is slamming into mine.

The sound I make is barely human, fingers clawing at the fabric of his shirt as his tongue delves between my lips. His hand cinches around my wrist, wrenching it up over my head. I drop the tea, the paper cup hitting the floor with a thunk, warm liquid splattering my ankles.

It's not that it feels good because it doesn't. These are not the tender, sensual caresses I just saw the Barons bestowing on their woman. He winds a fist into my hair, yanking my face up to him, and it stings. All of it does. When he palms my breast, tender for days now, it's all I can do not to shriek into his mouth.

Instead, I strike back. Reaching up, I jab my fingers through his hair, pulled back into his tidy bun, and rip it free from the elastic.

Lex grunts, pushing his hips into mine.

Only then do I lurch back, my shocked gaze locking on his. The hardness against my hip is as hot as a brand. "Are you... high?" I ask, my voice a mixture of fascination and horror. "Lagan." That's who's boxing me in against this door. Not Lex, but his feral, ruthless alter ego. "Don't do this."

A fist slams against the door, two inches from my head. "Don't ever call me that!" he roars.

I flinch, sensing that I'm wrong. His eyes are dark, but they're not the eyes of the crazed man who forced me over that table during the cleansing. They're two shades darker. I've seen it before. He's a man chasing a high—nothing will come between him and his next fix.

Which means he hasn't had one yet.

I tell myself that's why I surge back to him, taking his mouth in another hard, bruising kiss. But it's only half true. The other half has something to do with the gritty sound he makes, hands grabbing at me like a man possessed. One of them slides roughly under my short skirt, where he teases me through my panties. There's no warmth or tenderness in his motions. He's the silent beast that fucks me in his sleep—except here he's awake. He knows what he's doing. He just doesn't give a fuck.

This is not about want.

It's about need.

He chews his next words through clenched teeth, pushing them into my throat. "Fucking knew it. You're soaked. You walk around all day like that, don't you? Dripping wet, waiting for one of us to find you?"

"Fuck you," I growl, the anger belied by a sudden moan when he fists the gusset of my panties, yanking them down. His knuckles drag against my clit, and I chase the pressure, releasing a long whine when he slides two thick fingers inside me. He pumps them in and out, the shoulder blocking my vision, shifting and flexing as he draws me to the edge. My hand twists in his hair, and I'm panting, embarrassingly desperate to feel his cock inside. Like he reads my mind, he pulls his fingers out, loosens his buckle, and shoves down his pants.

I think I understand what's happening when I hear the clink of his belt buckle, the sound of his tense, rapid breaths as he jostles in closer, but it's too murky through this sudden fog of *wet-hard-need* to really register.

Not until his big hand suddenly hooks beneath my knee, hiking it up around his waist. Faster than I expect, the head of his cock is shoving through, spearing into me with a slick, powerful thrust. I open my mouth to tell him to stop, that I don't want this—or him—but his teeth bear down on my neck, sharp and painful, piercing my skin as he drives inside.

If I had a moment to think, I might consider how insane this is. How fucked up it is that we're doing this in the hallway. I hate this man. He hates me. We're bound by nothing but an archaic, deranged obligation.

But *god*, it feels good.

That's all I can think about as his hot breath washes over my neck. My cry bounces off the walls of the stairwell, but he's lost, an animal unleashed. His hips are relentless, pounding deep, meeting that spot that makes my legs weak. I struggle for tighter contact, feeling every muscle in his body flexing and bending in an attempt to fuck me deeper, harder. He holds me up, my body limp as a ragdoll, and I drag my nails over his neck, holding on tight.

The way I meet his thrusts with my own whimpers and grunts, hips grinding against his, might just be the first time my body has felt like *mine* in months.

This, the way he fucks into me, the shockwaves that follow every brush over my clit, my nipples hard, grazing over his chest. This body feels familiar. And as fucked up as it may be, when the orgasm crashes over me, it feels so right.

His spine immediately goes rigid, strands of his hair hanging in his eyes as they clench shut. My pussy clamps around him, and his mouth covers mine, a groan escaping as he comes, pinning me to the wall.

For a brief moment, it's just our hard breaths and the all-encompassing scent of him, clean and spicy and unmistakably masculine. If I had my wits about me, I might make some comment about him being a day late and a dollar short—I'm already pregnant. An 'organic' deposit is wasted on me.

But before I can, he's shoving away—violently—his hair wild as he tucks his cock back into his pants. "Your body doesn't belong to you, Verity. It belongs to me and my brothers. To East End." As I struggle to find my footing, the warm trickle of his cum dripping down my thigh, his shuttered eyes drop to my stomach. "It belongs to our baby. Don't you ever fucking forget that."

TOSSING the cum-stained tissue in the trash, I fish out my phone and shoot off a text.

Vivarium: *Beware the rose's thorns; a shadow dances among the petals.*

Instar: 🦋

Thirty minutes later, I return from campus to the loft, finding it overrun with high-ranking members of DKS.

"You okay?" Ballsack asks the second I get off the elevator. It strikes me how much he's let his hair grow out. Gone is the buzzcut that was given to him during pledge week last year. Now, it's so long on top that when he looks down, the ends brush the edge of a boyish cheekbone.

"I'm fine." I look across the room and see Kaczinski holding up the blanket Lavinia gave me. "Hands off, Doug. The Duchess gave me that." He drops it in a heap and moves down the couch, running his fingers underneath the edge of the end table.

"What tipped you off?" Ballsack asks, tattooed fingers prising open a jar of ginger. When he checks the contents, he pulls a face at the smell, instantly re-capping it.

"Lex." I push my hands through my hair, overwhelmed. "He knows things he *can't* know. He knows I've had coffee."

Ballsack pauses to give me a skeptical look. "That's it?"

Shaking my head, I pluck up the bottle on the counter. "He also knows I haven't been taking these stupid vitamins. He knows things no one but Stella should know."

Ballsack freezes. "You think Stella told him?"

"God, no." I wrench open the refrigerator and stare unfeelingly at the contents. I'm hungry, finally, but nothing seems appealing. "It's far more likely those intrusive little fuckers have the place bugged." I slam the door shut without taking out anything. "Find anything yet?"

Ballsack shrugs. "No. If there's any surveillance in this place, then it's professional work, that's for sure."

Pace. He either did it himself or got someone better than him to do it. But who? How? The Dukes have this whole block locked down tight.

"The Duchess and Remy are in your bedroom." Ballsack jabs a thumb in that direction. "She didn't want the guys in your personal space."

"Thanks," I say, giving him a little smile. But before I go find them, I assess him a little more closely, head tilting. "So, Eugene. What's going on with you and my handmaiden?"

He fumbles the jar of ginger, spitting a soft curse as he barely catches it. "What do you mean? What did she say?" His gaze snaps up, the fear there transforming to anticipation. "Wait. *Did* she say something?"

Chuckling, I shake my head. "I can't exactly expect Stella to keep my secrets if I don't keep hers."

His face falls. "Oh. Right."

I chuck him playfully on the shoulder. "Consider it a question from a curious bystander whose confidentiality works both ways."

After a long sigh, he says, "She's a cool chick." I don't miss the conflict in his expression as he idly juggles the jar. "But I don't know."

"Don't know what?"

"I had that thing with Laura," he explains. "And I know it's not, like... *cheating*, considering she ghosted me and all. I guess I just feel weird about it."

Shit. Everything in my life has been so crazy lately I hadn't even thought about Laura. "Still no word?"

Ballsack places the jar back on the counter. "Nothing."

"It happens sometimes," I try. The cutsluts are a loyal group, but they're largely impermanent fixtures in West End. For many, it's a stepping stone into the world before adulthood. Some girls stay within our boundaries, but most leave. "People just move on, and it's okay if you move on too."

He nods, expression pensive. "I guess so."

My stomach sinks at the look on his face. Here I am entirely unable to find one Prince out of three to give a shit about me, and Ballsack is stuck caring about two different women. It makes me wonder why Forsyth is like that sometimes. One extreme or another. Never anything gray.

I snatch up the jar. "Well, if it makes any difference, I'm in one hundred percent approval of you asking out my handmaiden."

He looks up, eyebrow arching. "Yeah? You think she'd say yes?"

I snort, remembering my weekend of being pelted with unsolicited Ballsack facts. "I think the odds are in your favor."

His mouth tips up into a small, conspiratorial grin. "Thanks, Ver."

The sound of something breaking across the room draws our attention back to the debugging process. "Jesus Christ," Ballsack mutters. "I have to supervise every fucking thing." He storms over to Weasel. "I fucking told you to be careful!"

I take the opportunity to leave the chaos of the living room and head back to my bedroom. I enter cautiously, still all too aware that this isn't my home, and find Remy peering into the mirror over the dresser. Lavinia stands over the bed, grabbing for a pillow, and it's only when I step inside that I notice the knife in her hand.

"What are you—"

Riiiiiip!

The knife cuts through the fabric, stuffing spilling out of it like a gutted fish.

"Really?" I ask her, looking at the mess. "You think they bugged my pillow?"

"No stone left unturned," she says, eyeing the mattress.

I start to jump in front of her, but Remy gets there first, plucking the knife out of her hand. He bends to place a gentle kiss on her shoulder. "You know I love it when you turn red, Vinny, but let's leave the bed intact. I'm pretty sure the padding would make a device ineffective."

"These guys are ruthless," she argues, looking frayed. "They'll do anything to keep an eye on her."

Remy and I share a look, but while his expression is full of confusion, I understand exactly what's going on.

"Lav," I begin, instantly feeling frustrated that we can't have any privacy.

But she curls her fists. "It's not fair."

"That she's being watched?" Remy asks, scratching his head. "I mean, she's a Royal, baby. Them's the breaks."

Lavinia deflates, but I give her a small nod to show her I understand.

It's not that I'm being watched.

It's that Lavinia is free, and I'm not.

Since I can't go into that with Remy here, I relent, "Pace would want everything as high-tech as possible." Thinking back to the security footage in his room, I remember that he always covers multiple angles, and the images are disturbingly clear. I look around the room, up in the corners, anywhere with a clear view. "He wants to see everything."

All the time.

"I already checked the toilet seat," Remy says proudly, spinning the knife around his inked knuckles. "Spick and span."

"Gross," I mutter, a heaviness sitting on my shoulders.

"Although I believe the jailbird has skills, this all feels next level." His eyes dart to Lavinia, a comprehension flashing between them. In a creepy unison, they say, "Charlie."

"Charlie?" I ask.

"He's Ashby's pet tech slave," she explains. "Creepy little fucker. I bet they're working together, even after Nick—" She clamps down on a growl. "I bet he's responsible. I told Nick he couldn't be trusted."

I hear what they're saying, but Pace… the way he talked to me that night in bed before I left the palace…

"He wouldn't leave all of this up to someone else," I decide, squirming uncomfortably. Sometimes, it's like I can feel his eyes on me. The energy of them. The intensity. It burrows into my bones like an inescapable hum, possessing me with the urge to look over my shoulder. "It's… personal for him. He's the cat, I'm the mouse. Even if we found every bug, every secret camera, he would have a backup measure."

"What?" Lavinia asks, studying me. "What are you thinking?"

I look at Remy. "How do you make sure Lavinia is safe—like all the time?"

His hand comes around her neck, his thumb gently sweeping the skin beneath her ear. "She's chipped," he says nonchalantly, then frowns. "They didn't tag you?"

"Of course they did," I answer, touching the same spot on my neck. "But I don't know very much about how they work. Can you use it to… listen to her?"

Lavinia looks alarmed at the implication, eyes pinning her Duke. "Wait, is that a thing? Have you guys been—"

"Fuck no," he says, thrusting his palms out defensively. "It's just a tracker. And the Royals only started using them because of your dad."

Her head snaps back in shock. "Excuse me?"

"You know," Remy says, looking almost as uncomfortable as I feel. "Because his vipers had such a fucking penchant for kidnapping."

Before Lavinia can spiral into the knowledge that her Father just found a new way of trapping her, I get back to the topic. "So it couldn't be capable of that." Biting my lip, I think.

"What about jewelry?" Lavinia asks. "The Lady is required to wear her cuff and—"

My stomach drops, and I whisper, "Oh, no."

All eyes go to my hand and the ring I was given at the ceremony.

"Take it off," Remy snaps.

"I swore that I wouldn't. The covenants…" I trail off. "Ashby takes them seriously."

"Then I'll do it." Lavinia steps forward and grabs my hand. Her fingers wrap around the precious metal, and she tugs.

Sharp pain like a hundred tiny pinpricks stab into my flesh. "Stop! Stop! *Stop!*" I shout, yanking my hand away. The pain instantly ceases, although the skin throbs. "Holy *fuck*, that hurt."

"What the hell?" Lavinia asks, gawking at the red dots springing up above the ring. "Did they booby-trap your ring?"

"Let me see." Remy holds out his hand. When I hesitate, he adds, "I'll be careful. I just want to look at it." He takes my hand in his and lifts it to the light. "I've taken several goldsmithing classes. Welding for jewelry and shit." He runs his narrow, skilled fingers over the metal, green eyes assessing. "It's impossible to tell from the outside, but if I had to guess, whoever made this created a trigger for when you take it off. Like those spike things when you go in and out of a parking lot? One way is fine. The other, your tire gets shredded."

Horrified, I snatch my hand back. "I can't take this off?" I feel sweaty, panicking. It may as well be a noose around my neck. "Ever?"

"There has to be some kind of lever that allows it to retract," Remy says, shrugging.

Groaning, I inspect the points of the crown. "So if this is a bug, then I'm screwed." But one look at Lavinia's ashen face drives it home that it's not just me who's screwed.

"I mean," Remy says, considering, "How attached are you to that finger?"

Lavinia hits him across the chest. "God, what's wrong with you?"

He rolls his eyes. "Please. You weren't upset with Nick cutting off Perez's finger."

Her jaw drops, but she turns away from him and says, "Did Prince Lex mention anything else? Anything... *specific*?"

That meeting...

"You're right," I rush out, holding her worried gaze. "It can't be the ring, or else Lex would have known about—" My eyes ping to Remy. "Er, other things. Way more private things. Things he definitely would have brought up."

Some of the tension disappears from Lavinia's shoulders. "I guess that's something."

"It has to be here," I decide, wrapping my arms around myself. I can't shake the sense that Pace is watching this right now like there's a phantom hand on the back of my neck.

Remy ultimately sighs. "Look, a lot of contractors are coming in and out downstairs. Nicky and I will put them through the third degree, make sure there's no one suspicious."

I nod, accepting it when the frat begins filtering out empty-handed.

Pace has made it clear that he'll be watching, and Lex confirmed it today in the stairwell. There's no getting the ring off, and I suspect even if we did find the surveillance, it either wouldn't be everything or Pace would replace it.

I can't control this, but I can control what I give them, what they see, and how to use it for my benefit.

7

icker

“SHE’LL PUT THIS ON.” I shove the garment bag into Simon Perilini’s chest, not even gracing my Princess with a look. “And do something with her hair. She looks like she belongs on a corner of the Avenue. Father won’t accept it, and neither will we.”

On either side of me, my brothers remain still and stoic, our postures a clear contrast to the three Dukes currently standing inches over the invisible boundary line, all hunched and leaning like they’re in some fifties flick.

Perilini pulls a face, holding the garment bag out like it might be infectious. “I’m not your fucking dog groomer. If you want to dress her up in pearls, then do it yourself.”

“As much as I can appreciate you acknowledging she’s our little bitch...” I gesture to the space around us, a little cut of cracked pavement that used to be a diner parking lot. Now it’s full of weeds and debris, playing host to four idling vehicles and a menagerie of Royals.

"We're under a treaty. The deal is that we get our Princess back on Monday, March 19th, at precisely 5 p.m." I jerk my chin at the small, sulking figure propped in the distance against Nick Bruin's SUV. "She's not crossing into East End looking like that."

I ignore the part of me that prefers her in what she's wearing. A short, pleated black skirt over lacy stockings is enough to get my dick full-throttle. But the higher my eyes climb, to her cropped sweater and plush tits, over the pale column of her throat, the more my libido remembers who she is.

The moment I lock onto those green eyes, my jaw clenches.

Tensely, Lex cuts in, "A Princess is a symbol of purity and grace. She's a *mother* now. If she comes into East End looking like a slut, it's an affront that won't be forgiven."

"Jesus Christ, you fucking psychos..." Perilini sighs, turning to hand the garment bag to his brother. "Go," is all he says, nodding in the direction of the three people waiting in the distance. It's not just Verity. Her handmaid is glued to her side while the little Dukeling-in-training, Ballsack, paces aimlessly around the truck.

Crossing my arms, I watch as Nick approaches her. The little confused crevice in her forehead deepens the closer he comes, but the moment he stops in front of her, too far away to hear what he says, her jaw drops in outrage.

"Here?!" she shrieks, swinging the full force of her glare on me.

I smirk.

Beside me, Pace snorts. "You actually included the pearls, right?"

I slide him a grin. "Of course I did."

In the distance, Verity huffily disappears into the back of the SUV.

Remington Maddox watches this exchange with an unimpressed look. "So, this is your plan, huh? Cage her up, cover her in gold, and pretend it's real. Is it always this fake with the Princes and their Princess, or are the three of you just especially talented at ruining good things?"

Emotionlessly, Lex answers, "Especially talented," his eyes trained like lasers into the dark SUV.

Five tense minutes later, Verity stumbles out.

The dress has a traditional cut, hugging her waist and falling just above her knees. It's a soft purple, with little white roses climbing up from the hem. The shoes are delicate little strappy heels, and she spends a long, stone-faced moment bent over, fiddling with the buckles. When she's done, she snaps upright, face red.

Raising my chin, I call out, "Don't forget your pearls, sweetheart."

Mouth pinched angrily, she reaches back into the car and whips them out. Thrusting the string at her handmaid, she turns to gather her hair up, rigid as Stella winds the strand around her pale neck.

Nick returns, his inked arms flexing. "You owe us something."

I cast a glance at Pace, arching a brow.

Pace plucks a small memory card from the inner pocket of his dark bomber jacket. "Here's everything I could catch about the vipers on surveillance." With a flick of his fingers, the memory card flies over the boundary line.

Maddox's hand snaps out to catch it. "Everything?"

Pace gives him a long, scathing staredown. "That's what I fuckin' said, isn't it?"

The clack of heels on pavement breaks the standoff, Verity finally approaching. I check my watch, tsking. "A bit late, but I suppose we'll let it slide. This time."

Perilini gives me a dry smile. "Next time, we'll remember the Princes need twenty minutes for collective primping."

I wait for one of my brothers to respond, but when I glance over, I realize they're too busy taking Verity in. I'm not sure why. She doesn't even look pregnant, her belly still flat. Plus, in that getup with her hair pulled up into a bun, that string of pearls sitting perfectly below her neck...

She doesn't just look like a Princess.

She looks like an Ashby.

A *real* Ashby—blood and bone, fair and prim—and Jesus fuck, it pisses me off that I have to think of my last name as more rightfully *hers*. Ashby has never been a name we wanted, but it was the one thing that tied Lex, Pace, and me together as family.

She's never had to kneel in front of a fireplace, or rot away in a cell. She didn't spend every summer being berated and bullied, a lash to her hand when she missed a note on the cello, or raged at for losing a game. She's never had to hear the phrase 'practice makes perfect' while holding in her exhaustion.

We earned the name Ashby with sweat and blood, torment and fury.

All she had to do was *exist*.

I reach out to rip the tattered duffel bag from her grip. "Get in the car."

She stumbles at the force as she tightens her grip, those high heels grinding awkwardly on the pavement. Bruin jolts forward, either to catch her or to strike out at me.

He never gets the chance.

Verity herself slaps my hand away, her eyes sparking hot. "I've got it myself." Then she squares her shoulders, lifts her chin, and marches right across the boundary line.

Her handmaid follows more reservedly, flashing me a wary glance as she passes. Ballboy is last, giving his King a reluctant nod before stepping over the line.

"Any attack on him or the Princess," Perilini says, voice hard, "is an attack on West End."

Nick Bruin touches the pistol tucked beside his hip. "If you forget that, we'll find a way to remind you."

I slide my sunglasses on. "If you taught him his manners, then there's nothing to worry about. And if you didn't..."

Practice makes perfect.

I let the implication linger, enjoying that split-second flash of doubt in Maddox's eyes. Yes, DKS boys aren't known for their good behavior. Having one in the palace will be like a bull in a china shop.

"If nothing else, you're guaranteed to get all of him back." Lex gives them a chilly grin, popping a square of gum into his mouth. "More or less."

~

WE EAT DINNER TOGETHER.

"As a family," Father had said.

It's a fucking joke.

He's at the head of the table, which has been decorated with roses and candles, the crystal chandelier overhead sparkling just as much as our glasses.

Across from me, Pace fidgets with the collar of his shirt. All of us were ordered to dress for the occasion, but Pace was the only one who actually needed to change. Verity sits at the other end of the table, gazing emptily at her salad course.

"How has your stomach been faring?" Father asks, cutting into his chicken.

Verity's eyes rise to stare at him over the absurd centerpiece. "It hasn't."

Humming, he takes a bite. "Pity. Miranda never had morning sickness. She stepped out of bed every day feeling full of life. So much energy, you'd think she was carrying a battery." His soft bout of laughter is met with silence. Father doesn't care. He sips from his wine glass, adding, "But your mother was of an inferior stock. It's a shame what some parents pass down."

Verity goes stock-still while Pace and I share a look. Miranda was Father's Princess, the mother of his first child, Michael. We're used to having her used as a low-key dig at us, but Verity is gripping her fork so tightly that her knuckles whiten.

She responds, "You have no idea."

"But those family dinners you attend in West End do seem so... *quaint.*" He says the last word like it's sour. "Since this is your home now, I thought we should offer you a similar occasion."

Verity glances at me, the corner of her mouth turning up into a tense grimace. "Thanks."

Fucking gag me.

Ashby's don't *do* family dinners. The closest we come are steaks at the Gentlemen's Chamber as naked women wag their asses in the background. Even those are more business dinners than anything.

This whole charade is another thorn in my foot because it's yet another reminder that he's changing things for her sake.

"I've let Frank go," Father suddenly announces. "The safety of the palace is a much higher priority than my own personal security. In his stead, I've promoted Thaddius to head of grounds security, so all matters concerning protection of our perimeter should go through him and his team." He glances at Pace. "Is that clear?"

Pace very badly hides a scowl. "Yes, sir."

Father dabs his lips with a napkin. "So who will it be for tonight then, Daughter? Lex?" He nods at my brother. "He can keep a close eye on you during the night to ease any," a wrinkle of his nose, "episodes. Although all three would be better."

Her brow furrows. "Tonight? What happens tonight?"

"Ideally, a full night's rest," Father says, reaching out to ring the bell for Danner. "You'll be given some warm milk first. A Princess may never retire alone."

"Retire?" Alarm spreads across her features, those green eyes pinging to Pace. "Wait. You—you were serious about that? It's a covenant that we have to..."

Pace very pointedly spears a carrot. "Sleep together. One or all."

"It's for the Princess' protection," Lex explains, not bothering to meet her gaze. He's glaring down at his mashed potatoes as if they've spent the whole dinner mocking him. "We've had break-ins in the past."

"Attacks," Father curtly corrects. "I won't have any Princess left defenseless in this palace, least so my heir and his mother. So make your choice, girl."

"I—I—" she sputters. "I can defend myself!"

Lex releases a quiet scoff, all of us remembering the nights he sleepwalked into her room and had his way with her.

Father's head snaps up, eyes tightening. "Don't be ridiculous. This is the way it's done. My sons have agreed to abide by the covenant and protect you, and they *will*. You won't leave this table until you've chosen one to bed down with. Unless you'd prefer I choose for you."

Danner strides through then, a steaming glass of tea on a tray.

Through the tense silence, he carefully places it on the table beside her plate, unbothered by the obvious discomfort in the room.

He recedes, disappearing through the door to the kitchen, and Verity swallows. "Wicker." The reply is so strained and hushed that I'm not sure I hear her right at first. Then she looks up, meeting Father's gaze. "I choose Whitaker."

"FUCKING *WOMEN*," I snarl, pacing back and forth behind Pace's chair. My fists are clenched, and from the leather couch, Lex is obviously laughing at me. Not outwardly, but I see it in his eyes behind his douchey glasses. "You treat them like garbage for weeks, and somehow, they still want you. The fuck is that about?"

Pace answers distractedly, tipping back a bottle of rum. "She doesn't *want* you. You're probably just the least threatening."

I stop short, jaw tensing. "Ex-fucking-*scuse* me?"

Lex, always the de-escalator, gets up to snag the bottle from Pace, giving it a furtive sniff, "It's more likely she thinks you want it the least. It's a tactical play. Go in there, fuck her brains out, and put her in her place." Shrugging, he takes a long gulp from the bottle. Ever since our old covenants expired, I doubt any of us have spent more than a 5-hour stretch sober.

"No." Shaking my head, I rip the bottle of rum from Lex's hand. "She's not getting my dick again. Not even if she begs for it." I'm not really sure when I came to this decision; I just know that I have. I gave Verity Sinclaire more dicking-downs than any other girl in Forsyth. And what did I get for it?

Contractual obligations and her knife in my back.

"Sure," Pace says, all drawn out and mocking. "You're going to go without any pussy for seven months. Uh-huh." I know why he rolls his eyes at me. I'm not exactly famous for my willpower—not when it comes to sex—but shit changed when Verity betrayed me.

I gave her that power.

With my *dick*.

"I am," I insist, and at the skeptical silence, louder. "I am!"

Lex sighs, taking the bottle back. "We've got a long way to go here, Wick. Do what you can to make it bearable, yeah?"

"Fuck that!" I snap. Beside me, Effie squawks, startled by the volume of my voice. Inhaling, I decide, "In fact, none of us should fuck her. We operate as a team here."

Pace turns to glower at me. "Leave my dick out of this. Some of us can rail a chick without divulging sensitive information to her in the afterglow."

I watch him for a moment, and then Lex, who's looking pretty fucking in agreement. "You want her," I realize, disgusted. "Both of you. Even after what she's done to us, you'd still—"

"No one's saying we want her," Lex argues, adjusting his glasses. He looks tired, even though Father cleared all of our schedules for tonight—for her. It's the only way I know for sure he hasn't been back on the Viper Scratch.

"Good pussy is good pussy," Pace says, shrugging. But it's a lie. I can see it in the way his eyes flick to the leftmost screen. It's eight blocks of CCTV footage, the middle being the Princess' bedroom, where she's currently occupying the window seat, gazing out at the gardens below.

He's *salivating* for her.

Unfortunately for him, she's not in the mood to sleep with her stalker. She made it crystal clear on the car ride home that she knew who was responsible for the surveillance in West End. Verity may be a bitch, but she's not stupid.

Obviously, she loathes Lex—you can feel the murderous tension brewing every time they're in the same room. They're in a power struggle over her body—and not in a sexy, fun way. If I hear another word about the benefit of folate, I'll shove one of those parenting books down his throat.

It's not like I don't feel the urge. I miss burying my cock in tight, warm spaces; pussy, asses, mouths, tits. But the last thing I want is to put my dick anywhere in or near that girl. She's toxic—the kind of poison that'll get a guy killed.

"You realize what she is, don't you?" I look between my brothers, waiting for them to come to the same conclusion I have. "She's Michael, but with tits."

In perfect synchronicity, Pace and Lex's faces scrunch into grimaces.

Pace levels me with a look. "*Dude.*"

I'm not sure any of us have ever hated someone as comfortably and reliably as we hate Michael fucking Ashby. Our whole childhoods, he was the ideal we could never live up to. Not a day goes by that some part of him isn't thrown in our face. We were raised in his shadow, under the boot of a man who will never stop grieving the loss of him. Perfect, flawless Michael Ashby.

"She's his flesh and blood," I explain, gesturing to the lazy curl of her body on the monitor. Her hair is down, cascading over her shoulders in loose, flame-like waves. "Half of her is Ashby. That means she'll always be more important than us." Shaking my head, I conclude, "You don't just fuck someone like Verity Ashby. She fucks you because she has all the power. You should know that by now."

"She's still *our* Princess," Lex says, but I can see the seed of indignation in his eyes. "A Prince always has dominion over his Princess."

I release a bitter laugh. "Bro, when are you going to get it? She was never ours. She's always been *his*." On the monitor, I watch her rest a temple against the window, palm reaching out to clear the fog on the glass. "Give me your words."

Pace turns away, angrily muttering, "Fine, we won't fuck her."

"Swear it," I demand, reaching for the knife he keeps affixed to the bottom of his desk. "Swear it on your blood."

Lex scoffs, watching me roll up my sleeve. "Come on, Wick. Aren't we a little old for this?"

"*Goddamn it, Wicker,*" Effie screeches, head thrusting with the angry inflection. Pace sends her a look, like he's agreeing with the sentiment.

But he still lumbers to his feet.

Thrusting out his forearm, I don't bother ignoring the slashed scars and inked tallies already marring his skin. She's the cause of every single one. What's one more?

It's what drives me to push the blade to my wrist. "It's her or us," I stress, slashing a shallow line into the thin skin. Then I flip the knife and hand it over to Pace.

He's always cut deeper than me or Lex. Some of those scars on his left wrist aren't tallies at all. They're promises—a roadmap of vows made in secret, hushed, dark places. I still remember the first time we did one of these rituals, back when we were barely pimply middle schoolers. That promise—to never let Father's punishments work—has never been broken.

Even more than a decade later, the sight of our bloody wrists still fills me with an odd sense of calm. Our bodies might have been made by different people, but the three of us bleed the same color.

Lex is the only one to pause, taking the knife with a furrowed brow. "Is this really necessary?" he asks. "It's disgustingly unhygienic, not to mention—"

"Do it," I snap.

Lex firms his jaw, cutting a shallow slash in his wrist. "Congratulations, you just bought us all tetanus shots." He punctuates this by grasping my forearm, our wrists pressed tightly together as we shake on it.

"On my blood," I say, holding his eye.

Lex's eyes drop to our wrists, the blood mingling. "On my blood."

Pace follows suit, his long fingers wrapping around my forearm. "On my blood," he swears.

Satisfied, I give his arm a shake, swiping up the bottle of rum. One by one, we drink from it, our throats jumping with grimaced gulps.

"Now," I say, fishing my phone from my pocket. "Pull up something recent."

Pace's eyes narrow. "Recent?"

I toss him the phone. "I want to see her tits." Specifically, I want to see if they've changed yet. And her stomach. All of it. I want to know.

Lex snorts, falling back onto the couch. "Well, that didn't last long."

"I'm not stone, prick. The pact is to not fuck her," I remind him. "Jerking off will be crucial to keeping my dick locked down. Practice," I remind them, "makes perfect."

Pace sends our brother an unimpressed look. "Yeah, this is doomed. But yeah, sure, fuck it. I've got the perfect spank bank material."

Five minutes later, he's copying a video that's clearly been taken through the window of that old newspaper building. Although it's now called *Royal Ink*, according to the articles of incorporation that were filed last month. Seems like the Dukes are turning Forsyth's ancient *Royal Gazette* into some shitty tattoo parlor.

And they've had our Princess showering in the loft above it.

"Here," he says, trading me the phone for the bottle of rum. "But take your dick into the other room. I don't want Effie watching you jack off. You've corrupted her enough."

As if to seal his point, the bird flaps her wings, trilling out, *"Suck my balls."*

"If only you could, pretty bird," I say, stroking her beak before leaving the room. My cock got hard the second I saw the first image of Verity stepping out of that decrepit West End shower. *Fuck*, it's been a while since I've seen all that naked, wet, smooth skin. I flop back on the bed and hold the phone in one hand while gripping my cock with the other. "Come on, Princess. Bend over and show me your sexy little ass."

This video was obviously taken before she realized she was being watched because she walks around the bathroom with a shamelessness she's never displayed here in the palace. There's not a trace of tension in her shoulders as she towel dries her hair, the red locks two shades darker and hanging limply down her back. Hanging the towel, she stands back in front of the mirror. The picture is slightly distorted, as if the lens is zooming to the edge of its capabilities. Doesn't matter. I can still see plain as day when she palms her tits, as if checking to see if they've grown. Then she drops her hand, skimming it over her belly. My cock thickens in my hand, and I give it a long, practiced stroke.

Since being liberated from the original covenants, I've used every medium to get off. Live shots from Father's Gentlemen's Chamber, hard-core porn sites, and even Pace's old-school magazines. But as much as I wish it didn't, nothing gets me hard like seeing the Princess unknowingly being recorded. She thinks she got one over on us by moving out of the house. Fuck that.

I didn't ask Pace how he got cameras into West End, but it does rankle to know she's not even covering her goddamn windows. She might not be ours in any true sense, but she's still meant for us and us alone.

I watch as she sighs, grabs a bottle of lotion, and sits on the edge of the bath, propping her foot up on the edge. She squirts out a white glob. Her hands massage the lotion down her calf, giving me a direct shot of her pussy. My cock leaks, and I spread it over the tip with my thumb, feeling my balls draw up tight.

"That's it, bitch." Her hands move higher, rubbing up her thighs. "Miss us? Wish that was some of your Prince's cum you're rubbing all over?"

I allow my mind to wander, remembering how good it felt to be balls-deep in that cunt. The sex was never anything to write home about. It wasn't athletic. It wasn't passionate. It wasn't even skilled.

So why does the memory of squirting a fat load into her make my balls draw up so tight?

Good pussy is good pussy.

And Verity Sinclaire might just have the best pussy in Forsyth. Unbidden, I wonder if it'll change like the rest of her. Experimentally, I imagine fucking her while she's round and full. Looking down and seeing her swollen belly, knowing I've put something inside of her. Her tits plumper than ever, maybe even weeping, engorged, and desperate for relief.

Dropping the phone, I grab my balls and squeeze, stroking my cock with wild abandon. Groaning, I pop off like a rocket, cum shooting all over my belly.

Jesus.

So I guess *that's* a thing I'm into now.

It doesn't take me long to clean up and strip down. I falter a moment as I pull up a clean pair of boxers. I haven't slept in anything more than this since high school. Gritting my teeth, I dig deep into my drawer for a pair of old running sweats, angrily jabbing my feet through the legs.

After, I march down the hall toward her bedroom, only to find Danner waiting just outside the enormous door.

He's balancing a glass and a mug on a tray. "Warm milk for the Princess," he says, nodding, "and a cup of sleepy-time tea for you." He reaches inside his jacket and retrieves a gun. "For the Princess' protection."

"Don't worry, Danner," I sigh, taking the tray. "I'm already packing."

The Princess' bed is equipped with hidden drawers and cabinets. Guns, knives, tasers... you name it, Verity's been sleeping on top of it. She doesn't know, of course, because she'd use them to castrate one of us in the middle of the night. But no one is getting to our Princess without a fight.

Securing the tray, I step inside without bothering to knock. She's sitting at her desk now, laptop open, a thick textbook fanned open next to it. She barely spares me a glance, but when she does, I see her eyes dart down to my bare chest, then back to my face.

Her eyes narrow. "What's wrong with your face?"

I snort. "You and I both know there's nothing wrong with my face, Princess. God broke the mold when he made this one."

"No." She closes the laptop and stands, revealing a silk robe and little fuzzy slippers. "You're all..." she waves her hand around her face, "flushed."

"You mean the natural, masculine glow of my seething hatred for you?" I drop the tray on the bedside table, liquid sloshing, and flop out on the bed. Placing one of the massive pillows down the middle, I rest my arm on top and pluck up my mug of tea.

Ah.

Spiked with bourbon.

Danner knows his stuff.

She gives me a suspicious look, lips pressed into a tense line. "Make yourself comfortable."

The suspicion, I get. I haven't made her bend over and assume the position. I haven't forced her to suck my dick. I haven't even whipped my cock out. Down is up, up is down.

Then she undoes the belt of her robe, the silk sliding down her shoulders. She's dressed in one of those delicate nighties Pace loves so much, with the scooped neck and the sheer fabric. Yeah, I get the appeal. Sweet little virgin.

Annnd bingo. My cock perks right back up like I didn't *just* rub one off.

No.

I'm better than this.

Better than *her*.

She may have the Ashby blood, but I have the Ashby training.

I shrug and sip my tea. "I'm just here to sleep, Princess."

She eases warily onto the other side of the bed—the one farthest from the door. The bed is made to fit four people. She could roll twice and not even graze me. Still, she lays stiff as a board right against the edge, arms crossed rigidly beneath her tits.

Rolling my eyes, I reach over to grab the milk from the tray, straining over the distance to hand it to her. "Drink up."

She eyes it disdainfully. "Do I have to?"

"Do you want to explain to Father why you're bucking his precious bedtime traditions?" I ask. Frowning, she thrusts out her hand, taking the glass. I give her a cold grin. "That's daddy's good girl."

Her eyes flash resentfully, but she tips the glass to her mouth, cringing through a sip.

We drink in silence, and when I'm finished, I try to settle in the bed. It's not as comfortable as mine or Lex's, or even Pace's couch. I'm used to bodies being around me, hard and solid. There's a reason I never slept with her while I was making my deposits. I like sleeping next to my brothers. The sheets in my bed smell like them, not the cloying rose that follows Verity around. The same scent that my cock responds to like a Pavlovian dog.

Her head pops up over the pillow barricade. "Stop shaking the mattress!"

I grunt as I violently adjust. "How is it shaking? I feel like I'm drowning in quicksand, *Christ*."

Huffing, she pointedly turns off the lamp, casting the room in near darkness. It takes a few minutes, but I finally find a semi-comfortable position, although I can tell sleep isn't going to come. I can hear the soft swell of her inhales and exhales like this frail little whisper, and that's enough to put me on edge. I've never slept beside a chick before. Especially not the kind seeking my demise.

"What did he mean about people breaking into the palace?" she asks, drawing me out of my misery.

My eyebrows slam together. "What?"

"King Ashby, at dinner?" Her voice is soft and hushed. "He said one of you needed to sleep here because of break-ins in the past."

I exhale, annoyed at the questions, and stare up at the dark ceiling. "Anytime a Princess is carrying a child, she's at risk. It's the perfect opportunity for some fuckwit to try to make a name for himself."

There's a tense pause. "You think someone would really try to kill me? Or the baby?"

"Kill?" I scoff. Bit of a drama queen, this one. "It depends on their goals. Are they looking to take down Father and make a run at his throne? Is someone trying to start a war? Or are they some low-level Royal trying to gain a little more clout? There are a lot worse things than death, *Princess*." She shifts next to me, but I refuse to look in her direction. "A while back, someone broke in and splattered the nursery walls in pig blood. Sometimes, a message is enough."

"Oh my god," she gasps. "Who did it?"

I roll my eyes. "Well, the pentagram and message they left pointed to the Barons, but I'm not convinced."

"Didn't Pace have cameras up?"

I grit my teeth. "Pace was in prison."

Her little "oh" emerges in a cautious whisper. Good. It's her fucking fault he was in lockup in the first place. "Who do you think did it then?"

Scowling, I snap. "How should I know? It was deranged enough to be your boy, Maddox, but he was probably locked away back then, too. Perez was too busy slinging Scratch and snatching women for the Counts." RIP fucker. "It's just too fucking obvious to be the Barons. They'd never leave a calling card."

"So... the Lords?" she asks.

Scoffing, I say, "Payne? No—definitely not his style. Mercer? Only if they set the house on fire when they left. But Rathbone?" I consider him for a long, silent moment. "I can see that fucker doing it. He's got a quiet flair for the dramatic. Not that it even matters. We'd need proof to retaliate, and there isn't any."

It still exposed a weakness in our defenses. Father had a false sense of security that our enemies wouldn't dare trespass through our exterior walls. Maybe in his day, Royals respected boundaries, but our generation has different priorities. As a result, Father immediately upped security and spent months trying to procure a new arms shipment from DKS. Nothing happened to the Princess that night, but there's no way in hell he's taking a chance with his daughter and heir.

That reminder turns my mouth to ash, and without another word, I roll on my side, away from Verity.

Sleep greets me like moth wings, fluttering in and out. Even when her breaths grow into shallow near-silence, I can still feel her over there, just... fucking... *existing*. I consider jacking off, but before the idea can bloom into anything actionable, I'm sinking past the moth-wing surface of dozing and entering proper sleep.

I've always been really good at dreaming.

Even back when my brothers and I were tiny little shits, and they were having these fucked-up, horrible nightmares, I could always conjure up something satisfying. The three of us in a house made of gingerbread. Slaying a dragon. Defeating our favorite hockey team. Then, when I was older, I could dream up tingly, tight, wet, delicious things. It was never like real sex. I have complete control in my own dreams. I'm the one tying people down. Riding them. Plucking painful pleasure from them like fingernails.

But sometimes I get these other dreams.

Soft. Warm. Safe. They're not images, just these impressions. The sense of being content and full of purpose. The knowledge that everything is right and okay. No jobs. No pain. No urges or frustration. It's a little like how I imagine death must be: dark and peaceful.

That's the kind of dream I have tonight, and even when I begin surfacing from it, the warmth remains.

There's a body in my arms.

Pulling it against me, my cock perks up like a hopeful, curious creature that's more alert than I feel. Sighing, I lazily palm the firm ass nestled up against my crotch. My breathing grows shallow, my pulse kicking up as I explore the curve of the body. Instinctively, I nestle my face into the warmth, pushing my lips against the neck in front of me.

What I get is a mouthful of hair.

Smacking my lips in irritation, I brace myself for Lex's annoyed grunt, his fist shoving me away as he grumbles about personal space and the persistence of my morning wood. None of that comes, though.

Instead, a hand lands on my outer thigh, gently running up and down.

My eyebrow ticks up sleepily.

It might be Lex, but hey.

Good ass is good ass.

Anticipation slowly climbs my spine as he turns in my arms, but —no, that's not right. This body is small, soft, and unbearably sweet-smelling, two plush lips brushing haltingly against my jaw.

My eyes blink open to a mess of red, tangled hair. "What?" The word emerges as a gruff rasp, gravel in my throat. For a long moment, all I can do is watch in bafflement as she swings a leg over my hips, the weight of her forcing me to my back.

As soon as I dig through the fog of sleep and lust to realize Verity is *mounting me*, she's grinding her hot pussy against the length of my cock. Her cheeks are flushed, eyes so heavy that I doubt she even sees who's beneath her. It takes some time for my brain to catch up with my body, which is the only reason my hips buck up, seeking and needing and so goddamn ready.

Her mouth parts, a breathy little moan spilling from between them.

It's only then that I jolt to awareness, clamping my fingers around her hips. "Wait, stop—" My words are swallowed by her lips crashing down onto mine.

My toes curl so hard that my legs shake. It'd take nothing—nothing—to push my boxers away and spear my cock into her tight, wet heat. I could fuck her hard, just like Lex said. Put her in her place. Bury my cum into her like a threat. Neither of them would blame me. I'm Wicker fucking Ashby.

This is what I do.

But when my hand rises, fingers clamping around the delicate column of her throat, it's to rip her from me with a rough, violent shove. The sound she makes, all confused and wounded, is like ice water being dumped over me.

She flies backward, landing on the end of the massive bed. "Hey!"

"What the *fuck*!" I drag my hand over my mouth, feeling the indignation grow to fury in the pit of my chest. My balls ache with the lost promise, and I fumble to detangle myself from the silk bedding. "*Not* happening. Not fucking happening!"

She looks confused. Join the club, my dick is super confused, too.

"You don't get to use me," I say, voice low and seething as I glare at her. "Not after what you did to me."

"Did to *you*?" she blinks, those green eyes becoming clearer, flashing hotly. "You used me like a sex toy for weeks!"

"No." I snap, towering over the bed. "I fulfilled my obligation. Whatever just happened, it's because you're a horny bitch looking to get off."

She looks crazed, her hair a wild mane of fire as her green eyes bug out. "And, suddenly, you find getting off *offensive*?"

"With you?" I release a dark, bitter chuckle, glancing at the time. It's past six in the morning. Our night is over. "Absolutely."

I circle the bed, stopping where she's still sprawled out, mouth fluttering in gawked outrage. It'd be so easy to spread her out, give her what she wants. Give my cock what it wants. Give my brothers what *they* want...

But then she'd win.

"I know you got a taste for our dicks, but let me make something crystal clear. None of us are ever going to fuck you again. I'm your Prince. You obey me and my brothers. You carry our child, and you pray that when he comes out, he's healthy. That's it. Nothing more."

"Fine by me," she says as I wrench the door open. "As if I'd want to fuck any of you, anyway!"

I slam the door on her enraged squawking, reaching down to press a palm against my hardness.

Verity Sinclaire can have our father. She can have his name. She can have his precious fucking heir. She can have the Purple Palace, East End, and everything that rots here.

But she can't have us.

8

erity

I POSSIBLY WANT to blame Regina and her Barons for what's happened to my body since seeing them in front of the elevator. That's where it started—this sudden, throbbing, low-burning want always thrumming through my veins now. I definitely want to blame Lex for sating it, his hard, sure body crashing into mine in that stairwell, the memory nagging at me like a video on repeat. I even want to blame Wicker because he comes in my room every night, shirtless and sculpted and so goddamn arrogant that it's easy to superimpose him in Lex's place, imagining him shoving me up against a wall and *handling* me.

But I can't blame any of them.

It's this *parasite* inside of me.

I wake up on Thursday morning the same way I have the past three days. Sleepy, warm, comfortable.

Horny.

So ungodly horny that all it takes is the gentle wash of Wicker's moist exhale against the back of my neck to turn my panties into a soaked mess. Just like yesterday, I lay frozen, blinking sleepy eyes at the cut of weak dawn light straining through the curtains. Wicker Ashby is so many terrible things. He's a liar. A womanizer. A bully. A spoiled brat with knives for words. For all I know, he's an actual murderer. This is Forsyth, after all.

But all that knowledge never prepared me for another horrible facet of him.

He's also a cuddler.

I never know when it happens. We fall asleep on opposite sides of this enormous bed, turned away from one another, and he always ends up on my side, wrapped around me like a sentient shackle.

In the dim light of morning, thoughts still thick with sleep, it's almost easy to fall into the fantasy. It doesn't last long, but for a split second, I let my eyes flutter closed and allow myself to pretend it's real. The warmth of his skin against my back, the breath that flutters my hair, the sleep-twitch of his fingers against my belly. His legs are tangled up in mine, a thigh thrust up against my core, and he smells sweet and masculine. He engulfs me so entirely that the thought of ripping myself away actually seems unpleasant.

None of Wicker's lies are as awful as this one.

I know he's awake when the chest against my back goes still. No expanded exhale. No contracted inhale. He freezes, the ensuing silence a palpable dread. I wonder if, in these two seconds where he doesn't even dare utter a breath, his broad palm rising to my hip, he's letting himself pretend a little, too.

And then he shoves me off the bed.

"Ah!" The ridge of my brow catches the nightstand as I tumble from the edge, a spike of lightning stabbing through my head. I don't even feel the landing, too busy clutching my forehead with a long, pained hiss. There's a moment where my vision swims and I panic, thoughts of concussions and brain damage forcing me to blink furiously.

But then a tear falls.

I realize my eyes are just watering.

I cast them upward slowly, all the hurt transforming into seething hatred.

Over the edge of the bed, Wicker is staring down at me with wide blue eyes, face pale. "Shit, I didn't realize you were—" That's all he gets out before my balled fist slams into his perfect fucking mouth. "Fuck!" he howls, lifting his hands to defend himself from my barrage of punches. "Ow! Watch the fucking face—would you just—!" Growling, he snatches both my wrists, yanking me close to bark, "Chill the hell out!"

I clamp down on the tangle of hurt inside my chest because it doesn't belong. Wicker can't hurt me there. I'd never let him. It was just the moment—that stupid fantasy—of warmth and comfort being shattered so wholly.

"Are you trying to kill me?" I roar. Or, I try to. In reality, my voice cracks, and I have to set my jaw to stop myself from showing this man something he doesn't deserve.

Wicker's eyes narrow. "If I were trying to kill you, you'd know it, what with being dead and all." He drops my wrists only to grab the front of my nightgown, hauling me close to inspect my head. "It's just a bruise. I've had worse from sleeping with Pace. Don't be such a baby."

"A baby?" I shove him away, sneering. "A *baby*. That's a good point. I wonder what Lex would think about you launching his precious fetus off the bed." When he freezes, I add, "Or your father."

I'm halfway to the door when I hear Wicker's feet pounding toward me, his body suddenly blocking mine. "Whoa, hold the fuck up." He touches my shoulders, eyes frantic. "You don't need to tell anyone."

I bark a low laugh. "Oh, I don't?"

"No, because," he wets his lips, eyes zipping side to side. "Because... because Lex, you know, he'll take you down into the exam room and poke and prod you, probably send you off for x-rays, and Father will..." A shadow falls over his expression, and I don't imagine the flash of horror in his eyes.

"What?" I smugly ask, possessed by visions of Wicker having his back whipped. "What will Father do? Hmm?"

Wicker's arms fall away, his blue eyes locking with mine. "Oh, you fucking bitch." His mouth pinches into a bitter, humorless smirk. "So this is the game now, huh? Gonna run to Daddy every time one of us makes you cry?"

Snorting, I reply, "I'm not crying."

"You were a second away from sobbing."

My fists clench. "You're a second away from losing that pitiful excuse of a dick."

He thumbs the corner of his mean grin. "Finally admitting you want my dick?"

"In a jar," I grind out. "On my mantle."

The standoff is atmospheric, like the crackle in the air right before a lightning strike. I can practically taste the ozone on the back of my tongue, watching Wicker's nostrils flare out.

"Fine. Name your price." Even when he relents, it doesn't look like it. Doesn't feel like it. He lifts his arms to lace his fingers behind his head, putting the full breadth of his body on display for me. "Want to grind on my cock? Use my body like a dildo?" After a moment of my gawking at him, he tugs his lip through his teeth, giving my body a charged once-over. "Nah, that's not quite right, is it? I know what you really want."

He locks gazes with me, slowly descending to a lazy-eyed kneel.

Maybe I'm actually still dreaming.

That's the only way to explain Wicker Ashby on his knees before me, a palm reaching out to curl around my calf.

"What are you *doing*?" I ask, incredulous.

"Don't pretend you don't want it. I eat your cunt, you keep your mouth shut. Fair transaction." The way he's touching me is electric, his tongue painting his lips with shiny saliva. Wicker is good at what he does, and what he does is this:

A single glance turns my bones to gelatin.

But I've been around him long enough now to understand it's just what he called it before. A game. Beneath the lascivious glint in his blue eyes burns spite that's hot enough to burn this whole city to the ground.

I should take it.

There's no way of cutting him deeper than this. To use him like a convenient, pretty body, just like those rich women at that party he took me to. I'd show him this is where he belongs; on his knees, between a woman's thighs. I'd ride his tongue and make him taste how bitter I am.

Instead, I place my foot on his chest and shove, watching him sprawl back with an affronted frown.

"Not happening," I say, mirroring his words from Monday morning. "I think I'll just ice it and have Stella do one of her fabulous cover-up jobs." On the outside, I'm the one smirking now. On the inside, I'm a warring conflict. "And you can hope none of the other men in this house find out."

Whipping off my nightgown, I almost enjoy the way his eyes dip right down to my exposed breasts. He can reject me over and over, but I know who is going to ultimately win this low-burning battle between me and Whitaker Ashby. There is no other option.

It has to be me.

~

"JESUS, IT'S COLD IN HERE."

"It's a hockey arena, Ballsack, of course, it's cold." I glance over at his beat-up leather jacket. It's thin and doesn't provide much warmth. "I told you to bundle up."

"Gloves are for pussies," he mutters, huffing into his cupped hands to warm them up. "And don't even get me started about scarves. Do you really have to come here every day?" Ballsy would never say it, but he's bored in East End. I see the restlessness in him, how he always falters when it's time to go back to the palace. Nothing there is familiar or welcoming, a stark contrast to West End.

He might be the only person in this city who comes close to understanding how I've felt these past three months.

"Not every day. Just when Lex has to work at the clinic." I've got my tablet open and should be working on a design for class, but I keep getting distracted by the sounds below. "You get used to it."

Surprisingly, I've started to like coming to the arena. Unlike Ballsy, I'm prepared, wearing a coat, hat, and gloves. The cold air helps with my nausea, keeping the sticky hot flashes at bay. And it definitely beats sitting around the palace all afternoon, aware that my every move is tracked on Pace's surveillance cameras.

The first week back in East End hasn't been easy. It's not just the cameras. It's Danner lurking behind every corner. It's Lex's stupid meal plans where every calorie, every ingredient, every nutritional component is measured and counted. It's waking up to a Prince wrapped around me and dreading his disgusted grunt as he peels himself off—or like this morning, lashes out.

"I eat your cunt, you keep your mouth shut."

On the ice below, Wicker is gliding effortlessly, almost lazily. Between drills, he spits out his mouth guard, only to then chew distractedly on the plastic strap, his obnoxious smirk amplified by pink flashes of his tongue.

The man clearly has an oral fixation.

My sudden shiver has nothing to do with the cold.

Ballsack chuckles and nods down at the ice. "At least there's the added benefit of watching the Ashby brothers chase each other in circles and get the snot beat out of them every once in a while."

I follow his gaze, watching as one of the big defender guys slams into Pace. Some of the other spectators dotting the stands flinch at the *crack* of the hit, but I don't. I'm used to watching guys beat the snot out of each other. I'm used to bloody grins and sweaty, stinky bodies.

What I'm not used to is one of them glancing constantly up at me from the ice, a thread of anxiety in his blue eyes. The ridge of my brow is still tender from the fall, but it's barely a knot now. Some of that might be attributed to the sweating ice pack that awaited me after my morning shower, sitting on the very same nightstand that necessitated it. No note. No barked instruction. No rose.

If I didn't know better, I'd think Wicker was worried about me.

Since I *do* know better, I understand that he's worried about himself.

"See, the thing is," Ballsack says, eyes tracking the players as they scrimmage, "I'm not discrediting their skills. These guys are tough, and if you put me in a pair of skates, I'd fall on my ass, but there's so much *bullshit* between them and their opponent. And I don't just mean all the pads and their helmets and protective gloves." He shoves his hands in his pockets and leans forward. "With boxing, every match is personal. Man to man. Fist to fist. Skin to skin. Bloody and fierce. There's no hiding. No penalty box. There's just the winner. Whoever lasts the longest."

I've slowly become obsessed with how the Ashby brothers move with one another on the ice, every pass and transition aligned. Even more so than they were when I first started coming back in January. They were still good then, but Pace was obviously rusty, and his frustration showed. Now they move like they're performing choreography—except only they know the steps.

Over the past two months, I've learned that this connection, this unparalleled bond, is the crux of their power. There's no relief from their oppression. If one lightens up for a single moment, the other snaps into place.

That's the lesson I learned from the Royal Cleansing.

"But if you go down in the ring, you're finished," I point out, carrying on the train of thought. "With this team, someone always has their back. You have to get through four more guys and the goalie. They're impenetrable."

The players zip around the ice, and I watch how Pace uses his body to keep the other side from advancing—boxing out, is what I think I heard one of them call it. He snags the puck and powers forward, arm rocketing back, and slings it over to his brother. Wicker moves so fast that I barely see the puck. One minute he's deking out a defender, and the next, he's slapping it into the net.

His blue eyes seek mine for the briefest moment, ticking an inch upward to where my bruise is hidden, but he quickly flits away, down the ice, all focus once again.

"They don't have to last the longest—they have to trust one another, work together, and stay focused."

I think about this long after we've left the arena, sitting in the SUV, trapped by the strong, clean scent of athletes just out of the shower. Wicker's glances have ceased entirely, but Pace's dark, piercing eyes are glued to me the whole way. He doesn't speak. He just watches unabashedly, gaze slithering from my mouth to my bare thighs, then back up again. My body has long since lost its impulse to squirm beneath the heat of his stare, but even worse is that I find myself growing confoundingly less tense when he does it so openly, right in front of me. At least like this, I'm not wondering if he's watching, always looking over my shoulder, feeling crazy that I sense the weight of it when I can't actually know.

The longer he looks, the more Wicker's expression becomes pinched.

It doesn't concern me—not until Pace suddenly grips my chin, wrenching my gaze to his. "The fuck is this?" he asks, eyes narrowed in on the lump.

I try futilely to squirm away. "What?"

"This weird bump." Scowling, he reaches out to poke the edge of my eyebrow, earning a pained hiss.

I swat his hand away, snapping. "What, you're cataloging my fun new hormonal zits now? Do you want to see the blemish on my back, too?"

He blinks twice. "Yes."

"*Ugh*," I grunt, shoving myself against the door to put some space between us.

The car pulls into the circular drive, and since I'm gazing out the window, pondering impossible things, I see Lex waiting on the front step doing much of the same. His hands are stuffed into his pockets, eyes trained somewhere in the distance. At some point, his expression became locked into a brood and never recovered.

He looks tired as he approaches the car, tugging open my door.

"You have an exam," he says, flicking his eyes to Pace beside me. "Father is... out."

Not understanding the emphasis but also somehow certain it's not meant for me, I accept Lex's hand and allow him to steady me as I climb from the vehicle.

I don't need to look at Wicker to know he's sweating. Lex has every part of my body documented, and Pace has every inch of my room recorded. That much is guaranteed. This means Wicker has to have erased the evidence. It means he's keeping a secret from his brothers. It means that for once—no matter how minor a thing—I'm not playing against a team.

My match against Wicker is personal now. *Fist to fist. Skin to skin. Bloody and fierce.*

And if you go down in the ring, you're finished.

"HERE," I say, holding out the cup of still-warm urine. "I hope it's enough. I peed before I left the arena."

"It'll do," Lex says, taking the cup and placing it in the refrigerator. He changed into his lab coat and set up the exam room while I was in the bathroom. "Undress." The command is firm but glib, his amber eyes fixed on the task of washing his hands.

It's all routine by now, the act of shucking off my clothes to the sound of running water. Lex's back shifts as he scrubs, and I unhook my bra, slide out of my panties, and remove my pearl earrings.

I'm used to the cold.

Before turning to me, he reaches over to rip a strand of paper towels from the dispenser. This part is always methodical. He never sets eyes on me until I'm naked and his hands are clean. Somehow I know this is a line—a boundary—not unlike the one the Princes and Dukes use to ferry me from East to West and back again.

The moment that wad of paper towels falls into the bin, we change into different people.

The scientist and his subject.

"First," he says, finally facing me, "we'll take your measurements and weight."

Ignoring the gooseflesh springing up my arms, I step onto the large scale, keeping my eyes trained on the wall. I feel his presence behind me like an ember, the heat of his body radiating just enough to lick at me, but never enough to warm.

His arm appears in my periphery as his fingers slide the metal weight, pause, then give it a couple of precise taps to the left.

The edge of his lab coat brushes my bare backside.

In a soft, deep voice, he notes, "Two pounds."

Sliding my eyes in his direction, I wonder, "Is that... normal?"

Lex is quick to temper in the exam room. He doesn't like apprehension or stubbornness. The one thing I've found he's entirely comfortable entertaining are questions made in the pursuit of knowledge.

He hates to accommodate me, but he likes teaching.

It makes him feel superior.

"Yes," he answers alongside the sound of a pen against a clipboard, "many women don't gain weight at all during the first trimester, especially with the nausea you've been experiencing. Arms up."

I lift them out to my sides, trying not to flinch when his fingers graze my hips, looping the measuring tape around my waist. I remain rigid as he brings it down to measure my hips, then slides it up around my breasts. He reaches over my shoulder to place it perfectly over both nipples, fingertips lingering until it's right. After, I feel him crouch, his touch like a livewire when he measures my thigh, and then a calf.

"Have I—" The question gets caught in my throat, but I clear it out. "Have I grown any?" I find myself looking for it now, inspecting the shape of my body more often than I'd like to admit. It's not vanity. A part of me just isn't convinced any of this will be real until I can see it with my own eyes.

"Nothing significant," is his short answer, and then, "this way."

When I spin, he's gesturing to the exam table, his gaze tracking me as I get into place. Even when I'm settling, paper crinkling below me as I shift, his eyes never once give me a reprieve, as if they're documenting every twitch and jiggle. It's not the same as when his brother watches me. With Pace, it's this sense of being hunted like prey, but with Lex...

With him, I'm just a bug under a microscope.

He clicks on the overhead lamp, blinding me. "Do you need me to administer an orgasm?"

My eyes fly wide. "*What*?"

Lex takes his stool, flipping through the papers on the clipboard. "Your labs from Monday showed hormone ranges trending above average. Considering I can smell your arousal from here, you're obviously struggling with your body's reaction to physical stimuli." Mechanically, he pulls on a latex glove. "I wasn't intending to perform a vaginal examination today, but if you need it—"

"Rest assured," I bite out, "there's zero arousal happening right now."

Lex's eyes lock with mine, flashing in irritation. "Suit yourself."

"I will!" Two offers of pleasure in one day are more than I ever got while any of them were fucking me. Then, his words more fully register. "Wait, so you're not even going to..." I glance down at the awkward feather of my still-growing pubic hair. "Then why am I naked?"

He shuts the clipboard, tossing it onto the tray beside him with a jarring clatter. "Because you were told to be that way. Now stay still and keep quiet."

I get the sense Lex isn't happy about me turning down his offer. Can't *possibly* imagine how I get that idea. Maybe from how he basically threw the clipboard. Or perhaps the way he tightens the blood pressure cuff, the edges digging into my skin as he pumps the balloon. Possibly even the fact he keeps taking these brief glimpses of my thighs, as if he's sure he should be between them.

"Let me make something crystal clear. None of us are ever going to fuck you again."

That's what Wicker told me on Monday morning. So why do I get the feeling all it'd take is the smallest gesture to get Lex Ashby's pants around his ankles again?

As he finishes up checking my blood pressure, there's a knock on the door.

"Come in," Lex calls, focused on the instrument tray.

It's Pace who waltzes through. He's wearing a navy blue hooded sweatshirt now, hands cradled into the center pocket. His eyes find me like a dowsing rod, locking right onto my fledgling thatch of pubic hair. An inhale gets trapped in my lungs as he comfortably crosses the distance, never releasing me from his stare.

"Had to check on Effie," he tells Lex in a low, reverberating voice. "Am I late?"

Lex is attaching a tube to the finger prick, which he clamps directly on my finger. "Right on time." The sharp stab into my finger is always a surprise, even when I know better. "Is Wick coming?"

"No." Pace's eyes are still glued to me. I force myself not to shift. Being alone with these two, down in this room where I always feel vulnerable, makes me uneasy. "He's in the solarium, playing for Michael."

Lex's mouth turns down. "Why? It's not Wednesday. It's not even the beginning of the month."

Pace shrugs, wetting his lips. "You looked in her pussy yet?"

My thighs slap together while Lex sends his brother a disparaging glare. "Vaginal exam. And no. I don't need to." Lex removes the clamp from my finger. "Wick hasn't fucked her."

For some reason, Pace deflates, spitting a curse. "Then how can you tell? Because I know when ten minutes of my footage goes missing."

"She doesn't have any bruising."

Pace stares at him. "So?"

There's a long, labored sigh. "I've done dozens of exams on her body after his deposits, Pace." Lex explains this as if I'm not even here. "Wicker always leaves a mark. Always."

Face screwing up, I start, "Wicker and I haven't—" but Pace interrupts me.

"What about this?" He marches up to me, uncaring of the way I cover my breasts, curling protectively into myself as if privacy or modesty is an option here. His dark twists fall in his eyes when he ducks down, pushing a thumb into my eyebrow.

"Ow!" I yelp, jerking away.

Pace gives his brother a look. "She's got a knot on her head." Lex immediately shoots to his feet, face stony and focused as he cradles my jaw, forcing me to face him.

"What happened here?" he asks.

"It's nothing," I insist, letting him look his fill. Anything else would be too suspicious. "It's just a zit."

Lex's jaw hardens. "Do I look like an idiot? Pace, get me one of those wipes. Let's see what's beneath all this makeup."

"Fine, okay?" I relent, dreading the ensuing fuss. "I fell out of bed this morning and hit my head on the nightstand."

Pace palms my cheek, tilting my face as he runs a wipe over the tender area. "Likely story," he mutters, his dark eyes honing in on what's revealed beneath Stella's cover-up job. "There," he says, looking all at once pleased and incensed. "That's a bruise."

When I dare glance at Lex, I find the anger I've been anticipating. "Fucking *liar*."

"I knew you'd make a big deal out of it," I snap, swatting Pace's hands away, "and it's *nothing*. Just a tiny bump!"

But it's like they don't even hear me.

"This is so fucking typical of him," Pace says, face tight. "Making us jump into a commitment he can't keep."

It's only then that I realize their anger isn't being directed at me.

It's for Wicker.

"And making more work for me while he's at it," Lex grits out, pulling a tiny penlight from his lab coat pocket. He shines it invasively into my eyes. "Jeopardizing *my* job."

I spend this exchange trying to figure out why Pace has even been invited to our appointment. Annoyed, I ask Lex, "Why is he even here?"

"Because I want to hear it," Pace says, overhearing. He raises his chin, dark eyes lingering on my breasts. "Because it's my right."

"Hear *what*?"

Lex snaps, "I'm checking for a fetal heartbeat today, and if you'll both be quiet and let me work, maybe I can do it before Father returns and demands to be in here, too."

The room falls so silent that we can hear the hum of the ultrasound machine when Lex flips it on. It's bad enough that Pace is here watching. The thought of Ashby standing at my bedside, his creepy eyes assessing my nude body…

It's all I can do to not retch.

There's a strange shift in the air with Pace here, a change in the routine. I'm never quite sure which version of Lex is going to show up: the cold, methodical doctor, or the dirty-talking Lagan. But Pace? He likes to be in control, and this isn't his realm. Lex grabs the bottle of gel and shakes it before squeezing out a glob on my stomach.

"What's the lube for?" Pace asks.

"It allows the monitor to glide smoothly over the skin." Lex picks up the wand and presses the end to my belly. "It also helps the sound waves carry."

He rolls the end of the wand over my belly, using various levels of pressure.

"Why don't we hear anything?" Pace asks, moving closer. His eyes dart from my stomach to the speaker, brow knitting up. "Is it broken?"

I wasn't worried coming in here, since the baby I'm carrying is still something of a foreign concept, but the sound of a hollow void makes me almost as anxious as Pace sounds. The only thing in this palace that's worse than being pregnant is *not* being pregnant.

"Shh," Lex says, tone soft. His eyes are fixed on my navel but unseeing as he prods two scant millimeters to the left. "The fetus is the size of a bean. It takes a minute to locate it."

He pushes down hard on my lower belly, and my bladder screams. The result is a sudden wave of noise.

"Is that it?" Pace asks, coming closer.

"No," Lex grinds out.

The speaker sounds like it's recording in a cavern, catching the sound of random warbling echoes.

Pace braces a hand on the exam table beside my thigh, squinting. "There?"

This time Lex snaps. "*Pace.* Chill the fuck out, brother."

Pace huffs but leans back, crossing his arms over his chest. He keeps his eyes on the speaker like he can see the heartbeat if he tries hard enough.

Woosh.

Lex's hand freezes and then applies a little more pressure. Pace crowds closer, turning his ear toward my belly. Holding my breath, I freeze, afraid to move and lose it.

Woosh, woosh, woosh.

It's faint. A small but distinct sound that seizes me like a fist around my stomach.

"There," Lex says, gaze rising to Pace. "I told you to be patient."

With his free hand, he presses buttons on the keyboard, recording something while Pace stares down at my stomach, expression hard and unreadable. I can't tell if he's angry, or excited, or what. Was he hoping there wouldn't be a heartbeat? The last time he said anything about the pregnancy, it felt more like a threat than anything.

"This baby inside you? I bet I'm the one who put it there."

"The heart rate is one-sixty-five," Lex says, muttering as he goes over some numbers.

Pace's deep voice rings out, "Is that good or bad?"

"It's very good," Lex says, giving his brother a decisive nod. "Strong. Perfect."

Pace tilts his head as he assesses my belly. "Is it a boy or a girl? I read that you can tell by the heart rate."

"You *read*?" Lex scoffs, head shaking. "That's an old wives' tale. We won't know that for another few weeks."

Pace seems to take this in stride. "And paternity?" he asks, his dark eyes abruptly pinning mine.

There's a tense pause before Lex answers solemnly. "You know the rules."

I don't know the rules. I should ask. I'm sick of being surprised, left in the dark, and expected to just know these things.

But I don't.

I'm too paralyzed by the gentle *woosh-woosh-woosh* filling the room. I saw it on the monitor days ago, but it wasn't anything then. Hardly a blob. I'm not even sure I saw the right thing. But this?

This is real, tangible proof that there's a heart growing inside of me.

When I was in West End, I missed the solarium, but I haven't visited it once since coming back. I felt the same about West End, pining for its loudness and grit only to spend my month there holed away in the Duke's loft.

That's the only reason I go down there Saturday morning. There are rays of light in these dark, dreadful places, and I don't want to lose them. The solarium, just like the gym back home, isn't mine, but it still holds a part of me—an imprint of my soul—and I still hold parts of them, these little marks inside that weren't made to hurt.

When I finally find the courage to step through the ornate glass door, my heart skips a beat.

There's *green.*

Stunned, I shuffle hopefully toward the huge planters, cautiously fingering a young amaranth's stem. It's not flowering yet, spring still peeking through the chill of a stubborn winter, but its fledgling leaves feel strong. So is the hibiscus beside it, small but spry, and the burgeoning ferns beside the gate to the gardens. I'd planted these without any rhyme or reason, snagging seeds from the Agri-building on campus that neighbors the Visual Arts department—something other than roses and wisteria.

"They've watered them while you were away." Spinning, I see King Ashby descending the steps, my pulse kicking up.

"You don't mean...?" But, of course, he means the Princes. I turn back to the hibiscus, noting the dark soil in the urn. "Why?"

"To create is to reign," Ashby says, as if this is obvious. "Also, I ordered them to."

My stomach swoops with disappointment, even though it's easier this way. "Thank you." The Princes don't care about this place, and if they did, I'd find it intolerable.

"I've been meaning to find a moment alone with you." He looks around the garden, to the new growth, then back to the other end where it's overrun with brambles and brush. "I assume you've done the math. About your mother and me?" He's watching me with a gentleness that feels too calculated, as if he's trying on an awkwardly fitting suit. "Perhaps she's already filled your mind with nonsense and lies."

"We haven't even spoken," I say, sensing that ignorance is the best way out of this. "But even if we had, I doubt she would have told me."

"Oh?" His eyebrows hike upward. "It's not so terribly salacious. Things were different then, and Miranda was a good Princess; faithful, healthy, and obedient." My belly curdles at his words, Ashby's long sigh rattling the stillness. "In my time, it was thought horribly improper to use one's Princess purely for carnal pleasure."

Every cell of my being rebels at having this knowledge. "I don't really need to—"

"There was a storm," he barrels on. "Hurricane Hazel. It might surprise you to know all the Royal houses—even Saul Cartwright and your mother—evacuated to the Barons' crypt for shelter. Yes," he says, noticing my shock, "we can occasionally put aside our differences and work together. You can imagine the tension."

South, North, East, and West locked in one room? "I really can't."

Ashby gives a small chuckle. "Oh, it was a sight to behold. The Bruins and their guns, South Side and its whores, Lucia and his Countess, the Barons and their shadows, and then there was us. *All* of us, except for my poor Miranda and our son, who I'd hidden away with my uncle, the old King. The roar of wind tearing the heavens apart. It was utter chaos that night." He smiles wistfully at the memory and adds, "You were created in the eye of a storm, Verity."

I pull forth the courage to ask the question that's nagged at me for weeks. "So you've known about me this whole time?"

"Sadly, no." He shakes his head. "Not until you were much older, truth be told. Your mother wasn't a Royal, and other than that night in the crypt, our circles didn't overlap. You know how Libby is," he offers a conspiratorial grin, "no one is going to find out a thing unless she wants them to."

Clearly, my mother is adept at keeping secrets.

He goes on, "Admittedly, I don't know how much it would have mattered anyway. I was focused on keeping my son healthy, not to mention my new fledgling empire and all the things that come with running a territory. By the time I'd learned about you, I'd lost Michael and adopted two of my new sons. I had my hands full raising the two of them to carry on the mantle." He laughs quietly and glances down at my stomach. "No, I brought you in when we were ready, and together you've achieved my greatest lasting accomplishment."

Pawns, I realize.

That's all we are to him. My mother, me, his sons...

Ashby comes to my side, making me tense, but one glance reveals that his gaze is far away. "My sons aren't good boys, Verity, but they'll do as they're told. You should take better advantage of them."

It takes a lot of energy to school my expression into something neutral. That might be the worst part about being around him. The exhaustion of pretense. "How so?"

"Each of them has their strengths," he explains, icy eyes scanning the garden. "Whitaker is excellent in a crowd. He draws attention and prestige because he's a jewel. Much like these flowers," Ashby fingers a green bud, "he blossoms in the sunlight. Having him on your arm will elevate your standing. You understand why that's important, don't you?"

Sourly, I reply, "Because in East End, image is everything."

"Don't be dim." His gaze falls on mine, making me shiver. "He's a flashy diversion. If you're struggling with the campus' attention, he will soak it up like a sponge."

I look away, feeling sick that he's aware of my movements outside this house. "Oh, right, of course."

"Pace is quite the opposite," Ashby continues. "Night-blooming, like jasmine. He'll keep you protected in places the others can't reach. Mind you, you don't require his *physical* presence, but you do need his watch." He says this a little too flippantly, tripping alarms in my head. "And Lex, well. He will nourish your body, and attend to its many needs. Creation is hard work. Consider Lex its humble servant." He tilts his head, studying me. "I get the feeling you're aware of this, and yet you've chosen Whitaker to bed down with this week."

Nervously, I try to glance behind me, hoping to see Danner's silhouette in the doorway.

He's not there.

I ask meekly, "Is that a problem?" I've covered the bruise on my head well enough that it can't be obvious. The knot has gone down since yesterday, and when Wicker awoke this morning, wrapped around me like a vise, he chose to fling himself away instead of me.

I've carved out some measure of understanding with him.

That's why I've kept Wicker in my bed.

"No, certainly not." Ashby gives me a grin that's anything but comforting. "I'd only want you to consider the function of a jewel. It's fun to look at, but its ultimate value is speculative. At the end of the day, a diamond is just a fancy rock."

I'm struck by the notion that I might be standing beside the only person in Forsyth whose opinion of Wicker is lower than mine. "I'll keep that in mind," I mutter, hoping that's the end of it.

It's not.

"Over the years, I've learned it's best not to show favoritism with my sons. It breeds jealousy and contempt—each of them vying for my attention and approval. It makes them sloppy and self-absorbed. Ruling a territory in Forsyth requires constant vigilance toward those around you. Are they enemies or allies? Do you have leverage or a weakness?" Ashby taps his temple. "My sons must be able to ascertain all of these in the blink of an eye. They must be sharp. They are my eyes, ears, and fists. They've been trained to be that for you, too."

I think back to Lex being lashed. Pace locked down in the dungeon. Wicker being sold. He's got them held tight, conditioned to his every whim, controlled to do his bidding. But I don't see the picture Ashby is painting. They aren't jealous and vying for his attention. His attention is the last thing any of them want. I've seen that myself. He hasn't bred sycophants, but instead a codependency.

Ashby walks down the path, hands clasped behind his back, inspecting the beds. There's an area in the back that I haven't gotten to. It's overgrown with wild, thorny vines sprawled across the top. He stops in front of it and rocks back on his heels.

"Do you know why, in each fraternity, the Royals are given a female of their own?"

I wrinkle my nose at the term. *Females*, as if we're a different species. A million reasons flood my mind, but none are good.

He explains, "The other houses are given a woman to fight for, to keep them in line, so their King has a string to pull. But East End isn't a house of animals. We're creators. We create beautiful things, like this palace. Or this garden." He nudges one of the tangled vines with the toe of his shoe. "We also create destruction. We create pain. We create power." He turns and walks back to me. To my horror, his hands reach out, palms pressing into my stomach. "We create life. My boys were raised to protect and nourish that life. In turn, you must protect and nourish them. *Equally*." His touch makes my skin crawl, like my body is emitting a warning. He holds my eyes, his voice growing disgustingly intimate. "I see so much of myself in you, in the way your mind works. I know you think that you're punishing them with these little games, but I won't have you toying with their delicate little psyches. I spent too long building them up for you to use your wiles to tear them down. I'm watching, Verity. Do your duty. Don't make me interfere."

My throat clicks with a gulp. "Yes, King Ashby."

"Oh, Verity." He grins, touching my cheek fondly. "Daughter. It's more appropriate for you to call me Father, don't you think?" I know instantly this isn't a suggestion.

"Yes," I swallow back bile, "Father."

His eyes spark with satisfaction. “Good. Now, keep up the work on the garden. It’s lovely to see. Although,” he tilts his head toward the back, “watch the bed on the northwest corner. It’s overrun with stinging nettles. It’s best you leave it alone and focus on the rest of the garden. Now isn’t the time for you to test your immune system in any way.” Winking, he strides away, hands clasped loosely behind his back.

I don’t let myself exhale until he’s out of sight.

9

Lex

SHE'S WEARING a low-cut sweater this evening. It's why I don't look at her directly, my gaze drawn to the crevice of her cleavage like a magnet. I watch from my periphery as Verity cuts through her chicken, her knife and fork scraping against the china. Good potassium, lean protein, and there are pumpkin seeds in the pesto, too. Her labs from Friday showed low magnesium. It's been stressing me out.

Which is good.

Stress, I can handle.

The way every cell of my being decides to go into stimulus overdrive the second I lay eyes on her? Not so much.

I lean to the side. "You haven't touched your sweet potatoes," I whisper. Father still hears, his head tipping up from his soup to watch our exchange.

Verity's eyes tighten. "I don't like sweet potatoes."

Reaching out, I nudge the plate of sweet potatoes closer to her. "The fetus *does*."

"Princesses have been eating Jay Cuthbert's meal plan since the seventies," Father says, pointing to her plate with his fork. "It's everything the baby needs."

Pace and I share a look.

Jay Cuthbert was a Prince back in the Stone Ages, and if Father actually knew anything about that guy's carefully constructed Royal nutritional plan, he'd know I threw that archaic bullshit out the night of negotiations. It's the twenty-first century. There have been a million studies done since Jay Cuthbert resided here. Luckily, Father had never dined with a Princess before his daughter became one. He won't notice anything amiss.

Across the table, Wicker is picking at his salad, casting Pace's plate of chicken a morose glance. "Sweet potatoes are gross," he grumbles. "And so is this salad. What is this? I'm not the one who's pregnant. Why am I eating rabbit food?"

Stiffly, I reply, "I'm not your nutritionist. If you don't like it, go get something else."

"At least you get cheese," Verity mutters under her breath. But I see the way she eyes the feta sprinkled over Wicker's salad. Like I'm letting her get listeria on my watch.

I avoid looking Wicker in the eye, because if I do, I'm going to fly over this table and strangle him. Neither he nor Pace understand how much harder I have it with this stupid pact. The first time my dick has worked in months, and now I'm not allowed to use it. They're not the ones spreading her thighs in the exam room, sliding their fingers into her soft, wet heat. They're not the ones palming her tits to measure her. They're not the ones who have to sit on that stool and shove down the need that's somehow become more potent than the urge for a hit of Scratch.

Apparently, Father isn't too happy with him either, his gaze burning into Wicker. "You've gained too much weight this season."

"I'm training," Wicker says through gritted teeth. "It's muscle mass. Practice makes perfect, doesn't it?"

Sighing, Pace curls over his plate, muttering, "He needs protein and carbs, or he's going to collapse on the ice. Coach has us practicing twice a day right now."

"He *needs* to trim up for Mother's Day," Father sharply insists. To Wicker, he explains, "You're escorting in four events that weekend, and I won't have you looking like some beast. They like you to be lean and unthreatening."

The table rattles as Wicker slams down his fork. "Am I your whore or your prestige athlete? You can't have both."

"You're whatever I damn well say you are!" Father roars. Beside me, Verity flinches so hard she drops her own cutlery. Father notices, too, visibly reining in his temper. "There has been far too much insolence from all four of you lately. Out of four children, at least one should do as they're told."

I glance up, locking eyes with Pace. Father has been pissed at us for listening to the heartbeat without him. Even knowing it's his grandchild, I wasn't expecting this level of possessiveness. It's almost like she's having his baby instead of ours. If it were up to him, we'd have no part in it whatsoever.

For a tense moment, I wonder what his precious daughter has done to earn his ire.

Not for long.

"Verity," he grinds out, glaring down the table at her. "I presume you have an announcement to make this evening."

Her green eyes rise, but only meet his for a blink before dipping back down to her plate. I'm not sure why she withers at first, her shoulders curling inward with a long sigh. "I choose Lex to sleep with me this week," she says, stabbing into her sweet potato.

"Oh, thank fuck." Wicker groans. "If I had to spend one more night listening to you puke up that milk..."

Her incensed gaze snaps to him. "Yes, I imagine not waking up to your face every morning will take care of the nausea."

Wicker's eyes burn with a vicious smirk. "And maybe without you hanging all over me every night, I'll actually get some rest."

Her jaw drops. "*Me* hanging all over *you*?!"

In the bickering, it's easy to miss the way Pace shuts down, pushing his plate away to glare at the table silently. Just fucking great. As if dealing with Father's possessiveness isn't bad enough, now I have to handle Pace and his sour grapes at not being chosen to baby her every night.

Dealing with their emotions is the last thing on my mind, what with Verity's tits threatening to crumble my resolve. Not to mention her announcement about sleeping arrangements—clearly set up by Father. I barely contained myself during today's exam and have forced myself away from her on campus, lest we have another run-in like the one in the stairwell.

My brothers and I made a pact, and those are taken seriously between the three of us. Trust and loyalty are all we have—because we sure as fuck aren't bound by blood.

Which is why Wicker's little stunt pisses me off so bad. It's why I don't believe him when he grins happily across the table, chewing a mouthful of his salad. Sleeping with Verity isn't an honor like Father thinks it is. It's a test.

And there's nothing I hate more than failing one of those.

I WAS nine when I told my father that I planned to enter medicine when I grew up. Although I can't remember the exact moment I made the decision, I do recall being in triage with Pace a week earlier when he broke his collarbone. There was no part of it that didn't capture me wholly, from the x-rays to the sharp scent of disinfectant to the pinch of annoyed pain on my brother's face when they strapped him into that harness and started cranking it back to set the break. I'd never seen that before—people being put back together instead of taken apart. His doctor was a small but stern Vietnamese woman who I'm pretty sure could still take me to this day. That was a part of it, too.

There's power in healing.

So when my Father collected us from the boarding school for

parents' weekend, gathering us in his office for our routine skill report, I looked him in the eye, squared my shoulders, and said that I wanted to start down the academic path of becoming a physician. I planned this meticulously, knowing that medicine would be a discipline that would serve him well. Father had no need for a bone-setter, but a doctor could do other things. If I'd understood better the nature of *creation*, I would have probably tried for obstetrics. But I was nine. Vaginas were gross. Bones were cool as hell.

Naturally, he laughed in my face.

"You're going to *take care* of people?" he asked mockingly. "You're going to hold their hands, patch their boo-boos, and dab away their little tears? *You*?"

"Why not?" I asked.

"If you really want to follow a path in medicine, I suggest you do a little research on genetics. I can only mold what I've been given, and you, son, will never be a healer."

That was the first time I understood that medicine required a certain emotional finesse that isn't innate to me. The older I got, the more I learned, and the better I saw how valid his cruel laughter probably was. I don't have it in me to be soothing and steadying.

Chilling.

That's what my case worker called me, believing her whisper to East End's King couldn't be heard through the cracked door of the police station. I only remember small snatches from the night my parents died, but that one might be clearest. I heard how the police found me secondhand; a toddler sitting among the bodies, tiny hands clinging to my mother's bloody dress. Sometimes, I wonder if it's part of the reason I wanted to be a healer. Not to prove them wrong, but to be on the other side of that door—someone who fixes instead of breaks.

Like everything else in my life, what I want isn't part of the equation. The pathway to medical school has a gatekeeper beyond passing Organic Chem, acing my examinations, and having the highest GPA in my class. The biggest obstacle to my future is my father. It's his money, his connections, his leverage that will get me in the door. Get me matched with the best program. Get me into the right clubs and situations where I gain acceptance and opportunity. Rufus Ashby, as always, holds the keys to my life, and I've had no option but to bend to his will.

I will not be a doctor who heals.

I'll be an instrument that suits the needs of a King and his territory.

Right now, that instrument is taking care of the Princess and our unborn child, and unknown to my father, it's peeled back the methodical way I've approached my goal. Verity is very real. Warm flesh. The baby's heartbeat, a drumbeat imprinted on my soul.

"What are you doing?" I stare at my bed, covered in the clothing Wicker is haphazardly tossing from the dresser.

He answers matter-of-factly, "Packing your shit."

"For?"

I spot the wild look in his eye, his blonde hair ruffled as if he's been combing his fingers through it for the past hour. I don't have long before I need to be down the hall, readying myself and Verity for bed. The mess isn't welcome.

"Northridge," he answers, throwing open another drawer, "Tidal Cove, the Briar Cliffs—anywhere but here."

I spring forward to stop him from rifling through my boxers. "Would you slow the fuck down? What are you talking about?"

He dives for the duffel I keep beneath my bed. "We did our part, Lex. We dressed up as Princes, we knocked her up, we gave him an heir. Time to scram, you feel me?"

"Father isn't going to let—"

"He doesn't want us!" Wick explodes, shoving shirts into the duffel. "And we sure as hell don't want him. We have enough leverage now to buy our freedom. Fuck the money, fuck the cars, fuck this whole fucking life. I mean," he turns to me, breathing hard, "Lex, what's keeping us here?"

This is not a rhetorical question, I realize.

'Father' is my instinctual answer, but I know it's not true. We've been planning to get away from him since middle school. School is a better answer. Graduation is in two months. I'm still waiting to be accepted into a good med school, and running now would be throwing away a decade of grueling commitment. That's reason enough.

But it's not the one that makes me lunge for the duffel, ripping it from his hands. I say nothing as I dump it out, and I don't need to.

No one knows me better than my brothers.

"*Her*?" Wicker's low, disbelieving laugh is like nails on a chalkboard. "Verity 'Backstabber' Sinclaire? You can't be serious. She wants us even less than he does! She betrayed you as much as she did me!"

"It's not about her," I snap, but before I can elaborate, I feel another presence in the room behind me.

"She's carrying our baby." Pace is in the doorway when I turn, his eyes fixed on Wicker like knives.

Wicker gives an aggressive, uncaring shrug. "So what? We don't even know whose it is, not that it matters. Fuck the kid, too. Let him have it."

The truth is, I can't even blame Wicker. This has been the unspoken plan even before Father announced us as Princes. It's why we tried so hard to succeed—why we made deposit after deposit, hoping someone's seed took hold in her womb. Because there was a light at the end of the tunnel, and it was illuminating a path to somewhere else.

But that was before we *created*.

"No." The word comes out raggedly, rough as sandpaper, and not even the way Wicker's face falls can shake my conviction. "After all we've been through, Wick? Are we really just going to let him do it again? Take someone's abandoned kids and make them into—" I can't even finish my thought. That's how vile it is to me. "No," I repeat.

"Am I tripping right now," Wicker asks, face screwing up, "or are you choosing some fucking bean-sized parasite over your real family?"

Snatching a pair of socks from his fist, I point out, "That bean-sized parasite could be the only genetic tie you have in this world. I'm doing it for you as much as me or Pace." This is a much easier explanation than the truth, which is that something nuclear happens in my chest when I imagine Father being the first person to hold that baby. To see it all covered in amniotic fluid. To wipe its eyes. To be the first thing it sees of this world.

It makes me want to kill someone.

"It's *ours*," Pace says, perfectly mirroring my thoughts.

I agree, "We created it, and I'll deliver it."

Wicker looks between us, that special unhinged gleam in his eye. "Have the two of you been freebasing? This isn't some innocent, cute little baby. It's the barrel of a gun pointed right at our heads. And since when do we give a fuck about genetic ties?"

If Pace is anything like me, he doesn't answer because he can't. Ten minutes ago, I didn't even know this was a line in the sand. How many times have I accomplished something, only for Father to swoop in and take the credit? The same man who laughed in my face at the notion of my becoming a doctor is the same one who brags about it at dinner parties.

I won't let him take this one.

"We're not leaving," I decide. It's kind of like when I chose medicine. It wasn't some grand epiphany where the heavens parted and granted me clarity. It just *is.*

The gleam in Wicker's eyes slowly melts away. "So that's how it is," he says, face hardening. "We made a deal to get out of here, and you're just—"

"Like we're the only ones breaking deals," Pace says, pushing into the room to stand beside me.

Wicker's eyes ping back and forth. "What does that mean?"

"Did you honestly think you could tamper with my footage and I wouldn't notice?"

I chuck the socks toward the dresser. "Yeah, we know what you did to her."

He wants to deny it. I can tell by the way he tightens his posture and drops his eyebrows. This is Wicker Ashby preparing for one of his signature slick talks. "I don't know what you—" Maybe it's the fight itself, or maybe he just knows we're not easy enough marks, but either way, he deflates like a sack of bricks. "That fucking narc."

"Oh, she lied," I grit out, "and tried to cover for your ass. Just not very well."

He runs his fingers through his hair, grimacing. "It was an accident. I was half asleep, and she was *right there*."

Pace scoffs. "So you lied to us like a pussy."

"I knew you'd blow it out of proportion," Wick bursts, throwing his hands in the air. "It's not like it hurt the baby. God forbid!"

I gape at him. "That's not the point!"

Wicker gives a humorless laugh. "The point is that you have a *real* family now, is that right?" He storms out, leaving Pace and me in the aftermath. For a house so tightly controlled, why does it always feel like we're in the eye of a storm?

"Wick," I try calling out, but he's long gone.

"He'll be back," Pace says, flopping down onto my bed. "Where would he go?"

I grunt, picking up my clothes and putting them back in the dresser in a twisted heap. I'll arrange them later. Right now, I have other things to attend to.

"Are you going to fuck her?"

When I look up, I realize Pace is staring intently at his phone. I don't need to see the screen to know he's watching her. I suspect he's doing that most of the time now; his evening reports growing more and more eerily detailed. How many times she brushed her teeth. If she flossed after. The precise material classification of the new underwear she's bought online. The amount of money spent on hot cocoa that morning. The shape and color of the blemish on her shoulder.

It's the unfortunate thing about being an Ashby—that we all absorb aspects of our father like a contagious sickness. Pace and his watching, Wicker and his attempt at locking down our dicks.

I guess that makes me the one who inflicts.

"Keep watching," I say, snagging up my blanket and pillow. "We're both about to find out."

~

By the time I get to her room, my muscles are coiled so tightly that I end up flinging the door open hard, the girl inside jumping in surprise at the sudden *bang*. She's perched on the edge of the bed facing me, her thighs parted. The little cream-colored nightgown she's wearing drapes into the space between her legs, and she immediately tugs it down.

Clearing the distance, I toss my pillow on the bed. "This is my side."

"Not you, too," she whines, flinging a hand toward the bathroom. "It takes me a century to get to the toilet from the other side of the bed!"

"I don't care," I snap, throwing my blanket down. "This side is the most vulnerable to entry attacks."

But Verity is staring in awe at the comforter I'm spreading out. "What's that? Did you seriously bring *your blankie*?"

I'm still fuming as I straighten it out, yanking hard at the corner. "You might be able to sleep on this slip-and-slide disguised as bedding, but I prefer to sleep on something comfortable."

"You slept just fine before," she mutters, rounding the massive bed to *her* side, closer to the windows. In an ideal arrangement, she'd have at least one Prince on either side of her. But nothing about this is ideal.

"Get ready for bed," I command, tugging off my socks.

She glances down at her nightie. "I *am* ready for bed."

Pausing, I take her in. It's sheer enough that the dark shape of her areolas is practically visible. Her nipples are peaked, a soft flush warming her chest, climbing her neck. When she reaches over her body to clutch an elbow, the bashful movement pushes her tits together, accentuating the plumpness of them.

My jaw clenches. "You actually sleep in that ridiculous get-up?"

"It's what was provided for me, so..." A small, careless shrug. "Yes."

I sneer at the empty glass on the bedside table, knowing there was warm milk in it not ten minutes ago. "What a good little poodle you've turned out to be."

Suddenly, she drops her arms, a defensive scowl setting her chin. "You want me to wear something else? Fine." She grabs the hem of her nightgown and pulls it up, whisking it off with a shimmy. Every inch of her body is exposed in slow motion, the light fabric fluidly caressing each destination. The soft planes of her belly, the gentle swell of her lower breasts, the peaks of her tight nipples.

There's a reason I never look when she's undressing in the exam room. Something about the way she does it, her body curving and squirming, is so inherently sexual that my cock jumps to life immediately, eyes glued to every exposed swath of skin.

The pact still means something.

That's what I tell myself as she flings the nightie away, a challenge in her eyes. But the challenge isn't for me. That much is clear when her cheeks grow even pinker, her arms crossing over her exposed breasts. This isn't the exam room. There's nothing clinical in the way I'm staring at her, lids falling heavy as my eyes descend her body.

"Actually, I was thinking," she begins, shifting her weight with a nervous jolt. "The other day, when you asked? Okay. Yes." She shrugs and nods at the same time, the motion a little too stiff to be anywhere near as casual as she's playing it to be. "I'll take it now."

My eyes are fixed on how her red hair drapes over each tit. "Take what?"

"You can... um." Some of her bravado fades when she tries to prop her hands on her hips. "Administer. The, er, thing we discussed." Her arms fall, hands wringing. "Before."

When I decipher this utter fucking gibberish, I raise my eyes to her, voice as stiff as my cock. "You want me to give you an orgasm."

"Because..." she begins, a touch of defensiveness in her stance. "Well, because of hormones and such. You're here to," her hand gestures at the bed, "attend to my needs. And that's... that's a need. So my answer is yes." She ends this barely coherent ramble with a hard, tired exhale.

I stare at her for a long beat, not because she's standing there like something out of an erotic Victorian painting, but because it's just so fucking insulting. Without answering, I turn, storming into the bathroom and slamming the door. I ready myself for bed with rigid, mechanical motions, brushing my teeth like they're the problem here. The whole time, I'm staring into the mirror, knowing my brother is watching me back.

"Shut up," I hiss, spitting a mouthful of toothpaste into the sink.

After, when I'm shirtless, clad only in a loose pair of boxers, I brace my hands on the counter and take a long breath. Wicker probably rode her hard and put her away wet, and now she wants me to slip on a pair of latex gloves and finger her until she cums thinking about it.

She's Michael, but with tits.

That thought has gotten me this far, but in mere minutes, it's completely lost its potency. I glance up at my reflection, noting my locked jaw and dilated pupils. My hair is still up, but the wisps around my temples are wild, damp from splashing water on my face. That day I fucked her in the stairwell, I was a mess, late to defend a lab assignment while Father was hassling me to make a visit to one of his clients. I was overbooked and jonesing for a hit of Scratch to make all the pieces fall into place, and instead, I fucked her. Against a door. Hard and fast.

And like someone trading one addiction for another, it's all I've been able to think about since.

Rapping my knuckles against the counter, I decide, "Fuck it," and march back out into the bedroom. I see her in my periphery, chest expanding with an aborted comment as I turn off the lamp beside the fireplace.

She begins, "You don't—"

"Shut up." I punctuate this by turning off the lamp on my side of the bed and then striding around to her side. She's shrinking in on herself, still naked but not nearly as comfortable about it, flinching when I reach around her to click off her own bedside lamp. The last thing I see before the room is bathed in total darkness is the spatter of freckles beneath each collarbone.

And then I can't see anything at all.

Neither can Pace.

She gasps when I reach out to grab her arms, shoving her down onto the bed. "Hey! What are you—"

I clamp a palm over her mouth at the same moment I pin her hips with mine. "Keep your mouth shut," I growl into her ear. "You're not on my exam table, *Princess*. As soon as I walk into this room, I'm not your doctor. I'm your Prince. That means you can't snap your fingers and demand anything from me." Her fingernails are digging into my shoulder as she puffs hard, angry breaths against my hand. "If I get you off, it's because I want to. Nod if you understand me."

The second I reach down to cup one of her tits in my wide palm, the sting of her nails eases, a sharp inhale swelling her chest.

She nods.

I roll her nipple between two fingertips, pulling in the sweet scent of her hair. "Are you going to fight me?" There's only a brief pause, and if I needed more evidence of how horny she's been, then it comes in the form of this:

She shakes her head.

When I crash my mouth against hers, it's hard and conquering, weeks of tension snapping as I overtake her, pinning one of her wrists to the bed. Maybe she was expecting it to be slow and methodical, the way she's used to having me down in the basement. Emotionless. Detached.

Instead, she gets my teeth on her lips, my cock—hard as fucking nails—grinding into her heat. There's a tiny punch of sound from her chest as she struggles to follow the kiss, her hips canting upward with a frustrated squirm, like she's hoping to meet me on even ground.

If Pace hears anything at all, it's little more than my rough panting as I reach between us to shove my boxers down, hooking two fingers into the crotch of her panties and yanking them to the side. All it takes is one crank of my hips to line my cock up to where she's slick and waiting. It might be pitch black in here, but I can almost see the whites of her widening eyes when I enter her with a hard, powerful thrust.

My vision turns to a static buzz as the tightness engulfs me, my eyes clenched against the sudden wave of pleasure. I'm prone to categorizing things into boxes—good, better, best—so the way my toes curl when I bottom out is a point of data. The night of her cleansing barely counts, the whole experience lost in the chemical fog of dead neurons colliding. *Good.* The day in the stairwell was over before it really had a chance to begin. *Better.* This, though. *This* is my body sinking into electric warmth, her damp exhalations like fire against my jaw.

Best.

The feeling doesn't lessen when her lips part, teeth digging notches into my shoulder. I feel the vibration of the sound she makes more than I hear it, and it makes me grunt.

I nose into the space below her ear, whispering, "Your cunt's been soaked all day, hasn't it?"

She shudders, a hand reaching down to grasp a tight handful of my ass. It tugs me closer, deeper, as her hips undulate against mine, seeking and desperate. I struggle against it instinctively, forcing her down with a sharp thrust. I don't know what it is about this girl that strips me down to the barest parts, but I know that I'm desperate to beat it.

I grab her by the chin and fuck her mouth with my tongue as I crash into her. It's how I taste the bitter edge of her little whimpers, too distracted with conquering her to realize her fingers are in my hair, loosening the tie that's binding it up. It falls around us like a shield, and then she's gripping it, the sting against my scalp only enhancing the ache in my balls. It takes everything in me to hold in my ragged groan—to not let Pace hear it—because suddenly she's a liar.

She does fight back.

Her hands grip my head as she surges up to control the kiss. It only takes me aback for as long as it takes her to fuck up against me. An infuriating question lingers in the background, and I begin to wonder if this is what it was like when I was sleeping. Did she pull my hair and growl into my mouth like this? Were her nails as sharp? Was I this deranged, slamming into her like a crazed animal?

Has she already learned what I like?

It makes me meet her pull with a shove, the two of us battling for the rhythm as I thrust into her heat. She's wild beneath me, a creature of instinct and frantic breaths. I almost forgot it could be like this, sweaty and painful and so fucking human that I don't think twice about trailing a path down her sternum with my tongue, taking the peak of a soft breast into my mouth.

When my fingers find her clit, I'm rewarded with the sound of her fist slamming into the mattress. I flick her nipple with my tongue, back and forth, relentless and unforgiving, and rest my fingertips against her throat just to feel it swell with a scream she'll never set free. She wanted to take it herself, but I'd never let her.

I'm the one who inflicts.

When she comes apart moments later, her body a quivering, seizing mess beneath me, I know I've won. I abandon her nipple for the refuge of her throat, burying my nose into her sweet scent as I fuck her limp body to my undoing. I tangle my fist into the crown of her hair and hold it too tightly as the first jolt of ecstasy takes me. I hide a grunt beneath her ear, slamming into her with a brutal thrust.

I can't even count how many times I've imagined filling her pussy up with my seed. Every squirt into that specimen cup. Every deposit made down in that cold exam room. Every time I'd hear Wicker's fevered panting in the next room as he emptied into her. Every morning I'd wake up next to her, not remembering how I got there.

Dozens, maybe even hundreds.

None of them compare to reality.

My cock swells with it, pumping her with a slickness that makes me wish I could get hard again right now. I indulge in it for so long that I don't even realize I'm worrying her earlobe between my lips like a mindless fidget as my cock gives its last feeble twitch. Everything feels quiet and soft, the kind of simple physical contentment that can only be achieved with a good, hard fuck.

And then she begins shoving me.

"Lex, get—" Her throat clicks beneath me, a palm pushing the center of my chest. "Get off. *Get off*. Get off!"

I make a tight, annoyed sound as I pull out, but I barely get to roll off before she's springing up. I hear her footsteps as she zips across the room, tripping over something with a panicked *oof* before the bathroom door slams open. The room blinks with the distant light, which I think I should probably do something about. No doubt Pace is getting an eyeful of my spent dick, knowing good and well how it got there.

Just as I'm tugging my boxers up, I hear an unmistakably wet heave.

Groaning, I give my temples a slow massage, kissing my afterglow goodbye. My legs feel like jelly as I trudge into the bathroom, finding her curled over the toilet in a sad heap. Just as I lay eyes on her, her spine bows with another retch.

My cum is dripping down her thighs.

Sighing, I snatch a rag from the shelf and begin wetting it, glaring at her reflection in the mirror. "A certain kind of guy could take that the wrong way."

Pace is probably in stitches.

"Oh, god, when will it end," she moans, using a trembling hand to gather her hair at the base of her neck. It tumbles back into her face as she heaves again.

From the sink, I toss the wet rag at her, not wanting to get any closer to all *that* than necessary. "Could end tomorrow," I tell her. "Could last until your third trimester."

In the middle of this, she begins jabbing a finger at her shoulder like she's trying to tell me something. Deciding that ignorance is bliss, I ignore it.

Until she gasps, "Could you... hold it. Hold it!"

I briefly consider walking away and getting into bed, falling asleep to the sounds of her gacking. Rolling my eyes, I trod over to her. She looks wretched and pale—quivering, and not in the good, sexy way she was mere minutes ago. Pointedly averting my gaze, I reach down to clumsily gather her hair up, jabbing the handle to flush down what's already been expelled. This isn't the part of medicine where I excel.

Crouching down behind her, I take up the wet rag, pull her head up, and blindly drag it over her face. "Maybe if you took the vitamins—"

"Finish that sentence," she growls, "and I'll find something in this bathroom to stab you with."

I snort. "Yeah, you're really intimidating right now, all clammy and pasty and covered in fluids."

"You're such a—"

I never find out what I am.

The word gets puked out with another round of heaving.

I spend it staring at her back, counting her vertebrae. She's too skinny. I make a note to increase her caloric intake.

"Lex," she pants, deflating as the round of heaving ends. "I know it's tradition and probably lost in some fine print inside the covenants, but..." She twists to meet my gaze through wet eyelashes, a despondent plea in her eyes. "Please. *Please* no more warm milk."

I blink. "What?"

Her voice is like gravel. "I'll take the vitamins, okay? I'll do the other stuff. But if I have to drink another glass of warm milk..." Somehow, her pallor worsens, her bottom lip trembling as she gasps. "It's killing me. I can't keep it down. Every night, I'm just..." Her lips press tightly together, clearly holding down another gag. "I can't do it anymore."

Spitting a curse, I mutter, "Jay fucking Cuthbert," and dab the corner of her mouth with the rag. "No more warm milk."

Her eyes track me carefully, even as they fill with hope. "Really?"

Giving the toilet another flush, I pull her to her feet. She wobbles but grabs onto my arms, staggering as I lead her to rest against the edge of the counter. I reach around her to wet another rag, ordering, "Hold on." I mean for her to grab the lip of the counter, but instead, she places each hand on my shoulders, her green eyes wide and wet as I crouch down.

It's the hottest thing I've ever seen.

I flex my fist around the rag as I spread her, cock already twitching back to life at the gleam of my seed. I've seen my semen dribbling out of her plenty of times, but never like this. She looks swollen and used, her pussy a bright, vivid pink, and when I finally bring myself to run the cloth over it, her thighs quake.

I clean her methodically from knee to groin, taking away every trace of myself. The gentler I am, the steadier she gets, widening her stance for my diligent scrubbing, and I become lost in the motions. It's odd, the way I'm able to know a twitch means something is ticklish, but it's odder that when it happens, I make a choice to readjust. To soothe instead of irritate. There's a reason every internship is mostly spent in labs, away from patients.

Chilling.

Other doctors sense that this isn't my area and keep me away from anything necessitating the human touch. This has never bothered me, except...

Except maybe I'm not *so* bad at it.

"I can have Danner make you some ginger tea," I offer, but when I glance up, my eyes meet her belly, movements slowing to a halt. We're not in the exam room, and we're not in the bedroom. We're in some inexplicable middle where she's neither patient nor Princess. For the first time, I look at her and am seized by the notion that my baby is in there. Right beyond this skin and muscle and sinew.

Right there.

My throat sticks with a dry swallow as it comes down on me all at once.

I'm staying for *this*. This bundle of cells and slowly forming neurons that are going to turn into a person has a grip on me before it even has hands. How does that happen? Why do I think of it in there and feel both filled with purpose and utterly fucking lost?

I'm only broken out of this revelation when a slow flutter moves through my hair. My eyes jump up to hers, caught off guard by the realization I'm framing her belly with my palms.

And she's caressing my hair.

Her guileless eyes are tracking the movements of her own fingers.

"I like it when you wear it down," she whispers, sounding tired and half-dazed.

The second I rise to my feet, she seems to snap out of it, a shadow passing over her features as she turns to rinse her mouth. A few minutes later, as I'm leading her into bed, both of us silent and fucked out, I cast my eyes to the ceiling—to where I know the camera is watching. I settle into my side of the bed, arm wedged up beneath my head, and wonder how I'm ever going to sleep.

I wonder if Pace feels this responsibility, too—that whatever is in her belly is worth killing for. Maybe that's why all he does anymore is watch. Maybe this fear gripping my chest has been chasing him for weeks.

This fear that we're not enough.

~

THE NEXT AFTERNOON, I walk back into her room without knocking. "Father wants us down in his office. He's requested that we draw the blood—" I stop in my tracks. "What the hell are you wearing?"

"I'm attending the home game," she says, grabbing a scarf off the coat rack. Her color is better this morning. After the initial round of milk exorcism, she seemed to sleep well enough, unbothered by my own fitful tossing and turning. "I'm just playing the part of the perfect, doting Princess."

She's nailed it—decked out in Forsyth colors, wearing one of Wicker's oversized practice jerseys, tied into a little knot at the small of her back. It's not my number, but seeing the name Ashby spread across her small shoulders sends a surge of blood right to my cock.

"Right," I say, dragging my eyes from her bare legs. "Like I was saying, Father wants to be present when I draw the blood for the paternity test."

She pauses with her bag raised halfway to her shoulder. "In his office?"

"Did you think he was going to go all the way to the basement?" I snort. "It's just a blood draw. I've already set up my supplies."

She grabs a knit cap with a fuzzy ball on the end and pulls it over her head. The beanie has the letters FU on the front, surrounded by crossing hockey sticks. I think about what it would've been like to have this girl sitting in the stands for me all those years while I tended goal. What it would have been like to come home to something soft rather than my father's incessant criticism and disappointment.

"What?" she asks when she sees me staring at her.

"Nothing." I swallow and nod at her jersey. "Wick's going to lose it when he sees you in that."

She rolls her eyes. "He gets mad about everything."

Mad isn't the right word, but I'm not about to tell her how it's really going to make him feel.

I lead the way downstairs to Father's office instead. I learned long ago to keep my composure in this room, holding my emotions close. Being here with Verity, knowing she's carrying our child, feeling the all-consuming need to protect the fetus as both a physician and potential father, it's hard not to feel an extra layer of stress.

Sweat beads up on the back of my neck. Everything must go perfectly.

Father rises from behind his desk, greeting, "Daughter." The word sounds foreign and awkward on his tongue as he pointedly assesses her outfit, his mouth pulled into a considering moue. I stiffen, expecting him to be upset. A Princess has a strict dress code, which is why, when he grins approvingly, I breathe a sigh of relief. "Supporting Whitaker today," he says. "I see you took my advice."

"What girl doesn't like diamonds?" she responds coyly.

What. The. Fuck?

"We don't want to be late to the game," he says, looking at me expectantly. "Are you ready?"

"Yes, sir." I gesture for Verity to sit in the leather armchair. It faces the fireplace, the spot where my knees have pressed into the floor too many times to count. She sits, crossing her fur-lined boots at the ankles. "Push up your sleeve."

Father watches my every move. The way I secure the tubing that attaches the needle to the vial. The way I fill out the label that sticks to the side. How I touch her arm, the way we interact. I know one thing for certain: he can't know the way I covet her.

He can't know how this process arouses both of us.

Because most of all, he can't know that I care about anything other than the health of the fetus.

Standing over her, I remind myself that Verity and I have done this blood draw a dozen times now. Maybe two. There's no surprise when I wipe the crease of her arm with alcohol or the way her nose wrinkles when I find her vein in one quick punch. I know her body inside and out, differently than my brothers. I know how the needle pinches when I'm taking blood. How her nipples rise when I stroke my thumb over her pulse. As much as this girl likes to be taken hard and fast, she gets turned on by the tiniest of touches. I know that when her eyes dilate, she's thinking about what could come next: release.

All of this knowledge should have my cock drilling into the seam of my pants, but in this room, I am in absolute control.

"Excellent work." Father hovers, watching the blood trickle into the tube. "How long until I receive the results?"

My eyes flick to hers, wondering if she catches the word he uses. Not us. Just him. "The lab said we'd have them back by next week."

It hits me. In less than ten days, we'll know who the father is. There's nothing I hate more than a mystery, and right now, this one is clawing at my insides. Whose child am I protecting here? In the end, Father will still be in control. It's his heir—he saw to that when he made his daughter Princess. A bone-deep urge to take her out of this room tightens in my gut. There's a part of Rufus Ashby I never thought I'd be able to relate to, but here I am, thinking unreasonable things. Like the three of us running away, but taking her with us, all the while knowing with complete certainty that Father would track us to the ends of the earth to get her back.

I know it because I feel the same.

If she ran, I'd chase her down, and nothing could stand in my way.

The vial fills, and I remove the needle while quickly covering the puncture with a cotton ball.

"I'll have Danner make my schedule for next week a little more flexible." Satisfied, he exits the room, surely to start planning whatever tortuous event will come with the results.

"Feel okay?" I ask quietly. I screw the cap on and secure the vial in the container that I'll have delivered to the lab. "Lightheaded?"

She cups her palm over the puncture, holding the cotton ball. "I'm fine."

I reach into my pocket and pull out a small piece of chocolate. "Eat that."

Taking it, she eyes me skeptically. "You're letting me have sugar?"

"You need to keep your blood sugar stable." I shrug as if it's nothing, but all of this is something. One more step, and we'll know.

"Nervous?" she asks as if she's reading my mind.

"About what?"

"Being a father?"

I look at the spot on the ground, the carpet slightly worn from the pressure of my knees. I was nervous last night. Today, I'm fucking terrified of this child being raised by the monster that just left this room. By the expectations that'll be placed on its shoulders. Of the consequences if it's a female. "There's nothing to be nervous about. I've prepared for this my entire life." I lift my chin and tuck the container under my arm. "To create is to reign."

10

erity

The envelope rests against my juice glass when I arrive in the dining room for breakfast. My name is scrawled across the pale pink paper in silver ink.

"What's this?" I ask Danner, who's standing by the door that leads to the kitchen. The sounds and scent of breakfast being cooked in the adjacent room waft in. My stomach growls.

"I haven't the faintest idea," he says with a small, secretive smile. "It was delivered this morning."

I'm trying to place the handwriting when Pace and Wicker walk into the room, although I catch the scent of them—sweaty and male —before I see them. Another perk of pregnancy is this horrifically heightened sense of smell. A wet stain of sweat makes Wicker's heather gray FU shirt stick to his sculpted chest. Pace is in the process of pulling his own sleeveless shirt on, arms raised to slip it over his head, and I can't help the way my eyes decide of their own volition to take a peek at his toned torso.

His abs are like warm, sculpted granite.

"Morning, Danner," Wicker says, walking past me without a glance. He leans over the table to reach for a muffin, but Danner, moving with a speed I didn't know he possessed, blocks his hand. Wicker glares at him. "Dude!"

"If you'd like to eat breakfast, then sit." His head tilts at Pace. "You, too."

"You know Lex won't let us eat upstairs without showering," Pace says, tugging his shirt down. "We just ran five miles. Can't you give us something to eat? I'm fucking starving."

"If only your brother's standards on hygiene were passed to you two," Danner replies dryly. "If it's okay with the Princess, then you can stay. I won't even remark on your attire," his nose wrinkles, "nor your stench."

They all look at me, but I'm still distracted by the envelope. "Sure, whatever."

The guys are in a fight.

I first noticed the tension on Monday evening during Ashby's sick and twisted version of 'Family Dinner'. That first night, I wondered if it's because I shook things up by choosing Lex, but now that it's been almost a week of him sleeping in my bed, I'm sure it's something else. It's been a point of fascination for me, being so close that I can feel the low-simmering friction between them, but not close enough that they'll drop the façade of unity. They still pretend nothing is amiss.

Or try to, at least.

Wicker drops into his regular seat and Pace follows, each grabbing a muffin and tearing off the paper wrapper.

"I'll tell the cook to make two more plates," Danner sighs, headed toward the kitchen door.

"Make mine with extra bacon," Pace calls out, grabbing the chair seat between his legs and scooting forward.

"Real eggs," Wicker says with a touch of brattiness. "I can't do any more egg whites."

"I'll see what I can do," Danner says, vanishing through the swinging door.

These two rarely show up for breakfast; the three of them usually hole up in their bedroom every morning. There have been no more morning-after gifts since the deposits stopped, so there's little reason to see one another until we get in the car for school.

Keeping an eye on them, I pick up the envelope and inspect it.

Pace doesn't talk to me directly that often. I can always feel him watching, but it's a rare occasion that he steps forward to interact with me like an actual person. Apparently, right now is one of them. "Where did that come from?" Pace asks, eyes narrowing.

Shrugging, I say, "I don't know. Danner said it came this morning." He leans over and snatches it out of my hand. "Hey!" I snap, lunging for it, but he holds it out of my reach. "It has my name on it!"

"You know he's got to know what's in there, Red." Wicker laughs darkly, slathering his muffin with butter. "He's like a warden going over prison letters. Gotta make sure you're not plotting a jailbreak, right?"

There's not a touch of humor in Wicker's voice. I'm starting to think he sees the palace for exactly what it is—a prison.

"It could be correspondence from one of your cubsluts," he grumbles, using the point of his knife to slide underneath the flap, opening it with a loud rip. "Or an assassination attempt."

The knife snags on the corner of the envelope, and a sudden shower of glittery pink and silver sparkles explodes from within, scattering all over the table. A fine layer coats the stick of butter, Pace frozen as he stares in bafflement at the crafty devastation.

I lean over and press my thumb into one, identifying the cutout shape. A stork.

"What the fuck?" Pace growls, looking at the mess.

"I don't think it's anthrax," Wicker adds unhelpfully. He leans over to swipe the card, his blue eyes darting over the words. "Oh. It's an invitation to celebrate your pregnancy. Gross." He flings it back at me like a Frisbee, and it lands on my placemat.

"An invitation from who?" I wonder, skimming the details. It's tomorrow, 4-6 p.m., held at the Gilded Rose Spa, and signed by 'The Court.' "What is this, and who are these people?"

"*Those people* are the other girls in East End," Wicker says, eyes rolling as he speaks in a tone intended for a five-year-old. "You see, effective little Royal cum dumpsters like yourself get a golden ticket to facial peels and pretense. It's a tradition; a women's-only celebration of the sentient creampie you're baking in that oven of yours."

Wicker, I've learned, is on a mission to goad me until I'm miserable.

I don't let him. "So it's like a baby shower?" My mother insisted on being involved with the baby shower.

"You think you're getting out of this with only one event commemorating your fertile eggs?" Wicker asks, snorting. "This is just round one. And speaking of eggs..." He turns to look hungrily at the door when Danner comes in carrying a tray with three plates.

If Danner notices the glitter explosion, and I'm sure he does, he ignores it, setting the plates in front of each of us. I eye theirs with jealousy. They both have a pile of cheesy scrambled eggs, bacon, and a couple of thick, buttery pancakes. In contrast, I have a bowl of fresh fruit, yogurt, and this terrible high-protein, vitamin-infused porridge Lex has ordered me to eat every day. Pace notices and snorts, shaking his head at my misery, then shoves a piece of crispy bacon in his mouth, licking the grease off his fingertips.

My mouth waters, and I'm not sure if it's the bacon or his tongue that I'm salivating over. Pregnancy hormones have been a roller-coaster of frustration, hot flashes, random crying jags, and, last but definitely not least, unimaginable horniness.

"Anyway," I say, dragging my eyes away from the food porn and picking up my spoon, "I don't think I'm going to accept."

"Why?" Wicker smirks meanly. "Worried Heather remembers you hit her with a frying pan when she was flirting with me?"

"No." I scowl. "Well, now I am." Shit, I forgot about that—about the whole night. I had to stake my claim with those vultures, and Wicker had been so turned on by it. He ate me out in the hallway and then carried me off to fuck me in someone's room. Sure, it was rough and impersonal, but now that I actually need it, he's on some revenge-based sex ban. With horror, I imagine that I wouldn't mind it so much if it happened again. "I mean, what do people even do at a spa?"

"Fuck if I know," Pace says, digging into his meal.

"Probably the basics," Wicker says, layering his pancakes with eggs and bacon, making a perverse and delicious-looking sandwich. "Pedicures and foot massages. A facial to clean up those pores. Gossip. Oh, and don't forget the pussy and asshole waxing."

Pace snaps his head at me. "Leave your bush alone. It's finally grown back out the way I like it."

"Jesus," I mutter, pushing my oatmeal away. My appetite has vanished. "Yeah, there's no chance I'm going to that."

"Oh, you'll go, Princess. It's tradition, and you know how Father feels about those." Wicker's damp shirt clings to his biceps, molding against his muscles. "But here's a little more advice—"

"*Unsolicited* advice," I make sure to note.

He takes a large, aggressive bite from the sandwich. "It's about time you made an effort with the other women in East End. They aren't your friends—they're your court. Now that you're knocked up and locked in the role, you just became their leader."

"But I don't want to be their leader." The thought is less appealing than the bowl of mush on my plate.

Wicker barks a sharp, humorless laugh, his blue eyes radiating hostility. "When are you going to realize no one cares what any of us want? Not me, not my brothers, and certainly not you."

Snagging up his sandwich, his chair skitters back with an awful screech as he rises, slinking from the dining room. Pace watches him with troubled eyes, curling closer to his plate as he wolfs down a forkful of eggs.

This is one of those moments where it's clear we're all on the same side of the coin—Ashby versus his children. We're all tied to his whims and directives. In a world where Wicker didn't blame me for it, it might even be the kind of thing that brings us closer.

You know, if they weren't psychopaths and I didn't have a plan.

"There's a cushion on the chair in the corner." Pace's voice draws me from the thought, his wiry, toned biceps flexing as he takes another bite. It's the first time I can remember being totally alone with him in weeks, and my heartbeat notches up at the intensity in his dark eyes.

"Cushion?"

"For your knees." He says this casually, the same way he might inform me my spoon is located beside my bowl. "I meant what I said, Rosilocks. I've been saving every drop for you." He leans back, spreading his legs. "Get under the table."

My answer is immediate. "No."

He takes a deep breath, pinning me with a set jaw and narrowed eyes. "It's been over a month. Our deal with Wick was that I wouldn't fuck you, but since both of them are weak bitches who broke the second they climbed into your bed, I'm giving that a little moral shift." His eyes dip down to my mouth, darkening. "I'm going to fuck your throat."

My thoughts stutter to a screeching halt before churning into overdrive.

Their deal with Wicker?

To not *fuck* me?

Pieces begin clicking into place. Pace and Lex's anger at Wicker during my exam. The tension between them. The more I calculate it all, the more I begin to understand. Lex has slept with me for the past five nights. There isn't always sex. Last night, he skulked into my room with his bedding and instantly fell asleep. But on the nights he waltzes through my door with that frenetic gleam in his eye, he begins by aggressively flicking out each light, neither of us able to see a thing when he shoves me down to the mattress and parts my thighs.

The sex isn't what I'd call intimate. It's done mostly to the soundtrack of fevered, frustrated panting, neither of us talking. The kisses are bruising. His movements are punishing. It's never anything less than clear that Lex is using me to get off.

Mostly, I just get a good grip on his hair and do the same.

Last night as I was falling asleep to the soft glow of his bedside lamp, I was unutterably disappointed.

"Wicker broke your deal," I say carefully, "by having sex with me."

The corners of Pace's eyes go tight, pinched. "Not that any of us were surprised. Apparently, all it takes is him being half asleep and having you 'right there.'" A sharp scoff. "He's never been good at covering his tracks, though. I knew the second I saw that knot on your head."

It's all I can do to hold my laughter in. All this time Wicker's been hiding that he knocked my head into the nightstand, his brothers have been thinking he had sex with me.

And the thing is?

It's working.

I've barely had to make an effort, and they're already fracturing, so paranoid and delusional that it's beginning to turn them on one another.

This might be easier than I thought.

Putting down my napkin, I say, "I'm not going to suck your dick."

Pace watches me for a long moment, his eyebrow twitching. "What makes you think you have a choice?"

Leaning forward, I prop my elbows on the table. "I am, as your brother so eloquently put it moments ago, 'an effective little Royal cum dumpster with a golden ticket.' So the real question is," I rest my chin on my folded fists, eyelashes batting, "what makes you think you can make me?"

His jaw tics. "You don't want the answer to that question."

"No," I decide, jerking my chin, "what I want is for you to go get that cushion."

Pace's brows knit up tightly, his eyes pinging to the chair. "For what?"

I smile prettily. "For *your* knees, of course."

It's evident when he comprehends, all mirth disappearing from his features. "You're overplaying your hand, Rosi."

"And you're under-licking my cunt."

"Monday will be me," Pace says, rising from his seat to tower over me. "That's when you make your choice, during dinner with us and Father." He holds my stare, tone brooking no argument. "Next week is mine."

I scoot my chair back and stand, taking the card with me as I crane my neck up to meet the challenge in his eyes. "That's for me to decide, and if I'm going by merit, then you should know..." I strain up on my toes to whisper, "Wicker licks my pussy like a hot sundae."

I pull away only long enough to catch the flash of murderous fury in his eyes before I sweep out of the room.

As Lex promised, I'm no longer greeted for bed by a glass of warm milk. To be fair, the milk is also on the tray, but he hands me the cup of tea and promptly takes the milk into the bathroom and dumps it down the sink.

"Don't tell Danner," he says when he returns with the empty glass. "He means well, but Father's rule goes above all."

I sniff the tea, smelling the ginger, and pretend like Lex didn't just reveal another secret being held in this house. "This isn't Wicker's tea, is it? I know it has bourbon."

"No, I prepared it myself."

I take a sip, the familiar, soothing taste warm all the way down. "Thank you."

As I'd promised, I've done everything he asked of me. I swallowed the prenatal vitamin the size of a horse pill and managed to keep it down. I ate the meals prepared for me without complaint. I monitored my sodium levels and wore the heartbeat monitor while I was doing my homework. And now, under the dim light of the bedside sconces, I pick up the pregnancy book he had delivered to me in West End. I won't admit it, but it actually is helpful.

On 'his side' of the bed, he strips off his shirt and the loose sweatpants that hang low on his hips. I'm aware of him all the time now, searching for the little signals. Is it a light on or light off night? Will he pull that hair tie out or wait for me to do it?

And exactly what will happen when I tell him no?

Because that's my plan, or so I remind myself as I keep my eyes on my book and not the thick bulge under his gray boxer briefs. Standing my ground with Pace this morning had an impact, and it's time for me to do the same with Lex, regardless of the way my body feels as he gets into bed, under the covers, and picks up his glasses and book from the bedside table. He slides the glasses on and goes to the bookmarked page in *'Deciphering DNA.'*

We sit beside one another in this amicable quiet until he closes the book with a snap, pulls out the tie in his hair, and reaches for the light.

"Not tonight," I say before he switches it off.

His forehead creases. "What do you mean?"

"Like I said, not tonight." He stares at me behind those glasses, a million emotions rushing across his face. A thick tendril of hair hangs by his cheek. "I know why you turn the lights off, so you're not recorded. I know you made an agreement with Pace and Wicker about no sex, and you're violating it."

"My arrangements with my brothers are none of your business." He reaches for me, but I move quickly across the bed, grabbing a pillow and clutching it against my chest. "You can't deny me, Princess."

"I can, and you know it." I lift my chin. Physically, he's right. I can't outmatch any of them. But sex is on my terms. It's in the covenant. "I said no."

His hands thrust into his hair, pushing at the auburn strands. "No one gives a fuck what you say, Verity. Take off those panties, or I'll do it for you."

I shake my head, pretending like my resolve isn't about to break.

Dark anger flickers across his face, and in a blink, he's on top of me, wrenching the pillow out of my hands and throwing it off the bed. His thick erection burrows between my thighs, and his wide hand clamps around my throat. With the heat of his breath fanning across my face, I see him for who he is under that careful façade.

Lagan.

"I need this," he growls. "I need your body—to feel your pussy clenching around me. I need to feel my cock balls-deep. I need every fucking ounce of me left inside." His mouth is on my shoulder, teeth bearing down. "I don't want it, Princess, no more than you do, but I can't stop until I've worked you out of my system. Just like the fucking Scratch."

He's wrong. I do want it. The rush of blood pulses between my legs like an erratic heartbeat, and I've been wet since he took off his shirt. This is bigger than biological need. This is about driving a wedge between these men—it's about me taking control.

"You can't," I tell him, placing my hands on his hard chest for stability as I force my hips not to rise, "you *promised*."

His teeth gnash, and a feral, dangerous sound rips from his throat. I wait for the invasion to come, those rough hands handling my body, the hard thrust between my legs as he takes me. But in a blink, he's gone, his hand snatched from my throat, his body weight, all of it. Lex is off the bed and up on his feet, scrubbing his face like he's trying to force his alter ego away. "Don't."

"What?"

His chest heaves, and I brace for him to pounce, but he turns away from me, facing the fireplace across the room. From this vantage, I see the criss-cross scars which mar his back, thick and gnarled. The top layer is still pink, healing from the last punishment. Bile rises to my throat now that I know what caused them. "Don't you dare question my loyalty."

"I'm not questioning you," I say, trying to keep my voice even. "I'm *reminding* you."

Silence stretches between us, and I watch the muscles in his back tighten and tense, making the scars ripple, as he struggles with his demons, a new one revealed when he said, *'I can't stop until I've worked you out of my system.'*

"Come back to bed." I clear my throat. "Please."

He doesn't acknowledge me, just walks into the bathroom, flicking on the light. I hear the sink faucet turn on, followed by a hard rush of water. A few moments later, he walks back out, seemingly more in control, picks up the pillow, and tosses it on the end of the bed. He returns to his side.

He burrows under the covers, flipping to his side, he hits the dimmer, and the room settles into semi-darkness.

"Goodnight," he says, the signal that whatever just transpired between us is settled.

On my own side, I turn my back to him and reply, "Goodnight."

Rattle...rattle...rattle

The noise cuts through the fog of sleep. Instinctively, I stretch my arm out across the bed. The space is still warm, but empty. Opening my eyes, I look around the room and see Lex standing at the door, fiddling with the knob.

His sleepwalking has lessened since we started having sex, although not entirely. A few nights when Wicker was here, he tried to get in, banging on the opposite side of the door. Each time, either Pace or Wicker gently returned him to his room, doing their best not to escalate the situation. Tonight, there's no one around to deal with him, so I rise to stop him myself, detangling myself from the blankets. Unfortunately, he gets the door open before I can reach him, his large frame ambling down the hall.

"Shit," I mutter, the cold air in the room slapping my bare thighs. I've seen how his brothers do this, quietly and without sudden movement. They don't want to wake him—just redirect him back to a safe bed. He moves quickly and quietly, passing his bedroom without a second glance. I expect him to stop at Pace's room, but he continues forward, headed to the back staircase.

I trail behind him like a ghost, not wanting to accost him on the stairs. He goes straight to the kitchen, pausing to snatch an apple out of the fruit bowl on the counter and taking a bite. The crunch echoes in the still room, his face and body lit only by a small light over the sink. As quickly as he picks up the apple, he drops it, the fruit hitting the tile floor with a thud and then rolling across the floor. Turning to the refrigerator, he opens the door and silhouetted in the light, I watch him remove a carton of juice and drink straight from the top.

Tentatively, I reach out and touch his back, feeling the rough ridge of healed flesh.

At my touch, he spins, juice dripping down his chin. He wipes it off with the back of his hand.

"Hey." I take the carton from him. He blinks, eyes glazed over, but I sense the shift when he notices me. He leans toward me, taking a long sniff of my neck. I fight a shiver and say, "Let's get you back to—"

His hands cinch around my waist, and he picks me up, placing me on the island in the center of the room. His hands flatten on either side of my legs, pinning me in.

"Lex," I say, setting the carton aside. A drop of juice is caught in his chest hair. "Let's get you back upstairs."

"Hungry." His voice is a low grunt.

"Then let's get a snack." I move to slide off the island, but he holds me still, hands moving up my thighs until they vanish under my nightdress. Roughly, he grabs the sides of my panties and yanks them down my legs.

I fall back from the force, and a rush of warmth pools at my core as he brings the white cotton to his nose and inhales, licking his lips on a hum. "You smell so good."

Fuck. I should stop this. Stop *him* before he breaks another promise... but is it? Is it breaking a promise when he's asleep?

Before I decide, a shadow moves on the staircase, and I freeze. If it's Wicker, he'll throw a fit. If it's Danner or Ashby, well, I'm already mortified. I squint past the refrigerator light and see the glint of black eyes peeking out from behind dark twists. Pace.

Well, that changes things.

"You hungry, baby?" I bend and lick the drop of juice off his chest in a slow, deliberate path. His Adam's apple bobs slowly, and I take it a step further, looking into his eyes. Spreading my thighs, I rub my fingers over my clit. "My pussy is wet and ready."

The words feel strange and out of character, but they're not a lie. I *am* wet and ready for him, and that dark look that I saw in his amber eyes earlier tonight returns. Swiping his tongue over his bottom lip, he hooks his arms behind my knees and pulls me to the edge of the table. The first swipe of his tongue over my clit feels like two exposed livewires meeting for the first time. I cry out and thrust my fingers into his hair, hips rising to meet his mouth.

There's nothing gentle about the way he tastes me, that ravenous hunger on display. His hands flatten against my inner thighs, spreading me farther apart, and the hot warmth of his breath sends a shiver across my flesh.

Turning my head to the side, I peer toward the stairwell for my dark Prince. I don't need to see or hear him to know what he's doing. I know his hand is down his pants, fingers wrapped around his cock in a tight fist. He's jealous, no doubt about that. Especially since I rejected him earlier, but I know he won't waste an opportunity to use my body for his own pleasure.

"You taste so fucking good," the man between my legs murmurs, tongue flicking over my clit. This man knows my body so well, each part studied like the textbook up in my room, but at times like this, when there's no lab coat or pretense between us, my body is rewarded for suffering through the cold sterility of the exam room. I don't have to worry about him not finding the right rhythm or toying with me. He gets me there quickly—fingers, mouth, tongue—working my body until I'm desperately close to the edge.

Standing, he lifts my hips into the air, eating my pussy with my thighs clamped around his ears. My fingers curl around the edge of the counter, our eyes meeting down the slope of my body, and I see it then.

No glassy surface, no foggy expression.

It's not Lagan fucking me with his tongue.

It's Lex, giving me exactly what I want.

The knowledge sends an orgasm crashing over me like a breaking wave. A moan rips from my chest, the sound echoing off the kitchen walls. My pussy quivers, desperate for him to be inside, and I wait for him to push down his shorts, to fuck me, but he slides his hand around the back of my neck and pulls me upright instead.

His mouth moves next to my ear, delivering a rumbling whisper, "You were right before. We made a deal. No sex while Wicker gets his shit worked out. But *my* shit is that you're under my goddamn skin. I want to be done with it. Done with you. There's no treatment for this. There's no group on campus where I can go to talk about the insatiable need I have to fuck my Princess, and *that* urge is worse than jonesing for a hit of Scratch." His breath is hot, tinged with the heady scent of my pussy. "Wick's relationship with sex is too fucked up to even comprehend. Pace is caught up in his own obsessions. I won't be denied, Princess. Not when it's my week. Not when I'm in your bed. Not when the urge strikes. Not," he says, drawing our eyes together, "until the baby gets here, or we're through. Whichever comes first."

My jaw drops, and he presses his finger under it, his mouth taking mine in a searing, unrelenting kiss.

I'm still sprawled on the table when he grabs the carton of juice, throwing back an aggressive swig as he stalks back up the stairs. I take a moment to compose myself, easing off the island and straightening my nightgown. He took my panties with him, but there's a streak of the glistening fluid between my legs that's also visible on the countertop. I find the cleaner under the sink and breathlessly wipe it down, then find the half-eaten apple on the floor and toss it.

You're welcome, Danner.

I survey the kitchen, satisfied it's in the same condition as when we entered, which is when I hear the shift of clothing behind me. I start to turn when a hard body slams into my back, a tattooed arm wrapping around my chest. A closed fist appears in front of my mouth.

I don't have to imagine what's inside.

"Nice show," Pace says, his voice rough.

"That wasn't for you."

"No? Because until you saw me, you were trying to get my brother to go back upstairs."

I gulp. "Not everything is about you, Pace."

"I think you like manipulating my brother." His teeth nip at my earlobe. "He's too wound up to see straight, but I see you just fine,

Rosi." My jaw clenches, but his fingers latch around my chin, wedging it open. He opens his hand, and I see the thick glob of semen threatening to drip on the floor. "Open up. I saved you a little treat."

"Gross." I squirm against him. "You're disgusting."

"Take it." He pushes it in my face, coating my lips. "All of it."

I know fighting is pointless. He'll chase me down and shove it in my mouth, or worse, cram his dick down my throat and drown me in his spunk. I stick my tongue out and take a lick, the salty tanginess assaulting my tastebuds.

"You like it, don't you," he says. "Tasting my cum. Licking it up like a fucking dog."

I fight a gag, but not from the semen. From his filthy, disgusting mouth.

"Swallow," he growls, fingers releasing my jaw. I swipe my tongue out and take in more, and his hand moves down to the column of my throat. "Every last drop, Rosi."

Already hard again, his cock drills into my ass, thickening with every swallow. Flattening my tongue over his palm, I get the rest, licking his hand bare.

He shifts, grinning at me with that handsome, smug face. "I think you fight me because you like it, but deep down, you want to be a good girl, don't you?"

What I want is to rip his eyes out so he can never watch me, or anyone else, ever again.

11

erity

Can't wait to see you!

The text came in about an hour before the start time. The group title is labeled '*The Court,*' and none of the girls are identified, but it's followed by a flurry of heart emojis, baby rattles, and gold crowns.

Kill me now.

Except now is too late because Danner is already pulling the car up to a massive Victorian house with pale pink siding and a wide wraparound porch. A sign hangs from the eaves: The Gilded Rose.

I did a little research after breakfast, discovering that the spa is owned by a former Princess, Adeline Beckwith, and caters to the women of East End. Her services cover everything from deep tissue massage and hot stone treatments to out-there shit like vagina cleansing and, just like Wicker said, pussy and ass waxing.

"I'll be outside if you need me," Danner says, opening the car door for me. I'd told Stella to stay at home. No need for her to sit around while I got pampered in home territory. If these women are going to be petty bitches to me, then there's no reason to offer her up for even more abuse.

The instant I step on the porch, the door swings open, and a big-haired, bleach-blonde woman lunges at me. "Verity Sinclaire!" She engulfs me in a hug. "I've been dying to meet you!"

I know this is Adeline, as her picture is displayed prominently on the website, and I try to wait an appropriate amount of time before disentangling myself. "It's lovely to meet you, too."

"Oh my gosh, you are the spitting image of your father," she says, taking me in. I do the same. She's younger than my mother, maybe in her mid-thirties. Every line in her face has been buffed out or smoothed away. "I should've known he was keeping a secret. Rufus Ashby is always full of surprises."

Holding back a grimace, I simper, "Isn't he?"

She gives my arms an aggressive rub. "You're just adorable, you know that?" Before I can think of a response to this, she laughs, flapping a hand. "Come in, come in!"

I allow her to usher me inside the foyer. A huge bouquet of white roses sits on the circular table in the center of the space—the fragrance overwhelming. A wave of nausea strikes, and I force it down. "This place is beautiful."

"It's been in my family for four generations. My great-grandmother started it, then my grandmother and mother continued, and then I became the keeper." She bodily shoos me past the foyer, and I send up a silent prayer of thanks that Stella stayed home. Their dual energy would drain me in one breath. "The girls are all waiting for you in the lounge. They're so excited!"

She leads me down a hallway, and I sense a theme. Everything is pink, from the patterned carpet runner on the floor to the brocade wallpaper. There are gold-framed photos on the walls, and from the hair and clothing being displayed, they go back decades. I pause in front of a black-and-white photo that's captured an image of twelve girls dressed in pristine white—their faces obscured with masks. I can't shake the knowledge that one of these delicate, poised girls walked out of that ballroom and sat on the same throne that ripped through my own hymen. Was it the one on the left? Or the small one in the middle? Maybe the curvy one in the back?

Was she as horrified as I was?

"This is... impressive," I say, surveying the artifacts. "It's like a museum."

Adeline nods proudly. "The palace is a shrine to the men of East End. They have their Gentlemen's Club and off-campus party houses, locker rooms, and trophies. The women in my family saw there was something that needed to be preserved—the history of the Princesses." She stops and looks at a photo taken of a Valentine's Day party. "We don't have a sorority house, but we do have this." She reaches out to carefully straighten a frame, and I get the sense she's downed a lot of the Royal Kool-Aid. This is sacred to her—worth memorializing.

I'm not going to find any allies here.

We enter the lounge where the other girls are waiting. My 'court' turns out to be a half-dozen semi-familiar faces. Most were at the masquerade, all of them at the Valentine's Day party as dates of the PNZ frat boys: the men who assaulted me at the Royal Cleansing.

It's immediately obvious I'm overdressed in the high-waisted linen dress Stella pulled from my closet. The East End girls aren't required to dress as properly as I am, setting their own fashion trends that they replicate like clones. This season they're all about pristine white, or pastel pleated tennis skirts. They're long enough to cover their asses, but flirty enough to give their boyfriends access to their cunts whenever they want it. Their jewelry is delicate, all gold or pearls. No silver. It's a sea of over-processed, bleached hair and bad tans.

I try to put names to the faces, but honestly, I never paid much attention. Although one girl does stand out—or rather, her rounded belly does. Her boyfriend Colby Harker is the guy who OD'ed last month. Hand resting on her stomach, she watches from the back of the room with a tight expression.

I'm about to call this whole thing off when someone gets the guts to step forward. Lakshmi, a standout with her dark hair, flawless brown skin, and curvy figure. I remember Wicker lusting over her in the footage of the dressing room that day. "Verity, you look amazing. Such a natural glow." Her eyes flit over me in assessment. "Pregnancy suits you."

Behind her, I see Gina and Heather, the latter sipping on a glass of champagne, expression blank, and decidedly not making eye contact. Fair. She could still be recovering from a concussion.

"Thank you, this is really nice of you to do," I reply, and a server walks over and offers me a glass.

"Sparkling cider, of course," Adeline says, then gives me an exaggerated pout. "No bubbly for you. Gosh, but you're such a tiny little thing! Are you sure there's a baby in there?" A boisterous laugh jiggles her stiff hair.

The room falls silent, as if they're waiting for an answer.

I give the sparkling cider a testing sip. "According to the blood test, sonogram, and hormonal changes, that's the verdict." Some of their expressions are satisfied, while a few other girls clumsily hide their disappointment. Clearing my throat, I do my best to cut through the awkwardness. "I was surprised to be invited to a celebration so early, though. This is so generous of you all."

"It's a tradition," Gina says suddenly, repeating what Wicker said this morning. "My mother still talks about her day out with the girls when she got pregnant. She was so excited to hear that I was going to be part of your special day." A few other girls nod, and it strikes me that any or all of them could be the result of a Princess pregnancy.

Well, that's a sobering thought.

I sip my drink just for something to do with my hands, wishing it was alcohol. God, this is a fucking nightmare. I have no idea how to talk to these people. How to, as Wicker said, lead them. Thankfully, Adeline steps in.

"I've planned an exquisite treatment for you all today. I've heard our mama-to-be has had a rough time with morning sickness, so I figured we'd start with a hot stone massage and facial. We'll follow that with a luxurious mani-pedi with one of our amazing nail designers, and then send you off with fabulous hair and makeup." She leans over and whispers. "Don't worry, your Prince contacted us with a very stern warning to leave you unwaxed. His demands will be honored."

I freeze, heat rising to my cheeks in mortification. "Oh." That controlling, obsessive freak of a man. In an effort to wade out of the humiliation, I meekly admit, "I'm not gonna lie. A massage sounds pretty awesome right now." I rest my hand on my hip. "Spending half the day bent over a toilet is murder on my back."

Adeline grins and then raises her glass. "To the Princess and her heir."

All six hands mimic her, glasses raised high, looking at me for... something. Approval? Humility? Gratitude? No, I realize, reading the expectation in their eyes. They want what Wicker said. A leader. Someone with the right words. Someone to carry on the *tradition*.

I hold up my glass and try not to gag as I give them what they need.

"To create is to reign."

~

WHO KNEW ALL I needed in my life was for someone to put hot stones all over my naked body and rub out all the tension? *Gah*. By the time the masseuse is finished, my arms and legs feel like they're made of gelatin. It's a shame when Adeline's assistants rinse me off and wrap my hair in a towel and my body in a white, fluffy robe before leading me to a room where the other girls are already sitting in comfortable loungers, their feet dipped in bubbling tubs.

Adeline doesn't provide the services herself. She's the commander of an army of assistants, each one focused on a different part of the body. Hands, feet, hair, everything buffed and plucked. I sit in the chair and sink my feet in the small whirlpool, exhaling in contentment.

This is a reason to be Princess.

Finally, some perks worth writing home about.

A woman with the name 'Carol' stitched on her smock stands

over me and begins applying a cool mask on my face. Closing my eyes, I relax and listen to the girls talk around me, discussing parties and classes and guys they're dating.

Across the room, a voice rises above the others. "I just think it's strange that he randomly has this new kink. Don't you think that's weird?"

I open my eye a crack and see all the girls looking at Heather. Lakshmi is next to her and asks, "Depends. What is it?"

Heather elaborates in an uneasy voice, "Well, you know how they're only supposed to come inside of us—increasing their odds for a baby—but lately, Tommy's been into something else..."

"Anal?" Someone asks. "Because Rory just pulls out and finishes inside."

"No," Heather says, lowering her voice so that it's hard to hear over the footbaths. "He's gotten really into jerking off and coming on me."

"On your tits?" Gina snorts. "I don't think that's a new kink, babe."

Everyone laughs, but Heather adds, "No. My collarbone. The same spot every time." Her voice wobbles. "You think he doesn't want to have a baby with me?"

"He probably just figures that since the Princess is knocked up, there's a little less pressure on the rest of the frat right now," Lakshmi says. Her eyes meet mine, and there's no time to pretend I haven't been listening. "Right, Princess?"

"Uh..."

Before I can formulate a real response, Heather's lip curls up, and she bites out, "I guess *your* guys never miss their mark, do they, Princess?"

"Heather!" Gina hisses.

She's not intimidated, though, raising a plucked eyebrow. "I'm just saying. You got knocked up really fast—faster than Piper even, and she was getting fucked by four men. Or is their kink fucking their sister? Is that what turns them on?"

Every eye in the room looks at me like they're waiting to see exactly how I'll react. With a frying pan? With sharp, bitter words? Will I cry?

I go with the truth. "None of us knew I was Ashby's daughter until I was already pregnant. In fact, you all found out at the same time we did and were probably less shocked than we were." Sensing that the other girls are listening intently, I weigh my words carefully. "The Princes are under a lot of pressure from their father to perform their duties, and trust me, they weren't happy I was chosen." Or that *they* were chosen. I think about Wicker's tantrums and Lex's concerns about my loyalty. "It may seem like all gifts and roses in public, but in all honesty, this is just a job. For them and me."

A little of the anger in Heather's eyes relaxes.

Frida, a short girl with a sleek bob, gushingly insists, "There has to be some romance, though."

I level her with a hard look. "Does there?"

Her smile falls.

"So, Princess," Lakshmi cuts in, "any guesses on who's the father?"

"Not a clue," I answer truthfully.

"You have to have some inkling," Kira says. It's the first time she's spoken to me all afternoon. "When Colby and I conceived, I knew right away. I could just feel it."

I hold back a statement about how getting railed 24/7 by three different men makes it hard to discern any special difference, and offer her a sympathetic smile instead. "I'm so sorry to hear about what happened to Colby. The guys were devastated. Particularly Lex. I know they were friends."

She gently strokes her stomach. "It's okay. I mean, I miss him, and I hate that this is the route he took, but I come from a long line of East Enders. If I carry to term, King Ashby will set the baby up with a trust fund, and I'll get an allowance. The Princes always take care of their own."

Of course, Kira understands what Frida apparently doesn't: that babies here are a business, not a declaration of love. Even so, Kira sounds naïve. Ashby doesn't have an altruistic bone in his body. Not unless it gives him what he wants, and I guess that's the catch. He just wants purebred babies to churn through this system. Boys to train for roles in PNZ. Girls to control. But I also can imagine this girl needs to know he'll support her and the baby when it comes. They all want the fairytale.

"I'm sure they will," I say, humoring her, even if uncomfortably.

An attendant moves behind my chair and unwraps my wet hair. "Carol," Gina says, looking at the woman behind me, "You should give Verity one of your amazing scalp massages. It feels *so* good."

The woman bends and asks, "Would you like that?"

I blink up at her, taken aback. "Uh, sure. That sounds nice."

Fuck.

Nice doesn't begin to describe it. She kneads and works my scalp from my forehead to my neck. It also has the advantage of doubling as an excuse to end my discussion with the other girls. Cutsluts wouldn't posture like this. They'd hound me until I told them all the dirty, gritty details, and they'd know when I was lying or holding something back. These East Enders are pros at artifice, however. They're happier with the illusion than the truth, and that makes honesty a tightrope walk.

I keep my eyes closed and drift off, barely aware of Carol's movements. At some point, the massage stops, and she begins applying something heavy and thick to my hair. The comfortable weight of it drags me beneath the surface of awareness, my late-night wandering the palace with Lex catching up to me.

My doze turns into a hard, dreamless sleep.

"Rise and shine, Princess," I hear, followed by a giggle and snort of laughter. My eyes flutter open to the sight of the rest of the party already dressed, hair and makeup flawless.

My jaw cracks with a wide, embarrassing yawn. "Ugh, I must have fallen asleep." I rub my eyes and sit up, feeling a heavy tug on my scalp. Frowning, I reach up to touch my hair, confused by the texture. "What the—" Jolting upright, I realize my hair is hard, caked in something thick and unmoving.

"Something wrong?" Heather asks snidely.

"What did you do?" I try to dig my freshly painted nails into my scalp. "What is this?"

Leaning back in her chair, she crosses her perfectly waxed legs. "What you deserve. You thought you were so smart going to the masquerade, pretending like you were some innocent little gutter virgin from West End. With your shiny red hair and perfect little womb. You knew all along he was your father, didn't you? This was your way of forcing him to claim you, by getting knocked up by one of his sons. A *double* heir. You just weren't happy with what you had—you wanted all of it, didn't you?"

"The gifts." Gina steps forward, snarling. "The boys—*our* boys—down on their knees, honoring you for being such a perfect Princess."

"Are you fucking with me?" I ask, trying to get out of the chair without tripping over the foot tub. The only ones in the room are me and the girls. Where Adeline and her assistants went, God knows. "I don't want any of that bullshit!"

"Jesus, you're such a spoiled, self-righteous bitch," Lakshmi adds. "You come here whining about this being a job? You can't even be grateful for what you have." She looks over her shoulder. "You know Chloe had two miscarriages? She's got one more shot before her boyfriend moves on to someone new." Behind her stands Chloe, her eyes shining with unshed tears. "So while you're flaunting your pregnancy, maybe you could show some tact by remembering that some people aren't as lucky."

"Lucky?" I gape at them, rage filling my chest. "How fucking dare you call me lucky. You think it's lucky to find out my father made no attempt to contact me until I could give him the only thing he wants? Or the fact that I signed a contract with the Princes using blood from tearing through my hymen? Or that my vagina was the target of a battering ram day in and day out?" To Chloe, I say, "I didn't know that about you, and I'm sorry. You shouldn't feel pressured to conceive a baby if it's dangerous for your health." I'm sure as shit going to talk to Lex about that. "But if you think being in that palace makes me lucky, then you've been lied to."

"Oh boo-fucking-hoo," Kira says, her quiet tone from before replaced with a bitter growl. "It's not even like your uterus is special. I got knocked up faster than you did, but my mother didn't *create* me with King Ashby, so it makes my child less worthy."

These girls are fucking nuts.

"You want to know how spoiled I am? How privileged my life is? What happens when I don't toe the line?" I turn my gaze at Heather, who's still staring at me like I'm the enemy. "You want to know why Tommy suddenly has this new kink?"

I grab my phone out of my pocket and search for the last text I got from the 'Court.' I've been saving this video file for my next stay in West End, trying to gather the courage I'll need to take away all of King Ashby's leverage against me. Who knows if I'll have what it takes to sit my mother down and reveal what happened that night with the frat.

I suppose this—uploading it to my Court's group chat—is a good start.

A series of notification alerts ping around the room. My heart pounds as they, one by one, pull out their phones.

"Go ahead and see!" I roar, a flood of rage unleashing. "Then you'll realize your sweet Tommy is reliving the best moment of his pathetic fucking life." Not all of the PNZ members seemed to take as perverse enjoyment in the act as others.

Tommy had his dick out before any of them.

"What is this?" Gina asks, voice a touch high. Her thumb is already pressing play. Around us, the room fills with the sound of deep grunts, the unmistakable precursor to a man ejaculating.

"Those are your boyfriends and your future baby daddies." I glare around the room. "Jerking off and spraying me with their cum. They call it the Royal Cleansing, and I had to sit there and take it, just like I sat here and took your petty bullshit all day." I finally get a look in the mirror, my stomach clenching. The green clay mask is still on my face, dried and cracking, and my hair is a slicked-back mess, looking like someone poured lacquer over it. "You can see this isn't the first time I've been covered in something sticky and disgusting. So whatever the fuck you did to my hair, I'll get over it. The same way I get over everything in this godforsaken kingdom."

I storm out, running into Adeline on the way.

"Verity?" She looks me up and down, eyes growing more horrified with every passing second. "Oh my god. What... who did this? Oh my god."

"Move, Adeline." I storm past her and open up the door, determined not to let the tears welling in my eyes fall. They'd think it's for them—that they have the power to hurt me—but that's not it at all.

Stupid fucking pregnancy hormones.

"Danner!" I call, craning my neck to search for the black sedan. I march up and down the row of cars, yelling his name, but just as his head appears around a truck, another car comes barrelling into the drive.

It's white and sleek.

I'd know Wicker's ridiculous Ferrari anywhere.

It careens to a dusty halt right beside me, my reflection in the tinted window taunting me further. When it opens, however, it's Pace who pops out, the sharp angles of his face hard as stone when he jumps out, not even cutting the ignition.

"Those fucking bitches," he snarls, glaring up at the house. "Why is this place so out in the goddamn boonies? I could have gotten here before you woke up."

Unable to handle him right now, I turn away. "Danner?" I'm not proud of the wobble in my voice, nor the way I flinch when Pace reaches out for me, snagging my wrist.

"Get in the car," he orders. "I'm taking you home."

"Home?" I explode, whirling on him. "Where is home, Pace? You're going to take me to West End where I'm a freak show? Or are you going to take me back to the palace where I'm a prisoner? Which is it? What fucking home?!" I punctuate the last word with a punching shove against his chest.

Naturally, he's as solid as a fucking tree.

His response to this is to lock his jaw and grab my arms, wrestling me into the breadth of his body. My instincts scream with alarm, but all he does is wrap his arms around me, hissing, "Chill, Rosi. Don't let them see they got to you." His chest smells like cigar smoke and cologne, and as I'm panting angry breaths into his jacket, I realize he's dressed in a suit, the knot of the tie beneath my ear loosened.

"Danner," I try, but Pace begins walking me around the car.

"Danner will follow us back," he insists, all but pushing me into the passenger seat. I'd gather more strength to argue, but the well, it seems, has run dry.

By the time Pace slams my door and gets behind the wheel, I feel too wrung out and frayed around the edges to fight him when he buckles my seatbelt.

Wrenching the gear shift, he peels out, tossing a confused Danner a wave as we fly by.

We're halfway back to the palace by the time he speaks, his deep voice cutting through the silence. "It's glue." His dark eyes flick to mine. "I saw the one chick take it out of her bag, but I didn't have audio, so I was too late to—"

"You were watching?"

He gives me an unimpressed look. Of course he was watching. Eyes everywhere. "While the Princess gets primped, the frat has their own tradition," he explains, wrist resting casually on the steering wheel. "It's kind of like a stag party. PNZ was hosting it at Father's club."

The strip club.

"Good for you," I mutter, reaching up to scratch my cheek.

Green clay flakes off onto my robe, and I don't need a mirror to know how insane I look. The mask, my matted, ruined hair. My eyes must be red from crying. But as Pace pulls into the palace driveway, the gate sliding open, I feel him watching me.

Always watching.

It's not his gaze that unnerves me. It's the look in his eye.

It never changes. Not when I'm in a ballgown, or when he has me on my knees, or when I'm walking across campus.

Not when I look like this—broken down.

Pace looks at me the same no matter the circumstances.

Like I belong to him.

12

Pace

"THOUGHT YOU'D BE INTO THIS," Wicker says, taking a long sip from a glass of something amber. Bourbon, probably. Through the dim, smoky ambiance of the Gentlemen's Chamber, I can tell his grin is full of displeasure. "Watching, but never touching. Isn't that your bag?"

From our leather booth, we watch the PNZ members cheer at the stage, Tommy Wright flinging a dollar bill at a lithe, big-tittied dancer. Another guy puts a bill in his mouth, making a 'come and get it' gesture.

"Here I thought *you'd* be into this," I mutter, turning back to my phone screen.

Wicker scoffs, downing another gulp. "Water, water everywhere, and not a cunt to drink. Might as well put a starving man in front of a steak dinner he can't have."

I flick my narrowed eyes toward him. "Yeah, you're real starved."

It doesn't even really bother me that he broke the pact. Wicker was the only thing standing between us and Verity's pussy, and now that's pretty much null and void. In another circumstance, he would have come to us to fess up, accepting the ribbing he deserves for being unable to control his dick.

The problem is that he keeps lying.

"Damn right, I'm starved," he says, eyeing a passing dancer hungrily. "It's been two months. You telling me you aren't about to jump out of your skin, too?"

"Some of us," I remind him, "have gone a lot longer than two months without pussy." Quieter, I add, "And some of us have gone a lot less..."

He pulls a face at my mention of prison but nods in concession. "Still can't believe you went all that time without at least chasing some hot felon ass. A hole's a hole. I would have found myself a nice, pretty little bitch ASAP."

On the screen, Verity is leaning her hair back for what looks like a scalp massage. "I already had a nice, pretty little bitch."

In my periphery, I see Wicker frown and then lean over the table between us to catch a peek at my screen. He instantly groans, flopping back into the booth seat. "Christ, can't you give it a rest? The whole point of this party is to forget about our own girls for a few hours."

Driving home this point, a raucous celebration happens in the middle of the room, one of the younger guys getting a lap dance from a tall, leggy blonde. We're in Father's club, but the frat is throwing the celebration. Happens to every set of successful Princes. While the Princess gets pampered with the girlfriends of the frat members, the guys escape for a night of liquor, cigars, and ridiculous debauchery. *Tradition, tradition.* They've probably been planning it since the throning ceremony, panting like dogs at the thought of a break from their women.

Every guy in this room has their balls in a vise, but only a select few have the guts to realize it.

My lip curls in distaste. "Not interested."

"The fuck has gotten into everyone lately?" Wicker asks, knocking back the last of his drink. "We used to have fun, you know. All three of us. Now, Lex is hiding in the back, making phone calls about lab results, and you're too busy stalking our ball and chain to notice the premium ass shaking in your face." His voice turns strained, pleading. "Come on, Pace. Can't we have one night where shit is normal?"

Distractedly, I reply, "It's my job."

It's not a total lie. Father has made it clear that if anything happens to her, we're accountable. This is an easier excuse than the truth, which is that every second I'm not watching her, I'm throwing away a valuable opportunity.

Today most of all.

"It's bullshit," Wick insists, scowling. "She's just getting her ass licked by the Real Housewives of Golden Row. It's not like she's in any danger."

I slump against the booth, lips twitching. "We'll see."

East End bitches are a rare breed. Not because they'll smile in your face while hiding a knife behind their backs, but because they're so convincing while doing it. I watched them all receive the Princess with their smiles and bland praise. I saw the way Verity tried to be honest and authentic, really buying into Wicker's advice to lead them. She's not used to dealing with our kind. She's treating them like cutsluts when they're sharks out for blood.

And when she comes back home with her hurt feelings and wounded pride, guess who's going to be there to dab the tears away?

Wicker slams his glass down suddenly, biting out, "You know what? Fuck this." He shoots to his feet, hovering over the table like a storm cloud. "Since all anyone around here seems to care about is *her*," the resentment is palpable, "you can just fucking—"

"Wait." I straighten, watching the screen as Heather pulls a large bottle from her bag. It's only now that I realize Verity has fallen asleep, her body lax as she lays back in the chair, hair wet. There's no staff around. That's the first thing that sends my hackles up.

The second is the devious, hateful look Heather shoots at the other smirking girls as she approaches *mine*.

I spit a curse, rising to my feet. "Give me your keys."

Wicker looks disheveled in a way that isn't intentional. His eyes are glassy from the brandy, hair tangled in the front. "No." Slurring, he adds, "Fuck you."

A glance at the screen confirms my fears, Heather pouring a white glob onto Verity's red, silky hair. "I don't have time for your sibling rivalry bullshit," I growl, lunging to jab a hand into Wicker's coat pocket.

"Hey!" he barks, punching my arm, but I've already hit the mark, clutching my fingers around a key ring. When I yank it free of his pocket, Wicker slams his fist into my shoulder, exploding, "Fuck it! Go ahead and run to her like the pussy-whipped shithead you are." He turns to where some of the PNZ guys are watching, shifting uncomfortably. "All of you! Probably had to get permission to stare at someone else's tits, didn't you? Weak fucking bitches." He stumbles as he backs away, throwing two middle fingers in the air. "Stay in school, fellas! Do your goddamn duty."

I lock eyes with Lex all the way across the room, the phone still glued to his ear.

Jerking my chin in Wicker's direction, I wait until Lex nods in understanding before I sprint out of the club.

RESTING my hand on the small of her back, I lead her up the main staircase, eyes flitting around like I'm doing something unspeakably illicit. My brothers are still at the stag party, probably wondering what made me leave in such a hurry, and Father's there with them. It just settles over me awkwardly, being away from screens and surveillance feeds. That must be it.

"In here," I say, knowing it's bad when she doesn't fight, allowing me to usher her over the threshold to her room. She's been quiet and tense, this little crevice set into the skin between her eyebrows.

She looks like she's absorbed in dreaming up some elaborate revenge plot.

And for once, it probably isn't against me.

When we enter her bathroom, I flick on the light, turning to assess her. She's a horror show, from the green mask that flaked all over the interior of Wick's precious car, to the matted hair. It's one thing to mess with the Princess. It's another to touch that shiny, red hair.

Mine.

When she just stands there, wooden and expressionless, I turn to the sink, snagging a washcloth from the little shelf beside the mirror. It takes a moment for the tap to run hot, and I keep my stare on her reflection as I wait, wondering what she's thinking.

That's the worst part of all this.

I can watch her every second of the day—and sometimes, I do—but there are parts of her I'll never have access to. Like that day down in the exam room, hearing the heartbeat on the ultrasound. Some intangible knot in my chest loosened. I took a copy of the initial sonogram video from Lex, but it's all blurry and confusing, and I'd rather punch myself in the dick than ask Lex to explain it all to me. It's not enough anymore to watch her like this. I need to see inside her. I need to know her veins and muscles and organs and sinew. I need to touch it, memorize it, map it out, and tape it to my wall.

Such a shame she can't get any x-rays.

"I left my bag." The words tumble from her mouth like a distracted afterthought.

I dip the cloth beneath the hot water, wringing it out. "Miss Adeline will keep it for you." I approach her like she's a spooked animal, showing her the rag before knuckling beneath her chin. The crevice between her brows deepens as I swipe it over her cheek, removing the mask. I watched Lex do something similar a few days ago, curved behind her as he cleaned her mouth of vomit. The flare of jealousy in my chest didn't make sense at the time—who the fuck wants to clean someone's vomit—but now I think I understand.

Inch by inch, I reveal her skin, pink and unblemished beneath the clay, and with each pass of the rag, another knot in my chest unwinds.

"There," I sigh once it's all gone.

Now I can see her.

There's a knock on the door.

"What?" I snap.

"Sorry to interrupt. It's Stella." The handmaiden. "I gathered the supplies. Do you need me to—"

"Leave them by the door."

"Yes, sir." There's a pause, then, "Princess?"

Verity's red-rimmed eyes hold mine, and she says, "It's okay, Stella. Thank you."

I wait a beat before walking to the door, opening it to find a caddy filled with everything I asked for. Mineral oil, acetone, a comb with thick teeth, and a special shampoo for damaged hair. I pick it up and step back inside, back to her.

I reach out slowly to grasp the robe's belt, half afraid she plans to shank me. "I'm just gonna..." I let my words trail off as I give it a gentle tug. "To clean you up."

Another knot loosened.

She averts her eyes, tipping her head down as the robe parts, but doesn't fight me when I gently nudge it off her shoulders, sending it fluttering to the floor.

She's stark naked beneath it.

I release a relieved breath when I see her bush is still intact, but my eyes instantly rise a few notches, landing on her belly. "I wonder how long it'll be," I say, brushing the backs of my knuckles over the flat of her belly, "until you get bigger."

She wraps her arms around herself, shivering. "I wish it were over with."

I don't.

That's what I think about as I fill the ancient porcelain tub. I want to see every second of her change. Every new inch. Each new curve. I'm already half hard by the time I open the bottle of mineral oil and turn to the steaming tub.

"Ready?" I ask, jerking my chin at the water.

She's still standing in the middle of the bathroom, her bare shoulders a dejected curve. "I'll just shave it off. Who cares?"

"I care," I snap, thrusting a finger at the tub. "Get in."

Snidely, she asks, "Why? Afraid I won't be pretty for you anymore?"

"Get in," I repeat, voice full of low warning, "or I'll put you in."

I only move one step before she growls, stomping her way to the tub. She jabs a foot into the water and then swings the other over the lip of the tub, dropping into the water with her full weight. It sloshes over the edge, splattering against the floor.

I release a whistle. "Goddamn, we have *got* to have Lex run a DNA test between you and Wicker. You're both such bratty little bitches sometimes."

She hugs her knees, fists flexing. "Fuck you."

"Exactly." I kneel on the floor behind her, gathering up her hair. It's tacky, not completely dry, which is probably good.

"Stella can do this," Verity says, shoulder flinching inward when my fingers brush her skin. "And Danner could have brought me home. You don't have to be here."

"Let me give you some advice—"

"Why does everyone think I need advice all of a sudden?" she snaps, hugging her knees tighter.

I try to stroke my fingers through her hair, snagging. "Because you're the Princess who accepted an invitation from your biggest enemies on April Fools' Day."

She goes abruptly still, and I don't need to see her face to know she's doing the math, realizing the date. Ultimately, she deflates, muttering, "They're not my biggest enemies."

"And Danner isn't your biggest savior." I grab the bottle of oil, thumbing the cap. "He's old. He can't protect you, and more importantly, he works for Father."

"Danner's always been nice to me," she argues.

"That's because Danner's a nice guy." I pour a generous stream of oil onto her hair, eyes dipping down to the mound of a perky breast.

"A nice guy who helped Father put you on that throne. A really stand-up dude who guarded the door during our cleansing. A true fucking hero, always making sure the whips and dungeon are in top shape."

She tries to twist, catching my gaze. "What are you saying?"

I wrench her head back straight, massaging the oil into the sticky locks. "Danner tries to do good within the narrow parameters he's given, but he serves Father before all else. He won't be loyal to you, or me, or even Wicker or Lex." This time when my knuckles brush her shoulder, she doesn't flinch away. "You should be careful about how much you show him."

She appears to take this in as I work the oil through her hair, trying to separate the strands. Eventually, she shrugs, saying, "I think he'd protect me."

"He'd protect our baby because it's Father's only priority right now. But you?" I scoff, eyeing the point of her soft knee. "You're just a vessel, Verity. You're disposable to all of them. Never forget that."

"Like I am to you?" she asks, voice bitter.

It makes me pause, jaw clenching, because it's been years now, and this girl still doesn't get it. "Have you forgotten?" I ask, leaning forward to drag my lips against her ear. "I made you mine long before I wanted to put that baby in you."

Now, she flinches. "I was never yours," she insists.

"Is that a lie you tell yourself?" Smiling darkly, I stroke her hair. "You were looking over your shoulder every night. Jumping out of your skin when I'd message you. Checking the locks on your doors. Hardly able to sleep, because you knew I'd be watching. Waiting." I pull in a deep breath, relishing the scent of her skin. Sometimes when I'm watching her, I forget this is better. The smell of her. The feel of her beneath my fingertips. "You couldn't think about anyone else but me."

Looking back, I can see it for the sickness it was. I was neglectful of my duties because every ounce of my energy was spent on *her*. It's why I can only have her now, when watching her *is* my duty.

"You think because you scared me, I was yours?" She jerks away to whirl on me, eyes flashing vehemently. "Fear isn't love, Pace."

I blink at her. "Love?" She grunts when I pull her back, oiled palms slipping over her shoulders. "Love is fickle and weak. People fall out of love every day. But fear?" I slide my hand down her chest, palming the curve of a tit, reveling in the weight of it. "Fear becomes a part of you, like a new molecule. No one has ever fallen out of fear."

Her swallow is loud in the silence of the room, reverberating. "Is that what you think? That fear is better than love?"

"I don't need to really think about it," I say, thumbing her nipple to a stiff peak. I wasn't really expecting her to let me touch her like this—not without a fight.

But she just sits in the water, tilting her head. "But you love your brothers."

"Plenty of fear involved in that, trust me." Sighing, I let her go, returning my attention to her hair. "Actually, we all had our fair share of hazing back in boarding school. Usually, that meant getting jumped, but sometimes you'd get a coward who'd sabotage stuff. Food, clothes, assignments." Meaningfully, I add, "Or your shampoo."

There's a stretch of silence as I work the oil into her scalp, and then a curious, "Whose hair got glued?"

"Lex," I smirk, shaking my head at the memory. "Wick and I always told him to shave it at the beginning of every year, but he never would. Sometimes I think he keeps it long because it's the only thing anyone let him have control over."

As I work my fingers down, dividing the sticky clumps in her hair, I think back to the last time Father ordered him to cut it. It was our freshman year of high school. Father pulled us out of boarding school to attend a local academy, allowing us to live in the palace until graduation. This was basically the fucking worst, which is saying a lot. In boarding school, we had more freedom. Living locally meant more rules—one of which was a strict dress code. So Father told Lex to cut it, but then Wicker stepped up to say he'd shave his own head if Lex did.

God for-fucking-bid Wicker Ashby do anything to diminish his attractiveness.

"Individually, we all had our specialties. Wicker had his music and good looks. I had my—"

"Stalking."

I snort and pour more oil into the palm of my hand. "Technological acumen," I correct. "And Lex was Father's robotic little academic. The long hair was a rebellion—until the glue incident."

"What happened?"

"I saved it." I chuckle, remembering the long nights in the communal shower, stubbornly combing product after product through his hair. "Took me a week, but eventually—"

She jolts forward. "A week?!"

"Different kind of glue. Chill." I ease her back to rest against the tub. "Lex's hair isn't like mine. It was a learning curve." I don't tell her about how Lex would later learn how to do my hair, too. That these twists swinging in front of my eyes are his, spun meticulously by his own exacting fingers.

There's a stretch of pensive silence as I let the oil soak in, smoothing it out every now and then. She breaks it with a soft, defeated sigh. "When I spent those weeks in West End, it was like people expected me to be upset about Ashby being my father. Because he didn't claim me when it mattered. Because I could've been living in the palace this whole time and not in my two-bedroom apartment with my mother." My fingers snag on a stubborn clump, and she hisses, "Careful!"

"There's no way out but through, Rosi," I mutter, but slow my movements.

"The truth is," she continues, shoulders relaxing, "I can't imagine growing up here." She shudders. "Sometimes I think he gave me a gift by not acknowledging me sooner."

Darkly, I confirm, "Trust me, he did."

People outside our family, including those in PNZ and wider East End, don't understand the quiet pressure that fills the house. They can't comprehend that the dungeon in the basement is there for us as much as our enemies, just like the whip in Father's office. The secret passageways. The barren solarium. The cemetery.

For a house built on the idea of creation, there sure as hell is an awful lot of destruction.

From there, I work quietly, methodically, separating the strands of hair until I can get the comb fully through it. Despite her red, angry scalp, with every pass, the tension in her body seems to loosen. She releases her knees, stretching her legs out to rest her heavy head on the lip of the tub. Her tits float in the water, perfect and round, her nipples bobbing in and out of the surface.

I can't tell if she's relaxed or given up.

"There," I say, looking down at her hair. "The ends are brittle as fuck, and you'll probably need to get them looked at or something, but I've reached my limits on white-girl haircare." I tap her shoulder. "Sit up so I can wash it."

She rises, and I use the shampoo Stella dropped off, something specifically for damaged hair. Carefully, I work it in, avoiding her inflamed scalp and focusing on getting thorough coverage.

The next time she speaks, her voice is slow, dazed-sounding. "You're good at this."

"I know." I watch the gleam of her tits as I rinse the suds from her hair, soap running like a stream down her chest. I'm in the middle of applying a thick leave-in cream when I ask, "What does Lex do when he turns the lights out?"

The question visibly throws her off, shoulders tightening. "What?"

It's a point of annoyance for me. A lot of the old analog cameras were built into the ceilings before infrared technology was a wider consumer option. Father refuses to let me retrofit them at such a critical time since it'd bring the system offline for days.

"I know he fucks you," I clarify, smoothing her hair back. I'd have to be a fucking idiot to think he's still held to the agreement. But Lex is smart. He won't leave evidence. "I just want to know how."

She shivers, the bath water probably lukewarm by now. "I'm cold."

So it's gonna be like that.

Bracing my hands on the lip of the tub, I push to my feet, snagging the thick white towel from a bar nearby. I grab her by the arm. "Stand up, and let's get you rinsed off."

Her skin does things to me.

It's silky smooth, alabaster perfection. She has these little spatters of freckles that fascinate me. I can't see them on the cameras so well, and I take them in slowly as I dry her. A spot on her chest. A patch on each shoulder. She can be so red sometimes, too. Like when I buff the towel over her back, a spotty flush rises in its wake.

Responsive.

That's what her skin is. It reacts to me instantly, pebbling with goosebumps or pinkening with a flush.

And when I take her to bed, she barely seems to notice when I start undressing.

Her eyes are heavy with exhaustion and thought, that crevice never leaving her brow. I leave her halfway beneath the sheets as I push down my pants, my hard cock springing free. I've been thinking of this at night, as I watch her curled into Wicker or twitching toward Lex, and when I climb into the other side of the bed, I don't bother bullshitting anyone like my brothers do.

I immediately clear the space between us.

She stiffens when I roll her to her side, so eager to feel all that bare flesh against mine that my breath grows choppy. "I don't want to have sex right now," she says, the words hard as steel, meant to repel.

But I grip my dick, slot up against her back, and whisper, "I know." I peer over her shoulder as the crease in her forehead deepens.

"I mean it," she insists as I spread her ass cheek, nudging her center with the swollen head of my cock. "I've had a really shitty day, Pace. I just want to—"

"Relax?" With a powerful push of my hips, the tip of my cock breaches her. "I know what you need," I assure her, pulling her into me. She releases a long, strained hiss as I slide inside of her. Despite the protest, she's plenty slick. Tight. Warm.

There's a moment when she grips my wrist, tendons taut from clutching her hip, and I think she might begin to fight.

But she doesn't.

There's no fight left inside her.

Only me.

"Sleep," I whisper, brushing my lips against her soft jaw. "Just like this."

I can tell when she realizes this isn't about fucking because her grip slowly loosens. I'm not Wicker, who's starved for the release, or Lex, who's feral for the catch. I'm here to fill the hungry, empty void inside her, and when her eyes reluctantly flutter shut, I content myself with holding her. Enveloping her. Possessing her.

I don't expect to sleep, but I do.

Maybe it's the scent of her all around me, or the way it feels to be buried so deep in her hot, wet cunt. Maybe it's that I haven't slept for more than random snatches of time in so long, consumed with the need to watch her every move. Maybe it's having her right here, my arms locked around her like vises, and knowing that I don't need to watch because I *feel*.

I feel every breath she takes, her back swelling against my chest. I rest my palm on her belly and think of the hidden mark inside of it. Once or twice, I even cup a heavy tit in my hand, just because there's no one to stop me. Mostly, each point of my focus is driven down to my cock, feeling every sleep-twitch of her body around it, her pussy clamped around me just as tightly as I am around her.

She looks so serene like this, eyes closed, breaths shallow, not even squirming when I run the wet flat of my tongue up the column of her neck. When the unavoidable pull of sleep takes me, it's all-consuming.

I don't remember having a dream.

It's not like when I was younger, waking up to wet shorts. It's just that I begin stirring, the scent of her hair still thick in my nostrils, and I feel how soaked she is. I awaken in stages, rocking my hips into her as my eyes open. It's dark. Pitch-black, how Lex likes it. It should bother me that I won't be able to go back to my room later and see it on the monitor, but it doesn't. When I shift, feeling how sticky we've become around my cock, it feels like a secret.

Because she's awake.

Verity makes a small, throaty sound, wriggling against me, but doesn't try to tug out of my grip. Maybe she awoke when the first surges of cum began to fill her. My cock can never give her enough. I went to sleep holding her, and I wake up in the exact same position, only now she's full of me. It feels important, heavy, as if our bodies are saying 'this right here, don't move a muscle'.

She disturbs the silence with a ragged sigh. "We missed dinner."

My cock is already half-hard again, swelling inside of her cum-soaked pussy. I skate my lips up her neck, whispering, "Are you hungry?"

If she hears the reluctance in my voice, then she can't possibly understand it. It's not that I'm unwilling to get out of bed. It's that I *am* willing. I'm sleepy and warm, clutching her against me, and Verity Sinclaire could snap her fingers right now and have me racing to the kitchen to make just about anything.

In my whole goddamn life, a moment has never felt as perfect as this one.

"He'll be mad," she says, not answering my question.

Shrugging, I pull her closer. "Let him."

I don't tell her that the dinners are probably more of a chore for him than they are for us. That they're an illusion—the pretense of giving her a choice, keeping her complacent. Which Prince will it be this week?

There'll come a day when he makes that choice for her.

Better I do it first.

"SHE DID *WHAT*?" Dorian Baxter is visibly caught between outrage and laughter. "Didn't you just buy that car?"

The whole locker room has turned to Tommy Wright, who looks exactly like a guy who just got his new Porsche keyed by his girlfriend. "That's not even the worst part," he fumes, pulling on his pads. "She dumped everything in my closet into the river. My whole wardrobe. The baseball card collection my grandfather left to me. All my shoes." He growls in frustration at a problematic strap. "All over some bullshit."

"At least she talks to you," Loeffler grunts, tying his skates. "Mine won't even answer my texts."

Wicker shoots me a tense look, and I keep winding the tape around my stick. I don't need my brother to tell me that Verity's little revenge stunt before storming out of the spa is causing waves. I can feel their pissed-off stares drilling into us—I have since we got to campus this morning. Maybe I could feel bad for them if I hadn't spent the night curled around my Princess, emptying my balls into her, but hey.

Not my fault.

At least, that's what I keep reminding myself during practice. It gets a little difficult when every scrimmage ends with me being battered against the glass by our pissy D-man. Wicker skates past me just as Coach blows the whistle, jaw tight.

"Keep your cool," he mutters.

"One more hit from him," I say, spitting out my mouth guard, "and I'm going to bury my skate in his fucking throat."

PNZ being pissed at us isn't even something new. Wicker and I were Ashbys long before we were Princes, so we've been dealing with bitchy Royals since high school. Guys who wanna put us in our place. Assholes who thought we weren't good enough for the name, let alone the Purple Palace. Becoming Princes created a social shift that was never natural or expected.

But it's still a problem.

The only thing that makes it worth it happens that night when I stalk down the hallway to her bedroom, Effie's cage rattling with every step.

When I push through the door, Verity is already in bed, blankets pulled up to her chin. She doesn't look at me for very long, her green eyes landing on the cage, but something behind them brightens.

"Oh." She scurries to sit up. "You're bringing her to sleep here?"

"Yes," I say, placing the cage on the dresser. It's covered with a sheet. "She's been a goddamn terror all day, and she'll be worse if I leave her alone another night. You can say hi to her in the morning."

From behind the sheets comes Effie's soft coo. "*Gentle, gentle.*"

Verity's jaw drops. "Oh my god, she sounds like me."

"All the fucking time," I mutter, pulling off my shirt. Effie doesn't hear many feminine voices. That must be why she's latched onto Verity's, because it's new and interesting. I make sure the sheet is secure before unbuttoning my pants and shoving them, boxers and all, down my legs.

When I turn, Verity is staring straight at my cock. Her throat bobs with a swallow. "I don't—"

"—want to fuck? I know." Possibly this is belied by the way I stroke myself to hardness as I walk to the bed, wondering what I'm going to find under that blanket. Is she in that sweet little nightgown? Or has she undressed for me?

The sheets are cool on my side as I slip in, and I let that knowledge penetrate. *My* side of *our* bed. Only that doesn't seem right, so I immediately discard it, clearing the distance between us.

I'm only mildly disappointed when I reach for her, feeling the sheer fabric of her nightie. "Turn," I say, catching her tired eyes before I roll her to her side, spooning up behind her. I heard the chatter around campus today about the Princess being frozen out—just like her Princes—not that I needed it. I saw her on my phone during Lit 311, disappearing into the bathroom stall she always likes to hide in for a good 15-minute crying jag. That's what makes my Rosilocks the perfect Princess. She's so good at hiding her misery. Her eyes weren't even red and puffy when she emerged from the stall.

Now, I lift a hand to brush a finger against the apple of her cheek, tracing the path a tear might have taken this afternoon.

"I'm going to put my cock into you again," I say, watching as her pale fist curls around the sheet. I rest mine over it, appreciating the contrast in colors. "I'll probably fill you up with more of my cum, too." I begin lifting her gown, my knuckles skating up her soft, silky thighs. "I can't sleep in your bed and not be inside you. You understand that by now, don't you?" Her troubled eyes remain fixed on the wall across the room, shoulders twitching when I finger the elastic of her panties, pulling them down over the round curve of her ass. Just as I nudge the tip of my cock against her warm hole, I assure her, "But I won't fuck you, Rosi. Not until you need it enough to ask for it. That's your call."

I enter her with force, curling an arm around her when she hisses, holding her tight. Making her take me. All of me.

Only when she settles, releasing a deep, unsteady breath, do I release her to rest my palm against her stomach. The baby should be enough. Rationally, I know that. But I can't shake this urge to be inside her all the time, feel her body grip me, feel her so close that our bones start to merge.

As I'm drifting off to sleep, I decide that, in the morning, when she's dripping with me, I'll plug her up to keep us together all the time.

~

THERE'S silence all around the room.

Every now and then, a PNZ member's eyes will flick to the throne at the head of the room. This parlor is an integral part of East End. It's played host to almost a hundred thronings. Dozens of Royal births. Plenty of Royal Cleansings. Probably a few orgies, too. The last Princess was relieved of her duties in this room.

I doubt there's ever been as much tension in here as there is now.

Lex clears his throat, shifting his notebook a couple of inches to the left. It's not often our brother fidgets. "I understand there's been a bit of an upset in the ranks lately."

Loeffler gapes at him. "A *bit* of an *upset*?"

"Your Princess showed the video of the cleansing to our girlfriends," Julian Carter says. He's a quiet sophomore who's never made any waves, and right now, he looks sick, eyes red and irritated.

From his chair in the front, Tommy Wright crosses his arms, chin raised. "A cleansing we were forced to participate in."

Baxter actually stands up, all the playful mirth from his eyes on Tuesday wiped away. "Every single one of us got dumped because of what she did! Aren't you going to do something?"

Wicker slumps down in his seat, scrubbing both palms over his face. "Jesus Christ."

"What do you propose?" Lex asks, voice turning sharp and accusing. "Another cleansing? Maybe we should bring her in to sit on the throne for a few lashes." He takes a long, significant pause. "Oh, wait. We can't. Because she's carrying *your* fucking heir. So sit the hell down, Baxter."

"You have to do something!" Loeffler cries, shooting to his feet. "We're PNZ! We can't just be single!"

It's all I can do not to laugh. If it weren't for my brothers, I probably would. But Lex looks hunted, and Wicker...

He's glaring at the floor, looking like he might not be opposed to that throne-lashing idea.

Rory Livingston adds, "Maybe she can tell them it was a trick."

Baxter perks up, looking over at me. "Yeah, she can tell them it was CGI or something, right? Just a fake. Then we can win them back!"

"Give me a break." It's only when all the eyes in the room swing to me that I realize the words are my own, spoken with low, cutting contempt. I don't regret them. Straightening in my seat at the head of the table, I announce, "Guys. Man the fuck up."

"Excuse me?"

"Your girls were bitches to her. Did any of them tell you what they did to her?"

"It doesn't matter," Livingston mutters. "A little hazing is normal for new—"

"What would you rather have?" Lex asks. "A Princess who's quiet and meek and afraid? Or a Princess who fights for herself?"

"Princesses are chosen for their charm and poise," Tommy says. "Which is why it was a fucking mistake to anoint a West End slut to the position. Heather was raised for all of this. She would have handled it with grace."

"Princesses are chosen for their fresh cunts," Wick chimes in. "Heather lost her virginity when she was fourteen on a yacht out on the river. I'm the one that popped her cherry. There is no universe where she was qualified for the position."

"You're blaming us and the Princess for this, but you're all to blame," I look out around the room at their stupid faces. "You couldn't keep your bitches on a leash, and they got on her bad side." I shrug. "I think it's fucking hilarious."

"Pace," Lex says, trying to regain some control of the situation. I roll my eyes but shut up. "We can't take back the fact the video is out there, but we'll all need to do what we can to mitigate the damage of the video being released. From this day forward, there can be absolutely no continued sharing of the clip. Not by your girls. Not by you. Delete it. Trash it. Pretend it never existed."

"What if it gets out?" Tommy says, already looking guilty.

"Then you and your girl better pack your bags and get the fuck out of Forsyth before we find out," Wick says, tone uncharacteristically serious. "This is an exileable offense."

Down in front, Livingston visibly swallows as he nods his head.

"And the Princess?" someone dares to ask.

"The Princess is Kevlar." I don't say it to whoever asked it. I say it to the room. "Same results. You mess with her, and you're gonna be de-crowned. Am I fucking clear?"

No one seems happy about it, but the arguing stops. After the meeting, the room clears, and the three of us remain.

"You think they'll follow orders?" Lex asks, the skepticism obvious in his expression.

"Most of them," Wick says, "but Heather may be a problem. She was convinced Tommy was going to be named Prince and she'd be named Princess. Her attack on Verity was more than an April Fools' joke. It was a retaliation."

"I'll keep an eye out online to make sure nothing is out there," I say. "And if I find anything, I'll trace it back."

De-crowning and failed Princesses happen but they're still allowed to live in East End; an exile from the territory is rare. This isn't just the Princess we're dealing with here. It's our reputation as leaders. It's Father finding out that we're losing control. It's reminding the men under our leadership exactly who we are.

Part of me almost hopes we get a chance to show them.

13

erity

"I WON'T FUCK YOU, *Rosi. Not until you need it enough to ask for it."*

I wake to Pace's words echoing in my mind, eyes clamping tight against the need, as if I can force myself to go back to sleep and forget the sensation of him inside of me, throbbing. It's not the first morning, either. This whole week has been an agonizing dance of resignation and restraint.

Resignation because I allow him in.

Restraint because I don't ask for it.

I blink my eyes open to the faint morning light, as annoyed about waking so early on a Sunday as I am about the burning need in my core. It doesn't help that Pace is confining me, like always. His arms are as solid and unyielding as manacles. The chest against my back is a cage. The breaths washing over my nape are liquid fire. His embrace is a prison.

So why do I always nestle back into him every morning?

How can having him inside make me feel so steady, yet so frayed?

I let myself blame Wicker and his lies because that's easy. He gave me all those stupid fantasies with his ridiculous morning cuddles, and now Pace is actualizing it—in his own way.

I've gotten used to Pace removing the plug at night before nestling himself deep inside my pussy, his hands cupping my tits, our bodies fused together as I fall off to sleep. Every morning, I wake up to the feel of him thickening, my walls stretching as he grows, and the smallest rock of his hips as we rouse together, bodies before our minds, the sensation all-consuming.

It's not sex.

Even when he comes, erupting in his sleep with a low, throaty groan, he doesn't *thrust*. He fills me without even enjoying it, always waking with a satisfied grunt when he pulls out, sliding the plug into me, and it's almost like...

It's like the orgasm isn't even the point of it.

This morning, I find myself wishing it were.

I whimper as I feel him stir, chuffing a breath into my hair as he rocks closer.

"Need something?" he asks, voice thick with sleep as he palms my breast. His skin is hot, and despite the chill in the room, I feel sweat beading up in the spaces where our skin meets. I'm not stupid. This whole thing has been one big, long tease. A way to break me down. This is a fight that'll have only one victor.

And it won't be me.

"Just fuck me already!" I snap.

There's only a short pause, his chest against my back stuttering on an inhale. Before I can wipe the sleep from my eyes and regret it, he grabs my hip, pushing me onto my stomach. There's an abrupt blast of cool air as he throws the blankets off of us, impatiently jostling me to my knees.

"Jesus," I yelp, nightgown bunching under my armpits. "What are you—"

"Gentle, gentle," Effie trills from under her sheet, my voice mocked back at me.

Ignoring the bird, he parts my thighs and pulls back, his cock dragging deliciously against my clenching walls.

And then he slams into me with a quick, vicious punch.

"Ah!" I cry out, fisting the sheets below me.

"Fuck yes," he mutters, exhaling loudly. His hands grab at my nightgown, and he curls over me, yanking it easily over my head. "Say it again."

I pant into the sheets, not bothering to raise my head. It's better like this; hiding. "Fuck me."

The plea emerges strained and ragged, and even though I'm expecting it when he slides back and slams into me once more, a cry still erupts from my throat, moistening the bed sheets. Shamefully, I open for him, back bowing as I meet his thrust. It's not something I can help, my brain fogged with sleep and days of pent-up lust, and here's the thing about Pace Ashby:

He's so fucking good at it.

From his grip on my hips as he fucks into me to the way he feels inside, Pace works my body like he's always known it.

Even when he roughly palms my ass, spreading me apart, his finger toying with the rim of my asshole, the teasing makes my pussy quiver, tightening around him. "I'd plug you up here if I could. Fill your pussy and your ass." His voice is so deep that I can feel it in my marrow. "Maybe next time."

Next time.

I have one week left in East End before I go back to the Dukes. Part of me is ready to stop walking around on my tiptoes, feeling like a monster is lurking around every corner. But the other part, the one that involves what happens in this godforsaken bed, is disgustingly disappointed.

It's the closeness.

It has to be.

A week of Wicker's touch. A week of Lex's gritty breaths in my ear as he fucked me relentlessly in the dark. A week in Pace's cage, his cock nestled into me like it's always belonged. I've gotten used to feeling full—either with his cock buried inside of me all night or with the plug he presses into me after he fills me with a thick stream of his cum. He's with me all day, this constant reminder that not only is he watching—not only could I be carrying his baby—but that we're bonded as one, whether I ask for it or not.

And now I have.

Come to think of it, maybe a break from their mind-bending touches is exactly what I need.

Until then, I take the fucking, not minding the different angle, the way the head of his cock knocks deep inside. My nipples feel extra sensitive, the cool air of the room teasing them into tight peaks. When he reaches beneath me to graze his palms over them, I groan, his touch like a current zinging down my flesh, the orgasm building.

"Tell me your perky hand-wench has some concealer that'll match my skin color." I recognize the tone of the voice before the source of it, bitter and impatient. When I glance over in confusion, I see Wicker striding through my door, fingers working down the buttons of his white shirt, untucked and wrinkled. His hair is pure chaos. "I need to cover this goddamn hickey."

Startled, I freeze, but Pace... well, he doesn't miss a stroke. Something—likely the sound of our flesh slapping together—makes Wicker's eyes snap up, landing on us with a stuttering step. He gapes, fingers suspended over a button as his eyes flick to my tits, swaying forcefully with every thrust.

"Dude!" His furious gaze swings to Pace. "What the fuck are you doing?!"

"Should be obvious," Pace replies, his arm sliding around my waist. He lifts me until I'm kneeling in front of him, lips skittering against my cheek.

Wicker's expression turns murderous. "We said none of us would fuck her!"

"No, you declared a sexile and then had the fucking balls to break it first." Pace never stops moving inside of me, his fingers dipping to brush over my clit. A quick glance over my shoulder reveals dark, vengeful eyes. "I mean, how long did it really take? Twenty-four hours? Forty-eight?"

Wicker's mouth gapes open. "Are you shitting me? My dick hasn't been inside anyone since the cleansing! You know that!" He shifts his weight, but it has to be unconscious, the way he does it alongside the rhythm of Pace's punishing hips. His expression is crazed, his well-crafted façade cracking. "The only action I've seen in over two months is my own fucking hand."

"Suck my balls..."

"Not now, Effie!" Wicker barks, but my eyes are drawn down, and I can't help but see that his cock is threatening to escape out of the zipper of his pants. God. He's horny right now.

Exasperated, I ask, "Do you mind?" and nod to the door.

Wicker, of course, ignores me, glaring at Pace. "Do you realize that I had to go see the team trainer about my wrist being overused?" he asks, voice getting louder, more indignant with every word. His eyes are bloodshot and a touch too wide, and it hits me that he hasn't just woken up. He never went to bed. "I blamed my incessant jerking off on hockey, when this whole time, there's been a fuck-for-all going on every night!" He punctuates this with a gesture toward me, the way my hips rock needfully back into Pace. The shame is probably there, but it's buried too far beneath the desperation to pay much mind to.

So close...

"What the hell are you shouting about?" Lex grouses, appearing in the doorway. His forehead is creased, but he takes one look at me and Pace, and another at Wicker, and quickly shuts the door. "Jesus Christ, seriously?"

I'm not sure which of his brothers he's talking to. The one throwing a tantrum, or the one who has finally ceased thrusting but is still firmly planted inside. Frustrated, I clutch at Pace's arm, trying to move his hand against my clit.

"Do you want Danner to come down here?" Lex asks again since no one responded to his other questions.

Wicker glares at Lex. "Are you fucking her, too?"

Lex goes stock-still, gaze locking with his brother's. Wicker probably doesn't need an answer, what with all the guilt etched into Lex's face. He may be stone-cold when he wants to be, but apparently, that doesn't hold up with his brothers. "I haven't been fucking her. Not since—"

"Last week," I finish for him, breathless and close to smirking. "Friday, wasn't it? You said you wanted to go again, but fell asleep before you could."

Wicker tosses his hands in the air. "Perfect! This is goddamn perfect. Betrayed by both of my brothers for some subpar West End pussy."

"Betrayed?" Pace repeats, his voice rough.

"Pace," I whine, so close to release that I can feel it in every tendon, coiled tight.

He growls, saying to his brothers, "Just... give me a fucking minute." He bends me over, his broad hand splayed between my shoulders as I release a soft, desperate keen. "I've got you. Gonna give you every drop." His hands grip my hips, and he pumps into me twice more before groaning loudly and seizing, warm cum exploding inside of me.

In the back of my mind, I understand that Lex and Wicker are watching as I fall to pieces. A better Princess—a better *monarch*—would play it to her advantage. But I just fold, rocking back onto Pace's pulsating cock as I tumble off the precipice, stars spreading like fireworks through my limbs.

"That's it," I hear Pace say, curling over my back to brush a clumsy kiss onto my temple. His whisper is meant for only me. "Such a good girl for me, aren't you?"

In a sharp, disbelieving tone, Wicker asks, "Are you done?"

It feels like an aching loss when Pace pulls out, leaving me empty and soaked, his thick semen oozing down my leg. Out of habit, I wait for the plug.

But it never comes.

Instead, Pace grabs my discarded night dress and wipes off his cock. "Let's talk about betrayal, huh? You covered your pathetic morning fuck by deleting it from my security files. Then you lied about it when we confronted you." Pace is leveling his brother with a flinty stare as he tugs up his shorts, stepping onto the floor with steadier legs than I'd expect. "*Then* you had her lie to cover your sorry ass."

Her. *Me.*

Not wanting to be involved in this any more than necessary, I keep quiet, watching as the brothers slowly tear each other apart. I'd laugh if it wouldn't draw their attention. I reach down unthinkingly, shoving two fingers into my hole as I roll to my side, fetal, still twitching with the aftershocks.

Wicker has also gone still. His body. His expression. His mouth. Everything except his eyebrows, which screw together when he says, "Wait. What are you talking about?"

"The footage you deleted during your week with the Princess," Lex says quietly, stepping further into the room. He crosses his arms as he faces Wicker. "We know you caved, and we figured all bets were off. So yeah, I fucked the Princess during my week. And obviously, Pace did the same. Now can we stop playing this game and move on with our lives?"

Wicker growls, thrusting his hands into his hair. "*Jesus,* I never fucked her. We slept in the same bed. That's it!" Due to my desire to be invisible, I don't point out the revelation that he's a cuddler. "The footage I deleted? That was from when I gave her a black eye."

"A what?" All control Lex possessed vanishes. "You gave her a *what*?"

"Accidentally," Wicker adds quickly. "It was a mistake. I apologized and everything!"

"Oh my god," I blurt with a choked laugh. Every eye in the room shifts to me. I'd tried to stay out of the fray, to let them fight this out amongst themselves, but fucking hell. "He absolutely *never* apologized."

His bloodshot eyes bug out. "I sent you ice!"

"That wasn't an apology." I rise off the bed, ignoring Pace's cum as it drips down my leg, likely leaving a trail on the rug. Grabbing Pace's hoodie off the floor, I feel their eyes on my spent body as I pull it over my arms and zip up the front. "*That* was like Pace said. You were covering your ass."

Pace tilts my head until he can see my face, his jaw hard as stone. "But you lied for him, too."

"You've got to be kidding me." I jerk away, glowering. "I told you he didn't fuck me. I said I hit my head on the nightstand." I look between them, scoffing. "Face it. The two of you were so hell-bent on getting laid that you believed what you wanted. *You* decided I lied. *You* decided he betrayed you. You never cared what I had to say about it!"

We all know the truth. They were just looking for an excuse to get their dicks wet.

Wicker's lips pull up into a sneer. "So that's what happened? I shouldn't even be surprised."

Lex has already crossed the room, sliding his fingers under my jaw and twisting my face as he searches for any lingering remnants of the injury. He already checked out the bump, but he and Pace were so incensed at the thought of Wicker fucking me, he never had the chance to check the bruise underneath. Even though his amber eyes are anguished, I know it's not meant for me. He's berating himself for missing it. Even in the exam room, Pace was the one who noticed the knot.

"The bruise was small," I bite out, letting him inspect me. "It was forever ago. Like Wicker said, it was just an accident."

Wicker begins a tight, frustrated pacing. "I knew you'd freak the fuck out if you found out that I—*accidentally*—hurt her. So I didn't elaborate."

"You're goddamn right about that," Lex seethes, turning his eyes on his brother. "She's carrying our baby. I know that doesn't mean anything to you, but it does to me and Pace, and it sure as hell means something to Father." His thumb rubs over the healed spot, angry eyes assessing. "Although the female body is strong and resilient, there's also a fragility here." Releasing me, he approaches Wicker, a cold demeanor settling on his features as he snatches his arm, stilling him. They're face to face, and I think for a second Lex may actually turn violent. "You touch her like that again, and I'll take action against you myself."

Wicker, clearly aware he's crossed a line, holds back the retort that's on the tip of his tongue. Instead, he nods, eyes tight. "It won't happen again."

"Good." Lex rakes his fingers through his hair, collecting himself with a steeling inhale. "All of this stays here. In this room. No one needs to know about it. Not Danner, not Father, and absolutely no one in the frat. Not after all the shit that's gone down this week. We need to keep everything locked tight."

"Oh, boo hoo," Pace says, eyes rolling. "Poor little frat boys lost their girlfriends. I'm sure the East End florists will take a financial hit, but I fail to see why I should give a fuck."

"Because the frat makes us!" Lex snaps.

"What's wrong with the frat?" I ask, picking up on a vibe I can't quite place.

"Nothing you need to worry about," Wicker says, dismissively.

Ignoring his brother, Pace turns to me, reaching up to tug at the zipper on my—*his*—hoodie. "Your little retaliation on The Court had fallout," he says, skating the zipper down a few inches. His dark gaze follows, tongue darting out to wet his lips. "Now everyone's balls are blue, and it's turned them into little bitches."

I'd been iced out completely at school last week, which wasn't a surprise. Not after the spa on April Fools'. "What kind of fallout?"

Lex rubs the back of his neck, looking away. "The girls were pissed about the cleansing, and they've been giving their guys hell about it all week. Breakups left and right. Property damage. Threats. Cheating."

"It's been a real shit show," Pace adds.

Thinking about this, I can't help the way my face brightens, lips pulling into a smile. "Excellent."

"It's not excellent, Red," Wicker says, eyes narrowed. "It makes us look like we don't have control—of our frat *or* our Princess. It makes us look *weak*."

"Weak?" Pulling away from Pace, I march right up to Wicker, fuming. "You want to know why those East End bitches came after me?"

"Because it's tradition!"

"Because of you!" I explode, whirling my gaze on Lex and Pace. "All three of you! You've shown East End that it's acceptable. That their Princess is trash and should be treated like it." It comes pouring out of me like an avalanche. "Day after day. Event after event. Wicker sneers at me on campus. Lex doesn't even acknowledge me until I'm on his exam table. Pace won't dare glance at me—not when he can look at me on a camera. They see injuries. They see contempt. They see Ballsack—a fucking West Ender—spending more time with me than my own goddamn Princes. But mostly?" I add, voice halfway to hysteria. "Mostly, they see the throning and the cleansing. They see you hurting me, again and again, because that's the only way any of you psychos know how to handle a woman!"

I pull in a long, hard breath, trying to get this maelstrom of emotions in check.

"Everything you've put me through publicly has given the implication that the mother of your precious heir isn't worth any respect. And if you don't respect me," I ask, challenging them all with a look, "then why the hell should they?"

The room is silent as that settles over the three of them.

"Precious heir..." Effie croons.

"See?" I snort, crossing. "Even the bird knows it."

Except then she barks, *"Just fuck me already!"*

I gasp at the sound, garbled but still sharp with frustration, just like I'd said it. "Oh no."

Pace grins like the cat who caught the canary. "I'm glad she caught that for posterity." Then, his face falls. "Fuck, that's really going to confuse my dick later."

"Verity has a point." Lex's jaw is tight as he looks between his brothers. "We've set an example."

Nostrils flared, Wicker buttons his shirt. "How exactly do you plan on changing this now?"

"Controversial take," I say, raising a hand. "How about stop being such massive dicks to me on campus?" To Lex, "Treat me like a human being?" To Pace, "Stop spitting into my goddamn mouth?"

Pace pulls a face. "Can't we just cut off some fingers?"

"We've had a lot of success with that in the past," Wicker agrees with complete sincerity.

"No," Lex decides, sighing. He looks almost as tired as Wicker does, pushing his hair back. "We've decided to see this thing through, and we're drifting around here like flotsam. If we're going to do it, we should do it right. Our job is to protect the Princess. They need to see that she's worth protecting."

Harshly, Wicker adds, "Or maybe they need to see their Princes are worth obeying. We're not the only ones setting an example here."

That word—obey—fills my mouth with ash. Even worse is the knowledge that Wicker is right. Among the social ranks of East End, the Princes only have as much power as the frat grants them. The more I fight, the more they have to punish and force me back in line. It's a vicious, never-ending cycle.

It's the only reason I square my shoulders and look into Wicker's blue eyes. "You're right."

He blinks. "I know."

Nodding, I agree, "I'll perform as your perfect, doting Princess so long as you treat me like one."

Lex thrusts his hand out. "Deal."

We shake on it, and before my hand can even fall, Pace's is there, his dark eyes gazing down at me as I grip his palm.

"On campus," he says, not releasing my hand. "But when we're alone..." His eyebrow arches expectantly. I conjure up the feeling that overcame me that day he rescued me. The humiliation. The hopelessness. The all-consuming rage against Heather and her friends. It's the only thing that allows me to part my lips, opening wide for him.

When Pace's saliva hits my tongue, it doesn't feel like that.

He pushes the tip of a finger beneath my chin, closing my jaw, and I don't see the need to humiliate in his eyes. I see a spark of satisfaction—the ripple of possessive glee—but it's not about me, I realize.

It's about him.

"Good girl," he rumbles, bending to brush the point of his slick tongue against my lips.

"In case you've forgotten," comes Wicker's voice, "I'm not the one who decided to stay. And since I already know what deals between you two are worth..." He yanks Pace away from me, his tired eyes glaring into mine. "My deal with you is that I'll treat you like any other girl I'm fucking. Take it or leave it. Anything more than that wouldn't be convincing anyway."

I give his proffered hand a dubious look. "That doesn't sound like much of a concession."

"Given that I'm not even fucking you, it should."

Supposing he has a point there—and knowing Wicker wouldn't budge regardless—I take his hand, shaking it.

"Deal."

WITH THE BOY-SHIT put away for the morning, I get in the shower, washing off the night spent with Pace. Unfortunately, when I get out, Wicker is sitting at the dressing table, rummaging through my makeup.

"What are you doing?" I ask, hastily wrapping the towel around my body.

"You think this matches my skin tone?" He holds up a tube of concealer. When I just stare at him, he yanks at his collar, revealing a purpling bruise on his throat. "A cougar got me last night."

A flicker of something angry and hot surges in my chest. "Where was it this time?"

His eyes darken, sliding to the mirror. "The opera. Mrs. Wilhelmina Johnson has season tickets and a private box." He waves his hand like it means nothing, but I know better. "The seclusion makes her bold."

"And after the opera?" I ask, nodding to his rumpled clothes. He's the very visage of a walk of shame.

"The afterparty ran over," he says, a touch defensively.

I stare at him for a moment, then grab my robe. Wrapped up, I cross the room to the dressing table and take the concealer from him. "This one is too light."

Bending over him, I pick through the makeup. This drawer is a mess. I should probably get Stella to do something about it, but we're leaving in a week, so does it really matter? Glancing up at the mirror, I see Wicker staring at the gape in the front of my robe, eyeing my cleavage in the reflection. Catching me catching him, he just shrugs and says, "They look bigger."

"They're not." I tighten the belt and resume my concealer search. Finding a couple of tubes, I say, "Push up your sleeve and give me your hand." He does as I ask, rolling up the white shirtsleeve and offering his hand. I flip it over to the smooth flesh of his inner wrist. Squeezing out a small dot, I tell him, "Rub that in." He does, working the makeup in with slim, quick, fingers. I shake my head and add a different color. "Try that."

We go through three more shades and his other wrist before we find the closest one.

"Jesus, you have a whole collection here," he says, surveying the bottles and tubes.

"What can I say?" I toss him a sponge, dryly explaining, "I have a lot I need to cover up."

Glancing at me, he catches the wedge, frowning. "How long are you going to give me grief about that shiner? You know it was an accident."

"Didn't make it hurt any less."

His eyes flick to me once, then twice, and when he mutters out, "Sorry," it's in this annoyed tone of voice. Before I can dwell on it, he turns the tube over and reads the name stamped on the bottom. "I should order a case of this."

The reality of that statement hits home. "How long does Ashby expect you to do this kind of thing?"

"I don't know," he answers honestly, staring at the wedge as if it's a particularly baffling, alien object. "I used to think they'd get tired of me, but if that happens, they'll just find someone else. It may as well be me."

I take the sponge back and dab a little of the concealer onto it, making a show of the process as I raise it to his neck. "Did you…" I swallow as he tilts his head, giving me access, "you know. With her?"

His throat flutters with a scoff. "I told you, the only action my cock has seen is my hand."

I feel his touch before I see it, his deft fingertips pulling at the collar of my robe. I don't stop him, letting it fall over my shoulder to expose my breast. His throat jumps with a swallow as I dab at the hickey, and in my periphery, I can see his gaze glued to my nipple.

"You know…" he begins, not hesitating to skate his fingertips around the underside of my breast. "Now that my deal with my brothers is functionally demolished, nothing is stopping you and me from fucking." Wicker has this way of being gentle but firm. His face is so close that I can count the wrinkles in his chapped lips, his exhale washing over me like fire. It's easy to want more, even if I know he's selfish and entitled and his desires will always come first. Beneath the expensive gray fabric of his pants, I see the growing bulge. "We could—"

"No." I jolt back, away from his touch, and quickly cover myself. It's harder than I think it should be, seeing him there all rumpled and hard—the embodiment of sin.

"No." He repeats, as if the word confuses him. "No?"

"You were right before," I rush out, clearing my throat. "We shouldn't do this."

He gapes for a moment, the confusion on his face transforming to anger as he rears up. "Why the hell not? Obviously, my brothers don't agree with the boundaries I made." He looks me up and down. "Your pussy is open for business."

Crossing my arms, I lift my chin, meeting his glare head-on. "Not for you."

"But it is for them," he guesses, smiling bitterly.

"Only because they know what to do with it."

He snorts, gesturing to the bedroom. "You didn't seem to have a problem with it three weeks ago when you were sleep-humping me."

"I didn't have any other options then." Shrugging, I explain, "Now, I do."

There's some more of that eye-bugging, and then Wicker sputters, "So, what? You're gonna make us compete for *the honor*?"

If the words weren't spoken with such dripping contempt, I might think to soften the blow.

"Oh, Wicker..." Tilting my head, I look up into his blue eyes, reaching up to touch the bruise hidden on his neck. "There's no competition."

When I leave, he's still standing there, gaping in outrage in my wake.

THERE'S NEVER BEEN A BIGGER and more absurd performance for a Princess than receiving my Monday morning offerings from the frat.

Lately, I've begun saving all the roses for compost in the solarium. It's a sort of catharsis, tearing them all to shreds as I plan where exactly to let them rot. There's something fitting about it, too—these symbols of my pain contributing to new life.

So when I arrive at the fountain this morning, I'm thinking of the warmth from the sun. Spring is coming, cutting its teeth in the ungodly chill of winter, and there's a row of zinnias in the garden that could benefit from some nitrate. The shredded, rotting roses will be useful there.

But I don't receive white roses.

Not today.

The first PNZ member to approach me is Tommy Wright, Heather's boyfriend. *Oops—ex*-boyfriend. "To my beautiful Princess," he says, eyes narrowed into slits. "May she reign." He all but hurls the rose at me. It's black and wilted, but the worst part is the smell; acrid and cutting, strikingly close to ammonia.

When I screw my nose up to pluck it from my lap, I gasp, thumb catching on one of its long, severe thorns.

Tommy is gone before I have a chance to react, and while I'm nursing my thumb, Dorian Baxter approaches to throw another one at me. "To my beautiful Princess," he snarls. "May she reign."

I get better at schooling my reaction by the third one, remembering Pace's advice from the spa.

"Chill, Rosi. Don't let them see they got to you."

"Thank you." To a glaring sophomore, I try to channel Stella when I gush, "Don't you just love black? It goes with everything!"

The bundle of roses eventually gets difficult to hold, not to mention absolutely rancid-smelling. These thorns are so unlike the soft ones on the white roses. Those thorns might still prick, but these *cut*. Halfway through the line of pissed-off PNZs, I make a point of shoving them to the fountain's edge.

Rory Livingston is the only one who goes off-script. "You know why we have Royal Cleansings?" he asks, squinting against the sun. The only reason I hold his gaze is because it's unlike the others. Where their expressions are stony and vicious, he just looks...

Sad.

"When a Princess breaks a covenant, there are only two options: de-throning or a cleansing." He looks off into the distance, eyes dark. "You've never seen a de-throning, Princess."

I cradle a stinging finger, squeezing a bead of blood from the tip. "I've seen a throning, so I can use my imagination."

"No, you can't." His curt voice draws my eyes up. "I've seen two in the last three years. A de-throning makes a throning look like a birthday party." Shifting uncomfortably, he goes on, "It's really hard on Royal girls. We saw it with Autumn, then again with Piper. East End has a habit of throwing its Princesses away." He looks down, and I realize he's holding a white rose. "The truth is, we haven't done a cleansing in a really long time, which is good, because it's barbaric and disgusting. But we did it for you. Not because we hate you." Meeting my gaze, he places the white rose on my lap. "But because we don't."

I clench my jaw against the wave of dueling emotions, but one wins out. "You're saying you participated in that barbaric and disgusting act for *my sake*?" Raggedly, I laugh. "This must be why men have testicles. They need somewhere to store all the fucking audacity."

Shoving his fists into his pockets, he shrugs. "You're not the only one with contractual obligations, Princess. A cleansing can only be done with full fraternity participation," he says, nodding. "We both know there are guys who did it for those other reasons. I won't defend them. But I wanted you to know... not all of us were there just to hurt you."

When he turns to leave, I catch a glimpse of the remaining PNZs, all but maybe two of them holding the painful black roses, and my stomach sinks. Just as I'm bracing myself to receive them, someone begins pushing through the line, the knot atop his head the only thing I can make out.

Until Lex stands before me, brows crouched low in annoyance, a cup of coffee clutched in his hand. Pace and Wicker file in behind them.

Someone has the balls to clear their throat—a boy from the line of PNZs—and one by the one, the Princes turn a slow, menacing glare on him.

Pace is the one to approach the guy, staring him up and down. "Hughes. Do you have something for the Princess this morning?" he asks in a low, threatening voice.

The guy backs up a step, glancing at me over Pace's shoulder. "Favors are compulsory," is his answer, but even though the words are confident, his gaze drops. "Sir."

Lex marches forward to rip the rose out of his hand, not even wincing at the thorns. "This?" he demands, furious gaze passing down the row. He holds up his hand, which is when I see the blood beading on his palm. Raising his voice, he barks, "There must be some mistake, Hughes. Surely my frat brothers wouldn't give our Princess something that would cut her." There's silence along the row as Lex glares them down. "Because such an act goes directly against the orders we explicitly gave you, not to mention your fraternal covenants." He reaches back to point at me, holding their gazes. "I'm about to check her hands. If there's one scratch on her, you're all getting de-crowned." He glances at his brothers, lips twitching. "Unless someone tells us who organized this."

Hughes immediately drops the rose, raising his hands. "It was Tommy."

Wicker's cold eyes snap to him near the back. "Well, then Tommy can spend practice on his knees cleaning the locker room with a toothbrush. And the rest of you," his eyes scan the group, "for violating a direct order, are skating lines until you puke, then Tommy can clean that up too."

"Get this shit out of here," Pace barks.

With a speed I've only seen them commit to on the ice, they rush to the mound of roses beside me, gathering them up before taking off.

"We didn't tell them to do that," Lex says, scowling as his frat brothers scurry away.

"Obviously." I try not to laugh as Baxter trips over a cobblestone and slams into Livingston, knocking a bunch of the roses to the ground.

"We'll hold them to the punishment." Lex is dressed a little more casually today than usual, in a white t-shirt and loose, low-slung jeans. It's how I know he won't have clinic duty or lab work, the particulars of these men's lives becoming so entwined with mine that all it takes is a glimpse of a loose lock of his hair to signal that today is a light one.

When we arrived in the parking lot twenty minutes ago, Lex and his brothers instantly separated, each going their own way, leaving me to handle my Monday morning favors alone. This has been business as usual since my return to East End, but the gesture still rankled. If they'd been with me, none of the frat members would have—

"Here." Lex thrusts the cup toward me. "It's for you."

I look between the cup and his amber eyes, my stomach uneasy with suspicion. "What is it?" After weeks of ginger tea, it's become impossible to separate the taste from the slow-rolling nausea. One day, I just woke up and hated it.

His brows crush together. "It's coffee." When all I do is stare skeptically, he releases a hard sigh. "It's my morning favor, Verity. Not a trap."

With wide, stunned eyes, I reach out slowly, as if he might snatch it back. "*Really*?"

He lets me take it, his eyes tracking the way my lips purse, blowing over the hole in the lid. "It's half-caf, light syrup, whole milk, full-fat cream, no additives—honestly, it's a glorified milkshake, but Pace said you like those flavors." More begrudgingly, he adds, "One a day won't kill you. I guess."

I can smell the hazelnut wafting up, excitement clenching my gut. The fact that it's a small doesn't even register. It's been impossible to orchestrate a coffee delivery while living at the palace, so it's been nearly a month since I've had anything so utterly decadent. One sip has my brain zapping in pleasure. "Oh my god," I moan, feeling the cream foam on my upper lip.

Before I can lick it away, Lex makes a sharp, disapproving sound. Before worry can capture my gut—panic that he'll take it away—he grabs my chin, tipping my face up. I don't have time to really think about it when he dips down to push his lips against mine, but I know that it starts out stilted and testing, his eyelashes fluttering as he tastes the cream on me.

Wicker is the most skilled kisser, but Lex is by far the sweetest.

He cradles my jaw as he deepens it, his tongue rough and slick as it meets mine. It's all too easy to get swept up in it, opening up for him, but when my hand goes for his hair, he snags my wrist, pulling back.

"No more secret deliveries," he says, his voice low and gruff—meant only for me. "From now on, I'm the only one who gives these to you. Understand?"

Dazed, I offer him a slow nod, blinking my eyes into focus when he pulls back.

Behind him, Pace is wearing his bomber jacket and dark jeans, eyes pink-rimmed in the special way that suggests he's been hitting a vape pen. Even stoned, he looks intense, his dark eyes fixed on my mouth. "I got you this," he says, extending an envelope.

The nervousness returns. Aside from the public humiliations, my Princes haven't bothered with public favors since the deposits stopped, and even those were usually humiliations in their own right. I'm thinking of the necklace Pace gave me a few months ago—the collar—as I tentatively rip open the envelope.

Cheery pink text on the card declares, 'Princess for a day!'

If only.

My stomach drops when I see the name of Adeline's spa. "What's this?"

Pace pushes his hands into his pockets, clearing his throat. "Adeline is shitting her pants about what happened, so she wants to make it right. You'll get a full hair treatment. Masks and trims and whatever-the-hell." At my worried gaze, he frowns, rocking back on his heels. "Don't look so fucked up about it. I can even come with you this time. Nothing is going onto that hair that I don't personally approve of."

"Oh." I glance down at the card, biting my lip. Taking the other girls out of the equation, it really had been a lush experience. "Okay," I decide, slipping the card back into the envelope. "But only if you'll come with me."

Pace blinks, his eyes locking with mine. There's a long pause, and then, "Yeah?" He sounds as skeptical as I was about the coffee.

"You're going to be watching anyway," I muse, tucking the envelope away. "I'd rather feel 'watched over' than 'spied on.'"

His head jerks back, more of those rapid blinks happening. "Really?" It's as if this thought had never occurred to him, the difference between feeling protected and feeling hunted.

Before I can elaborate, Wicker lets out a huff, shoving him aside. "Here," he says, throwing a paper bag into my lap. "Don't say I never gave you anything."

My eyes flick to Lex, but he just gives me a knowing look, dipping his chin in a nod.

Okay. So whatever is in here probably won't kill me.

But when I unfold it, peering inside, all I see is another bag, this one smaller, the size of an egg, and made of cloth. Warily, I pluck it out and turn it over, dumping the contents into my hand.

Seeds.

When I look up, Wicker looks away.

"What are these?" I ask.

"They're seeds," he answers dryly. "You can plant them in the solarium."

Narrowing my eyes, I ask, "What will they grow?"

He finally meets my gaze, blue eyes flashing in irritation. "Well, it's a surprise, isn't it? If I just told you, what would be the fun in planting them?"

Our gazes lock in a challenging stare for all of three seconds. "I'll just ask Danner," I say, dropping the seeds back into the pouch. "No doubt he got it from the same catalog as my new pruning shears."

Wicker meets my challenge with a steely smirk. "Danner didn't get them. I got them myself, from the Ag department's heirloom seed depository."

I frown, looking the pouch over once again. "What could they be?" Then, my head snaps up. "Oh god, it's not more roses, is it?"

"It's not roses," Wicker insists. "It's a surprise."

I tilt my head, assessing the size of the seeds. "Is it fruit?"

Wicker's eyes bug out. "Do you understand what a surprise is? Jesus Christ."

"I'm just asking—"

His hand snaps out, cradling behind my neck, and he mutters, "Just shut up and take it," before tilting his head and slanting his mouth over mine. The battle between us is short-lived. I'm pressed against his hard body, clutching the gifts in my hands, being forced to admit I asked for this. Trading one complication for another.

As Wicker slowly pulls back, a satisfied smirk lingering on his lips and the thrum of blood pumping in my veins, there's no doubt that out of the two, this complication feels so much better.

14

icker

THURSDAYS SUCK.

Usually, my brothers and I will run jobs together, but they're both busy with their own bullshit on Thursdays, leaving me to take care of Father's petty chores on my own. It's right after my last class that I'm walking across the quad, ready to get this fucking errand over with, and I see her standing near the fountain.

My stride falters when I see what she's wearing; a skirt two inches shorter than what I know is standard in her closet and a soft gray sweater. It looks sweet, but the way it clings to the growing curve of her tits is nothing but pure temptation. Same goes for the over-the-knee boots. It's not the first time this week she's turned up at school like this. It's like she's inside my fantasies and putting them on display.

I'm starting to wonder if I talk in my sleep.

Catching her like this, all carefree and easy, red hair cascading down her back, is even more jarring since I'd left the house early for morning practice. I haven't seen her since we detangled from one another in the bed, her warm body like a siren's call. Predictably, I've been dealing with a semi all day, even after rubbing one out in the shower. You'd think after sleeping next to my finely sculpted, shirtless body for four nights, some of that staunch refusal in her eyes would have faded some.

It hasn't.

If I don't get my dick in a hole soon, I may explode.

Her laughter carries over, and I frown when I see that the person she's with is her DKS lackey. It's not his presence that annoys me. I'm used to him lurking around and adept at ignoring him. It's the easy smiles they share. The way they laugh together like they've got inside jokes. Want her or not, she doesn't belong to them. She belongs to us.

It's that primal need that takes over as I approach her. My movements are seamless, taking the backpack off her shoulder with one hand and lifting her chin with the other. Her mouth parts in surprise, and I take advantage, bending my head and sweeping my tongue inside. Her entire body tenses, and her nails dig into my bicep. She hates it when I do this, but this is the deal everyone wanted. On campus, we treat her like she's our Princess, and this is how I do it: massive amounts of PDA, and my wicked, skillful tongue. With every stroke, she starts to loosen until she's kissing me back. Dropping my hand from her jaw to her ass, my fingers graze the flesh just under the hem of her skirt.

A cough draws us apart.

When I rub my thumb over her bottom lip, she looks up at me with dazed eyes. She's not the only one. Several groups of girls in the general area are giving me heart eyes. Jesus. Chicks are so easy.

Without looking at the DKS, I say, "You're dismissed."

"But I'm supposed to—"

"The Princess and I are running an errand, and then she'll be back home." I lick my bottom lip, tasting her fruity lip gloss. "Don't you have some potluck to go to or something?"

Verity blinks at me, then looks over at him. "It's your night off. Go have fun at Family Dinner."

"You sure?" he asks. "I could have Sy put in a call. See if you can come?"

Before I can fully rear forward to interject, Verity touches my chest, shaking her head at him. "No, thanks. I'll be back in West End soon enough. Better to stay here and tie things up with Stella."

The reminder that her month with us is coming to a close evokes conflicting feelings. There's relief since we won't be on round-the-clock guard duty, but also a thread of deep annoyance. If it were up to me, my brothers and I would be long gone. But it isn't, and we aren't, and if we're going to stay and keep playing the part of Princes, then we should at the very fucking least have a full-time Princess and not this ridiculous halfway situation.

Before he even walks away, I've tossed her bag over my shoulder and taken her hand, intertwining my fingers with hers. Full boyfriend mode. If there's one thing I'm good at, it's this.

"So where are the guys?" she asks, wiggling her fingers uncomfortably. I tighten my grip, holding her close enough to get a whiff of her shampoo as we walk to the parking lot.

"Lex had a meeting. Pace has tutoring."

Her brow arches. "Tutoring? Isn't he, like, crazy smart?"

"Yeah, Princess." I unlock the doors of my car. "Turns out no one is teaching advanced calculus in prison."

Her face falls. "Oh."

It never gets old, reminding her that she's not the center of the universe. I know she thinks she is, especially with that abomination growing in her stomach, but we all have shit going on. School, hockey, Prince obligations, meeting Father's demands...

I open the passenger side door and toss our bags in the back. Before she moves to sit, I grab her by the hips and bring her in for another kiss—this one observed by a passing group of sorority girls. Verity makes a small, surprised sound, but melts into it faster than the last one, her fingers twisting in my designer shirt. I've only got two more nights to convince her a ride on my cock could be advantageous to us both. The hornier I leave her today, the better my chances become.

When her chest is heaving and gasping for air, I pull away, nudging her into the car. Slamming the door, I exhale, taking my own deep breaths before getting in the driver's side.

Now we can drop the pretense.

"Where are we going?" she asks, turning her legs away from me. Inside my prized Ferrari, our body language is the polar opposite of outside. As much space as possible.

"Picking up my new tux." I press the button to start the engine, and the steady beat of music spills from the speakers. "Despite Father's efforts to keep me the physical dimensions of a ten-year-old, I've grown an inch in height and across the shoulders."

From the passenger seat, a deep sound rumbles through the air. I glance over and see Verity clutching her stomach.

"Oh, hell no," I snap. "Don't you fucking dare puke in my car!"

"I'm not going to puke," she says, grimacing. "I'm starving."

"Doesn't Lex send you to campus with some kind of snack?" I ask, pulling into Forsyth Center. The shopping promenade is located just off campus, in undesignated territory. It's filled with high-end boutiques and upscale restaurants.

"I already ate it," she says, eyes flashing guiltily. "Hours ago."

"Sucks to be you." Driving straight to the valet, I stop, stepping fluidly out of the car. And since I'm good at what I do, I walk around, opening her door and offering her my hand.

After a skeptical glance, she takes it, but as soon as she's standing on the pavement, she releases a long, desperate groan.

"What's your deal?" I ask, impatiently ushering her toward the shops. I'm not pushing the PDA out here. That deal was for campus.

"That *smell*. God, I would literally die for a burrito right now." She looks longingly at the Mexican restaurant across the plaza.

I freeze, a light bulb going off in my head. "Yeah?" Turning to her, I take her hand and place it on my belt, just above my cock. "What else would you do?" Pointedly, I drop my gaze to her soft lips.

Her green eyes stare up at me, growing wide at the implication.

"I'm not sucking your dick for a burrito!" She snatches her hand away.

"Fine," I say, casual as I please. "Even though this will probably be your only chance. Lex will never let you have one."

She pauses like she's actually considering this, her gaze dropping down to my belt. She gnaws on her lip a second, shoulders drooping. "No," she grumbles, kicking a pebble across the sidewalk. "Can't do it."

Yeah, I thought so.

"Why do you want to eat something that already looks like vomit, anyway?" I ask, lip curling. "You're just going to puke it back up."

She shakes her head. "It's been days since I felt morning sickness. Guess I'm moving out of that phase."

I'm unwilling to discuss these 'phases'. There are these little things about her that are changing. Or maybe not so little things. Like her tits. They're bigger. I know it. It's like a disturbance in the Force or something. I sense their growth.

And her nipples are so fucking sensitive. High beams all day long. And when I woke up in bed with her this morning, my arm wrapped around her stomach, she felt... thicker.

I don't like it. I mean, fine, the tits aren't the worst—*not* that she's letting me touch them. What I don't like is the reminder of *why* her body is changing. Of what's growing inside or how our lives are fucked the instant the thing comes out. My brothers are already goners. I know they'll change their minds once it gets here. Once Father ruins our lives even more. They'll regret being pussies, refusing to run while we had a chance.

She glances at the Mexican place again, mouth twisting hungrily, and then peeks at me. "One burrito hardly seems worth it."

I do a double take, realizing this chick's seriously down to whore herself out for a burrito. The fuck is Lex doing to her? I raise my chin. "Name your price."

"Two, with all the fillings and toppings I want," she demands, crossing her arms over her chest, pushing up her tits. "Two per *week*. And you can't come in my mouth or on my face."

"Deal," I say, or rather my cock says, before I even think it through. I'm that fucking desperate.

That is until we're sitting at a small, festively decorated table at Señor Mexicana, and I see her massacre the burrito. Like, literally take it down like a wild animal. Her eyes go feral the second the waitress sets the plate in front of her, and she tears into it with one giant bite after another. I watch in equal parts disgust, fascination, and terror.

She stuffs the burrito between her teeth and tears through it like sinew.

"You know what?" I say, eyeing the glob of guacamole on her cheek. "I'm good."

"What do you mean?" She swipes her finger into a pool of sour cream and shoves it in her mouth.

Grimacing, I tell her, "I'm not putting my cock in there. You're like a fucking piranha. Consider the bj declined."

She freezes mid-chew. "Seriously?"

"Dead serious." I gesture at the carnage in front of her, and she rolls her eyes.

"I'm sorry if my *eating for two* repulses you."

I scoff. "Convenient excuse."

She takes a big, deliberate bite. "I'm also hating for two."

I distract myself by scrolling through my phone. "What's so great about West End anyway?" She makes a muffled, questioning sound that doesn't even resemble words. "At the palace, you're basically waited on hand and foot. Safer than houses. Groomed and plucked and adorned with jewels. Not to mention, apparently having your choice of premium Prince dick." Baffled, I wonder, "Why do you even want to go back?"

She gives me an obvious look. "You just tried to sexually extort me for a burrito. Gee, I wonder."

Jaw locking, I lean forward, voice low and cutting. "My whole family chose you over me. Did you know that?" Of course, she didn't. I can see it in the dull confusion in her eyes. "I sleep in your bed, I put on a convincing performance for the frat, I protect you at all fucking costs, and I do all of this despite the fact you stabbed me in the back. You took something I gave you—intel that was meant for your own fucking sake—and used it against me." I almost enjoy how her face falls, gaze falling to her plate. Leaning back, I conclude, "Maybe I don't roll out the red carpet for you like everyone else, but I've never tried to get you killed. I'd say I treat you just fine."

After a long moment, she reaches for her drink. "I wasn't trying to get you killed."

I shrug. "Couldn't care less if you were."

"I wasn't," she repeats, trying to catch my gaze. "It was never about that."

She doesn't elaborate, and I don't ask her to. It wouldn't matter. If life has taught me anything, it's that people are always looking for something to take. At the end of the day, the fault lies with me. I looked into these big green eyes and saw someone worth giving something to.

My mistake.

The tension lingers in the background as she finishes her second burrito in silence.

Kind of.

"It's something poisonous, isn't it?" she asks, but even though she narrows her eyes, there's something playful about it. "Like belladonna or foxglove."

I roll my eyes. "Like Lex would let me get away with that."

She's been pestering me about those seeds for days now. God knows why she doesn't just plant them, and wait and see.

When she finally pushes her plate back, she slumps into her seat with a long sigh. "That was amazing," she says, sticking out her chest and messing with something on her back.

I take a surreptitious glance around us. "Look, I know you were raised in the equivalent of an apocalyptic world, with no social graces or manners, but what the fuck are you doing?"

"This bra is killing me," she grunts, shifting uncomfortably.

"You're awfully hyperbolic today."

She grimaces, squirming around. "The elastic is gouging into my skin."

I signal to the waitress that we're ready for the check, muttering under my breath, "Jesus, just buy a bigger one."

"What did you say?"

When I turn to her, she's frowning. "Red, it's obvious your tits are growing. Just like how I need a bigger suit to contain my manliness, you may need to buy a bigger bra to contain," I look at her and wave my hand around, "all that."

"All *that*?" Her jaw drops. "Are you saying I'm fat? Because I'm wearing the exact same size clothes as always."

Groaning, I drag a palm down my face. "Red, don't make me do it."

Her head tilts quizzically. "Do what?"

"You asked for it." I stand and drag her to her feet. Lifting her shirt, I point out how she's secured the button of her skirt with one of Lex's hairbands to extend the space. "Stop kidding yourself. You're growing."

She bats my hand away, but I don't miss the way her eyes water. "I'm not ready to get fat. I just started the second trimester!"

"Don't you dare start crying," I growl, panicking. "You're not fat. You just..."

She grabs her boobs, wincing as they squeeze together. "And what the hell is this? They hurt all day. My nipples have a mind of their own and..." She reaches under her shirt, fumbles with the clasp, and exhales, eyes rolling back. "That feels so much better. I'll just stop wearing it."

"Like hell you will!" Realizing we're drawing attention to ourselves, I pull out my wallet and throw some bills on the table. Her tits are spectacles enough when they're contained. The thought of her walking around with them bouncing all over the place? If I think my brothers are whipped now, the Princess going around braless will make their minds melt. "Come on," I insist, spinning her.

"Where are we going?" she asks as I grab her arm and lead her to the door.

I know women. I know how to make them swoon. I know how to

make them feel better. To help them push aside those little insecurities like crow's feet, or sun spots, or whatever it is I'm not supposed to notice.

Right now, there's only one thing that will make Verity feel better.

"Shopping."

~

It's not until later that I realize how stupid I've been.

I took her to the lingerie store and pressed the credit card in her hand, but didn't go inside with her. I've shown Herculean magnitudes of willpower the last few months, but lingerie shopping is a level of torture I'm not prepared to suffer through. She shopped. I picked up my tux. When we met at the car, she seemed to have calmed down.

But now I can't stop wondering what she bought. Lace? Satin? Cotton? My fingers twitch as I busy myself getting ready for bed, listening to the sounds of her doing the same through the bathroom door. Like my balls weren't in enough pain, now I have that on my mind. And even if I asked—fuck, demanded it—there's zero chance of me getting some. She's made that perfectly clear.

Instead of wondering how her tits would look squeezed between my hands, or with my face buried in between, I comb my hair back with my fingers. Then check my cuticles. Then brush my fingers over my jaw, wondering if there's stubble. It'd be a lie to say I don't put a lot of effort into my looks, but usually, it's just an enhancement of what I know to be true. I'm a goddamn specimen.

So why isn't she on my dick yet?

I check my reflection in the dresser mirror, seeing the hard ladder of my abs, the bulge in my boxer briefs, and my hard pecs. I've definitely put on some muscle mass since the season started, and my shoulders are a touch broader than normal. A little nagging voice in the back of my mind—a voice that sounds just like Father—whispers to me.

They like you to be lean and unthreatening.

Frowning, I flex my chest, wondering why I suddenly feel shitty about new muscle. Even after arranging my pillow and sliding under the covers, it nags at me, face set into a deep frown as I consider this... what's the word?

Insecurity?

Gross.

"What's this?" The thought shatters when I look over, seeing her standing inside the bathroom door. She's holding a Royals jersey, black, purple, and gold, with the name Ashby on the back.

And the number 2.

My number.

Smirking, I wedge my arm behind my bed. "I had your wench put that out."

"For... your game?" she asks, brow furrowed in confusion. "That's not until next week."

"For you to wear to bed."

My week. My name. My number.

She may not let me inside her, but I can force these little bits of dominance where I can. It's her fault, really. I haven't stopped thinking about her wearing my jersey since she showed up in it at my game.

She gives me an unimpressed look. "You can't be serious."

"Oh, I'm always serious about fashion, Red." Arching a brow, I add, "I never got compensated for the burritos."

Rolling her eyes, she doesn't even bother stepping back into the bathroom to pull off that little silk nightie. I make a low, pleased sound as I stare at her tits, full and heavy-looking. It's only for a flash. She pulls the jersey on at lightning speed, her expression set into an unamused scowl.

"Happy?" she says, spreading her arms.

I reach down to give my dick a squeeze. "Getting there."

With another eyeroll, she climbs into bed, the hem of the jersey grazing the top of her milky, smooth thighs. "I was going to thank you for the food and the shopping today," she grumbles, wrestling the blanket toward her, "but now I think I'll just try to forget it ever happened."

"Good luck with that," I say around a jaw-cracking yawn. Despite the urge to keep her up and goad her some more, I'm fucking exhausted.

Each of us turns off our lamp, but since we both know how this is going to end up, I immediately roll to the middle of the massive bed, reaching out to grab her hip and haul her toward me. After that morning I shoved her right off the edge, I try to keep us in the middle. The bed's the size of a goddamn elephant. Who wakes up in a bed this big and expects to be right on the rim of it?

She makes her customary noises of complaint—a groan, a grunt —but ultimately settles into the cradle of my body, sniping, "Watch the hair!"

I don't watch it, though.

I smell it.

God, girls smell good. All clean and sweet, like they're fruit just waiting to be peeled.

"Cactus," her voice rumbles sleepily.

I snort. "Nah."

There's a moment of silence, and then, "Is it a tree?"

This has been our nightly routine for the week. I make her cuddle with me, then she drives me crazy. "You really can't handle surprises, can you?"

I feel her arm shift as she fidgets with a thread on her pillowcase. "I used to be able to," she says, shoulder jerking with a shrug. "But there are no good surprises in this house." There's a flicker of melancholy to her voice that I know all too well. She doesn't need to tell me.

Huffing, I relent, "It's a flower. Not a poisonous flower. Not a disgusting flower. Just a flower."

She goes still. "Really?"

"*Yes.*"

I can tell she's hoping for more. The truth is, I don't tell her because the flower isn't even about her. I just think it'll be ironic to have it growing in the palace's solarium. If she knew the intent behind it, she'd hesitate to see it through.

"Okay," she says, nestling down into her pillow. "I'll plant them and wait."

"You do that," I grouse, throwing my leg over hers. It's not long though before that nagging thought begins picking at me again. Maybe it's the dark, or the rhythmic way her chest rises and falls against my arm, or just *her*, all solid and sweet-smelling and obscenely comfortable. But eventually, I whisper, "Hey, Red?"

"Mm?"

It takes me a second to form the question. "Am I... too big?"

She groans. "Wicker, it's too late for dick jokes."

"No, I mean my muscles," I say, frowning. "Do they make me look... worse?"

There's a beat of stillness, and then her head turns like she's trying to catch my gaze. "Is this about what Ashby said to you a couple of weeks ago?" When I don't answer, she turns a little more, a little divot in her brow. "Because he was wrong. Sy and Killian Payne are the most muscular people I know, and look at them. They're Kings."

I scoff. "Yeah, they're really rolling in pussy."

"They could be," she insists, her fingers brushing against my forearm. "Muscles mean strength, Wicker. Power. Security. Protection. And that's hot as hell."

My lips twist into a wicked smirk. "Oh, really now?" It's all too easy to skate my palm up, getting a nice handful of her tit.

"That's what I get for inflating your ego," she says, yanking my hand back down and turning away. "Go to sleep." But minutes later, just as my eyes flutter shut, she inhales. "Your body is a work of beauty, Wicker. If you had a heart to match it..."

She never finishes the sentence.

It's still ringing in my ears as I nod off.

I WAKE to the smell of lavender in my nose, my cock hard as a rock, and the incessant sound of rattling across the room. Groaning, I mutter, "Fucking hell, Lex."

At least twice a week, I have to take my brother back to his room. He's less combative and violent now that his dick is functional again, but it's still dangerous for him to be roaming around alone at night.

Unwrapping myself from Verity's warm body, I get up, rubbing my face as I walk to the door. "Bro," I say, twisting the knob. "I need my beauty rest just like everyone else."

But when I swing the door open, the hallway is empty. I peer toward the other bedrooms, the shadowy area lit by a small light down by the stairwell.

"What the hell?" I mutter, wondering if I dreamed the whole thing. Behind me, I hear the rattle again, and I turn, waking up a little more. My eyes land on the windows.

In the bed, Verity sits up. "What's going on?"

"Nothing, go back to bed," I say, eyeing the way my jersey falls off one of her shoulders. But a flash of light from the window has my head snapping toward it. Not lightning, but a beam—like a flashlight.

Just as the hair on the back of my neck stands on end, I hear footsteps racing down the hall. A dark silhouette skids to a stop in the doorway, hand racking the slide of a pistol. "Code purple."

"What?" I ask, trying to catch up.

Pace, eyes thin and tense, begins snapping his fingers in my face. "Code fucking purple!"

Any lingering sleep is gone as I spring into action, rushing over to Verity. She's more awake now, forehead furrowed. "What's a code purple?"

Yanking her out of the bed, I lean over and press the center jewel in the headboard with my thumb, and then two other, smaller jewels. A panel slides open to reveal a small alcove. I push Verity into it.

She stumbles into the compartment, ducking. "What the—"

"Someone's trying to breach the palace," I explain. "Stay in here until we come back. Don't make a fucking sound."

Panic flickers across her face, green eyes shining up at me. "You're locking me in here?"

"It'll be okay," I say the words so mindlessly that she can't possibly draw any comfort from them when I close her in. Heart hammering in my chest, I push aside the image of her wide eyes and put on my game face. Not even bothering to dress, I reach under the bed, unlatch the weapons cache, and pull out two guns and a knife.

I start down the hall, mentally getting myself in the right headspace. We've trained for this, hours of drills commanded by Father's security experts. Pace meets me at the top of the staircase, eyes wild. "The alarm went off five minutes ago. Someone tripped a motion sensor outside her room."

"Yeah, I woke up to the sound of someone trying to get in. I thought it was Lex." I tuck one gun in the back of my boxer briefs. "Where is he, anyway?"

Pace is dressed much like me, which is to say *not*. Boxers and a Glock, the outfit of choice for any Prince at 2 a.m. "He had an overnight shift at the clinic. Father is away at a business meeting in Northridge, and I've got Danner locked in. Same with all other staff." He lifts something in his hand, nodding to the door on our right.

The palace's skeleton key.

We start down the hall, moving quickly. He unlocks a door, and then I push it open for him to clear the left of the room, his gun raised as I clear the right side. After the last break-in, every ingress has been updated, but anything is possible. Particularly in this wing.

"Didn't the Duke's ball boy come in late tonight?" I ask as we descend the staircase. Suspicion thrums in my veins. "Did he bring back friends?"

"No." Pace shakes his head, eyes scanning the corridor before us. "I saw him come in."

"But he could have left the gate open, or maybe a window?" I don't trust those fuckers for a minute. Especially not Maddox. Something about him sets me on edge. "Maybe they're tired of waiting for her to come back."

"It's not him." Pace stops in front of a door that leads to the fighter's room. The hand-wench's room is on the opposite side, connected by a bathroom. "I'll prove it."

Using the skeleton key, Pace slides it into the lock, giving me a nod as he pushes it open.

The first thing I see are legs. Long, smooth legs with their soft thighs spread obscenely, a gown rucked up over slender hips. Her head snaps up at the sound of the door opening, a shocked gasp falling from Stella's lips.

Ballsack's head is buried between her legs, his mouth full of pussy.

I groan, gesturing limply to the tableau. "Great, so I really am the only one not getting some in this house." Well, maybe other than Danner.

Frantically, she begins shoving his head out from between her thighs. "Prince Whitaker! Prince Pace! Oh my god..." She springs up, breathless, cheeks red as tomatoes as she tugs the hem of her gown down. "I'm so sorry, I know we shouldn't—"

"What the hell?" Ballsack stands quickly, his eyes dropping to the guns. "What's going on?"

"Shut up," Pace snaps, already coiled tight. This is his worst fucking nightmare. "There's an intruder on the property."

I march over to the closet, open the door, and press a lever. The back slides away, and I look at the girl, waving the barrel of my gun at the hole. "Get in. Follow the passage until you get to a dead end. There's a nail on the left side. Pull it down, and the wall will move. The Princess is on the other side." I remove a flashlight from the closet's false floor and offer it to her, along with the knife. "Take this, lock the two of you inside, and stay until someone gets you."

"Yes, sir." When she takes the knife, it looks huge in her small hand. God help us. She gives Ballsack a lingering look and vanishes inside.

"You," I say, walking over to him. "Wipe the pussy off your mouth." I remove the second pistol from my waistband, turning the butt toward him. He reaches for it, but I don't release my grip, forcing him to see the threat in my eyes. "Use this against us, and PNZ will burn West End to the ground." I jerk my head toward the closet. "Including the girl."

"I hear you," he says, and I give him the weapon. He slides out the clip, then snaps it back into place. "Who is it?"

"No fucking clue," Pace says, heading out of the room. "But the zone lighting up was outside the Princess' room. I have to assume she's the target. Head up there and guard the room. Protect her like your life depends on it."

"Got it." He takes off back upstairs, and we continue to check every inch of the house, every closet, every hidden passage. With every room we clear, the more angry and anxious I get, wanting to be upstairs to make sure everything is okay.

We make our way through the dungeon and solarium, where Pace stops, turning to me with a grim look. "Ready?"

I glance down at his hand, poised over the knob, and pause. This isn't part of the script. We're supposed to wait until Father's security arrives and let them handle the exterior. But it only takes one glimpse of Pace's dark, murderous eyes to understand he's not getting out of this situation without some bloodshed.

"Muscles mean strength, Wicker. Power. Security. Protection."

Apparently, neither am I.

I grip my gun tighter, nodding. "Let's go."

He pushes the door to the gardens open, snapping his gun up to scan the area before crouching down. Together we move along the southern wall toward the Princess' room. The trees are steady and still, not even a breeze to contaminate the silence, and thorny vines scrape the bottom of my bare feet. The adrenaline has my senses on a razor's edge. Even in the dark, everything feels crisp and sharp, little puffs of steam punching from my mouth into the cold night air. Pace stalks ahead, hunched over like I am, but when we reach the western wall, he jerks his head, motioning me to clear the corner for him.

I duck around him, flattening myself to the stone wall. Holding my breath, I peer around the edge before jolting along the wall, gun raised toward her window.

Fuck.

There's nothing out here. Just shivering roses and moonlight. I'm going to be so pissed when we find out it was just a raccoon or some shit.

Just as I deflate, exhaling a cloud of mist, a deafening *crack* rings out.

I spin so fast that I stumble, panic rising in my chest when I realize Pace isn't behind me. I lurch up, all thoughts of remaining hidden dissipating as my feet pound painfully against the bramble. "Pace?!"

Another *crack* pierces the silence, and then a third, and by the time I reach the corner where I'd left him, I'm fully expecting to see my brother in a pile of dead leaves, riddled with ragged holes.

Instead, I'm greeted by the sight of him in the garden, crouched behind a statue, pulling the trigger a fourth time. "Fuck!" he spits, turning to press his back against the marble. "I got the fucker. I know I did!"

"You saw him?" I ask, rushing to his position. Only when I'm pressed against him, shoulder to shoulder, do I finally look him over, collapsing in relief at the realization all the shots came from Pace's gun. "Who was it?"

He's reloading, face set into a scowl. "Couldn't fucking see. He was fifty yards out, going into the trees." Again, he stresses, "I got him."

But when he goes to run out toward the trees, I grab him, yanking him back. "If you shot him, he won't get far. Let the paid team bat cleanup."

His eyes are black, burning into mine. "I want that motherfucker in the dungeon *tonight*."

"Then get up there and do your thing," I say, pushing him toward the house. "Search him out. We're not running into the woods in the dead of night to chase an armed intruder without at least some fucking shoes."

He lowers his gun, knowing I'm right. "Motherfucker," he growls, trudging back to the solarium.

By the time we get back inside, some of Father's security has already congregated at the front door. Thad, who Father recruited to head the palace's exterior security, is a massive former goalie who once captained the Forsyth hockey team. Unlike us, he's dressed in black tactical gear and moves quietly around the property like a ghost. Seeing him like this only confirms how unusual this is.

"The grounds are clear," he tells us when he returns, holding up a long cable with a hook on the end. "Whoever it was came in through the southern grounds and made an attempt to secure entrance on the second floor."

"That must be what woke me up," I say, nodding at the hook. "How many?"

"From the footsteps, possibly two. Obviously, they didn't realize the windows are fortified." He points toward the west. "We found the blood trail in the woods—your boy definitely got a hit—but it leads right to the brook."

Behind me, Pace spits a curse. "He escaped."

Thad sighs, nodding. "Unfortunately, that looks to be the case."

"Shore up everything," Pace barks. "The fencing, the windows, every goddamn weakness on the perimeter."

"Yes, sir."

Back upstairs, Pace strides into his room and goes straight to the monitors. "Whoever this fucker is, he had to leave some kind of trace. If he lost blood, he could have lost something else."

"You don't think this is retaliation for the cleansing fallout?" I ask, watching him scan the feeds, the screen reflecting back in his dark eyes. I see the glint of his paranoia ratcheting up. This is going to be hard for him to let go of until he's found out who made the attempt. "One of our own?"

"They're pissed but not stupid."

Honestly, I'd rather it be someone inside, because an outside enemy making a move this bold... there are too many variables to consider.

"What do you need me to do?" I ask, feeling the adrenaline waning.

"Get back to her." He never looks away from the screen. "Stay with her all night."

I nod, for once not angry about doing my duty.

"And you?"

His jaw is set. "I'll rest when I find out exactly who tried to fuck with what's mine."

15

erity

I DON'T KNOW how long I stand in the dark, back pressed against the wall, nothing but the sound of my heartbeat to keep me company. It feels like an eternity before I hear anything, but even though I'm hoping for a thump, a voice, *anything*, the sound of approaching footsteps makes me stiffen in terror.

The hiding spot Wicker shoved me into is the size of a coat closet, with only a tiny sliver of light coming through the baseboards. I have no weapon. No fucking clue what's going on. I didn't even know this hidey-hole was here, right behind the bed.

A scrape comes, but not from outside.

From behind me.

Twisting my head, I silently wrap one hand over my stomach and ball the fist of the other. Maybe it's a mouse. God, let it be a mouse. I grip the flashlight tightly, wrapping my fingers around the heavy metal shaft.

There's a snap, and then an awful *creak*, and suddenly I'm blinded by a bright beam of light. "Princess?" I slacken at the sound of Stella's frightened voice, raising my flashlight to see her. She's holding a flashlight too, much like mine.

And also, a massive knife.

"Jesus," I exhale, my heart threatening to explode out of my chest. "It's you."

"This place is like a maze." She quickly closes the hatch, snapping the wall back into place. "Are you okay?"

I point the flashlight away, letting it bounce off the walls. "I'm fine. Just..." I don't know how I feel. Scared? Worried? I look down at my hand on my stomach and wonder when I started doing that. "What's going on out there?"

She crouches down beside me, our shoulders brushing. "Princes Pace and Whitaker are searching for the intruder," she whispers. "I was told to come here and wait with you."

I nod, glad to know they took care of her. "Where's Ballsy?"

"Close, I think," she says, looking away. "After they told me to come in the passage, I heard Prince Whitaker ordering him to guard your room."

"So I guess we wait." I gesture to the floor, and we both slide down, knees bent and cramped together.

We sit quietly for another long moment, listening but unable to hear anything. The wall of my bedroom is insulated heavily—clearly meant to keep anyone from discovering someone hiding inside.

"They seemed very in control," Stella reassures, holding the knife so the light reflects off the sharp blade. "Like they were prepared. I'm sure it'll only be a few more minutes. Probably a false alarm."

But I doubt that. "They've had break-ins before. Someone vandalized the nursery a couple of years back."

I wait for her shocked reaction to something so awful, but instead, she giggles. "I heard about that. It was quite the drama at the Hideaway. It's not confirmed, but my sister thinks it was Dimitri Rathbone and his Lady."

"Story?" Wow. Wicker called it.

Stella's shoulder grazes mine when she shrugs. "That's the rumor. I mean, there are *a lot* of rumors that go through the Hideaway, especially about the Royals."

Since this seems like a good avenue to distraction, I turn, wondering, "What do they say about the Princes and their Princess?"

"About... you?"

Hearing the confusion in her voice, I shake my head. "No, I mean in general. Everything I thought I knew about this Royalship was wrong, and I'm pretty sure no one else knew either, you know?"

Stella hums, tapping the knife against the floor. "Just the usual, I suppose. Everyone thinks the Princes are just weak pretty boys with too much money and hair gel," she says. "No one had ever heard of the throning, or the deposits, or—gosh, definitely not the cleansing. Although it explains some of the Hideaway's PNZ clientele."

After a beat, I ask, "Have you... told anyone? About what's really happening?"

She turns, her big eyes blinking at me. "Only when I had to, Princess."

I know without needing to ask that she means the cleansing. She told Lavinia and Story, and while they were orchestrating my escape, I was orchestrating my revenge. "Thank you," I say. "Not for telling, but for... *not* telling them." Because I know that's the harder task. Especially now, as I'm sleeping beside the Princes, making deals, and capitulating for the sake of the endgame. "I don't think they'd understand."

Her brow puckers. "I think you underestimate what they've gone through, too. That's part of the sickness, isn't it? That women in Forsyth are humiliated so much, we can't bear to humiliate ourselves by bringing it into the light."

Snorting, I say, "There are a lot of other factors to consider. Like... take my mother, for instance. Or your sister. Or the Dukes. Or hell, even Lavinia and Story. If everyone knew what happened in this house, they'd want to get me out of it." I squirm, trying to stretch out in the cramped space. "But I made the decision to see this through, and finding out Ashby is my biological father only reinforces my commitment. We have to find a way to stop this cycle, and the only way out is through."

I think back to what Rory said on campus the other day. *'East End has a habit of throwing its Princesses away.'* But it's not just the Autumns and Pipers out there. From Leticia and Lavinia Lucia to Story Austin, the sickness Stella speaks of doesn't know Royal class. It doesn't know blood. It doesn't know names.

It only knows gender.

It probably knows where these missing girls are, too.

"I'm tired of women in Forsyth being disposable." I reach out and take her hand, squeezing it. "Royal or not."

She squeezes back, but then abruptly blurts, "We were together when the Princes came in."

I frown. "We who?"

"Me and Eugene." Even in the dim light, I can see the blush rise on her cheeks. "They walked in on us together. I mean, we weren't like *that*," she rushes to add, her words getting faster as she tries to explain, "but we weren't *not* like that either. It was after-hours, you know? And you were already in bed. I know it's inappropriate, especially with the delicate nature of our houses not being aligned—"

"Stella." I squeeze her hands together. "Breathe."

She takes a deep breath. "Okay."

"I think it's good. Eugene is a great guy. He's sweet, which isn't something I can say about all of the guys in DKS. He'll treat you right."

She straightens, her grin wide. "He's so nice, isn't he? I've never had a guy want to do that to me before, and oh my god," she gushes, "he has such a good tongue..."

"Okay!" I hold out my hand. "Ballsack is like a cousin to me. I'm happy for you, but I really don't want to know *anything* about his tongue."

She giggles. "Gotcha."

A moment later, there's a grinding sound, and Stella and I both spring to our feet, her hand brandishing the knife. But when the wall slides away, it's just Wicker, still shirtless and pantless, his blonde hair even more disheveled.

"Whoa, yeah," Wicker says, plucking the knife from her hand. "I'll take that."

"Everything okay?" I ask, feeling his gaze sweep down my body. I got the feeling before that he made me wear his jersey just to piss me off, but seeing the glint of satisfaction in his eyes makes me wonder if he's just getting off on it.

"Everything's clear. Whoever was on the property is long gone." He offers his hand, and I take it, allowing him to help me out of the compartment. Ballsack moves around us, fluidly offering Stella his own hand.

Aww.

"You can go," Wicker says to Ballsack, who moves to hand him the gun. But Wicker shakes his head. "Keep it. Just in case there's another alarm."

"That was bold," I tell him once they've left. "Letting Ballsack keep a weapon."

"They're loyal to you," he says, checking the window. "I don't trust him, but I trust that he doesn't want to see you dead, which is a sentiment East End is running a little low on." Glancing back, he explains, "A couple of people on the security team were at your cleansing."

"Oh." I tug at the hem of the jersey, realizing this means I'm responsible for what's probably their messy breakups. Not that I feel much sympathy, but I suppose I didn't do myself many favors with the frat. "Where's Pace?"

"Obsessing." Wicker drops heavily onto the bed, raking his hands through his hair. He looks exhausted, and the fact it's the middle of the night hits home. We've all had a long day. Tomorrow's going to suck. "This kind of shit fucks with him. He'll blame himself even though no one got in because of all the measures put in place."

Frowning, I glance at the door. "Should I go talk to him?"

He considers it. "Probably wouldn't hurt. Let him know you're okay."

But I don't get the chance. He appears in the doorway as I'm watching it, Effie's cage in one hand, a tablet in the other.

Unlike Wicker, Pace has gotten dressed. Fully. Dark hoodie, a pair of gray joggers, socks, shoes, and all. "Is it okay if she stays in here?" he asks, setting her cage on my dresser. He fidgets with the placement for a beat, his twists falling in front of his eyes. "I'd feel better knowing she's in here with someone."

"Sure," I say, perching on the bed. Wicker is already leaning back on the pillows. "Are you going somewhere?"

He adjusts the sheet covering her cage and stalks over to the windows, checking and rechecking the locks. "I'm just going to keep an eye out. I don't like that we didn't catch the son of a bitch who did this. If his body pops up, I want to be the first to spit on it."

"Thad will call if they find it," Wicker says, yawning. "Just go to bed."

He glares at his brother. "Not an option."

"Pace," I gesture to the room, "we're okay. No one got in. All the measures you had set up worked." His anxiety is making me anxious. "I agree with Wicker, just... come to bed." It's an invitation I'm not expecting to give, but when it tumbles free, I let it.

His eyes dart to the mattress at my choice of words, then down to the tablet in his hand. "Why don't you two sleep, and I'll stay up and keep watch."

Wicker and I share a look. Any wariness I might feel about inviting Pace into the bed with us is clearly unnecessary. Wicker makes space.

"Are the alarms set?" I ask.

Pace presses something on the pad. "Of course they are."

"Is the security team outside?"

"They fucking better be," he mutters.

I pat the mattress. "Then come lay down."

His forehead puckers angrily. "I can't sleep! Someone is out there!"

Stubbornly, I raise my chin. "Then keep watch from here."

Wicker flips his pillow over and curls on his side, ab muscles clenching with the move. "Come on. There's a reason Princes sleep with the Princess: to protect her. Get your ass in the bed."

Pace sighs, turning to survey the bed. I take the opportunity to scoot up next to Wicker, leaving Pace the spot closest to the windows. His dark eyes pass over us before he says, "Fine." Not even taking his shoes off, he eases onto the edge of the bed, back straight, eyes focused on the screen. "But I'm not sleeping."

This is the most we're going to get.

Wicker dims the light, shrouding us in near darkness.

Whatever threat is outside, I know I'm safe.

I WAKE to the brash tug of my panties being jerked to the side and the thick fullness of a cock stretching me from the inside. My eyes flick open, and the first thing I see is Wicker sleeping across from me, bare-chested, those long eyelashes soft against his cheeks. His wrist is slung around my waist, and I try not to jostle him while shifting enough for Pace to push in as deep as he can go.

"Didn't mean to wake you," Pace whispers in my ear. "I just needed inside."

It's been almost a week since he's slept in my bed, since he filled me with his body and cum. I'm not sure how to feel about my body accepting him so freely, almost like a warm, comforting blanket.

"What happened last night..." he continues, nose skating up my neck to my ear. His words feel unbearably quiet, as if he's divulging an unforgivably shameful sin. "If someone hurt you or our baby, I'd lose my fucking mind."

Wicker's eyes flutter open suddenly, back arching as he drags himself out of sleep. He's like that, I've noticed, always waking up like he's forcing it, fighting with himself. It's not long before his blue eyes lock on me, and then Pace, and then lower, blinking rapidly as he realizes what's happening.

As he takes in me and his brother, I wait for the tantrum to start;

how unfair it is that he's not getting his dick wet and how utterly deprived he's been. Poor, cockblocked Whitaker Ashby.

Instead, he stretches on his back and props an arm behind his head, the other dipping into his tight boxer briefs. "She wet?" he asks his brother, stroking up his length.

"Dripping," Pace replies, perfectly still. My pussy aches, desperate for him to thrust. "She always acts like she's not into it, but I feel her clench around me at the smallest movement." His hand travels up the jersey I'm wearing, fingers pinching my nipple. I wince at the sharp stab of pain. "Fuck, just like that."

"Too much," I murmur, still wading in the fog of tiredness.

Wicker licks his bottom lip and rolls toward me, temple propped on his fist. "What happens if I do this?" he asks, bending to capture my mouth in a kiss. His tongue sweeps against mine, warm and diligent. My body heats, electricity running across my skin as my tongue seeks his unthinkingly.

Behind me, Pace groans, my muscles clamping down on him. A kiss shouldn't feel this good—*none* of this should feel so good—but Wicker touches my cheek and strokes his tongue across mine, and just like that, I'm utterly lost.

By the time Wicker withdraws, we're both breathless, but I'm the only one in a soggy daze.

"You like that, huh?" His wicked smirk is tempered by the way his thumb presses against my bottom lip, catching our saliva. I don't wonder why for long, watching as he pulls his cock from his underwear, all pink and stiff. He rubs his slick thumb over the tip, hissing, "*Jesus*. Just fuck her already."

Pace's deep chuckle tickles my ear. "That's not how it works, is it, Rosi?"

Wicker and I stare at one another, his half-lidded, lust-filled eyes boring into mine. "No," I admit.

"What do you have to do for me to give you what you want?" Pace's long fingers dip into the crease of my ass, and I tense as he brushes my puckered hole, restraining the need to arch against the touch.

Swallowing, I take control. "I have to ask for it."

"Is that how it works?" Wicker asks, holding my gaze. "If I ask you to get me off, you'd do it? You want me to say please?"

I shake my head. Those rules are between me and Pace. But Wicker and I? If sex were a religion, we'd be in purgatory. He might be slightly less mean to me, buy me burritos and appropriately sized bras, but I don't trust him. Not with my body.

Still, he's so fucking pretty.

"You see how it is?" Wicker says, looking over my shoulder. "Maybe she just doesn't know how to please a man without him taking control."

"Is that the problem, Rosi?" Pace asks, removing his hand from under my shirt. I watch, confused, as he reaches not for me, but Wicker.

I gasp as his slender fingers expertly fist Wicker's cock. Wicker groans, abs flexing as he lets his brother take over. "Fuck, yeah."

My body reacts, some mixture of shock and indecency twisting deep in my belly. Pace groans into my hair, his gruff voice announcing, "Fuck, she *really* likes that."

"Yeah?" Wicker's eyebrow quirks up, tongue darting out to wet his bottom lip. "We used to do that, you know. Go to parties and make out for the girls. Got so much pussy." He comes forward again, but this time, it's not for me.

He and Pace meet right over my shoulder, their mouths colliding in a slow, wet kiss.

"Oh," I breathe, close enough to see when their tongues meet. "Oh, *god*."

It's beyond hot. What's hotter than hot? Scorching? It doesn't do it justice. Pace groans into his brother's mouth, only to turn away, instantly capturing my lips. I gladly chase the taste of Wicker on his tongue.

Pace growls. "Holy fuck, she's gushing, Wick."

Wicker bucks into Pace's fist, smirking. "Me too, Red. Me too."

This time, Wicker's kiss is hard and bruising, his breath hot as he pants, reaching up to palm my breast. Slowly I unwind, caught in this circle of muscles and body parts. Full of Pace, mouth occupied by Wicker, I'm trapped by their connection. After all the fear and tension, I let them take the lead, curious about where the electrical current will end.

Wicker's mouth blazes a hot trail down my neck, and I can't help but watch the way Pace handles him, mesmerized. There's no gentleness, just firm control as he draws Wicker closer to the edge, their breaths growing ragged. Pace's cock swells inside of me, thickening until his need to thrust builds into these tiny, rocking punches. My clit throbs, desperate for touch, but when I drop my hand between my legs, Wicker's fingers cinch around my wrist.

"Ask me to do it." His voice is strained, clearly close to coming to his own release. He grunts and repeats, "Ask me, Verity."

Maybe it's that he's using my name—not Princess, not Red—and the fricative falls off his tongue like a bolt of lightning, but I find myself wanting to chase, not run. "Touch me," I demand. "*Please.*"

His lips look so red, twisting into an evil grin when he finally relents, slipping a hand between my thighs. I cry out at his touch, but he swallows it with his mouth, using a thumb to toy with my clit. That would honestly be enough to do me in, especially with Pace sucking a mark into my neck as his brother rubs me in these small, delicious circles. My mind starts to melt, the orgasm a breath away, but then I feel it: the stretch of Wicker's forefinger joining Pace's cock, slipping in beside it.

It's nearly too much, my mouth gaping open on a whine as Wicker licks against my lips.

"Still so tight," he rumbles.

Pace growls into my ear, his voice more ragged than I've ever heard it. "You have no fucking idea."

It's too much to bear, and the rush crashes into me, a shattering jolt that's followed by the deep, guttural groan in my ear. It's the signal to brace myself for Pace's unrelenting surge of cum. I'd close my eyes, but I'm too enthralled by Wicker's gorgeous face, seconds from release. He closes his hand over Pace's, the two of them gripping his shaft as he explodes, thick and dripping over their combined hands.

The shockwave of it keeps rolling on and on, the gradual pressure of fullness drawing a cry from me.

Wicker's stunned eyes take me in, but it's only when he says, "Goddamn, bro, you're still going?" that I realize his finger is still inside, feeling Pace pulsate as he pumps into me, wave after wave.

Pace releases a shuddering breath, his palm curling around my forehead to press me closer. "Get her plug," he grunts, shoving his hips into mine. "Top drawer, on the right."

Wicker looks flushed and lewd as he eases his finger free, twisting to wrench open the drawer of the nightstand. He returns with it, all golden and gleaming, and I can barely understand the way something in my chest eases at the mere sight of it.

"That's right," Pace whispers into my temple, brushing a kiss there. "Gonna let you keep it today."

But it's Wicker who rises, nudging my knee into my chest so he can get a good angle to watch as Pace slowly eases out of me. I feel the growing, gnawing absence, unable to help the way my body clutches at him.

"Shh," Pace soothes, asking his brother, "Ready?" At Wicker's nod, Pace warns, "Don't let her lose any," and then drags his cock away.

Whatever Wicker sees makes him spit a low curse, jerking forward. His bicep flexes as he forces it into me. "Fuck," he breathes, fiddling with the base. "She's really going to hold that in all day?"

Pace grabs my chin, turning my dazed eyes onto his. "Are you?"

I give a heavy blink. "If you ask me to."

His kiss is slow and achingly sensual, a palm coming down to push against my inflated belly. The pressure makes me whimper. "All day," he affirms.

I'm given a reprieve from the two of them when their alarms go off, signaling a morning workout. I lie back in the bed, feeling both strung out and full, the image of the two of them seared in my mind.

My goal has been to drive a wedge between them, but if what I just witnessed is the depth of their bond, there's no way I can break it.

But the way it felt between us opens up another possibility, one that's more and more inviting.

Maybe I don't need to break them apart, but instead, figure out a way to tie us all together.

~

ONE REASON I kept asking Wicker about the seeds is because I wanted to know the best place to plant them. There was a small card on the inside of the bag, advising optimal growth conditions—medium sunlight, perennials—but for the solarium, I need more than that, like how much room does it need? How much space for the roots to dig into the soil and latch on? Would it crowd out the rhododendrons? Or creep along the ground? Putting together a garden is like snapping together the pieces of a puzzle, all the different cutouts and shapes needing to align symbiotically.

"What do you think about over here?" I ask, looking at a patch of dirt that I've cleared and cultivated. The soil is dark brown, and it's ready for planting. "Or should I get closer to the begonias?"

"Just fuck me already!"

Effie's voice—*my voice*—echoes off the high glass ceilings. No matter how many times I hear it, I still find it startling.

"We talked about this." Eyes narrowing, I walk over to her cage. "If you want to stay down here with me, you have to be nice."

She bobs her little head. *"Effie's a good girl..."*

I can't help but squirm at her version of Pace's voice. It's easy to imagine him saying that to her because he says it to me often enough.

That's my good girl...

Clearing my throat, I nod. "That's right, a good girl who isn't going to tell her daddy I let her come down here, right?"

Since the break-in, Pace has been keeping Effie in my room. It's almost like he feels better having us together, his two prized possessions rounded up in one place; easier to protect. His paranoia is almost visceral, and although it may sound crazy, I think his energy affects her energy. She's been restless all day, rattling her cage and ruffling her feathers.

I'm not the only one who feels trapped and stir-crazy inside the palace walls.

Earlier, as I pulled on my gardening clothes, I found myself sympathizing with her. I've told Pace before that I thought it was wrong to keep her in the stuffy upstairs bedrooms while there's a perfectly safe place for her to explore. It's not exactly fresh air, but it's *fresher* than being cooped up in the house. The solarium keeps me sane while I'm at the palace.

And right now, she's *basking* in it, wings extended as her head jerks around, eyes taking everything in. She hops from one perch to another, then back again, emitting sounds I've never heard before. Trilling, musical, *happy* sounds.

"*Pretty bird!*" she exclaims in a thin imitation of Pace's voice, hopping to her other perch. "*I'll tell you anything!*" I'm not sure exactly whose voice that is, but afraid the sentiment is a plea, I frown.

"I'd let you spread your wings, but your daddy would absolutely lose his shit," I say, sticking my finger through the bars and rubbing her head. "Maybe next time."

I wait for her to mimic me, but she just bobs her head in agreement, fluttering wildly to the other side of the cage.

"What the *fuck* are you doing?"

I spin to find Pace sprinting down the pathway between garden beds. His eyes are wide and wild, and when he reaches around me to slam the cage door shut, snapping the latch into place, Effie squawks, "*Gentle... gentle...*"

His gaze burns murderously as he towers over me, the vein in his temple popping out. "I made it perfectly clear how I felt about you bringing her down here!"

I shrink back instinctively, heart in my throat, but I take one glance at Effie, so happy and delighted, and gather my courage. "You know I wouldn't hurt her or let her get hurt," I say, *gently*. "She needs sunlight. She needs to spread her wings."

"*Sunlight,*" Effie trills, stretching her neck.

"She needs to be where I leave her!" he snaps, pulling a treat out of his pocket and giving it to her. "I checked the live feed on her cage. Do you have any fucking idea how it feels to expect to see a bedroom, but instead, it's... this?!" He gestures to the glass, the sunlight, the plants. My stomach drops, realizing he thought she'd been taken. But before I can apologize, he keeps hurling his rant at me.

"You know the solarium isn't monitored, so I can't see you when you're in here. I gave you a direct order, and you disobeyed it!"

"I'm sorry I scared you," I say, squaring my shoulders, "but you left her in my room. You want me to watch her, but only on your terms. There's no reason I can't bring her down here other than the fact you're scared!"

He snarls, "I'm not scared."

"Oh, god, please, no!" There's that weird voice again.

Turning to her, Pace pulls in a steadying breath. "It's okay, baby. You're okay." He speaks calmly, but I feel the rage vibrating off him. "Everything's okay, we'll get you back upstairs, and everything will be fine."

"Is this how you plan on raising your kid?" I blurt.

His hand clamps around the top of the cage, but he looks at me, eyes narrowed into dangerous slits. "What does that have to do with anything?"

"It has everything to do with it," I insist, mind whirring. It's the first time it's really hit me that these three men might be responsible for the life growing inside of me. Not just responsible for creating it, but raising it, too. It makes anger flare in my chest. "Are you going to hide our child away like you hide Effie? Are you going to watch them twenty-four hours a day from your little security cave, more focused on screens than reality? Are you going to be too scared to let them experience life?"

"You know what I'm going to do?" He sets the cage back on the ledge and strides over to me. "I'm going to do everything I can to keep what's mine safe, even if that means putting in measures other people think are insane." His finger pushes at my belly. "Just by existing, this baby already has a target on its head, and if you think I won't do everything in my power to protect you both, you don't understand me."

"Protection doesn't always mean locking something up in a cage." Angry tears burn in my eyes. "You can at least give Effie the illusion of freedom, can't you?"

He explodes, "You don't get it, Rosi!" and I flinch back. He bears down on me. "This is *all* an illusion. We're all in cages. Some are bigger than others. Some, like ours, are gilded and comfortable. But that's how being a Royal works. We're trapped behind territory lines. We're in our brownstone, or tower, or crypt. We may be sitting on bombs waiting to go off at any fucking moment. We fight for our brothers, blood or other. We fight for our Kings," he curls his fingers against my belly, "for our heirs. Effie doesn't need to get her hopes up that there's something more out there, because it doesn't fucking matter. This is it for us, Rosi. All of us."

At some point, I realize we've stopped discussing Effie altogether, and my heart sinks. It's Pace's turn to flinch when I reach up to cup his cheek, willing him to see the conviction in my eyes. "I refuse to let that be this baby's future."

He jerks away, jaw set. "There you go again, thinking you have a choice."

It's not the threat he probably means for it to be.

It's probably not directed at me at all.

When he grabs the cage, hauling it up the steps to the house, I know I'll be haunted by the fear in his eyes. It's a fear that's only now forming in my own gut, this gnawing suspicion that I'm growing something in my body that I won't have the right to.

And maybe its father won't, either.

Later that night, the rain beats a staccato against the parlor window, as distracting as it is mesmerizing. Outside, through the dark and the mist, I see Thad, Ashby's head of security, standing watch in the gardens.

"Read 'em and weep!" Stella says, fanning her cards out on the table. "A straight flush!"

I blink at the cards, glancing at Ballsack, who looks just as flummoxed.

"I think we're being hustled," he tells me, throwing down his hand. A pair of aces. Better than mine: a pair of fives. "To the victor," he sighs.

Clapping her hands, Stella rakes in the pot, which consists mostly of pennies, gum, and since this is Five Card West—a special Duke variation of poker that DKS likes to play—also light ammunition. "This one is so shiny!" she gushes, no doubt clueless as to what the shell goes to.

"It's a nine millimeter Luger," he says, shuffling.

Stella and I share a grin. "It's shiny."

Ballsack rolls his eyes, dealing another hand. "Gambling my best ammo to a couple of girls who don't even know how to use them."

When I peek at my hand, I bet a twenty-two cal, four pennies, and a stick of Big Red.

Ballsack folds.

"Sorry," I say, restraining a smile. "I know you'd rather be at the aftergame party with the guys." The Forsyth Royals won their second game of the championship, which I spent beside Lex, watching as Wicker and Pace stole the show on the ice. I squirm, once again remembering how in sync they are. How in sync they *were*, in my bed two mornings ago.

Ballsy makes a gagging sound, falling back in his chair. "Partying with a bunch of prissy East Enders? No, thank you. I'd much rather be here getting my balls handed to me by actual hard-asses."

"Don't you forget it," Stella says, and then, "Oooh, a big one!" She holds another bullet aloft, this one coppery and long, and scrunches her nose. "Aren't they all so phallic? Do you think it's a metaphor? Like, for manhood."

Ballsack looks like he's got a comeback for that, but thankfully he doesn't get the chance to make it.

My Princes come barreling-stumbling-slinking through the door.

Wicker is the stumbler. He's wet from the rain, his blonde hair dripping a raindrop down a defined cheekbone. He draws up short when he sees us, doing a triple take. "The fuck is this?"

Pace, the barreler, enters in a Forsyth hockey sweater, the hood pulled up and glistening with rain. Without a word, he marches to the window and pulls the curtain back, surveying the gardens, which Thad is surely patrolling. Slowly, he looks at me, his tense shoulders beginning to unwind. Not too much, though. He's still pissed at me for taking Effie to the solarium this afternoon.

Lex was the slinker, and he's already reaching up to pull out his hair tie when he walks in, ruffling the dampness from his auburn locks. He takes in the scene—Ballsack, Stella, the cards, the stakes—and freezes, a dangerous glint in his eyes. Wordlessly, he reaches down to pluck up a bullet from Stella's pile, fixing Ballsack with an incredulous glare. "You're using *live rounds* as poker chips? With our *pregnant* Princess?"

Ballsack snorts. "They're centerfire cartridges, not explosives. Perfectly safe."

Lex always gets this way about him when he's about to lose his shit. It's taken me a while, but I'm starting to see. He gets eerily still. More composed than usual. Silent.

But the back of his jaw tics.

"Calm down," I tell him, shuffling the deck. It's monumentally difficult to look at Lex when he's like this, all rumpled, hair down, eyes intense. "I've been around bullets my whole life. They're only dangerous when they're in a gun."

Lex clenches his teeth. "What if there's a fire?"

"Then I think I have bigger problems," I say, deadpan.

Ballsy pipes in, "That thing about fires shooting bullets is a myth, anyway. It's the high velocity from a gun that makes it lethal."

"Oh, shit," Wicker says, stumbling to the table we've set up beside the settee. "You're playing poker, right? That DKS one—Five Card West." He drops beside me on the settee, which is when the smell of beer and vodka hits me.

He is *wasted*.

Wicker slaps the table. "Deal me in. I got ammo." But when he starts patting his back, he snorts a laugh, gesturing to Lex. "Gimme my gun, bro."

Lex scoffs. "Yeah, that's gonna happen. I wouldn't even trust you with a blow dryer right now."

Wicker thrusts a finger at him. "That was one time. *One time.*"

Rolling his eyes, Pace pulls a pistol from his own pants, his deft hands unlocking the clip. "Just let him play. We've been babysitting him all night. Let them have a turn." He throws the clip to Wicker.

It hits him in the chin.

"Ow," he says, but in a worryingly chipper tone.

I wrinkle my nose, leaning away from the toxic cloud emanating from him. "How much did you let him drink?"

"*Let* is a strong word," Lex grumbles, dragging a chair from the corner closer to our twisted tableau. "Wicker's never met a win he couldn't regret in the morning."

Ballsack says, "Hell yeah, to the victor go the spoils," and extends a fist.

To my shock and deep concern, Wicker springs up to bump it. "To the fucking victor, baby! Now deal me in."

I give Lex a dubious glance, but ultimately deal the hand.

Thirty minutes and five hands later, Wicker is going on a slurred diatribe about the thing he loves most. "No, no, no, North Side has the best pussy—or they used to. But West End has the best dick. That's a cop-milent." His pronunciation leaves a lot to be desired.

And the more I think about it, so does his conclusion.

Ballsack humors him with a wary nod. "Thank you?"

Wicker puts his hand on his heart, eyelids slumping. "You're very welcome."

"Hey, Wick?" Lex says, coaxing but obviously fed up. "You don't think you might wanna head to bed?"

Wicker immediately waves this off. "Bed's not where the pussy's at. I mean, it's there, but it's not for me. It's for you. But not for me." He twists to look at his other brother, camped out at the window, still hidden beneath his hood. "It's for Pace. But not for me." He brings a hand down on the table. "Deal me in."

I palm my face. "Good grief."

Stella politely clears her throat, rising from her seat. "I'm actually pretty tired." She badly fakes a yawn.

Ballsack rises with her, agreeing, "It's late. We should rest. Be alert in case there are any more incidents."

From his perch at the window, Pace throws a lazy salute, not looking away from the rain-soaked grounds.

"Oh." Wicker frowns, but seems to bounce back pretty easily. "Okay then. Far be it from me to keep you from fucking like rabbits." He gives them a sloppy, lewd grin. "Wrap it up, kids. Don't wanna find yourselves shackled down to a glorified parasite, do you?"

No one shares his bitter, wheezed laughter.

At least he seems to settle down a bit after they've left, fidgeting with the cards as his demeanor deflates. Despite obviously being three sheets to the wind, he expertly shuffles them in one of those fancy, showy ways that has always eluded my fine motor skills.

I don't know how tonight works. It's my last night in East End. Tomorrow, I'll be ferried back to the territory lines, traded to the Dukes for another case of weapons. It's Wicker's week, but one sniff of him makes it clear I won't be able to stomach it. Already, I'm feeling queasy. And while Pace has slept with us for the past three nights, I hardly expect him to now, given how pissed he is at me.

The silence stretches on, and I'm just about to give Lex a pleading look when his quiet voice rings out. "He got the lab results today." Pace glances at him, his eyes tired and hard, and Lex clarifies, "Father."

"Which ones?" Pace asks, turning more fully.

Wicker gives the deck another flourished shuffle.

"Paternity," Lex answers, tipping his head back against the chair. He massages the bridge of his nose. "Sex."

My stomach is suddenly in my throat, although it strikes me how useless such a reaction is. "He's not going to tell us," I guess.

Lex's eyes drop to mine, his amber stare dark through his eyelashes. "Paternity? Not until the birth. But the sex?"

Pace makes a low, disgusted sound. "He's already setting up for the gender reveal party when you get back to East End. All the streamers, balloons, and ego that can fit into the ballroom."

"So we'll find out then," I say, sighing. "When everyone else does."

Pace and I share a look, and I hear his words seeping through my head like venom.

This is it for us, Rosi. All of us.

Wicker shuffles again.

"Fuck that." It takes me a second to figure out who said it, the words so quiet and sharp. But then Lex jerks up, scrubbing his palms over his face. "Let's find out now."

Wicker chuckles darkly. "What are you gonna do? Break into his office? Hack his files? You'd have an easier time storming Fort Knox. Probably get off lighter, too." It's the first sign he's even been listening to the conversation.

But Lex's eyes are clear, locking on mine. "Father won't be home from his trip for another hour." His eyes flick to Pace. "I've got the ultrasound machine downstairs."

Pace steps away from the window, brows knitting together. "You can tell on that thing?"

"Already?" I gape at him, my heart beginning to flutter again.

Lex shrugs, rising to his feet. "It's early, but still possible."

"Here's a question," Wicker says, fanning the cards out. "Who cares? Girl, boy, it's all the same."

Glaring at him, I reply, "I care," and stand, striding to Lex. Pace gets there first, the three of us pausing to look back.

"Wick," Lex says, rubbing a thumb into his eye. "We do this together, or we don't do it at all."

There's a tense beat where Wicker just dances a card along his knuckles, the curve of his shoulders tired and dejected.

I don't exhale until he pushes to his feet.

~

"COLD," I hiss, clenching up against the ultrasound gel.

Rubbing it in with the wand, Lex says, "Sorry," but it sounds more like, "Deal with it."

Pace is on my other side, hovering over me like a bat. "Is that it?"

"No," Lex says, sliding him a warning look. He pushes the wand harder, the pressure almost too much to bear.

"I should have peed first," I lament, grimacing.

"No, it's good," Lex insists, adjusting his elbow. "The waves travel better through fluid."

From the other side of the room comes a metallic *clink-clink*. "Jesus, this is some medieval shit. We should put one of these down in the dungeon."

Without even glancing away from the screen, Lex says, "Leave the speculum alone, Wick."

He's squeezing it like scissors, and then making a hole with his hand and shoving it through. "Christ," he says, pulling a face. "Another check in the 'glad I have a dick' column."

"That's it, there?" Pace guesses, pointing to the screen.

But Lex shakes his head. "Give me a second."

Huffing, Pace checks his phone. "We've got thirty minutes. You wasted all that time disinfecting—"

But he falls silent when the *woosh* begins filling the room. I'd know that anywhere, even though it's more defined now, louder, thrumming hard like hummingbird wings.

Lex's whole body is tense, like he's straining to hold the position. "There it is," he says. "Right in the center."

He doesn't need to tell me. It's a bigger blob than it was the first couple of times, but most of all, I'm struck dumb by the shape of it. "There's a head," I say, utterly awed. Later, I'll think back on that and laugh. Of course, there's a head. I just couldn't see it last time.

This time, it's so obvious.

The baby has a head.

My baby has a head.

That head could have red hair like me. Or—I think, glancing at a similarly stupefied Pace—curly and dark like him. Or wavy and auburn like Lex. Or blonde like Wicker. It's overwhelming to think of all the potential that head could hold one day. Knowledge. Feelings. Personality.

"I think I see... *oh.*" Lex adjusts, spine straightening, and he glances at me first. That's what I'll remember about the moment, later on—the way his eyes locked on mine before sliding to his brother. "It's a boy."

A loud *clank* makes me jolt, Lex losing the image, but it's just Wicker, casually tossing the speculum aside.

"Hooray," he mutters, and his back might be turned, but I hear the displeasure in his voice. "Another little Ashby soldier."

"Wicker," Pace snaps, not even bothering to glare at him. He's too busy staring at my stomach, his face so stricken that it makes my belly clench. "Fuck," he breathes, pushing away. It's only then that I can place the expression on his face.

Disappointment.

"Why the long face?" Wicker says, holding his arms out limply. "Look at it this way. If it's a girl, she'll be a whore. A boy gets a thirty-three percent shot at being something else." The smile he gives is pure agony.

Suddenly, it's all too real; the heartbeat, the shape of the body, the sex. A boy. God help us all. All the angst, the emotion, the fucked-up-ness of it all slams into my chest, and as much as I hate crying in front of these assholes, I release a choked-up sob.

All three of the brothers' gazes snap toward me, but after a stretch of silence, Lex is the one to speak.

"Get the fuck out," he barks, tightening his grip on the wand and yanking it away from my stomach. "Both of you, get the fuck out of here before I toss you out myself."

"Chill out," Wicker drawls. "Just because—"

In a flash, I see why Lex was a goalie. His reflexes are lightning-fast, his body coiled and ready to strike. One thing is certain, no one is getting between him and me. Not even his brothers.

"Go," he repeats. "I know you're both fucked in the head over this, but that doesn't mean you get to upset her. For everything this means to us, it means a thousand times more to her."

I look away, wiping my eyes, not seeing but hearing them leave. After a tense moment, there's a long, tired sigh, and then Lex returns to my side. "I'm sorry about that. They're just..."

"Scared," I answer, knowing they don't deserve an ounce of grace. "I know. This is so scary."

He looks at me, his wild hair framing his face, and then reaches forward to cup my cheek, thumb wiping away a tear. All the rage that he showed his brothers has vanished. "Pace knows what it means to be a boy in this house. He just has to process it in his own way. And Wick," that tic in his jaw returns, "he'll come around."

I'm not sure either of us believes that.

"Can you..." I look down at the sonogram wand, gulping down the remnants of a sob. "Can you show me again? The baby?"

He blinks, fingers sliding away from my cheek. "Of course."

"And show me everything? All I really saw was a blob." I brace myself for another squirt of the cool gel, but this time when he squeezes it out, it's less startling. Lex presses the wand over my belly, and he's faster this time, locating the fetus—no, locating *him*—quickly. The *woosh-woosh* of the heartbeat fills the room.

He clears his throat. "So here's his head, obviously," he says, pointing to the screen. "And the heartbeat, see it move?"

I watch the tiny vibrating spot thud faster than I'd expect. "Yes."

"Then we have the spine and the other organs. They're hard to see because they're all smushed together, but this," he grabs a pencil off the cart and taps it against the screen, at what looks like an elbow or knee or maybe a tail, "that's the sex organ. His tiny penis."

"So it's really a boy."

A grin tugs at his mouth as he assesses the screen. "It really is."

It might be the first time I've ever seen him smile a *real* smile. No bitterness or spite or malice driving it. Just this small, delighted quirk of his mouth.

He looks beautiful.

I wait for the wave of fear and upset. The doom of reality at knowing I'll bring another spoiled Royal into this world. It never comes. Instead, I'm struck by a sense of awe, protectiveness, and truth.

I just see my baby boy.

Our baby boy.

16

Lex

It's still raining the next morning, when I park my SUV in the old diner parking lot. The service road we took to get here is flooded out, not to mention half of South Side. Over the speakers, the DJ—a creepy junior who runs the underground college radio—is talking about the crisis not so unlike a stoned art major. The broadcasts are more riddle than news, but Verity has taken a strange liking to them.

"Seventy-two more hours of rain," the radio crackles. He sounds like he's inhaling from a cigarette or a blunt. "Grab a boat and some critters, because Forsyth is going biblical. If it doesn't wash away our sins, they'll probably bob to the surface and start floating down the Avenue like discarded Scratch baggies. If that worries you, then you're a Royal. If it doesn't, then congratulations. You're nothing. Can you think of anything better to be?"

Through the fog of the windshield, I see Nick Bruin and Remy Maddox just standing out beside their car, not even caring about how soaked they're getting. Their King, Sy Perilini, is smarter, waiting in his own SUV.

I twist to look at my brothers in the back seat. As I fully expected last night, Wicker looks miserable, his pallor a touch green. He's wearing a pair of designer shades, as if the sun would dare peek through the thick, gloomy clouds. "Go check the supply," I tell them.

Without a word, Pace raises his hood, wrenching his door open. He's been quiet since last night—or, come to think of it, since yesterday morning.

He doesn't even give Verity any parting words.

Wicker groans, wrapping his hand around a white umbrella. "I'm too hungover for this shit," he grumbles, opening his own door. I could tell him it's his own fault, but it'd be pointless.

When their doors shut, Wicker battling with the umbrella outside the windows, I turn to her, noting the dark circles under her eyes. She's not the only one fighting through the exhaustion of a restless night. I made her ride shotgun this morning, just so I could steal glances at her belly.

A boy.

I hadn't really given much thought to it one way or another, only now that I know, it feels absolute, as if it could have never been any other way.

Now, I cut the engine, nothing but the low volume of the DJ's rant and the sound of the rain pelting the roof to disturb us. "That's for you," I say, nodding to the cup of coffee in the center console.

Her eager green eyes jump to it. She was in the car when I made the order and picked it up, but she's waited, strangely obedient about the process of my giving it to her. "Thank you," she whispers, reaching to take it. For a long moment, she just clutches it close, letting it warm her, and there's a curl to her lips that I'm not used to seeing.

Odd how she latches on to such a small pleasure.

"Why did you do it?" I don't want to ask the question. It's not how I work. I'm a studier; the kind of person who'd rather solve a mystery than ask for the answer. But I find myself suddenly needing to know. I jerk my chin toward Wicker, who's trying very hard to saunter up to the boundary line, but mostly just looks like he wants to double over and barf. "Why did you tell them his secret? You clearly don't like him, and he probably treated you like shit during the deposits, but you don't want to see him dead."

"Wicker?" she asks, expression souring as she watches him lope up to Bruin. "What if I do?"

My reply is matter-of-fact. "You don't." This is what's been bugging me. Hatred is easy. Forsyth is drowning in it, body after body, and it doesn't need a calculation. Survival is easier; animals just wanting to come out on top to see another day. But Verity told the Duchess about Wicker being a Kayes, and I need to know.

I need to know which it is.

"Was it revenge?" I press. She had a million ways of getting back at us over her weeks in the palace that wouldn't have left a trace. Why that one? I gesture out the window. "You sleep with him. You let him hold you. You might hate him, and you don't let him fuck you, but you don't want to see him killed over what you did."

She scoffs. "How do you know?"

It's been bothering me, the fact that I do. It was her wide, glistening eyes as she took him in that day he got beat down on the ice. She was careful, so fucking gentle as she straddled him, drawing his deposit out of him like a thorn, all because she didn't want to be the cause of someone's pain.

Not even his.

Looking at the Dukes, Maddox hauling a crate from the vehicle, I wonder, "Or was it just allegiance? You're that loyal to them?" It doesn't really hold up, either. Someone that loyal would have fought tooth and nail during negotiations, and I've seen the footage of it. She basically let her mother negotiate on her behalf. She wanted to go home, but she wasn't willing to go to war over it.

"That's between me and him." She glances at me, eyes hardening. "Why does it matter? What's done is done."

That's the crux of it. Truthfully, any one of those reasons would be valid and sensible. "Because I need to know what the mother of our son is capable of." That's the cause of my sleeplessness: that this wild, heavy, aching thing in my chest has attached itself to the baby she's carrying, and I don't know if she'll love it for being hers, or hate it for being ours.

Her gaze snaps to me, flashing in outrage, and in that second, I have my answer. "Why did *you* do the cleansing?" she asks, the fire in her eyes hot enough to boil the flooded streets. "Because I know just what the fathers of my son are capable of, and it's far worse than locker room gossip."

This is easy. "Because it's not just between you and him. That's not how we work." When she looks away, I reach out to touch the tense line of her jaw, drawing her gaze back to mine. "You understand that now, right?"

Her green eyes blaze into mine, but it's not just anger I see. "I understand that every time you fuck me in the dark, all I can see is the way you held me down and hurt me."

I jerk my hand away from her like she's lava.

"What I did..." She gives a grim chuckle, glancing out at the trade-off presently happening. "This may come as a shock to someone like you, but I didn't actually do it to hurt Wicker. I didn't do it to hurt any of you." Reaching down, she grabs her bag, voice thick with unshed tears. "That's all you need to know about the mother of your son. That she's human and has a soul, which is more than she can say for his fathers."

Gripping the wheel, I say, "That's not fair."

She explodes, "Nothing about this is fair, Lex!"

We're both tense, breathing hard, and I find myself too tired to tolerate it. "Is this how it's going to be? You hating us for fulfilling our obligation, fucking us over because of it, and then us getting our payback?" I turn my head, locking onto her miserable gaze. "We know how that will end."

Bloody, probably.

What's another body or three to float down the flooded streets?

"You tell me," she says, a challenge in her eyes.

But all I can offer is the way I cradle her cheek in my palm, drawing her soft lips to mine. "We're trying," I say, never closing my eyes. The kiss is testing and too brief, her jaw still clenched when I pull away. In that moment, I wish I were Wicker, who can reduce girls to a pile of goo with nothing but a look. I've never been able to do that.

Verity's eyelashes flutter, but her expression is shuttered. "I've never tried harder at anything in my entire life."

Maybe I'm not the only one afraid of letting shit go.

The sound of her door slamming reverberates hard enough to jostle me in my seat. I watch soundlessly as she trudges through the puddles toward her Dukes, the DJ's voice rolling through the cab.

"The river is rising," he says. "Now it's your turn. Wake up and smell that beautiful decay, Forsyth..."

"HAVE you seen any of my hair ties?" I ask, rummaging around the drawer of my bedside table. "The ones I use at night?" I'm in pajamas, ready to settle down for the night, but I don't want to sleep with my hair down, and I'm not willing to risk split ends on a shitty rubber band.

"Sorry, I haven't," Danner says, resting the tray of bedtime drinks on the dresser. There are three, one for each of us. It's a rare night that we're all at home.

The only glass missing is Verity's disgusting milk.

The first time she left the palace for West End, it was a relief. Everyone was bitter and raw after the cleansing and Valentine's Day. I know I was pissed, my anger consuming me as I plotted ways to hurt her the way she hurt me.

But this time, things feel different. All week, the palace has been quiet, devoid of her little movements through the halls, around her bedroom, the high-pitched incessant chatter of her handmaiden echoing off the vaulted ceilings. More than once, I'll catch the scent of her perfume and head into the corridor, thinking I'll get a glimpse of her before remembering she's gone—back to her people.

"Would you like me to look in the Princess' room?" he asks. "It's possible they got mixed in with her personal accoutrements."

I grunt in irritation, but say, "I'll go. Thank you, Danner."

It's amazing how many ways she's infiltrated our lives. Her scent, her belongings, *our* belongings mixing with hers. It strikes me again as I step across the threshold to her room. The bed is made up, but Wicker's pillow is neatly leaning against the headboard, my blanket is still folded at the foot, and Effie's cage is near the window. Much to my brother's irritation, after leaving her in the Princess' room, Effie has started shunning her live feed, preferring the view outside this window. Even at night, it's the best view in the house, so I can't blame her. Something tells me Effie prefers the bright daylight and soft colors in here over the dark, screen-filtered light in Pace's room.

"Pretty bird," she croons when she sees me.

"Sure are," I say, walking over and getting a treat out of the pouch. "A very pretty bird who hopefully hasn't been hiding my hair ties."

Effie, the impossible klepto she is, goes through phases where she likes to knick various baubles. *"Oh, god,"* she squawks. *"I'll tell you anything!"*

Grimacing at the weak imitation of Gary Troy's voice—a job we had months ago to extract information regarding adultery and some light embezzlement—I narrow my eyes at her. "You wouldn't last three seconds in the dungeon."

It's then that I pause, noticing the sound of running water.

We'd know if she was back. Pace wouldn't let that slip past him, but still, my pulse thrums at the possibility of her being here. I didn't leave things the best when we traded her back to the Dukes. I've taken her coffee the past two mornings, but all I've gotten is a grateful nod and more of her 'performance' as Princess. It's new and annoying, the scratching *need* in my chest to settle this constant friction.

For the sake of the baby, of course. Seeing her on campus, getting remote updates on the heartbeat, and trusting her to stick to the diet while she's gone doesn't satisfy my need to keep track.

Any hope for that shatters when I find a pile of clothes on the floor: jeans and a pair of three-hundred dollar limited-edition sneakers.

You've *got* to be kidding me. I open the shower door and stare blankly at Wicker, who's lathered hair to toe.

Unflinchingly, he nods. "Hey."

"What are you doing?" I snap, harsher than I should.

He tips his head back under the spray, looking totally fucking euphoric. "Have you taken a shower in here? It's huge. There's a fucking bench. I mean, really, a *bench*. Perfect for fucking. Dual shower heads, waterfall feature..." He points to the ceiling, then grabs a bottle off the shelf and squeezes a large dollop into his palm. "And her shower gel really makes my skin soft. It's not like she's using it, right?"

I'm about to suggest he buy his own bottle of shower gel, but there's no point. Stepping back, I leave him soaping up his balls and wander to the vanity. I dig around, looking for a hairband, but the only ones I find are too small and not my brand.

Damn it.

"I'm finished," Wick calls. "Want me to leave it on?"

Rolling my eyes, I call back, "No, I'm just looking for a hairband."

"I saw some the other day," he says, shutting off the water. There's some intermittent dripping, and then, "Top drawer of her bedside table."

Shit, my dick gets hard thinking about how Verity likes to let my hair down when I'm fucking her. Probably got lost in the sheets. Of course, the second I lay eyes on the bed again, I'm reminded of her barbed words from Monday morning.

"...every time you fuck me in the dark, all I can see is the way you held me down and hurt me."

I stare at it for a long second, that place in the middle of the bed where I'd usually drag her, taking my fill. The sex is always hurried and hungry, and despite fucking myself into exhaustion during my week, the need is already building again. It's the only time I let myself separate her from what she is. When I'm inside of her, crashing into her body, she's no longer the vessel, a patient, or my duty.

She's just the woman who turns me into the worst parts of myself.

I've just opened the drawer when Wick walks in, dried off and in a pair of boxers.

"Found it," I say, snagging the silk tie. Wicker approaches the bed and pulls back the covers. "What are you doing?"

His hair is damp, tongue prodding the corner of his lips. "I special ordered these sheets that first week I slept in here. They finally came in." He sprawls out languidly, running his hand over the pale blue sheets. "Holy shit, feel that. It's like petting a baby lamb."

After tying back my hair, I roll my eyes but touch the sheets. "That's nice." Better than the silk. *Better for fucking*, my brain unhelpfully provides.

"Right?" He stretches out, resting his head on his hands. The lure of Egyptian cotton is too much to bear, and I pull back the rest of the blankets and get in. He slides me a slick grin. "Nice, huh?"

"Pretty fucking nice." Definitely better for fucking.

"Jesus Christ, what the hell is this?"

We both look over at the doorway, Pace glaring at us like we've lost our minds.

"Just fuck me already!" Effie snaps.

I don't think I'm the only one whose balls tighten up when we hear Verity's voice mimicked.

"No," he says, crossing over to her cage. He's dressed for bed like we are, shirtless and weary around the eyes. "I told you not to say that anymore."

"We're testing Wicker's new sheets," I say as if that justifies the situation. I lean over and pick up the book on the bedside table. It's one of the pregnancy books I gave her, and a flicker of annoyance runs through me at the fact she left it. We made a deal.

Flipping through it, I note the pages are creased toward the end.

Huh.

Maybe she finished.

Across the room, Effie rattles her cage, letting Pace know she doesn't want to leave. "*Sunlight!*"

"It's the dead of night!" he argues.

She retorts, *"Oh, god, please, no!"*

He throws his hands in the air. "Fine! You can stay, but don't freak out when you're all alone in the middle of the night."

"What's in that book anyway?" Wick asks, noticing me flipping through it.

Shrugging, I reply, "Mostly just an overview of what new mothers should expect during pregnancy. It goes week to week covering body changes, do's and don'ts, things you should prepare for, lists of supplies."

Wicker props on his elbow, a little divot appearing between his brows. "So... what about this week?"

Since I've already taken out my contacts, I reach into my pocket and pull out my glasses. To my surprise, Pace opens Effie's cage, beckoning her to hop onto a finger, and then carries her over to the bed. Without prompting, she jumps to the footboard, extending her wings as Pace shoves me over.

"Okay, here we go," I say, thumbing through the pages. "Week fourteen of pregnancy marks a significant milestone for both the expectant mother and her developing baby. You're experiencing a whole new set of changes. Your baby is moving their arms and legs, and is developing their senses of smell and taste."

Wicker looks grossed out. "Does that mean she can feel it moving around in there?"

But I shake my head. "He's still too small. She probably won't feel movement for another few weeks." Clearing my throat, I continue, "At this point, the fetus is approximately the size of a lemon, measuring about 3.4 inches and weighing around 1.5 ounces."

Pace, who's laying on his back beside me, screws his face up. "I'll never get this obsession with comparing fetuses to fruit. Wasn't it just a plum a couple weeks ago?"

"It's a visibly accessible sense of scale," I insist. "Next week will be... uh, apple."

Wicker fluffs his pillow grumpily. "This shit is really ruining pies for me."

Snorting, I continue, "In terms of prenatal care, week fourteen is a good time for expectant mothers to discuss various screening options and genetic testing with their healthcare provider. These tests, along with parental familial health history, can provide valuable information about the baby's health and any potential risks, allowing parents to make informed decisions about their pregnancy journey."

A tense hush falls over the room.

In some ways, I know too much about my parents' history, but in others, I know nothing. Looking over, I know Wicker is the same. He's a Kayes. But what is a Kayes, exactly? No one knows. His family line is known best for being elusive and mysterious. There won't be much medical history on them anywhere.

And Pace...

His dark eyes are distant, lost in thought.

Until suddenly, he looks at me. "Michael's cancer."

Shrugging helplessly, I confess, "All I've been told is that there weren't any abnormal genetic markers."

Pace exhales, which is when Danner appears, stopping in the doorway with an unblinking stare. "Boys," he says, waddling into the room as he balances the tray with our drinks. "I've been searching high and low for you. Your erratic sleeping arrangements never fail to keep one on their toes."

Frowning, I insist, "We're not sleeping in here."

"Of course." Danner arches a brow before setting the tray down on the nightstand.

Pace reaches for Wicker's first, straining over my body to hand it to him, and then mine. The three of us watch as Danner leaves, silent until the door has closed.

It's only then that I keep reading. "Your little one is beginning to look more and more like the person you'll meet after birth. As a bonus, you may have increased energy and more lustrous hair and nails during this trimester."

Beside me, Pace groans.

"What?" Wick asks, blue eyes flicking to him.

Scowling at the ceiling, Pace reaches down to adjust his junk.

"You know how her hair does it for me. Shinier and more lustrous? I can't take it."

"That's how I feel about her stomach," I admit, leaning back as I remember gliding the ultrasound transducer over the slight swell of her belly. "I thought it'd be weird seeing her get bigger and... I don't know. Thicker? But knowing it's because our baby is growing in there..." I shrug, face feeling suddenly warm. "It's hot." Then I turn to Pace, wondering, "Isn't it?"

He swallows. "Yeah."

Wick pulls the sheet up over his abs. "Well, I bought her new bras because her tits were trying to wrestle their way out of the old ones. *Expensive* ones. You're welcome, by the way," he says, "since I'm not going to get to enjoy them."

"I doubt she's going to let me back in here," Pace says, glancing around the room. His eyes are heavy, drooping. "Not after the fight we had in the solarium."

"What was that about anyway?" I ask, placing my thumb in the book to hold the page.

There's a long beat where Pace just chews on his bottom lip, a hardness to his brow that suggests he's fighting sleep. "She asked if I was going to treat the baby like I do Effie, keeping her locked up all the time."

"Obviously, yes." Wicker snorts, and when Pace swings a glare on him, adds, "Come on, you're a control freak. It's why you'd rather sit in your room all day watching security feeds than be an actual part of the world."

"In there, you control all the conditions. You're a *god*. All-seeing, all-knowing. But out there?" I gesture vaguely toward the window. "Out there, you're just a whim of fate. You can't handle it. You can barely handle it when Wick and I go on jobs without you."

Pace's frown darkens with each word, but I'd be lying if I said I haven't been thinking about it. We're going to have to wind all our neuroses into a single knot in order to raise a kid together. I don't know what that looks like, but I know it won't be whatever our son needs.

"How else do you keep something safe?" he asks. As if she understands him, Effie hops onto his ankle, walking up the long length of his shin. He strokes his hand down her inky feathers. "How do you live the life of a Royal, see all the jacked-up shit we have, and not be fucking terrified sending something you care about out into that sewer of depravity?"

"Hell if I know," I say. "That's why I just focus on her health. It's what I *can* do."

"Why are we acting like this matters?" Wicker's low, cutting words draw my gaze to him. "You keep talking about this thing like it's already ours."

"Because it is," I argue.

His blue eyes flash in frustration. "It's *his*. You really think he's going to let any of us raise this thing? He probably already has every second of its life all planned out." Raising a hand, he lists off on his fingers, "Nanny, nanny, special academy, nanny. We're a non-factor. Which, personally, works fine for me."

"No." My reply is hard as nails. "I won't let that happen."

But Pace's low voice rings out, "Wick's right," and when I glance at him, all the pensive calculation in his eyes has disappeared. "We're not going to have a choice in anything. The sooner we accept that, the easier it'll be when it happens."

But I won't accept that. Not for a fucking second. I don't know where it comes from or why, but I know I'd go down swinging for the right to my own goddamn son.

I start to close the book, but Wicker's hand comes down over the top. "What are you doing?" he asks. "Cliffhanger much?"

"It's late." I'm tired, and I blame being in this bed for making me feel, well, *things*... other than sleepy.

Pace carries Effie over to her cage and closes her in. He drapes the cloth over the top and returns to the bed, nudging Wicker to the middle. "One more chapter, bro." He stretches out, resting his head on his bicep. "I need to know what to expect next week. You know, other than the apple thing."

Sighing, I flip the page, and start, "Week fifteen is an exciting time, as you're well into the second trimester..."

At what point do I get used to this, I wonder? The repetition. The sense of dread. The slick sweat on my back that appears the second I step into Father's office.

I smell my brothers before I see them, the faint scent of nerves striking as I shut the door behind me. They're stiff and in position, standing in front of Father's desk.

It makes it worse that I haven't the faintest idea what this is about, and from the crease on Pace's forehead and the twitch in Wicker's fingers, they don't either. There's a terrified part of me that wonders if this is about getting knocked out of the tournament. They lost their game two days ago and although Pace and Wick hadn't been happy about it, I got the sense they were both happy to be done with the season. I'd been waiting for Father's commentary on the loss, and maybe this is it. None of that blame belongs on me, but that's not how this works. My brothers failed to secure the win. That fallout may land on my back. Literally.

"Sorry I was late," I say, stepping into place. "My lecture ran long."

Father is busy writing in one of his ledgers, and the twist of anxiety in my stomach threatens to go straight to my bowels. We stand in silence, the clock ticking behind us, until he shuts the book, caps his pen, and glances up.

"I've been going over what occurred while I was away on my business trip. The security footage, the evidence found on the grounds by Thad, and of course, your own reports." He glances at Pace, then Wicker, while I slowly process that this isn't about hockey. "The timing is surely suspect, and I can't rule out that it wasn't orchestrated to happen in my absence from the palace, but from my audit of the events that happened that night, it seems things were handled well." He focuses his attention. "Whitaker."

He stands a little straighter, even though his heart doesn't look in it, a little sigh falling from his nose. "Yes, sir."

Father's gaze takes him in for a long beat. "It was your quick action that corralled the Princess to the safe room. And although the decision to arm the Bruins' boy was risky, in this circumstance, I approve."

Wicker loses some of his stiff posture, but it's not relief. It's as if he's too tired to hold it. "I'm glad to hear that."

Father adds, "His loyalty to the Princess is clear. Adding another man to protect her while you and your brother searched the grounds was smart. The heir is our number one priority, and you acted beyond reproach."

Wicker dips his chin. "Thank you, Father."

He shifts his gaze next to me. "Pace, it's my understanding that you managed to land one of your shots."

Pace is stiffer, eyes fixed on Father's desk. "Yes, sir."

Father taps the wood with his pen. "I'm disappointed we weren't able to recover the intruder." The statement hangs in the air. Father's disappointment is always worse than his anger.

"Yes, that was my failure," Pace says in a subtle attempt to cover for Wicker. "It was dark, and the cover was limited. I should have done more. I wanted to follow, but the conditions didn't make a pursuit safe or practical, and we really wanted to get back inside with the Pri—" he swallows, "*heir*."

"As you should have." His agreement startles us all. "Your aim was true, and the injury was substantial enough for a blood sample. You and your brother both acted exactly as we'd practiced, and I'd like to reward you for your discipline." He stands, reaching for a gold case on his desk, and holds it out to Pace. His smile is wide and bright, sending a chill up my spine. "For being the first to sound the alarm and for hitting your target, I felt like it was time."

Pace regards the box before warily reaching out. Only when Father nudges it closer does my brother finally grasp it, a skeptical slant to his mouth as he turns it over, inspecting it. Slowly, he unlatches it, lifting the lid to reveal a key.

There's a shiny metal crest on it.

Plucking it from the box, Pace frowns as the crest spins, the other side bearing a golden bull and a single word.

Lamborghini.

"You got me a car?" he says, gaze snapping up in shock. After his arrest, Father sold Pace's prized Mustang. Since returning home from prison, he's only been allowed to drive one of the vehicles in the garage downstairs. "A Lamborghini?"

Fully understanding the fear in Pace's eyes, I edge a little closer. A gift this nice from Father doesn't come without strings.

Even when he insists, "You deserve it for your hard work over the past few months. Your dedication to East End is worth rewarding."

"T-t-thank you," he stammers, looking equal parts surprised and nervous.

"And for Wicker..." Father announces, complete with a dramatic pause. "One night off, any event or obligation of your choosing." My eyes ping between Wick and Father. This is big. Bigger than a Lamborghini. Father fixes him with a stern look. "I get veto power, naturally."

"Of course," Wick says, shoulders still tense. "Thank you for your generosity."

There's a long silence, and then Father says, "You're both excused. I need a moment with Lagan."

My stomach drops. Paces' fingers pinch around the key ring while Wicker gives me a long look. I barely lift my chin, letting them know it's okay. Whatever's coming, I can handle it.

My brothers passed the test, but I wasn't here. Anxiety rolls through me as the door clicks shut, and I'm left alone with Father. I force my gaze forward, away from the box in the corner. Will he make me go get it myself?

For the first time in my life, I wonder what would happen if I refused.

Standing, he rounds the desk, looking dangerously casual. "I'm aware you were at the clinic when the intruder breached the palace walls."

The back of my neck prickles. "Yes, sir."

"But," he adds, "You promptly, and without arousing suspicion, searched the hospital records of various medical facilities to see if anyone was admitted."

I nod. "Yes, sir. Unfortunately, there were no patients with gunshot wounds that night, nor in the following days."

He hums, seemingly aware. "Even more evidence that it was an attack from another house. Most, if not all, are equipped with medics that can attend to a gunshot wound." He leans against the desk, pressing his fingers together in thought. "Thad tells me that you took possession of the DNA and immediately secured it."

"Yes, sir." I swallow. "It was a solid sample. If you'd like me to hand over a portion to the police, I can."

But he shakes his head. "No. I'd prefer not to get them involved at this point. There is another option, but it requires absolute discretion." His eyes dart to the door. "Even from your brothers."

My mind swirls, mostly from the realization that I'm not being punished. But what is this? What is he ordering now?

I bite back a sigh. "Whatever you need me to do, Father. You know I'm at your service."

He nods, as if that's all he needed. My absolute fealty. "I'm giving you full access to the palace blood samples. The likelihood that the intruder was someone we already have in our system, or a relative of someone in our system, is high. I'm sure you'd agree. I'd like you to begin running these against one another and see if you can find a match."

My gaze whips to him, widening. "The entire database?" There are hundreds, if not thousands, of blood samples that Father has taken over the years. Every member of PNZ. Every man or woman tortured in the dungeon, every employee, every whore, every person father deemed necessary.

"An attack on my heir requires me to use the full force of my resources." His eyes meet mine, a warning glinting through. "But you are the only one I can trust with this. And that includes the privacy of the donors of the samples and any connection to others. As the revelation about Verity being my daughter has proven, bloodlines among the Royals are thinner than the space between each territory." He clears his throat, straightening. "Pace would love to get his hands on any bit of leverage he could use against our enemies, but he's still too brash and impulsive. Whitaker doesn't need any other excuse for petulance. The less he knows, the better. But you," he gives me a knowing grin, "you understand the oath between a patient and their doctor. The sensitivity of this kind of information can't be overstated. You'll look at it under the lens of a scientist and find the bastard that dared threaten my blood."

Reeling, I agree, "Yes, sir. I will."

He hands me a slip of paper bearing nothing but a code.

A code that I know will open the security lock on the refrigerator where he keeps each and every sample he's ever taken. It's not a new car, or a night off, but it's something much greater.

Trust.

17

Pace

I HATE WAITING.

Something about it feels wrong, like I should be using my time more wisely. Part of that is the conditioning I can't seem to shake off from my time in prison, sitting in a cell for eight hours and wasting away the hours on any little thing. A bigger part is the way Father is always sure to fill every block of each day with *something.* Today's outing was approved weeks ago, but it still feels illicit, as if I'm shirking some greater duty.

There's a bench beneath the awning of the student union that has a complete view of the courtyard, and that's where I sit, staring off into the distance at somber clouds and the occasional flash of lightning. I'm both exhausted and wired, fueled by little more than caffeine and spite. It's Tuesday, and there may have been a time I looked forward to the weekend, but I can't remember it.

"You're late," I say as Verity walks up, sparing her a discreet glance.

Everything feels wrong.

"I had to pee," she says, tugging at her black leggings. To my annoyance, her belly is hidden under an oversized sweater, just like it has been for the past two weeks. The crew neck does nothing to hide her tits, however. It's a West End outfit; tight in all the wrong places and street-casual, including those scuffy sneakers she likes to wear. Nose wrinkling, she squirms. "Apparently, your son likes to sit on my bladder like a bean bag."

She glides past me, opening her umbrella and stepping out in the rain. Her casual use of those words—*your son*—shakes me, and I run after her, stepping foot first into a puddle.

"Damn it!" I sidestep it, but not before tepid water seeps into my boot. I shake it off and jog toward her, trying to catch a glimpse of her belly. "Wait the fuck up."

I slide under the umbrella, wrapping my hand around the handle. She cuts me a smug look at being so close to her.

"I'm still pissed," I tell her, eyes dropping to her stomach, "but I already got soaked waiting for you to get out of class." I direct her toward the road that cuts between buildings. "I parked over there."

The black Lamborghini sits next to the curb. Slick and shiny from the rain. The inside is top-of-the-line, all leather and chrome with updated features, wireless access, and a screen in the dash. Jesus, the first time I sat in it, I basically got a boner.

The only thing that would be better is actually getting off in the car. I peek over at Verity, at those soft, plump lips, remembering how good they feel wrapped around my cock.

Nope. *No.*

Not after what she did.

"What the shit?" I ask, darting out from under the umbrella to the side of the car. A yellow, rectangular piece of paper is stuck under the wiper. I snatch the soggy paper out and read the blurred print. "A parking ticket?"

"You're in a fire lane, dumbass," Verity says, continuing past me to the passenger side.

Crumpling the paper in my fist, I intercept her, blocking her before she opens the door. "Show me." The demand is gruff, impatient, and more than a little aggressive. Oh well.

It's been a shitty day.

I deserve it.

She squints up at me, face twisted in confusion. "Show you what?"

I gesture to her belly. "*Him.*"

Her cheeks pinken, eyes casting around the parking lot, which is practically deserted. Heaving a sigh, she reaches for the hem of her oversized shirt, yanking it up. "Happy?" she mutters, tugging it back down.

Or, she tries to.

I jolt forward to catch her wrist, rucking the shirt back over the swell of her belly. Half of it's hidden by her pants, and I don't think twice about hooking my fingers into the waistband, tugging it down.

Once I have the bump of her belly exposed, I pause.

Fuck.

"You've been hiding the way you're growing," I say, unwilling to mask the anger that rises at the thought. "That's a problem. We're entitled to see this. To feel it." Unthinkingly, I press my palms to it, dwarfing her belly with my wide hands. "You should come back early."

"What?" She tries to jerk away, green eyes flashing in panic. "That's not the deal."

"It's only a couple weeks," I argue as I tug her back, but it's weak. I already know it's not possible. "It's... warm," I say of her belly, forehead screwing up. "Is it supposed to be this warm?"

In a wry voice, she offers, "I do have body heat."

Oh.

Right.

There are long creases in her skin where the waistband of her leggings has made an impression, and I wish I could smooth them away. My fingertips glide across them, watching as her stomach twitches in reaction.

They look like scars.

Clearing my throat, I release her, reaching behind me to open her door. "Try not to get everything soaked," I mutter as she snaps the umbrella shut and stuffs it on the pristine floorboard.

"Me?" she snorts, adjusting her pants again. "I'm not the one who can't control my fluids."

"Yeah, well," flustered, I start the car, the windshield wipers scraping smoothly across the window, "I don't hear a lot of complaints out of you when you're begging me to plug them inside."

She scowls, but I bet if I checked her cunt right now, she'd be dripping, dying for me to be inside her.

No. God, stop thinking about her pussy.

It's impossible, though, with her sitting next to me, her scent ripe and raw from the rain. She's been away from the palace for two weeks, and I don't like it. My hands tighten on the wheel as I remember waking up in her bed this morning—just like I have for the past week—Wicker clutching me like a fucking octopus as Lex showered just beyond the bathroom door. That's another change. It barely feels like 'her' room anymore. How could it, when she's not in it?

Wicker's new sheets don't even smell like her.

And it pisses me off.

I force myself to focus on the drive, not the girl next to me, ready to tick this chore off the box.

"We don't have to do this," she says suddenly. Her hair is damp and frizzy, the humid May heat rolling into Forsyth like a damp exhale, and she's staring at her fingernails, picking at a cuticle. "You don't want to. I don't want to. You should just take me back to campus."

I glance over, trying to suss out what's going on here. When her expression reveals nothing useful, I break, too impatient for games today, "Because you're desperate to get back to your gutter rats, or because you're scared of going to the spa? Because I assure you, nothing's happening to you at the spa except some garden variety pampering."

It's a little comical, stepping away from all my obligations in order to have my Princess plucked and shined. Danner or her handmaid could have taken her, but she asked me to be here. Specifically. And now that I'm here beside her, something inside the core of my being begins unwinding. Relaxing. Calming.

It's the first time I've seen her in person in *days*.

There was a time when a glimpse of her on the monitors would have settled the restless storm in my chest, but it's stopped being enough.

I need to touch her.

Reaching over, I place my hand on hers, stilling her picking fingers. "We're here."

I ease the car to a stop in front of the Gilded Rose. The only private appointment we could get was during her time in West End. It didn't seem like a big deal at the time, but that was before she risked Effie's life.

Her palm flattens over her stomach, green eyes scanning the parking lot. "You promise you won't leave?"

So she *is* scared. Begrudgingly, I promise, "I'm not leaving you in there alone."

"It's just..." She chews on her lip, eyes tight. "The girls are still really mad about the whole thing."

"Have they done anything—*specifically?*" I ask, willing to go nuclear on some prissy bitches if I have to.

But she shakes her head. "No. Just bitchy girl stuff. They're pros. I know their anger is misplaced. I didn't force their boyfriends to be total jackoffs, but things are tense enough that if they found out I was coming back here, they may look for a way to retaliate." She looks at me, holding my gaze. "And things are hard enough, you know?"

Looking at her then might be the hardest thing I've done all week because I know that look in her eyes. Tired but persistent, weak but fierce, defeated but determined. This is how it gets you. First, it's the obligations, and then the enemies, people on all sides. One day, my brothers and I just stopped caring about the future because we didn't have the capacity. Not when all of our energy was spent making it through the week—the day—the hour.

Now more than ever before, she has the eyes of an Ashby.

"Rosi, do you know how freaked out Adeline was when she saw what they did? In her business, and not just to any client, but the fucking reigning Princess?" I shake my head at the way she pretty much groveled when I came to make the appointment. "Even if I wasn't here, I can promise you that woman isn't going to let a hair on your head get damaged."

She takes a deep breath, lashes fluttering. "I know. I'm just being paranoid."

"Yeah," I mutter, looking out the window, "this city has a way of doing that to people."

The rain outside has decreased to a drizzle, so there's no need for the umbrella on the way into the spa. Adeline meets us at the door, immediately fawning over Verity.

"Oh my goodness, you're glowing even brighter, Miss Sinclaire!" She glances up at me and smiles, taking my limp hand in a firm handshake. "Mr. Ashby, it's so good to see you again." She tilts her head. "I have to remind you that there's a no-weapons policy inside the spa."

"Why do you assume I'm carrying?" I ask, crossing my arms over my chest. "Because I have a record?"

"Because you're a Royal, of course," she says lightly, pointing to a lockbox next to the door. "It should be secure in there." Adeline has this energy about her that makes me nervous. She looks all sweet and eager to please, but every request she makes brooks no argument. Part of me wonders what she'd do if I made a scene.

A bigger part of me really doesn't.

Annoyed but still weirdly cowed, I pull out the gun tucked in my waistband, and then remove the switchblade from my pocket, placing them both inside.

"Thank you," she says, returning her focus to Verity. I don't miss the worried look she gives to her damaged hair. "There is no apology good enough for allowing such treatment to a Princess at our facility. I was remiss to leave you alone. I just hope we can make it up to you today."

"I just want to forget about it," Rosi says, giving the woman a smile I'm not sure she deserves. "And take care of these split ends."

"Well, prepare yourself for an afternoon of pampering." Adeline gestures for Verity to head toward the back of the house. But when I step forward, the woman pauses, blocking me. "Prince Ashby, this should take a couple of hours. I can call you when she's ready."

I look at Verity, jaw tensing. "I'm not leaving her."

Adeline's expression never falters, and the grin never fades. "I love your dedication to your Princess," she says, "but we have a strict 'no males beyond the foyer' policy. What goes into making the women of East End the most beautiful creations in Forsyth stays behind closed doors."

I scoff. "Sounds a little sexist to me, Addie."

That gets a response: the tiniest raising of an eyebrow. And not just from Adeline. It feels like every woman in earshot stops to turn a flat, disbelieving stare on me—not least of all being Verity herself.

I could hear a goddamn pin drop.

My shoulders turn inward as I stuff my hands into my pockets. "Fair enough," I admit, shuffling my feet. "But if she comes back out here with a single strand of hair to her disliking, you're not going to be happy with the result."

Adeline waves this off. "I assure you both, the Princess will be treated with the utmost care. I have a whole team ready to knock her socks off."

I look at Verity. "You okay going back alone?"

Her lips tip up into a small grin. "Yes, it's fine."

As Adeline whisks her through the forbidden door, I drop into a seat in the front lounge, trying to ignore the prickle of discomfort whenever a staff member darts past. In an effort to focus, I pull my laptop from my backpack. I have an assignment due for Calc at five, which gives me an hour to experience a different sort of discomfort. I've been in tutoring for three months, and have only just managed to catch up to the syllabus, which means I'm going to have to stay on the ball if I have any hope of—

No.

The document glares back at me from the screen, the deadline reading Tuesday at five.

Five *AM*.

Motherfucking shitfucker of a fuck, who the hell sets a paper deadline for five in the morning? First, the ticket. Now this.

Father is going to crucify my ass.

I shoot off a letter to my professor begging for an extension. Her son was in PNZ a few years back. Surely that can curry some favor with her. Closing out the tab, I pull up the live feeds and click through them mindlessly, like an idle fidget. The exterior of the palace, then to the main rooms, checking on Effie, who refuses to be anywhere other than Verity's room, looking out her big window. She seems content, so I flip over to Lex's bedroom, where Wicker is currently lounging, flipping through one of my magazines.

I shoot him a text.

Pace: *If you get jizz on Miss July 1973, I'll kick your ass.*

I watch on the screen as he pulls out his phone, eyes scanning over the message. Then he glances up, right into the camera, and flips me off.

Jackass.

Across the room, Lex is bent over the computer, missing our exchange. Wicker and I both thought a punishment was coming when Father told us to leave his office, but when Lex came out, he simply said Father gave him a project to work on. I zoom in, trying to get a better look, but it's just columns and numbers. Science shit, I guess.

Everything at the house seems fine, so I move over to Father's other assets. It's late afternoon, which means nothing much is going on over at the Gentlemen's Chamber. There are a few patrons watching a dancer up on stage, and then a foursome of men playing cards. Back in the private room, I see one of the girls, Lexi, mid lap dance. When she moves, I get a look at Tommy Wright's stupid lust-filled face. Guess shit's still bad with Heather.

Moving to the bar, I can make out Monroe, the bartender, and the ancient stool squatters who have been there since the dawn of time. These old timers are alcoholic sex addicts who can't even get their limp noodles up anymore, but can still tell you the exact measurements of every girl who's ever worked the stage, because they're always there- rain, shine, or Armageddon.

That's when I discover the feed is fuzzy, glitching out. I try another angle, and it's the same.

Shit.

This better not be another rat infestation.

The bigger problem is that I need to deal with this before Father finds out and loses his mind. The parking ticket is one thing. The missed Calc deadline is another. But shirking on my job is a surefire way to make him go nuclear.

I snap the laptop shut and stuff it in my bag. How long did Adeline say this was going to take? Could I pop out and back before it's over?

No, I decide, leg jittering nervously. I promised, and we may not be on positive terms right now, but I'm not going back on my word.

Plus, I'm not sure I trust a place that only allows women inside.

I circle around the lounge, checking out the photos on the walls, realizing for the first time they're not just decoration but actual photographs.

"Mr. Ashby, can I get something for you? A drink? I have kombucha." Adeline appears suddenly, as though she never left. Her eyes rake down my body appreciatively. "A strong hockey player like you probably needs a lot of calories to maintain peak performance. I'd be happy to whip up a protein shake for you if you'd like."

"I'm fine, I just," I stop, taking in the impressive wall of photographs. Girls, girls, and more girls. "These are all from East End?"

Adeline follows my gaze, beaming. "Yes, I keep a history of the

Princesses and their Courts. The women in my family have for decades."

I'm drawn to the photos like a magnet. Some are in black and white, others in color but dull, lacking the vibrancy of modern-day processing. Over an antique cabinet, I get to a row of photos, each framed the same, each woman in the same position, and I recognize it as the coronation. These Princesses all conceived.

"It's very thorough." Admittedly, I'm a little annoyed. This is the kind of collection that should be in the palace archives, but our information leans heavily toward the Princes—not the Princesses. The more I look, the more I realize there's something off about the display. There's a discolored area on the wallpaper underneath the frames. It's like they've been shifted at some point, or maybe a photo has been removed. "I see you nixed Piper's photo." I tap on the last frame. I recognize Princess Carolyn—the girl before Autumn was the last to conceive during her timeline. "And where's Verity?"

"These are just the women who conceived and delivered healthy *Royal* babies." She smiles knowingly. *Yes, Piper was a cheating whore. We all know, Adeline.* "I'm sure your Princess will be on the wall in a few months." Something flickers in her eye, her gaze growing less horny housewife and more curious. "You know, it's interesting you should ask about these. I've been thinking about your eyes..."

"What about them?" I ask, realizing I've wasted enough time. I need to tell Verity to speed it up so I can head to the club.

But then Adeline says, "Your eyes look very familiar."

There's a thing about being adopted. About not looking like anyone in your family, not sharing hair or eye color, the same bridge across the nose, or eyebrows. It's a million pieces of a puzzle, and none fit.

So when I hear Adeline say that anything about me looks familiar, it triggers something unknown deep in my chest. The only other time I've felt this way is when we were down with Bruce in the dungeon.

I'd been standing over him with the branding iron as he begged and bartered with dirt about my birth parents. He'd bragged that he'd heard his father say that my father was a Duke, which was shocking enough, but it was the rest that haunted me at night. *"Man, I don't know! I just heard it was a huge scandal. If I had to guess, I'd say she was someone important." His eyes flicked up to mine. "Someone Royal."*

I swallow, careful to keep my voice even. "Really?"

"Yes," she says, more confident now, but a line crosses her forehead. "I know I shouldn't say anything. It's not my place." I think she'll end it there. I don't like the wave of panic that thought sends through me. Fortunately, she releases this little self-deprecating chuckle. "But I've been dying to know, and who among us can resist solving a mystery?"

She turns down the hall and gestures for me to follow. Cautiously, I do, allowing her to lead me to a closed door off the hallway. Giving me a conspiratorial grin, she opens it to reveal the most hideous office I've ever seen. The walls are hot pink, while the furniture is a glaring white, including large bookshelves and cabinets on every side. She strides over to one and presses her thumb into a security pad. The light blinks green, and the lock disengages, revealing a massive filing system. For a brief second, I wonder if, despite Adeline's blonde hair and hazel eyes, we're actually related, because this is a woman after my own heart.

"There's the history we present," she says, her long pink nails flipping through file folders with precision and speed, "and the history we censor. The miscarriages and stillbirths, the infidelity and accidents, the Princesses who never conceive and are removed, you know."

I do.

"So you keep the censored history in here?"

"I do." She pauses, turning to me with a reluctant tilt to her mouth. "You might already know this, but I was a Princess once."

My head snaps back in surprise. "You were?"

I can't tell if she's more disappointed or relieved that I didn't know. Eventually, Princesses fall out of generational gossip. In twenty years, no one will remember Piper, either. "I conceived, but it wasn't meant to be," she says, glancing at me with a sad smile. "I lost the baby in my tenth week."

I'm struck rudely dumb as I process this. The thought of going through everything we have, only for Verity to lose our son...

Panic wedges itself into my throat.

"I—I'm sorry." The words are weak and selfish because I'm not even thinking about Adeline or her Princes. I'm thinking about *us*. I'm thinking about how I can lock Verity up, watch her every second of the day, kill anyone who even looks at her, and even then, there's a possibility it won't be enough to keep the baby safe.

"Thank you. It was a long time ago," she says, turning back to the files. As I'm lost in this loop of utter fucking dread, Adeline exclaims, "Ah! Here it is." She pulls out a photo—a portrait—and I recognize the setting like I'd know the specific texture of Effie's wings. It's the palace's ceremonial room, and just like others, the background suggests it's the night of the masquerade. The white dress, the tuxedos, the candles, and the roses; they're all there. But this photo is taken up close, the woman's face clear and crisp.

She's black, her complexion darker than mine, with a wide smile revealing a warm umber blush on the apple of each sharp cheekbone. She has full, round lips that tilt a little, her expression some mixture of elation and wryness. Her hair is relaxed but set into large, voluminous black curls. She's wearing a pearl in each ear, staring straight into the camera with dark eyes that glitter against the flash.

Too stunned to speak, I remain frozen as Adeline holds the photo up to my face. "It's not just the eyes," she says, her tone giddy. "It's the bone structure. The way your lips turn down slightly, see? Don't you think so?"

I snatch the photo from her. "Who is this?"

"Careful," she says, looking alarmed. "That's the only photo I have of her."

"*Who* is she?" I repeat.

"I wish I knew." She looks down at her files. "Sometimes, it's easy to track them down. They have family still involved or powerful enough to salvage their reputation. East End is fairly incestuous enough that everyone knows, or is related, to whoever is involved." She touches the edge of the photo in my hand. "But occasionally, we have a mystery. This woman, clearly someone you're related to, is a mystery. We've got no information on her at all. I was hoping you might know." Her expression turns careful, just like her voice. "Do you happen to have any information on your biological family?"

Shaking my head, I inspect the photo voraciously, looking for any little signal that this is *her*. "How the hell do you just erase a Princess?" I ask, unable to tear my gaze away.

Adeline gives a weak chuckle. "You know King Ashby better than I do. I assume it would be on his order."

"Or maybe she just didn't want to be found," I offer, that same rush of dread from before taking over. "Maybe she walked away. Abandoned her duty."

Abandoned *me*.

"It's possible," Adeline says, "but you know nothing is that easy here. Especially for the women. No one walks away from your father."

Then she ran. Packed up her things, dropped me off at the children's home, and never looked back. Maybe Bruce was right. She fucked a Duke, abandoned me, and bolted, both of them traitors —*embarrassments*—to their houses.

Reaching into my pocket, I take out my phone, lay the photo out on her desk, and snap a photo. With a few taps, I have it sent to an encrypted email that no one, not even Father or my brothers, can access.

"Do you want to keep it?" Adeline asks, watching me closely.

I shake my head. Adeline has kept this photo safe for years now. If Father really had something to do with erasing her, I'm not about to take it back to the palace. "This is an impressive collection. I wouldn't want to remove anything. Keep it safe." I step toward the door, pausing. "And let me know if you learn anything new."

"I will." She reaches out to squeeze my arm, her eyes full of sympathy. "I'm so sorry if seeing this upset you. I shouldn't have—"

"It's fine," I assure.

Adeline knows this is a lie. Luckily, she just nods. "I'll go check on your Princess."

I'm still staring at the photo on my phone when Verity walks out. Could this be her? My mother? Or maybe Bruce was full of shit, mixing up shitty West End gossip, and this is someone else. An aunt? A cousin? Even a sister. That's the fuck-you when you know nothing about your history. There's no thread to pull, no dot to connect.

"Well," Adeline prompts, "did we make up for the fiasco?"

I drag my eyes away from the screen, and my heart skitters like I'm in a goddamn movie. Everything is suddenly in slow-mo, from the way she ducks her head to the nervous smile touching her lips. There's no denying Verity is my dream girl. I knew the minute her picture popped up on that app, hair like fire and skin like ice. Back then, she was cute. Innocent and pure. But right now, with that red hair all shiny and curled over her shoulders...

Fuck. She's a knockout.

Too bad my mind is on other things.

"Good job," I say, grabbing my backpack and slinging it over my shoulder. "We done here?"

Adeline's forehead creases. "I think so."

Verity's smile falls, but she quickly recovers. "Thank you, Adeline," she says, turning to her. "I really do appreciate it."

"Anything for you, Princess."

They say their goodbyes, and I slip Adeline a tip so absurd that even she does a double take.

Verity and I are both silent on the way to the car, her footfalls dragging behind me. There's a small part of me that's bursting to tell her—*anyone*—what I just learned from Adeline. How after all this time, I get a morsel about who my mother may be, and it turns out she's a traitor to East End.

To me.

But this feeling in my chest is too raw, too exposed, and I'm not ready to share it with anyone. Worse is that, in the back of my mind, buried beneath the ragged panic and stomach-churning despair, this little thought is screaming at me to, at the very least, turn to her. To take her face in my hands and tell her that she's the most gorgeous fucking thing I've ever laid eyes on. To bring back that shy little grin that I shattered with my apathy.

But I can't seem to make myself stop, feet pushing one step in front of the other. I can't think. I can't talk. I can barely even breathe until I find out the truth.

~

I WASTE no time dropping Verity off back at campus, ignoring the worried glance she sends my way before climbing out of the car.

It's torture not to glance at her in my rearview as I speed away.

The lot of the Gentlemen's Chamber isn't even half full. It's still early, but the post-work crowd will start rolling in soon. The bouncer has the door open before I even reach the steps, ushering me inside with a nod. The half-naked women might as well be wallpaper for all the attention I pay to them on my beeline to the back.

Much like the bouncer, Monroe pours me a shot of whiskey before I've even reached the bar. "You look like you need this."

I throw it back mechanically, glancing up at the camera in the corner. "More signal interference."

Monroe shrugs, drying off a glass. "Probably this wiring. It's older than I am. Might as well—hey, whoa!" He lunges for me as I climb up on the bar, stomping down the length until I'm within arm's reach of the camera. "You spoiled little shits too good for ladders now?" he snaps. "This isn't exactly code-compliant."

Ignoring him, I strain up on my toes, grabbing the camera and ripping it straight off the ceiling.

Monroe glares at me. "Too good for screwdrivers, too, huh?"

I leap down, whipping my phone from my pocket. "I don't have a lot of time," I tell him, frantically pulling up the photo. This is the only camera covering this corner of the bar, but the longer it's offline, the higher a chance Father will find out about it. "Do you know who this is?"

Monroe squints as I turn the phone to him, zeroing in on the image. He's been working this place since before I was probably born. It's a risk. Father has spent decades culling his crews. Much like Danner, Monroe's loyalty goes to one man and one man alone. If it didn't, he wouldn't still be wiping down this bar.

I know I'm right when Monroe looks away, shrugging. "Never seen her."

His mustache twitches, though.

Horrible tell.

"Cut the shit," I hiss, grabbing a fistful of his shirt. "You can't tell me who she is—I get it. You know me, Monroe. I wouldn't ask you to put your neck on the line like that. Just give me *something*. Point me in a direction, and I'll do all the footwork myself."

His faded eyes look into mine, eyes that have seen more women than the Crane Motor Inn, and then flick just over my shoulder. One blink and I'd miss it. "Sorry, kid. Got nothing to tell."

Releasing him, I glance behind me, spotting one of the ancient stool squatters, curled over his glass of bourbon like a wrinkled goblin. "Thanks," I tell Monroe, giving him a nod. "I'll get this camera fixed up for you."

"You do that," he mutters, spitefully spraying down the bar.

I don't know the squatter's real name. I know that he likes his women the way he likes his liquor, brown and fiery, but for as long as I can remember, he's just been Ole Boy. He never comes to the club in anything less than his finest suit, pressed and starched and soaked in cologne. He's loud when he's sober, and louder when he isn't.

Thankfully, it's easy to get him into my new car.

"Goddamn, sonny." His whistle is half garbled, the guy already a dozen thumbs deep on the drink at four in the afternoon. He smells like a distillery. "You pull a lot of trim in this thing?"

"Sure," I say, eyes rolling. "But I had a question for you."

Ole Boy squints harder than Monroe did when I show him my phone's screen. "Who's that?"

Stomach dropping, I say, "I was hoping you could tell me. Chances are you might have seen her twenty-ish years back?"

Watching his milky eyes search the photo, I press, "A Princess, maybe?"

I can tell when it clicks for him, some of that drunken stupor sharpening to fear. Pushing the phone away, he says, "Oh, I don't think I'm supposed to talk about that one, sonny."

"Why not?" I ask, shoving the phone closer. "Who is she?"

Ole Boy has jowls that flutter when he swallows. "Sad thing, that one. Gams for days, but sad, sad thing."

Annoyed, I snap, "Give me a name. I need a *name*."

His glazed eyes land on mine, blinking heavily. "You're a sad thing, too, aren't ya, sonny?" I push the phone closer, and he sighs, moving his gaze to the photo. "Her name was Odette," he says. "Odette Delisle."

MOST OF THE county administrative offices are located in North Side, which might have been a problem before Lavinia Lucia blew her father to smithereens. Unfortunately, the drive from the ass end of the East to the elbow of the North takes a good forty minutes, leaving me barely twenty minutes before they close.

I park haphazardly, springing through the rain up the steps and through the glass doors, hood raised.

"Vital records," I pant to the receptionist, who points me through to another lobby.

More waiting. *Great.*

It's ridiculous, really. I've hacked this place weekly since the age of fifteen and know damn well their cybersecurity has more holes than Swiss cheese. But the thought of searching her out anywhere near Father's network makes me twitchy. Even now, I glance around at the security cameras, wondering if he'll see me.

I tap my foot and huff as I wait for the person in front of me—some rube who needs a birth certificate—and listen plainly as the man behind the counter informs him that birth records are confidential. He then snidely explains all the hoops he'd have to go through to obtain access.

Fuck that.

I leave out the door and into a corridor, stopping by the lobby.

The fire alarm clicks as I slam it down, disappearing into the restroom as the mechanical wails throb through the halls. Just beyond the bathroom door, I can hear the scuff of shoes as the building begins emptying. I give it a solid three minutes before ducking back out.

It's easy to get through the door to the back, easier to find a secluded bank of computers, and easiest to type in one of the twelve access codes I already know.

Odette Delisle, I type in, not knowing if I have the spelling right. I'm drenched, either from the rain or sweat, and as the computer lags, I growl in frustration.

Then, a list of entries flies up.

If you can call two entries a list.

There's a birth record.

There's a *death* record.

Everything is automatic after that. I print it out, although later, I won't remember why I bothered. It's like being a piece of machinery, the belts turning as I go through these practiced, routine motions. Get the mark's information. Avoid detection. Clear my access code. Go out through the back. Inhale and exhale, the way a body should.

It's all a dull blur as I walk out into the back alley, rain beating like knives against the pavement. I hear it dabbing against my hood in rapid little thumps, the fabric growing heavier as I wander out to the front of the building. A fire truck has arrived. No sirens. Just lights. It's sitting right where my car should be, in fact.

My car, which is hitched to the back of a tow truck and already halfway down the street.

I feel in the back of my brain that I should run and catch it, but just as fast as the thought arrives, it's discarded. That's proof. Father will get a call. He'll know I was here.

At best, I'll be punished.

At worst, Lex will be the one to take it.

So I begin walking.

I don't know at first where I'm going. My feet lead me south because that seems like the thing to do. The palace is South. The strip club. Campus. Spa. My brothers. *Her.*

I walk for so long that it grows dark, the streetlights popping on around me. The rain becomes a part of the weight of me, dragging me closer and closer to the earth. By the time I get anywhere recognizable, it feels like a million pounds of water has seeped through my clothes, and my feet are numb.

It's cold.

It's only when I find myself in the old diner parking lot that this wildly spinning compass in my chest fixes on a direction. I don't even pause over the invisible territory line, stepping over it like it's just another crack.

~

THE LOFT above *Royal Ink* has a weird smell.

I wander around for a few minutes, trying to reorient the scale in my head. From the cameras Charlie stashed in the building across the street, this place looks small. In person, it's big and empty, a throw rug, a couch, an armchair, and a coffee table. There are no trinkets or baubles. Her laptop is resting half-closed on the arm of the couch, the charging cord draped dangerously around a lamp, but other than that and a throw blanket, it'd be easy to think no one lived here at all.

Idly, I detangle the charging cord before moving to the kitchen, noting the clean countertop and a single bowl resting in the sink.

A wall over, the pipes whine as the shower cuts off.

It's only then that I allow myself to enter the bedroom, gaze passing over the rumpled bed. The sheets are pink, which strikes me as odd. I stand numbly as I watch myself drip a splatter of water into the cotton, blossoming out like blood.

Behind me, her gasp cleaves through the silence like an arrow.

"Security here is shit," I say, my voice jagged and unfamiliar. "I gained entry in three minutes flat." When I turn to look at her, I'm expecting the fear. The way she's clutching the towel to her body. The wideness of her eyes. The paleness of her cheeks.

I'm *not* expecting the relief that seeps into her face when she realizes it's me. "Pace?" she says, shoulders falling. "God, I thought you were that old serial killer Lav keeps plastering articles about all over the walls." The relief doesn't last. She lunges for me, slamming a fist in my shoulder. "What the hell are you doing here? If anyone catches you, all hell is going to break loose!" Each word is punctuated by another pound of her fist.

I take each of them limply, frowning. "You washed your hair."

Nothing is going right.

She releases a tight, frustrated growl, flicking water from her fist. "Why are you so soaked?"

"Because I walked here."

Her eyes bug out. "From East End?"

"From North Side."

She just looks more confused. "What? Why? *What?*"

Collapsing, I land heavily against the mattress, feeling like my chest is caving in. "Everything is so fucked up. The Calc deadline. The parking ticket. I left my gun in Adeline's safe." I glance at her, feeling sick. "Then I forgot to tell you how pretty you looked at the spa." I prop my elbows on my knees, dropping my face into my hands. "Plus, my car got towed, along with my phone and my wallet, all so I could find out—" The words get caught somewhere in my esophagus. Pushing them out feels like being strangled. "I think I killed my mother."

There's a long stretch where I struggle to breathe. I inhale these tiny, ineffectual gulps, and the truth is, it hurts. Like, physically. Right in my sternum. What the fuck is that? I haven't felt like this since those early days in prison, waiting for the next shove or fight, so alert that it drained me. Now, it hits me like a sack of bricks, banging ruthlessly against my ribcage.

I think I might die.

"Pace, calm down." Her voice flutters in and out like a butterfly's wings. "Hey, look at me. Can you look at me?"

I shake my head, unwilling to lift it from my hands.

"Okay," she says, voice gentle.

Gentle, I hear in Effie's approximation of Verity's voice. *Gentle, gentle.*

"You're having a panic attack or something. Just... here." There's the soft shifting of fabric and then something over my head. The towel. Verity is wringing the rain from my hair. "Let's get all these heavy things off you."

I don't fight when she unzips my hoodie, slipping it off my arms. I pant down at my waterlogged shoes and give her access to my arms. My shirt comes next, and then she whispers, "Lay back, okay?" and what else am I going to do?

I flop back, struggling to breathe as she pops the button on my jeans, working them over my hips. It feels so much better once it's all gone, without the weight of it dragging me down. I hear more than see them land on her floor, the heavy *plop* of the fabrics ringing significantly.

I wish she could take my skin, too.

That thought, *skin*, draws my eyes up, realizing that she's used her own towel to dry me. She's between my legs, worrying her lip as she watches me, her body completely bare. My gaze instantly snaps to the curve of her belly, so small a thing.

Just a tiny little bump.

Just...

Just an apple.

I'm drawn to it like a magnet, holding her hips as I press my forehead to the small swell of her belly. Father preaches a lot of bullshit, but I think I see it now. The power of creation. It sinks into me like a soothing balm, much like the flutter of Verity's fingers in my hair, stilted but unwavering.

She whispers, "Why did you come here, Pace?"

"Because I'm a fuck up." Her skin is soft. So fucking soft. Sometimes I touch her and wonder if it's wrong—if I'm tarnishing the very thing that drew me to her to begin with. "Because I needed to know he was okay," I answer, remembering Adeline's confession from earlier.

Her baby was only ten weeks.

Strawberry.

I look up, brushing my lips against the bump of her belly as I meet her gaze. She looks scared, her brows knitted together, but she also looks beautiful. Fiery, like an avenging angel. I almost regret coming, dimming her brightness with all my darkness. Maybe that's why, for the first time in my life, I decide to be brutally, painfully, terrifyingly honest.

"Because the only time anything feels right is when I'm inside you."

Her hand is warm when she cups my cheek, her expression collapsing in despair. "Pace..."

I clutch her hips, willing to beg. "Don't make me leave."

She sighs, her thumb rubbing the tender, tired spot beneath my eye, and I'm pretty sure I see her make the decision in her mind, the crevice in her forehead smoothing. "Get under the covers. You're freezing."

I tug her with me as I go, curling around her body like a desperate, needy thing. She's warm and soft against the cradle of my body, a contrast in all the ways that matter, and if it takes me a few minutes to get us both ready, then she doesn't resist.

She nestles back into me as I get her wet, my cold lips skittering up the column of her neck.

When I finally push inside, pressing her close, it's just like I knew it would be: hot and slick and *right*.

18

erity

IT'S THE SCENT, I realize.

Ever since coming back to West End and reacquainting with the Dukes' loft, I've been trying to find out why sleeping in this bed is so discomfiting. Not discomfiting in the way it used to be, either. It's a discrete dissonance, like something's been missing. Not *bad*, just not quite right.

It's only now, with Pace's scent on my pillow, that I think I know what it is.

My Princes, for all their flaws, always smell so good. Masculine but clean, spicy but fresh. I slept in those scents for a month. That shouldn't be long enough to form associations, but apparently, it was, because I draw in Pace's smell with a quiet gasp and almost forget where I am.

"Oh my god," I whimper, digging my teeth into my bottom lip.

Between my thighs, Pace makes a rough, gritty sound, his fingers digging divots into my hips as he spears his tongue into me. Through the foggy haze of sleep, all I can think is, *wow.*

What a way to wake up.

I can't even see him as my eyes flutter open, straining against the morning light. He's beneath the sheets, the shape of him as unmistakable as the way he touches me, greedy and unyielding. I'd never admit it, but I've been achingly horny for the past two weeks, the pregnancy hormones working their dark magic against my libido.

I struggle to fling the sheets off, feeling hot and too crowded. I see his hair first, the texture coarse but plush beneath my fingers as I thread them into his twists. His arms are hooked beneath each of my thighs, holding me open as he licks a hot path to my clit. I get a crystal clear look at the tattoos on his arms and the way they shift with his muscles and tendons.

It's like a lightning bolt when his sleepy eyes open, rising to lock with mine.

I wonder if he's eating his cum out of me.

The thought sends a frisson up my spine, back arching as he licks a slick circuit around my clit. "Pace," I whine, throat clicking with a swallow. "Don't—don't stop."

The assenting noise he makes is a low, deep vibration that draws a moan from my chest. It's easy in that thin barrier between sleep and wakefulness to chase the ache in my core. Pace eats my pussy with outright leisure, like this is something to be savored, indulged in. His black eyes hold mine, every flick of his tongue meant to elicit a response, and I give it to him in spades, spreading myself out obscenely, too caught up in the moment to feel something as trivial as shame.

"Oh," I breathe, panting as he tips my hips upward, fucking his tongue into me. "I want—I need—"

There's a deep, guttural sound, and then he's springing up, looking so human as he grips the shaft of his cock that it overwhelms me. The muscles in his torso tighten and flex as he enters me with a sure thrust.

"Like this," he rasps, licking at my mouth just like he had my pussy. "Come on my dick, just like this."

It's not the sex I'm used to—especially not from him. It's unbearably close, our breaths mingling in the scant space between our mouths. If I had half a mind to, it might even make me uncomfortable. As it is, I indulge in it just as much as he is. His body rocks into mine, claiming but not owning, coaxing me to join him. And his eyes...

His eyes are fathomless pits of darkness, never blinking, not giving me any respite from their intensity. Best of all is the way he feels inside, thick and swollen and ripe.

I've never been so wet in my life.

I grab onto his shoulders and listen to what his body is saying. *Follow me*, it demands, and I comply, heels skidding against the sheets as I buck up against him, powerless against the pull of ecstasy.

He captures my gasp when I seize, the orgasm throbbing through me like sharp, silken threads.

I'm too lost in the starry rapture of it to know exactly when he comes, but I eventually feel it. The growing fullness. The twitch of his cock as it pulses. The clipped grunt that punches from his chest. The way his fingers flutter through the crown of my hair, holding me fast as he buries himself deep inside, panting into my flushed cheek.

I soothe him through it mindlessly, turning to skate my lax lips across his tense jaw. Here, in the sleepy stillness of the loft, having him inside me feels normal—*sweet*—an act between lovers instead of Royals.

It's... nice.

When his muscles finally loosen, he breathlessly rolls us to our sides, face to face. It doesn't matter that his eyes are closed now, fingers grasping my hip to keep me close. I still remember with sharp clarity the way he looked last night, wet and shivering and terrifyingly *lost*.

Idly, I reach up to rest my fingertips against his forehead, my touch no more than a glancing caress as I bring them down, mapping the shape of his face. "What happened yesterday?"

His cock is still softening inside, and he sighs, dark eyelashes fluttering as they open. "I've been thinking about that." He looks better than he did last night, at least. The dark circles are gone, replaced with a pensive tightness. "I can bribe them."

Frowning, I ask, "Who?"

"The tow company." He releases my hip to stroke his fingers through my hair, eyes calculating. "It's probably not even in the impound yet. I can spare a few G's. Or threaten them—Father will respect that."

"Oh." I blink, trying to catch up. "I meant—"

But he continues, "Then I can swing by the spa, snag my gun, take care of the speeding ticket before it hits the wire, and make it to campus in time for Professor Piresh's office hours to make a case for my extension." There's a new looseness to him once it's all out, as if having a plan was all he ever needed.

As much as I want to ask about his mother, I can't bear to transform him back into the miserable, desperate man I faced last night. I barely know how to handle Pace on a good day. But on a bad day?

His calf rubs against mine as he stretches, a hand wandering down to press against my belly. His eyes follow it, something soft in the way he blinks, slow and heavy. "Have you thought of a name for him?"

I squirm against the tickle of his fingertips. "I'm still getting used to the fact it's a boy," I confess. I hadn't really had time to land on a preference.

His hand looks so striking against my belly. His dark skin against my pale. His scars and tattoos against the unblemished swell. "Tell me when you do," he whispers, nestling into the pillow.

Cautiously, I wonder, "Would it matter?"

His eyes flick up to mine. "What do you mean?"

"I mean…" I shiver when his fingers skate up to my breast, his rough knuckles dragging over the soft underside. "I guess I figured whoever the father ended up being would get to decide."

Pace stops, staring. "I named my bird after a keystroke. Do you really want to find out what I'd name a baby?"

I laugh without meaning to. A really bad laugh, too. It's a deep, snorting bark that immediately makes heat rise to my cheeks.

It also makes his mouth form a slow, sinful grin, his hips rocking into mine. "Christ, you look—"

Bang-bang.

"Rise and shine, bitch!" comes Lavinia's muffled voice.

There's a moment where we both freeze, our eyes flying wide with panic, and then it's a flurry of limbs as we spring from the bed. "One sec!" I cry out, throwing him his jeans, the denim still damp.

"Shit," he hisses, stubbing his toe on the bed frame, but at my distressed glare, clamps down on it, hopping into his boxers.

"Hurry, hurry!" I whisper, chucking his shirt at him.

It lands on his head, and he yanks it down, muscles twisting.

"Verity!" Sy's annoyed voice rings out, the bang louder now. "We're ten minutes late already. Somebody—not naming any names —wouldn't let me leave the house until we went eight rounds over possession of my jacket. Again," he adds, "not naming any names."

And then Nick's wry, "It was the Archduke."

"Archduke?" Pace mouths, jamming his foot into a shoe. "Recruit?"

I punch my arms through my robe. "Cat."

"Fuck." He angrily pulls on his hoodie, brows crouched low. "Goddamn it. That's a good name."

I usher him into the living room. "Go, go, go!" Only, I stop, spinning in alarm, because he can't exactly go out the front door, can he? "Shit! How did you—"

But Pace is already pulling a chair to the middle of the room, jumping on it, and looking upward.

To the skylight.

I gape at it. "You came in through the *roof*?"

He bends before springing up, catching the edge of a beam and doing a pull-up that looks criminally effortless. With a twist of his hand, he has the pane of glass hinging upward, feet swinging as he works up the leverage necessary to vault his weight to the opening.

He glances down before pulling himself through, adding, "I'll be watching if you need me," before slipping away the same way he came in.

It's in that harried moment as I'm scanning for any further evidence of Pace's presence that I find it: two pages of paper, folded into eighths. It must have fallen out of his pocket, I realize, half expecting to see a parking ticket as I unfold it.

Instead, what I find is a damp death certificate, the ink fuzzy from moisture, for someone named Odette Delisle.

Under the cause of death is typed a short, unfeeling passage.

Complications related to childbirth.

"Is that the hardest you can go?" Remy's voice echoes against the rafters. "Because if that's all you've got, we're going to need a case of bleach to clean up all the blood after LDZ is done with you."

It's training day, and the Dukes are all working with the recruits. The closer we get to graduation, the less they'll fight. Sy's already pulled back. With the Bruin ring on his finger, he's got nothing to prove. Nick would rather do his fighting out of the ring. But for Remy, toying with frat boys seems to give him a perverse sense of pleasure—one he's passing on to the next generation.

With the sounds of the gym behind me, I stare at the door to my mother's office, unable to actually go inside.

She's in there. I can see her movements behind the slats of the blinds.

We haven't spoken since the negotiations. Neither of us have made the effort. Things were too raw. Too humiliating. The pieces of my life laid out on that cherry wood conference table, signed and sealed by the men that rule Forsyth.

I'm not sure if it's the fact Mother's Day is around the corner, or if I just miss her that got me to ask the guys to bring me to the gym with them. Whichever it was, now that I'm here, I'm having second thoughts.

My hand flutters over the tiny bump that's started to emerge on my lower belly. Things are different now. None of this is abstract anymore. Not since the four of us snuck down to the medical room and Lex said the words, "It's a boy."

I take a deep breath and grip the knob, entering without approval.

"I wondered how long you were going to stand out there." She licks her thumb and flips through a stack of invoices. "Thought maybe you were waiting for an engraved invitation. Maybe a bouquet of white roses?"

"You know what?" I say, feeling instant regret. "Never mind. It was stupid to come in here."

I spin, too tired for my mother's East End jabs.

Outside the door, I hear her chair push back, the screech like nails on a chalkboard. "Verity, wait."

Over by the ring, Ballsack watches, eyes tracking me. I know he'll take me out of here if I ask him to, but I don't. Not when my mother's hand touches my shoulder, and I catch the scent of her perfume. More softly, she repeats, "Wait."

I turn and face my mother, trying not to squirm as she assesses me. She's always been impeccable, and I've always admired that about her. I've never been good at the glamour of femininity. Makeup, hair, jewelry. All of that stuff seems to come so easily to her. I remember so many nights, watching her apply moisturizer, and even more mornings watching her put on her war paint. Because that's what it is to my mother. The teased hair, the red lips; it's armor.

I wish I were better at it.

"Your tits are finally bigger than mine," she says, lips quirking.

Clearing my throat, I hold her gaze. "Yeah, well, all I had to do was get knocked up."

We stare at one another, a million unspoken words hanging between us. We'd always been close, or so I thought. Obviously, she had an entire life I never knew about. A dark, royal-filled, secret life that included Rufus Ashby being my father.

Something in her eyes softens as we stand there, assessing one another. "Are you still having morning sickness?" she asks.

"No," I admit, clamping down on the urge to cry. How many times have I wanted someone to talk me through this? To tell me they understood? "The opposite, actually. I'm fucking ravenous all the time."

She turns abruptly and starts marching across the gym. Halfway there, she jerks her chin for me to follow her into the kitchen. By the time I get there, she's already opened the refrigerator, a bowl cradled in her manicured hand.

"What is that?" I ask, hands wringing as I try to get a peek.

She smirks. "Banana pudding."

"Oh?" I couldn't hide the anticipation in my voice if I tried. I've tried to stick to Lex's dietary plans while in West End. That's part of the deal. But the thing is, my mother's cooking is my kryptonite. *Especially* her banana pudding. It's freshly made, set aside with a note on top: *Do Not Touch-Mama B.*

She removes the lid and grabs a plate out of the cabinet, scooping me out a large helping. My mouth waters looking at the mushy vanilla wafers lining the edge. Gesturing to the small kitchen table, she carries it over and places it in front of me when I sit down.

The first bite is better than an orgasm.

"Oh my god," I whine, savoring it. "It's even better than I remember."

"I'll admit to having done some stress cooking." She sits across from me, arms crossed over her chest, bracelets clinking against one another. "You're too thin. Is that bastard starving you?"

"No," I say, taking my time with the pudding. I want this to last. "But it is all very healthy. Greens and antioxidants and stuff."

She snorts. "Like he has any clue how to nourish a pregnant woman."

I glance up, catching her glare. "Actually, Lex makes the meal plans. It's not all bad." I scoop up another spoonful, making sure to get whipped cream, but before I eat it, I ask the question that's been hanging over me since Valentine's Day. "Is there a reason you didn't tell me?"

Sighing, she looks away. "Yes. One simple reason. Because I didn't want that monster anywhere near you." She shakes her head. "Whole lot of good it did. He got you anyway."

That angry knot in my chest returns. "I keep telling you, I made that decision on my own."

"But he sent you that invitation. You had the title of Princess before you walked in that door." She huffs and slinks back in her chair, looking more exhausted than I've ever seen her before. "This isn't what I wanted for you, Ver Bear."

The old nickname makes my stomach warm. "Isn't it?" I ask. "All the dance lessons and etiquette classes weren't for this? What about the metaphorical chastity belt you shackled on me since puberty?" Pointing my spoon at her, I accuse, "You *groomed* me, mother."

"For them!" She shouts back, gesturing to the gym where the guys are training. "I trained you for one another. I knew even being with a Duke wouldn't be easy, but it wouldn't be..." She can't say it. However much she knows about my time in East End, she can't admit it, but she knows it's been hard. More than hard. A literal nightmare. "That man is evil. He is *vile*. And you can see what he'll do if you share his blood. He doesn't have family, Verity; he has possessions." Her eyes flick to my belly, darkening. "And that baby doesn't belong to you. It belongs to *him*."

Tell that to Lex, I want to say. Or Pace, who looked so eager to see me name the life growing inside of me. My Princes—or two of them—are consumed with the idea of fatherhood. Do I think they'll be good at it? No. At least, not yet. I'd meant what I'd said to Pace that day in the solarium. His flaw is being too protective, but that doesn't come from a place of malice, does it? And Lex... he has this intensity about him. He's devoted to this child. I can feel it.

They will fight for their son.

But I know my mother won't listen to that. The Princes are an extension of their father, if not by nature, then by nurture.

"He told me about the hurricane." It's almost imperceptible, the way she stiffens. "About your... night together."

Her jaw tics. "I very much doubt what he told you resembles the truth."

I put my spoon down, the sound loud in the stillness between us. "Then you tell me. Tell me the truth for once in your life." I place my hand on my stomach. "How am I supposed to make smart decisions if I have no idea what's actually going on? It's too late to protect me, but maybe if you'll stop covering up the past, you can help me protect my child."

Her palm lands on the table, her talon-like nails digging into the top. Even before all of this, my mother was a steel trap, keeping her personal life sacred and hidden. It was easy to do in a gym full of men who probably never thought of her as more than the mama bear to their den of cubs. And even the cutsluts viewed her more as an authority figure than one of the girls.

But now, with this little human growing in me, I see her differently. I see her as a woman. The same kind of woman I am now. A *creator*. I just want to know that person. How she became the woman in front of me.

"There was a hurricane," she says, jaw tight. "That much is true. The river breached the banks, spilling into the streets, sweeping trees and cars with it. The whole city had been told to evacuate, but when did the Royals ever listen to caution? So the Barons' King opened up the crypt, inviting everyone to shelter down in the catacombs. A hurricane party," she says, barking out a mangled laugh. "Any excuse to cross territory lines, drink, and get a little fucked up with the enemy."

"Everyone was there?" I press when her eyes get foggy, faraway.

She shakes her head. "Davis and Manny had left by then. Sarah, too. They were off building their own lives, outside the Royalty. There were so many new Kings back then," she muses, brows knitting together. "Not just Saul, who had barely started working for the university, but also Daniel Payne. He'd taken over the Lords just a couple of weeks earlier. And then there was Lionel Lucia, who'd taken over North Side a couple of years before that. And Rufus... he wasn't King yet, but we all felt it was coming. His uncle was sick." She looks at me, raising her chin. "It was an exciting time. New blood. Youth taking the city back from the decrepit monsters who once held their leashes. I think you understand now how that feels. Not just the energy, but the sense that Forsyth is balanced on the edge of a knife. What will it be? Revolution, or more of the same?"

Stomach twisting, I guess, "It was more of the same, wasn't it?"

She picks at a fingernail, shrugging. "It's hard to explain, but back then, I was... adrift. I wasn't Royal, and I was getting too old to be a cutslut. But this," she gestures overhead, to the gym, or maybe even West End as a whole, "this was all I knew. I wasn't ready to walk away from it—to stand on my own." Her eyes meet mine, pleading, "You know what I mean, don't you? How easy it is to cling to this?"

Slowly, I nod, because I get it. West End is more than a phase. In many ways, it's grafted into our bones.

She leans back, face twisting. "I didn't expect Rufus Ashby to be there. Everyone knew his wife had a toddler. He made sure both of them were out of the way." Snidely, she adds, "He would've held a goddamn parade in that kid's honor if the Mayor would've approved it. Apparently, he made sure they were somewhere safe, outside of Forsyth, and then he slinked in, wet and windblown, just before they sealed the doors, locking us in." She pauses then, eyes locking with mine. "Do you really want to know this, Verity?"

I nod without reservation. "Yes."

She almost looks stricken at the answer, folding her arms around her middle. "It was... cold down there. Clammy. A little damp." She runs her hands up and down her arms like she's back in that time and place. "Dust covered everything. That place is a maze, all these little nooks and tunnels. When Rufus offered me a drink from his flask to warm up, I took it, but I wasn't drunk." Her eyes hold mine. "I said no."

Uneasiness unfurls in my stomach. "You mean he..."

But I can't say the word.

She averts her gaze, a grim smile touching her lips. "It's probably hard now to imagine his charm back then, but he had it in spades. A little bit like your blonde Prince, actually. He easily got me away from the other cutsluts and the protection of DKS. It wasn't hard. It was crowded and dark, and Saul had lost interest in me, just like the rest of the frat. People were fooling around. Making out, having sex. It felt like we were at the edge of the world, chaos above us, emptiness below." The muscles in her throat tighten. "There were other Royals there. He took me right up against a stone wall, ten feet away from Jacob Oakfield, his hand clamped over my mouth as he explained to me that his wife couldn't fulfill his needs. She was too occupied with caring for their son, you see." She looks away, blinking rapidly. "Apparently, that gave him the right to take whatever he wanted. And the others..." A shiver wracks through her. "Honestly, I couldn't name them all if I tried. Daniel Payne, certainly. Clive Kayes. Maybe even Lucia. There must have been half a dozen, but maybe more. Too many to fight. At some point, I blocked it out."

"Mom," I say, choking out her name past the lump in my throat. "I didn't know."

"Because I didn't *want* you to know," she snaps, visibly trying to regain her composure. "Being a woman in Forsyth teaches you that your body is never your own. I wish I could say Rufus was the only man that took what he wanted from me. What I *can* say is that he's the only one who left something behind more important than life itself."

I wrap my arm around my stomach. "How did... why didn't you..." I can't say the words, but I need to know.

"Why didn't I terminate?" She shrugs, eyes devoid of emotion. "I thought about it. Even made the appointment up in Northridge. But I couldn't do it. For once in my life, one of these men gave me something that was mine and mine alone." Reaching over, she takes my hand, some of the color returning to her cheeks. "You were a gift, Verity. My lifeline. You gave me the guts to stop playing around and become someone. A mama. Not just to you, but to a whole den."

"I thought about it, too," I confess, my own eyes welling. "For a minute."

Her face collapses at the admission. "Baby, all I ever wanted..." Her eyes shine with unshed tears as she holds my gaze. "All I ever *needed* was to know you would never be the girl against that cold wall, scared and lost." She tightens her grip, her voice as hard as steel.

"Verity, if you want out of this, tell me. I'll make it happen. I was powerless then, but I'm not now. I've been collecting leverage for years. I can burn East End to the fucking ground."

I don't doubt her, but...

"I don't want out of it." I swallow and move her hand, pressing it against my stomach. "It's a boy."

"Oh, Ver," she whispers, wide eyes fixed on my belly. "That's exactly what he wants."

My voice is fervent as I declare, "He's not taking my baby, Mama. I won't let him."

But she looks at me like I'm missing something crucial. "Do you realize there are no Royal women past a certain age? Before Lavinia Lucia and Story Austin, there were no Queens in Forsyth. There were only gaping holes. There was no reigning Lady or Duchess. Queen Lucia was murdered by her husband. Miranda Ashby has been dead as long as you've been alive. And if there's a Baron Queen, I've never seen her." She turns her wrist, showing me the DKS symbol branded on her wrist. "You asked me about this once. Remember? You said it seemed like I was a Duchess in all but name." Her eyes grow flinty. "Saul gave this to me because, after that night, I begged him for protection. But it didn't come free. I had to barter myself. My body."

I stare at the brand, aghast. "Oh my god, Mama..."

"Nothing is free," she stresses. "A brand, a ring, a tattoo, a wrist cuff, a necklace... every Royal woman pays a price for those symbols. I paid mine."

"Things are changing," I tell her, willing her to see the promise in my eyes. "Sy isn't going to give up Lavinia, and I can't see Killian Payne walking away from his Lady. It's different now."

She pushes against the bulge of my belly. "You think the women before them didn't think they were different? Why do you think Sarah ran with Nick and Sy's fathers and never turned back?" She's not just being harsh. I hear the fear in her words. "Royal women don't survive, Verity. Especially once they birth an heir."

Desperately, I wonder, "Is that why you never told him about me?"

"There was nothing to tell," she snaps, yanking her hand away. "You could have been Lucia's just as much as his. How was I to know? Your looks favored me more than any of them. You were *mine*."

"This is Forsyth," I stress. "You know it's not that simple."

"He would have killed me," she says, her voice rising into near hysterics. "Who would have protected you then, and what price would you have paid for it? And if he knew—if any of them knew—you'd have a target on your back."

I think about betraying Wicker—revealing to Lavinia his Royal lineage—and my heart sinks. I've been so fucking foolish, playing games where lives were at stake. Why? Because I was too embarrassed to admit that I may have actually felt sympathy for him?

It all feels so silly now.

"When did you know?" I wonder, feeling sick. "When did you realize Ashby was the one who..." *Created*, I want to say, but it's an East End term she won't welcome.

She stands up then, walking over to the ancient fridge. Opening it up, she pulls a bottle of vodka from the freezer, her movements slow, as if she's drawing out the process of filling a shot glass. Glancing over her shoulder, she admits, "I'd had some suspicions ever since his kid died. Miranda, as you know, wasn't far behind. East End grieved them so publicly that it became a spectacle." She snorts, mouth curving derisively. "'The year the roses died.' That's what the *Royal Gazette* called it. In any case, photos of them were plastered everywhere. You couldn't get away from it; those green eyes of Michael's, always watching you. Eyes," she stresses, "that looked *exactly* like yours. We were just lucky so many wrongly assumed you got your green eyes from me." Throwing back the shot, she finally turns to me, stone-faced. "But you were four when I knew for sure."

Stunned, it takes me a moment to find my voice. "How?"

She fills the shot glass again. "Because Rufus showed up on our doorstep, demanding to see you."

My chest clenches just imagining it. *Four*. She would have thought she was home free. "He found out?"

"Of course, he did," she snarls before downing the second shot.

"Bribed your goddamn dentist for a cheek swab and confirmed paternity. Why not? He'd already managed to take two of those orphaned Princes of yours. It probably distracted him for a while, but they weren't what he wanted. He wanted Michael. He wanted an heir—a true heir." She points the glass at me, a fuming sort of satisfaction in her eyes. "That's part of how I was able to fend him off. A King has no use for a daughter."

"A *part* of it?" I ask, catching the glint in her eye.

Arching a finely plucked eyebrow, she pops out a hip, drawing my attention to the pistol holstered there. "Well, he did bring a dick to a gunfight."

A reluctant smile tugs at my mouth imagining my mother pulling a gun on King Ashby.

How differently things might have turned out if she'd pulled the trigger.

"I still worried there'd come a day he'd return, but year by year, I grew more and more prepared," she continues, laughing darkly. "A lot of secrets come in and out during the Furies. I gained my leverage and waited to use it, to keep us safe. And then you grew up," she adds, gesturing to me. "You became a woman, and I stopped looking over my shoulder."

Frowning, I pick at my pudding. "And here I thought you were just trying to get me into a Royalship."

She shakes her head, looking tired. "The truth is, I saw that night in the crypt how Royal women were protected. Not just Miranda, but the Lady, the Countess, the Duchess—all of them. I didn't groom you to be a Princess, Verity." Her voice cracks. "I groomed you to be *loved*. Cherished. Protected, like the Mirandas and the Lavinias."

"Loved," I clarify, "by monsters."

"By fighters," she argues, nodding toward the gym. "By *victors*. At least," her eyes roll, "that was the plan."

Pace's rant rings in my ears.

"We're all in cages. Some are bigger than others. Some, like ours, are gilded and comfortable. But that's how being a Royal works. We're trapped

behind territory lines. We're in our brownstone, or tower, or crypt. We may be sitting on bombs waiting to go off at any fucking moment."

"Things are going to change," I tell her, pushing to my feet. "I know you can't see it. I know revolution never came for you, and I'm sorry, Mama. But I'm not in this alone. This baby has more than just me."

"For all of our sakes, I hope that's true," she says, capping the bottle of vodka. "Because as loyal as I am to what I've built here, I couldn't ever not love something you made." She glances down at my belly, a sad smile touching her lips. "Not even the heir to East End."

When I rise from the chair, lunging for her, she meets me halfway, the embrace as hard as it is sweet. She smells like cinnamon and cloves, and even if only for a moment, it's the smell of home. I pull it in, hugging her close, feeling lighter now that some of the secrets of the past are lifted between us.

I know that there's one more bridge I need to rebuild.

I just have to figure out how to do it.

19

Verity

CLASSICAL, subjective, or empirical probability.

That's the bane of my Friday afternoon in stats class with the ex-Prince, Professor Winston. The lecture is drier than sand, and I spend the first ten minutes of it trying with all my might not to nod off to the sound of his droll voice. Sometimes, like an intrusive thought, I imagine what he must have been like in the palace during his Princeship. Who was his Princess? I'll have to ask Adeline next time I'm at the Gilded Rose, even though it'll just make the visualizations worse.

Not that they aren't already awful.

I picture him giving a 'deposit', all sweaty and red, panting as he regales the poor girl with the statistical probability of successful insemination.

The disgust is almost strong enough to keep me alert.

The only thing that truly rouses me is a sudden knock at the door,

Professor Winston pausing with his hand poised over the whiteboard. "Enter!" he calls.

And when the doors swing open, Lex is the one walking through.

I straighten in my seat, freezing when his amber eyes land on me. Him showing up in my stats class is unexpected enough, but that's not what makes heat rise to my cheeks.

His hair is down.

Lex slides the professor a look, something passing between them, and then Winston nods, continuing his lecture. Confused, I watch as Lex climbs the pitched floor to my row, dropping his bag on the table and taking a seat beside me.

I gawk at him openly, watching as he tucks a strand of hair behind his ear. "What are you—"

He slides a cup of coffee to me, leaning over to whisper, "I was late this morning."

I take the coffee automatically, because, yes. I waited for him in the courtyard, achingly disappointed when he never showed up with my daily dose of caffeine. I almost thought of paying a low-level DKS to snag me a cup from the cart, but I resisted, keeping my promise to only get coffee from him.

"Thank you," I whisper. I wish I could say that the first delectable sip is the most indulgent part of the moment, but it'd be a lie. I slide a furtive gaze to him, noting his sleeves have been rolled up, the cordy muscles in his forearm twisting as he twirls a pen between his long, precise fingers. A fidget, perhaps? "How can you be here?" I wonder.

"OChem let out early," he explains, reaching up to run his fingers through his hair. Down the row, a girl watches him with a slack mouth, practically salivating. A quick glance around the room shows she's not the only one. Lex Ashby, to my knowledge, has *never*—not once—worn his hair down in public. "Winston doesn't mind. He'd probably suck my toes if I asked nicely enough."

I recoil. "Please. No more visuals."

He tucks that lock of hair behind his ear again, only to rake his fingers through it and send it tumbling back into his face.

Now *that* is a fidget.

"What's with you?" I ask, more fascinated than suspicious. That is, until his weird jittering sends up an alarm. Frantic but quiet, I ask, "Are you on drugs?"

His amber eyes snap to mine, full of outrage. "Of course not!" When his reaction draws the attention of a few surrounding students, he huffs, draping his arm over the back of my chair. Just like that, he's the very picture of casual, a finger winding idly in my hair. "I'm not used to having an hour to do *nothing*."

"Oh," I breathe, inhaling his clean, spicy scent.

Suddenly, I wish we were in bed.

Which reminds me...

"Uh, so... how's Pace?" I ask, speaking the words to his smooth cheek.

He turns to meet my gaze, so close that I can see his eyes track my swallow. "Why do you want to know about Pace?"

"Just..." I swallow again, wondering how much Lex knows. "The last time I saw him, he seemed upset."

"The last time you saw him," Lex repeats, twirling my hair around and around. "And when was this?"

My answer is purposefully vague. "Few days ago."

Pace's smell is already disappearing from my pillow.

Lex watches me carefully before saying, "Well, Pace is fucking fantastic." A shadow falls over his face. "Wicker's the one I'm worried about."

"Why?"

The crease in his forehead deepens. "He has all those functions to attend this weekend."

I wait for him to elaborate, but nothing comes. "That's new?"

He holds my stare. "It's Mother's Day weekend, Princess."

"Oh." I blink, the conversation from Ashby's sick version of family dinner—god, more than a month ago—coming back to me. I wince. "Is it going to be that bad?"

Snorting, he says, "A bunch of horny, middle-aged socialites who are gagging for his dick, but are told they can't have it? Yeah, it'll be a blast." He rolls his eyes. "Father gave him a get-out-of-jail-free card, but he won't use it."

My face screws up. "Why not?"

He gestures to the whiteboard at the front of the room. "Subjective probability. This weekend will be bad, but next weekend could be worse. He's saving it for something unbearable."

I think about this for a long stretch as Professor Winston goes on about empirical probability. "I wouldn't have expected that from him," I admit. Wicker's always so impulsive, driven by his base needs. The thought of him hoarding a treasure instead of consuming it...

My stomach twists.

Shifting, Lex whispers, "He's been..." but trails off, something complicated crossing his features.

"He's been what?"

He glances at me, eyes shuttering. "He's just been unhappy." I realize then what's happening. Lex doesn't want to divulge too much about his brother to me. It's the same protective glint I see in his eyes whenever Ashby is sniffing around.

"Unhappy." I frown. "Like Pace."

Lex scoffs, giving my hair a mindless tug. "Pace isn't unhappy. Probably because you let him fuck you on Wednesday."

My head whips toward him, jaw dropping. "How do you know?"

"Please," he says, giving me a look. "I can spot his post-coital nap fest from a mile away. He was practically comatose until yesterday."

I wrench my eyes to the front of the room, cheeks warm. "That's between me and him."

"What did I say about that?" His fingers touch my chin, forcing my gaze back to his. There's something calculating in his eyes as he scrutinizes me. "I didn't realize your month in West End was open for fucking. If I had, I probably wouldn't have spent the last three weeks crawling out of my goddamn skin."

"Oh my god," I breathe when it hits me. "Is that what this is? The coffee, the touching, the hair..." I shove his arm away, hissing, "You're trying to get into my pants!"

"Obviously," he says. And then, a glare. "You like my hair."

My face must be glowing crimson. "Oh my god, and in stats class!" It's a struggle to keep my voice low when I want to yell at him. I settle for punching his thigh.

He doesn't even flinch. "Winston? I could fuck you where you sit, and he wouldn't bat an eye."

I sink down further in my chair. "Lex! Stop."

For a while, he does. He heaves this big, laborious sigh, and listens to the lecture. All around us, people steal glances—usually other girls. If Lex notices this, he doesn't show it, his fingers fluttering through my hair every now and again.

Until abruptly, his breath caresses my ear. "I'll finger you first." The whisper is deep, smooth like velvet, my core clenching at the vibration as much as the words. "Make you come on my knuckles like a desperate little slut. I know you like that, the same way I know you're embarrassed right now, but also getting off to the thrill of me talking to you like this in front of a room full of people." Reaching up, he touches my neck. "I can see your pulse jumping, pupils dilating, and there—your thighs rubbing together. You're *drenched*." Close enough that his lips brush the shell of my ear, he whispers, "No one knows your pussy as well as I do, Princess."

I gulp.

"I don't like flirting," he adds, skating his fingertip down my collarbone. "As you've just witnessed, I'm not good at it, which is fine by me because I'm more of an empirical probability guy anyway. I'd much rather do *this*." This time when he touches my chin, turning me to face him, the tips of our noses bump together. "Come with me, and I'll fuck your brains out."

My brain shorts out at his filthy mouth, but my body spurs into action. I have my laptop in my bag so fast, I almost spill my coffee in my haste. "Let's go."

The heat on my skin as we leave the lecture hall isn't from embarrassment. It's sheer want. I start to the door, but he grabs my hand, walking straight past Winston, who never stops teaching, to a door behind the lectern.

The professor's office.

"In here?" I ask, my voice a squeak as he shuts the door. "They'll hear."

"Good, they'll spread the word that the Princess is getting her needs met."

He pushes me against the desk, hands bunching up my shirt to reveal my stomach. He bends to press a kiss against my belly, that long hair grazing my skin. A different sort of flutter builds inside.

"For the record," he unzips his pants and pulls out his thick erection, "what I'm about to do to you isn't going to hurt the baby."

He spins me around, flattening me over the desk, hands dragging both my leggings and panties down with a hard yank. He enters my wet pussy with a swift, deep punch.

I bite down on an exhale of relief, just grateful to feel him buried inside. I never know which version of this man is going to show up, but more and more, it doesn't matter. My ache for him rivals the one he has for me.

Doctor, father, lover... they're all the same; a man capable of giving me everything.

"THANKS FOR THE RIDE." I tug at my dress as we approach the gated building. "I know this is a little weird."

"If I get jumped on the way home, I'm not going to be happy about it." Sy eases the car up to the guard shack. A shiny Mercedes idles in front of us. For the second time, he asks, "Seriously, did you get called to come here? Because it's our month. They can't make demands of you."

"No one is forcing me," I insist, yet again. "There's just something I need to do, and it happens to fall on one of the days I'm in West End."

"A Mother's Day event," he says dryly.

A tea party, to be exact, held at the marina clubhouse, and by the grace of the Forsyth gods, it's finally stopped raining.

Turning to Sy, I take in a deep breath, willing him to hear me. "I know this is hard for you all to understand, but I'm taking my role as Princess seriously. I appreciate everything you've done for me, like having me regularly come back to West End. I never want to give up my family for my position, but I also have obligations now—things that are important to me."

Today isn't an obligation. It's righting a wrong, but I know Sy can't understand any reasoning I offer. The Royals exist in black and white. Them versus everyone else. North Side turned their back on Lavinia long before she turned her back on them. She found a home with her Dukes. I was lucky enough to have a home and a mother who loved me, but the last few months have shown me a life outside the only one I'd ever known.

"You're right. It's weird as fuck, Ver," he admits, watching the car in front of us get waved through. "Seeing you with them." His eyes dart down to my stomach. "Seeing you pregnant with their kid."

"I know." I place my hand over the growing belly. The baby still isn't very big, but like his fathers, he's making himself known. "It's weird for me, too."

Sy pulls up to the shack and rolls down his window, the security guard pausing at the sight of him. Even though he's a King now, he doesn't wear the uniform. There's no slick suit or expensive shoes, just a sleeveless shirt that shows off the roaring Bruin tattoo on his bicep.

The security guard frowns at the muscle car. "Can I help you?" he asks, in a tone that implies he knows we don't belong.

"I'm dropping off the Princess." Sy jerks his thumb at me. "She's going to the party."

The guard drops down, looking across to the passenger seat. I'm a comical contrast to the fighter in the driver seat, in my pretty dress, string of pearls and all. To my relief, the guard blinks in recognition when he sees me. "Oh, yes, of course," he sputters over the low rumble of the engine. "My apologies. We didn't know you were coming."

Wincing, I offer, "Last minute decision."

"Drive straight to the entrance," he says, stepping back, "and Happy Mother's Day, Your Highness."

"Thank you," I reply, giving him a tight smile.

We're waved quickly through, but not before I see him pick up a walkie-talkie.

Sy coughs a laugh into his fist. "Fuck, Ver. You're kind of a big deal around here, huh?" He snorts. "'*Your Highness.*' I thought he was going to shit his pants."

I groan, slumping in the seat. "I assure you, I'm *not* a big deal. If anything, I just broke a million rules by showing up unannounced." And I'm about to enter a room filled with members of my Court, who hate me, while also completely blindsiding my Prince. "But again, thanks for bringing me."

Sy pulls into the motor court, and my door is quickly opened. "You need a ride home?" he asks, "Or I can pick you up at the boundary line."

"Maybe." My stomach flutters with nerves. "I'll let you know."

I take the hand of the attendant, accepting his help out of the car. With one last nod, Sy revs his engine and wastes no time peeling out of the portico. The guard clearly let everyone know I was coming, because, on the way in, everyone seems to recognize me.

"Princess," the attendant greets, and then the doorman, and then a smartly dressed woman who ushers me down the hall. I never get a chance to touch a doorknob or ask for directions. It's as if they hand me off, one by one, in some twisted Royal relay.

According to Adeline, the Mother's Day tea party is a long-standing tradition in East End. Pregnant Princesses aren't graced with an invitation unless they're past the twenty-week mark, which is an indicator of a healthy fetus. That, or they're attending with their own mothers. It's not just women, though. Sons are included as a way to show off the young men of East End, as well as providing an opportunity for matchmaking.

None of those reasons are why Wicker is here.

He's a diamond, flashy and bright, used to make one or more of these women feel special.

The room is crowded and a little warm, a group of women by the door gossiping about the cake table. "Twenty-four karat gold flakes on some of the petit fours," one is saying. Another offers, "I heard she paid the patisserie an extra five grand to cut in front of a Senator whose daughter is having a sweet sixteen." A third gushes, "She's really outdone herself. Last year's cakes were half the cost, and already the talk of the town."

I recognize more people than I expect, probably a sign of how long I've been in East End. The women in my Court are scattered throughout the room. No tennis skirts and crop tops today. Everyone has on their Sunday finest, floral-print dresses that come at least to the knee, if not the ankle. I see Kira, her belly even bigger than before. One of the women fawning over the cakes bears the same features and flawless brown skin as Lakshmi; she has to be her mother. Near the dining room doors is a short, squat woman with a rope of pearls around her neck, and two feet away, looking uncomfortable and bitter, is her daughter, Heather.

But I'm not here to see my Court. Those cunts can all go fuck themselves.

I spot my target right by the absurd dessert display, past one of the enormous flower arches. They're roses, obviously, but not the white shade of purity I've grown resentfully accustomed to. These are a subtle shade of blush pink; a maternal color.

He's in a pale blue suit, looking as if he just walked off the pages of a spring menswear catalog. He is, as expected, surrounded by women. The event may be a tea, but he's holding a flute of champagne in his hand. I recognize the woman on his arm from the fundraiser: Trudie Stein.

I observe nervously as she leans into him, touching his shoulder. Taking a deep breath and straightening my shoulders, I approach the circle and squeeze in next to him. "There you are," I say, pushing up on my tiptoes to press a kiss on his cheek. "Sorry for being so late."

I wobble at the height difference, but almost as if he's expecting it, his arm circles around my waist to balance me. The only hint of surprise Wicker allows is the smallest lift of his brow. He's too good, otherwise. Good at faking it. We're practiced from the shows on campus.

The women around him are less adept. There's a ripple of horror spreading through them. I don't belong here, and with the way Trudie is staring daggers at my hand on Wicker's arm, she's making it clear I don't belong near *him*, specifically.

Wrong, bitch.

"Princess," he says, casually scanning the room. "I was starting to worry about you."

I take his stiff hand and pry open his fingers, flattening them over my belly. "Turns out none of my dresses fit anymore, so I had to go out and get something for this special event."

"Well, you look breathtaking," he says, taking in the pale green wraparound dress I bought on a last-minute trip to Forsyth Center. *Shit*. Did I take off the tag?

"Princess," Trudie says, lips pressed into a coldly polite smile. "I wasn't aware you'd passed the twenty-week mark."

"Not quite," I admit, rubbing my palm over Wicker's knuckles, "but when I found out about the tea, I just couldn't resist making an appearance in support of all the mothers in Forsyth." I glance around dramatically. "Are you here with your own children? I'd love to meet them."

The other women watch our exchange like volleys over a net.

Trudie doesn't give an inch, still shoulder-to-shoulder with Wicker. "Sadly, they couldn't be here. My daughter Brooklyn is finishing up her coursework in Scotland, and Armand is in Asia."

"Oh," I ask, feigning interest. "Also studying?"

There's a soft snort from one of the women, who quickly covers it up with a cough into her handkerchief. Trudie shoots her a glare.

"Armand is on a journey of self-exploration. I'm sure he'll return soon." She smiles at Wicker, reaching up to straighten his collar. "I'm grateful Mr. Ashby has volunteered to be my escort in their absence."

Volunteer, my ass. Wicker hasn't moved his hand from my stomach, and he's gone strangely quiet. Okay, maybe not strangely. I've placed him in the middle of a rock and a hard place. Chances are, he's not overly fond of either of us.

Up front, the orchestra wraps up their song.

"That's the signal for us to head to the dining room for the tea serving," Trudie announces. Everyone starts toward the double doors that lead to the adjacent room. From here, I see dozens of circular tables, laden with fine china and centerpieces. Trudie lingers, casting me a sympathetic smile. "I apologize, Princess, but you weren't on the list, so you'll be unable to sit at my table. I can squeeze you in the back if you'd like." A hand flutters at her chest. "Oh, I hope you won't take offense if you're not offered a petit four. They were custom ordered and exquisitely designed for only those who RSVPed." She looks at my Prince. "Whitaker, are you ready?"

"I need a moment to speak to the Princess," he says, sliding his fingers off my belly and down to my hand. "Go ahead without me."

I'd like to say Trudie's displeasure was obvious, but the Botox injections make expressive cues impossible to read. Her anger only comes through when she steps up to him and flattens her hands over his lapels. "Don't make me look foolish," she quietly says, leaning in to kiss his cheek. "Today, you belong to me." I don't miss the icy look she shoots me, nor the scorching fury it ignites in my chest.

"I'm so sorry," I cut in, matching her tense, frigid smile. "But Wicker belongs to me first and foremost, especially on an occasion meant to honor the mother of his child." Raising my eyebrows, I adopt an innocent, guileless look. "But I can always call my father and double-check. He certainly wouldn't want any misunderstandings as to the priority of his Prince."

She turns the full force of her stare on me. "Maybe you're mistaken, Princess, because much like the catering, I paid five figures to have something pretty on my arm today." The smile might still be plastered on her face, but the words she speaks are gritted through clenched teeth.

So are mine. "Then maybe you should have bought a watch."

Her eyes spark, a vein in her forehead popping, and for a split second, I really think Trudie might throw down.

And then Wicker steps between us, whisking me away as he calls out, "I'll find you shortly, Trudie."

I'm fuming the whole time he leads me out into the corridor, mostly because I can't believe she had the fucking nerve, but also because I'm a daughter of West End. I was learning punches and grapple holds at the age of nine. I could rearrange the plastic in her goddamn face.

But I'm pregnant.

And I can't fucking *fight*.

It's only when we reach the middle of the hallway that Wicker whirls on me, face pinched as he hisses, "Are you fucking serious?"

"Me?!" I shriek, gaping at him in outrage. "That woman deserves a heel in her eye socket!"

His eyes widen in disbelief. "Why? Because she made a deal with my Father that forces me to pretend I'm a doting lover to her in public?"

"Yes!"

He snaps straight, blue eyes pinning me. "So only you're allowed to do that."

"Yes!" The answer is instinctive, but as his response sinks into my brain, I add, "No!" And then, "Wait—what? That's not the same!"

But for a moment, I'm not so sure. There's this thing I've noticed about Wicker when we're performing as happy Royals on campus. He always touches me—fingers entwined with mine, a hand on the small of my back, or sometimes, even a kiss—and he's good at it. Practiced, fluid, just like he is on the ice.

But his eyes, as beautiful as they are, are always fixed somewhere in the distance.

Just like they were with Trudie.

The realization grips my chest like a fist.

"What are you doing here, Red?" he asks, sounding tired. "This isn't the kind of party you break *into*."

"It's..." I swallow, trying to shake the sick feeling from my stomach. "It's Mother's Day, and you're my—well, *one of* my baby's daddies.

I know you may not want to spend the day with me, but you sure as fuck shouldn't spend it with that predator."

"Still, after all this time, you think I have a choice." His chuckle is devoid of any humor, barbed and jarring as he advances on me. "You come waltzing in here like you own me, but the truth is, you can't pay the price. So if you want to piss on my leg because you're jealous—"

"I didn't come here because I'm jealous!" I squawk, leaning away. "I came here to apologize. And to rescue you."

"Rescue me?" he scoffs, lip curling snidely. "Because I need rescuing."

"Because you're more than this!"

The snarl on his face deepens. "Don't you dare tell me what I am. You think the way you're whoring yourself out is more righteous than mine because it makes a baby?"

"That's not what I mean," I say, rubbing my forehead. It's beginning to throb. "None of this is coming out right."

"Let's hear it, then," he snaps, eyes wild. "This apology—the one you're so willing to get me in trouble to give?"

I can't help the way my lip wobbles, but I do try to tamp it back. Holding in the way my voice wants to crack, I rasp out, "I-I wanted to say—"

But he barks, "Speak up, Red! Can't hear you over the violins."

"When I told Lavinia about you..." I try, my body strung tighter than a piano wire. "I wanted you to know I didn't plan it."

He releases a low, cutting chuckle, his eyes tracking the way my eyes water. "Oh, Red. I'd respect you so much more if you had."

My shoulders sink. "Don't say that."

"Why?" he asks, never relenting. Not until he has me backed up against the wall. "Because you can't handle how dirty you played me?"

Fervently, I say, "That's not how it happened."

His palm smacks into the wall, right beside my head. "That's exactly how it happened!" He fumes at me, inches from my face, "You want to apologize? Then be honest, for once in your goddamn life. You told them because you hated me. Own it, Red!"

"I told them because I *didn't* hate you!" I explode, shoving his shoulders. As he stumbles back, it all breaks free. "You were awful to me. For *weeks*. Every deposit was another reminder that I was just a thing to you, and I couldn't do *anything*. I had to take it, day after day. Even when it felt good, it was torture. And you know the worst part?" I ask, throat clenching. "You probably know that feeling better than me!"

He finds his footing, eyes flashing in vicious satisfaction. "So you admit it."

"It wasn't that." I shake my head, feeling abruptly wrung out. "Suddenly, I became putty in your hands. That night at the fundraiser, in the swimming pool, then in the car, and back at the palace..." The anger leaves me raw and ragged, staring into his eyes as if I could possibly find him again. "I saw you, Wicker—the *real* you—and everything felt different. You weren't a monster anymore. You were just..." At first, I think I can't possibly find the words. But he's so close—close enough to reach out and touch, my palm cradling his pale cheek. "You were sad, and genuine, and scared, and beautiful, and..." His eyes are wide enough that I could count the capillaries if I tried. The truth is, I could go on and on, finding new words to describe the man I catch these stunning glimpses of. Maybe that's part of the reason I confess, "You were someone I could feel myself falling for."

He's still, utterly silent for so long that I let my hand slip away, fingertips dragging over his smooth jaw. Wicker was terrible to me, but never because I gave him the chance by letting him in. That's what stings, deep down in my soul. He trusted me with something precious, something meant to help me, and I mangled it.

In a way, I cut him deeper.

"Lavinia clocked it before even I did," I say, ducking my head, "and I felt so fucking stupid. Weak, like a failure. How can so much pain be wiped away so quickly? Who falls for someone like that?" I ask the question as if he could possibly answer.

He doesn't even twitch.

"You're very good at what you do, and I understand that the way you learned it, and the reason you learned it, is heinous, but it's also a weapon." Sighing, I admit, "So when I told her about you, I just... panicked. I was trying to prove to myself you were nothing because the truth hurt too much. Maybe you know what that's like. Maybe you don't." Steeling myself, I find the courage to lift my chin, meeting his frozen gaze as the tears finally spill over, trailing down my cheek like fire. "It's excruciating to care about someone who hurts you."

There's a long stretch where he just watches me, and even though I try to swat the tears away before they become obvious, I know he sees them.

It doesn't matter.

Laying myself bare like this, trying to salvage the unsalvageable, was the worst idea.

I realize that now.

"I'm sorry, Wicker," I say, "if I ever became that person for you. I know you didn't want this. I wish..." I shake my head, laughing grimly. "I just wish everything had been different—for both of us. I think, in another life—"

But I never finish the thought.

I can't bring myself to.

Instead, I pull in all the misery and guilt, tucking it up inside. It's what allows me to meet his eyes. "I'll call King Ashby and take responsibility for ruining your night with Trudie."

That's what sticks with me as I walk away: the way he just stares at me, emotionless and frozen, not giving an inch. It's only then, as I'm marching for the doors, that I allow myself to imagine that other life. What would Wicker be like without the resentment and obligation?

Without the past.

Without Rufus Ashby.

"Verity," comes his voice, from behind me. It's jagged and quiet. "Hold up."

When I turn, he's not looking at me. He's in perfect profile, from the curve of his nose to the swoop of his blonde hair. He's looking down at his shoes, and for a long moment, he doesn't say anything else. This is the most complicated part about Whitaker Ashby.

How someone so beautiful can be so unreadable.

Finally, he turns to me, locking those blue eyes on mine. "Wanna go eat all those ridiculous petit fours with me?"

The answer falls from me clumsily, *recklessly*, like a boulder. "God, yes."

20

Wicker

My cheek is still humming where she touched me before, even long after we've set off for the dining room.

She rushes after me, her heels clicking like automatic gunfire, until we reach the dessert table. Trudie and the rest of these bitches have been going on and on about the food all afternoon. Aside from the booze, it was the only thing about this stupid tea I was even looking forward to. Father has had me on his salad diet for fucking *weeks*.

I snag one of the platters and begin emptying decorative tiered trays onto it, little petit fours and cookies tumbling together.

Beside me, Verity wrings her hands. "We won't get in trouble?"

Touch me again.

"You're the Princess, for fuck's sake." I shoot her an annoyed look, nudging a tray toward her. It's filled with finger foods. Little sandwiches with the edges cut off. "I don't know why you tiptoe around

East End like a mouse. No one in this whole godforsaken town is as bulletproof as you are. You could probably strangle one of those bitches in broad daylight, and the rest of them would just worry about your manicure."

There's a moment where she soaks this in, her brow all knitted up, before she slides me a sly look that sends my skin fucking aching for another touch.

She grabs a platter and starts dumping. "They do look good."

"I've been smelling this stuff for *hours*." Platter in hand, I turn, nearly running into a server. The man darts a gaze between us and the pilfered table, mouth going slack in shock. Shrugging, I gracefully pluck a bottle of sparkling water off the tray. "Perfect. The Princess is gonna be parched."

Verity almost topples her platter when I hand it off to her, our fingers grazing in a way that nearly makes me shudder. The bottle of champagne chilling on the table comes with me. Without missing a beat, I lead her through a side door that goes to the kitchen.

"Richard," I greet the stoner in a hairnet and apron, both of us pausing. There's a bit of a complicated history. "How you been?" I ask. "How's Klancy?"

"Not bad," he says, glassy eyes darting to me. "Heading upstairs?"

"If that's okay," I say, lifting the tray in offering.

Perking up, he takes some cookies. "Go for it, man." The large stainless steel shelf is easy enough to wheel away from the wall, revealing a squat hatch. Glancing at Verity, he even does me the courtesy of holding open the door. "Princess."

Verity's heels click-clack warily behind me, but go silent as we're faced with the staircase's sharp incline. I duck under the frame, balancing my tray and bottle of booze carefully.

Turning back, I see her glaring into the darkness. "You're always taking me into creepy hidden passages," she grumbles, carefully following my lead. My fingers buzz with the impulse to grab onto some part of her and drag her the rest of the way. It's not impatience or irritation, but instead, this nagging, clawing need.

Touch me, touch me, touch me.

She waits until we're halfway up to ask, "That guy, Richard… he's South Side, isn't he?"

I answer the unspoken question. "We took a couple of classes together freshman year. Usually, when I make a run at a guy's girlfriend, I expect violence, but Richard took me aside and asked me to show her a nice time. Called it a birthday present. It completely ruined the conquest for me, so I never ended up actually fucking her." I turn to toss her a smirk. "But I got a pretty nice hookup out of the deal."

We turn twice, eventually getting to another door. I open it with my elbow, and bright light fills the stairwell. Stepping out, we're greeted by a blue sky and an incredible view of the river.

"Whoa." Verity gapes as she takes it in. It's difficult to watch her here, all sun-soaked and fiery, because that finger-buzzing crashes into me full force. Her skin looks smooth and radiant, and I can just imagine the feel of her body against mine, all soft and warm.

Touch. Me.

"Expecting a dusty attic?" I wonder, leading her to the back corner. There are a few pool lounge chairs that have seen better days, and a rickety-looking table with one leg bound with duct tape. I clear away an overflowing ashtray before setting the food down.

Verity follows suit, looking nervous once her hands are free. "Do you come here a lot?"

From anyone else, that'd be a horrible pick-up line.

From her, it's sincere.

Maybe that's why it's so easy to reveal all these secret, hidden places to her.

I shrug. "I've got escape routes in almost every function hall in Forsyth. Maddox Hotel's basement rec room is the funnest, but this is the best view." I loosen my tie, watching as she casts a glance out over the water. "It's like I can't fucking breathe down there."

As I'm undoing my top two buttons, Verity bends down to unbuckle her heels.

Great idea.

I kick off my own shoes and sit in the lounge chair, hoping it doesn't collapse under my weight. "Thailand," I say, suddenly.

She frowns. "Er, what?"

"Armand. *Armie*. Trudie's son," I clarify, watching her hands. I wonder if she'll touch me again. "He's fucking his way through Thailand."

"Oh." She wrinkles her nose, perching on the other seat. "I guess that tracks."

"Yeah, he's a prick. A former Prince, actually. One of Autumn's. He took off the minute he was cut loose of his duties." I pick up a tiny sandwich, giving it a sniff, but instead, swap it for a petit four. Cruelly, I wait until she's tipping back the bottle of sparkling water to ask, "So you're in love with me, huh?"

She sputters, spraying it into the breeze. It's all I can do not to howl with laughter. "What?!" she coughs, eyes wide and glistening. "I didn't—I don't—I *never said*—"

The laughter finally breaks free, tasting just as sweet as the chocolate on my tongue. "Christ, you're such an easy mark." Then, quietly, "It's why I believe what you said down there."

She blinks, wiping her chin. "You do?"

I'm starting to think I've been reading her all wrong, which is embarrassing. I've been seeing her as a woman first and a West Ender second, but the truth is, she's both things at the same time. She's vulnerable, and she's defensive about it. She's pliable, and she's fighting it. She's desperate for companionship, and she resents it.

She's not Michael Ashby with tits.

She's *me* with tits.

"You're thinking it could have been an act that night," I say, taking a swig of the champagne. Meeting her gaze, I lift an eyebrow. "I'm good, but not '*divulge a decades-old family secret to sell the moment*' good."

She looks down at the finger sandwich in her hand. "Oh."

It really hangs there.

I thought of trying to be a boyfriend once, back in high school. I didn't even have anyone in mind, but I felt the pull of the idea; one person to fall into, soft and familiar. The concept of a non-brotherly love. Something warm and comfortable and safe. Just one problem with that.

"I wasn't built for attachments."

She looks up slowly, like she's afraid to meet my stare. "I wasn't asking for one. I just needed you to know why I did it. That I'm not just a traitor. Things had gotten confusing."

"I get that," I say, looking down at the ganache on my fingers. "The way I was with you... during my deposits..." I don't know why it bothers me how she brought it up down there. She knows what she was brought into the palace for. She signed the covenants. I did my job the only way I knew how.

Resentfully.

"You were mean." There's a shadow in her eyes when I glance over.

"I was pissed," I admit, kissing any hopes of being touched good-bye. "But it wasn't actually about you. Being told when and who to fuck is nothing new."

Her face does something complicated. "So I was just another client?"

"Client?"

She nods toward the door. "Like Trudie, and the rest of them."

I shake my head, snorting. "Oh, Red, you were so much worse. You weren't some old woman to parade me around on a leash to make her feel young again. You were this ridiculously hot redhead, all innocent and pure. Someone I might have actually wanted." Giving in, I finally reach out and touch her leg, running my fingers over the pale skin. The frantic buzzing eases. "You're defiant and determined. You're all the things that he beat out of us a long time ago."

"I understand," she says, blinking down at my hand.

Touch me touch me touch...

I slide it away, fingertips dragging against flesh. "No, Verity, you don't."

But her green eyes snap abruptly to mine. "Over here, I'm a

symbol of health and fertility—of the future. But it's all false imagery to convince the rest of Forsyth that the Princes are above the rest. That we're more civilized, with our masquerades and ceremonies. That he's a loving and doting family man, when really, it's the opposite. He's a monster, and he's created more monsters who, deep down, are rotten to the core."

"So you think I'm a monster?" I bare my teeth, willing to take the title. I deserve it.

Some of that fire in her eyes bleeds away. "That's the problem, actually. I don't think you need to be. None of us do."

"Us? You including yourself in that?" I ask, raising an eyebrow.

She sighs, leaning against the back of her chair, her hand resting on her belly. "You're not the only one he created, Wick. He's my father, too."

It rankles inside, this thought that she sees herself as one of us when she's only been his daughter for five months. *Try nineteen years*, I want to say. But my brothers and I... maybe we were the test run. The exercise to work out all the kinks. If he's created us, then in some way, we've created him. Taught him all the best ways of controlling hurt, angry, lonely people.

Already, he's made her into something to be used. Isolated.

"God, we're really all fucked, aren't we?" I take a bitter swallow of champagne and stare across the river, looking at the sun as it dips behind the trees. Trudie is probably losing her shit downstairs. There will be consequences for abandoning her, but I just can't seem to care.

She's not the one I want to touch me.

"Julian," Verity says suddenly.

I lower the bottle. "Huh?"

There's this very particular way her hair sways in the wind. Not heavy and full of hairspray, but light and floating. Right now, it's billowing around her shoulders, her eyelashes fluttering as she basks in the breeze. "For the baby's name. Julian. What do you think?"

I pull a face as she looks at me. "I think he'll get his ass kicked on the ice with a name like that."

"Hmm." Her lips purse. "Pace told me he thinks I should pick out a name. It wasn't really on my radar before, but now I keep thinking about it." She wrinkles her nose. "So that's a 'no' on Julian?"

At this moment, after dropping all this truth on one another, I want to be able to tell Verity I care, but I just can't. I don't want anything to do with this baby. It's just another cuff linking me back to Father.

"Call it whatever you want." I pick up a tart and give her a wink. "As long as it's not Julian."

She picks up a macaroon and tosses it at me, but I snag it easily out of the air and pop it in my mouth.

"You're a pig," she mutters, the playful glint in her eyes softening any sting to it.

"*I'm* a pig?" I gesture to the trays. "You've eaten a dozen of those little cake things in ten minutes flat."

Her jaw drops, laughter spilling from her throat. "I had to! You were going to eat them all!"

A gust of wind blows off the river, and Verity shivers, wrapping her arms around her upper body.

Inspiration strikes.

"Come here," I say, beckoning her over.

The look she gives me is wary. *Fair.*

"You're cold, but I'm not ready to go back down there," I say, shifting my legs to either side of the lounge chair to make room. "I won't bite," I smirk, "hard."

There's one long, last beat before she rises off her chair, turning to sit between my legs. *Finally*, I think, wrapping my arms around her. It's just as good as I remember from those short nights in her bed, folding her into me like a new organ. Nudging my nose into her hair, I pull in the scent of it, different from how she smells when she's in East End. There's more lavender now, but the scent of rose is still there, peeking stubbornly underneath.

The buzzing roar beneath my skin quiets entirely.

"Better?" I ask, feeling her slowly relax.

"Yes."

In some ways, it's even scarier to know this is all it takes now. There was a time only one thing could ease the raging disquiet in my blood, the need to fuck as strong as the urge to breathe. But as we sit there, watching the sky's fiery glow over the water, I think I might prefer this. A lot less messy.

"You didn't have to come today, so..." It's a struggle to get the words out, to let them nestle into her hair like a devastating secret. "Thanks for rescuing me." And then, as stubborn as the scent of roses clinging to her, "Even though I didn't need it."

She releases a silent laugh, like it's obvious I was hanging on by a thread. It probably was. "You're welcome. Although maybe next time, I'll wait for you to actually ask." She turns just enough to show me the pensive curve of her frown. "Everyone's gone out of their way to make it seem otherwise, but I'm starting to think we're on the same side, Wicker." She glances up, meeting my gaze. "Maybe we should start acting like it."

~

Like a well-oiled machine, Lex and I handle the trade-off with West End, everything going off without a hitch. The gun transaction happens quickly, loaded from one vehicle to the other, and for once, even Maddox manages to keep his mouth shut. Verity emerges from the back of the SUV appropriately dressed, with a container tucked in the crook of her arm and a baby bump that even I can't ignore. It's strange to think this is already becoming routine.

All but one very noticeable thing.

The anger I expect every time I see her has simmered off since Mother's Day, a week ago. Shifted, maybe. I don't know what she is to me now, but I can't muster up all those bitter, burning feelings of hatred anymore.

I think I might pity her.

Not because of the parasite, or the way it was made, but because she hasn't realized what it means yet. Even as she walks the distance from the Dukes to us, she has one hand on her belly, like she's protecting it absentmindedly, a new habit.

She thinks she gets to care.

"Ready?" I ask as she approaches, my eyes scanning the lot.

But Lex is the one to touch her, ushering her toward the SUV with a hand on the small of her back. On the way, she shoots me a quick, conspiratorial smirk, reigniting the memory of that evening on the roof of the marina, both of us cramming sweets down our gullets.

But the thought of Lex finding out isn't what has my stomach all twisted up. It's the way she openly talked about Father's demands on me, how sad she seemed for me to be in the clutches of women like Trudie.

Pity.

That's what it was.

The things I do aren't something I think about. We each have our roles. Our skills. We fulfill our duties to the Kingdom.

This just happens to be mine.

Verity's comments picked at a festering wound, one I've kept bandaged and covered up since the age of ten. In one sugar-fueled conversation, Verity Sinclaire ripped off that bandage and let the wound ooze freely.

"What's that?" I ask from the backseat once we're on the road.

"Banana pudding," she says, eyes flicking to Lex's in the driver's seat. She holds it a little tighter. "My mother made it for me. It's my favorite."

The thought of ball-busting Mama B wearing an apron and whipping up food for her daughter is laughably foreign. Maybe that's because all we've ever had is Danner and a series of nameless cooks cycling through the palace.

"Never had it," I mutter, thinking that it sounds gross, like something served at a trailer park or smelly gyms.

"Too bad," she clutches it closer to her and smirks, "it's delicious."

Lex's eyes ping between us, probably trying to figure out which to suss out first; the fact Verity is smuggling in unapproved food, or the fact she and I aren't going for each other's throats.

In the end, he opts to keep quiet about both.

Smart.

Her growing belly isn't the only reminder of the way the parasite is overtaking our lives. Back at the palace, trucks take up the circular drive, their sides adorned with business names: East End Catering, Bouquets by Fran, Mercer Pyrotechnics.

"Oh my god..." Her words drift off as Lex passes them, heading straight to the garage. "Tell me that's not for—"

"The gender reveal," Lex finishes with a glower. "They've been here for three days. It's like we're hosting a state dinner or something."

"Yeah, if you thought the masquerade and Valentine's Day were a big deal, then get ready." I snort, head shaking. "Father's been preparing for this day for twenty years. It's going to fucking suck."

Once inside, we dodge staff dressed in white and black, carting in enough food and drink to feed an army. When we pass the ballroom, she gets a horrified glimpse of the explosion of pinks and blues. Not exactly subtle, but when has Rufus Ashby ever been accused of that? He's notorious for his extravagance, but not for actually having any real taste.

Ducking around the heightened security, Danner stops us at the end of the stairs. "Your suits are waiting for you in your room," he says, then turns to Verity. "And the Princess' team is in her suite. Welcome back, Miss."

"Thank you," Verity sputters, watching Danner bow. "Team? There's a team?"

"Hair, makeup, stylists. Your handmaiden is already organizing them." He looks down at the container. "Shall I put that in the refrigerator for you?"

Her grip tightens, fully aware that if the pudding goes into the kitchen, she's never getting it back. I reach out and snag it out of her hands. "I'll take that."

"Wick!" she grabs for it, but I hold it over my head, taking way too much satisfaction in the way she hops.

"Chill, Red. There's a refrigerator up in Pace's room. I'll keep it safe for you there."

She frowns but exhales in resignation. "Fine, but you better not eat it."

I wrinkle my nose. "You really don't need to worry about that."

Upstairs, she parts from us outside our room. Pace looks up as she passes, dark eyes lifting from the screen where he's been watching us until now.

Down the hall, Verity stops in her doorway. "What the—"

There's no doubt what she means. Over the past three weeks, we've overtaken her bed, dragging in our own pillows and bedding, not the least of which being my Egyptian sheets. Lex brought in the fan that helps him block out the sound of Effie in her cage, his pile of parenting books and hair ties growing on the bedside table. In the bathroom, I've added my bottle of conditioner and shaving gel on the marble shelf next to hers. Pace hasn't brought it up yet, but there's a new monitor, still in the box, that I just know is going to make its way in there eventually.

Her room has, with varying degrees of embittered defiance, become our room.

She looks down the hallway at the three of us, her lips pressed into a thin line, but says nothing before stepping inside.

"How much time do we have?" I ask, stepping into the room and securing the food container in the refrigerator. I grab a bottle of beer and sit on Pace's couch. Popping the top, I take a long swig, knowing it's not enough to get me through the night. I reach for the box on top of the coffee table, but Lex's hand comes down on top of mine.

"No weed. Not tonight. We need to be present. No slip-ups." He looks toward the door. "For *them*."

"Them?" I ask, but the confusion is short-lived. *Her and the fuck-ling*. Groaning, I fall back onto the couch. "Seriously?"

I look at Pace for a little help, but he shrugs. "He's right. Everyone is going to be under a lot of pressure tonight. A clear head is probably for the best." Lower, he angrily mutters, "Reckless bullshit. Can't even vet all the people coming through here. Security this week might as well be a wet paper bag."

Running my fingers through my hair, I look between them. "Who the fuck are you people?"

That sets the tone for the rest of the afternoon. We dress quickly, and *soberly*, pulling on our tuxes and tying ties, until we're waiting out in the hallway for Verity to get this night over with.

She emerges from her room in a white, lace dress that hugs the swell of her belly like a glove. The neckline is low, giving an appropriate but all too enticing peek at her tits. I swear to god, they doubled in size while she was over in West End.

My brothers both react to the sight of her in their own way. Lex is strung tighter than my cummerbund, the shell of his ear a glowing, blushing red. Pace stares at her like a heat-seeking missile, raking his bottom lip through his teeth. There's no doubt in my mind he'd fuck her right here if he could.

How did I become the least horny fucker of the three of us?

Pace is the first to crack, stalking forward to meet her. His hand is curled around her neck before he even stops, hauling her into him for a hard, audibly wet kiss. Her fingers grip his shoulders hard, like she's caught off guard, trying to stay balanced.

I run two fingers under my collar, trying to get air.

This night can't end soon enough.

"You look..." Lex falters when Pace finally releases her, reaching up to rub his blushing ear. "Er, you look nice." His gaze is fixed right to the swell of her stomach. After a beat, he adds, "Pretty."

I scoff. "You've been around me far too long to have so little game."

He shoots me a glare, but that ear-blush has traveled to his neck. Like Pace, he obviously wants to nail her regularly. Lex has always seen sex as an unavoidable, if fun, biological function. Watching him stammer, and, like... *try*?

This girl has no idea their balls are in the palm of her hand.

"Thank you." She pushes a curl behind her ear, the Princess ring catching the light with the movement. "Maybe this white dress will make it through the night without getting blood on it, unlike the others." The words could be barbed and acerbic, but they're not. She says it airily, her gaze dipping to the floor, and an awkward silence envelops us.

Once again, I'm reminded of my role in this. In some ways, I've treated Verity no better than the men and women of East End have treated me. The thought leaves an aftertaste that I don't particularly care for.

Kind of sour.

Instead of acknowledging this, I link my arm with hers, shrugging. "Bloody dresses are a requirement of any Royal event in the palace. But in case you didn't know," I add, leading her toward the stairs, "the blood doesn't necessarily have to be your own."

She glances up at me with a dark smile. "I'll keep that in mind."

MY BROTHERS DON'T ATTEND as many black-tie events as I do, and it shows. It's painful to watch Lex move about the room with an overly formal stiffness, his motions perfunctory and robotic. Sure, he knows the right things to say and do, when to kiss cheeks and when to offer a firm handshake, but there's none of the finesse that comes with years of weekly practice.

Across the room, Pace is in the middle of a conversation with one of Father's CIOs, looking like he'd rather take a walk off the balcony than spend another moment engaged in small talk with a corporate tool.

And Verity...

You'd never know she's the same woman who endured all the trials and abuse that come with being a Princess. We've watched them come and go over the years, and none of them have taken to the role with equal parts feisty independence and determined perseverance like she has. In a way, it's a little unnerving, how well-suited to the role she is.

Maybe it's in her blood.

There's a small part of me that realizes this whole thing may come to fruition. That she'll carry the baby to term, survive labor, and hand over the first true Ashby heir in a generation. Maybe she'll get her wish and name the baby something meaningful to her.

Then I remember how this obligation will do nothing but fuck up our lives.

"Whitaker," I hear, wincing at my name. I've kept to the edges of the room all night, snagging flutes of champagne, doing my best to avoid cougars—particularly Trudie Stein, after standing her up at the tea. The voice doesn't come from a woman, but a man, and I glance over and see Darnell Livingston approaching, expertly draining a glass of bourbon. "Tough loss the other night. That was a beautiful goal. Too bad you came up short. The instinct you and your brother have together… well, it's a goddamn sight to see."

"Well, you know what Father says." I peer across the room at him, lip curling. "Practice makes perfect."

He claps me on the shoulder with a meaty paw. "Good thing you've got one more year to claim that title from Easton."

I try to muster up some team spirit. "That's the plan."

He nods. Rory's father was a D-man back in the day. He even played professionally for a few seasons up north; opportunities me and Pace won't have even if we wanted them. A drop of sweat glides down my back.

He looks around the room and whistles loudly. "Fuck, Ashby went all out on this shindig, didn't he?"

"Ah, you know Father," I say, rocking back on my heels. "He's never met a balloon arch he could resist."

He laughs the way all guys his age and class do: uproariously, as if they're the star of the show. "I have to tell you, my wife was disappointed when Rory wasn't chosen as Prince, but I was relieved. It's a lot of pressure you guys are under. School, hockey, East End obligations, and then a fucking kid on the way." His gaze sweeps over Verity in the distance, and then he leans in, eyebrows wagging. "Although, your Princess sure is a looker. If she's anything like her mother, I bet she's a fucking tiger in bed."

Annoyance pricks along my skin. I get this mental flash of what it'd look like to break the stem off my champagne flute and bury it in his neck.

Ungodly messy.

"No offense," he continues, like he's not a heartbeat away from bleeding out on the parquet floors, "but these gender reveals are some kind of youngster bullshit if you know what I mean." He waves over a waiter and drops his empty glass on the tray. "Back when we were having kids, we'd find out or not, pick blue or pink for the nursery, and move on with life. All this," he waves at the grandeur, "it's ridiculous. What's your father going to do when the baby gets here? Have a parade?"

"More than likely." There's not a trace of humor in my eyes.

Darnell sees it, grimacing. "The good news, I guess, is that as long as the paternity test pans out, your Princess will be set for life."

Unless it has my DNA, and then it'll be a Kayes, looking over its shoulder just like I have.

The loud clang of metal against glass ricochets through the ballroom.

"May I have your attention!" Father's voice rings out over the crowd, his eyes pinging around the room. First to Lex, then Pace, then me, and on to Verity. He makes a beckoning motion. "Children, please come forward."

Thankful for the escape, I nod at Darnell and set across the room to meet the others. Lex and I share a long-suffering look, but Pace is too wound up to convey any message to. His eyes keep scanning the room, a fine sheen of sweat building on his forehead. He looks sick, dark circles under his eyes. With so many people in and out of the palace, his paranoid mania has gone into hyperdrive.

Verity settles between them—Lex and Pace—and I hang off to the side, doing anything I can to not be a part of this.

The glance she tosses at me could be full of irritation or anger.

But it isn't.

She just dips her chin before turning back to the room, her belly on full display for the masses.

Up on the platform, Father addresses the crowd more than us. "I know what you're all thinking," he begins, waving his champagne flute toward the room. "That this is the tackiest show of self-indulgence you've ever seen. And to that, I say," he pauses dramatically, "...wait until you see the first birthday."

The room fills with titters and claps.

Gag me.

"You only have your first grandchild once," he goes on, his tone growing more serious. "I know Forsyth enjoys its rumor mill, so I won't pretend you don't all understand my predicament. The King of creation, unable to bear fruit." There's a hush in the room, and I slide my gaze toward Lex, who's stiffer than a statue.

Father never discusses this privately, let alone publicly.

"Evidently," he goes on, "it was my lot in life to create only twice, but really, such miracles they were." He reaches out to touch Verity's shoulder, and she flinches. "Blood begets blood, and though I already know what this child is, I must say that either possibility would see me equally pleased. Sons are muscles and bones bearing the strength to not only carry on legacy, but also protect it. And daughters..." He pulls his hand back, stroking her hair. When she takes an almost imperceptible step away from him, he doesn't even notice. "Daughters are the heart—the beauty—which bears the soul to nurture it."

I roll my eyes as the crowd applauds.

Luckily, he raises his glass, beaming out over the guests. "Now, if everyone could please move to the balcony for our grand announcement."

Even though it's an invitation for the audience, they watch the four of us like we're the entertainment, their stares like hot pokers on my neck as I file out behind my brothers and Verity. The bruised shadow of dusk has already taken the sky, the late May air full of moist warmth.

"Act surprised," Lex says quietly as we move to the railing. He catches my eye as if I'm the one who'll screw up. Okay, fair. In a show of cooperation, I bend down to brush a featherlight kiss against Verity's temple, ignoring the zing of heat that sparks when my lips touch her skin.

Strains of dramatically uplifting music swell from the orchestra within the ballroom, but it's the first firework, popping off like a warning shot, that sets me on edge. The bang ricochets off the stone exterior, a green explosion blooming across the sky. The dark, still waters around the palace reflect it like toxic radiation.

The music is timed with the fireworks, the tempo and explosions gaining in frequency. I look over at my brothers, at Verity, their blank expressions awash in a rainbow of colors. Verity's fingers find mine. I'm not sure who is anchoring who.

"Here we go," Pace mutters. He'd helped program the show, sending Father's plan to Mercer Pyrotechnics. As the first blue hits the sky, a strange feeling hits my chest. It's only then that I realized I sort of liked having this secret between the four of us, something sacred and ours alone.

But now, it's out there.

Now it belongs to them more than us.

AFTER THE FIREWORKS display announcing to the world Rufus Ashby is expecting a grandson, Father approaches Verity with a box. The four of us are in the middle of the room, accepting congratulations and back pats. A box of cigars from Darnell Livingston. A bottle of aged whiskey from a tipsy Coach Reed. Books. Cufflinks. A weekend getaway package from Professor Winston.

As if we'd ever get a chance to use it.

But while the men in the room are giving my brothers and me gifts, Father approaches Verity with this box. The packaging is blue. No more playing coy.

"For my grandson," he says, beaming.

"Any idea what that is?" Lex whispers, the three of us standing to the side.

"None," Pace says.

Verity gives Father the presentation he wants, slowly running her nail under the tape and unwrapping the gift. Inside the box, she reveals a small sterling silver cup and bowl.

"An heirloom," Father says, taking the cup from her. "It was a gift from my uncle—the old King of East End—when Michael was born."

Verity shifts the cup, revealing an engraved monogram:

MAC.

I'm familiar with the trickle of white-hot anger that seeps into my veins, which is why Coach Reed really should have chosen someone else to give that aged whiskey to.

I have it uncorked in record time, turning away from the scene as I tip it back.

"MAC… is that…?" Pace breathes.

"MCA, actually." I swallow the whiskey like fire. "Michael Claudius Ashby."

"It's an heirloom," Lex says, but I hear the tension in his voice. "Giving gifts like this is common. One generation to the next."

I take a sharp, ineffectual breath, my muscles wound so tightly that it's an ache. "He's staking his claim, and you know it."

"Chill out," Pace whispers, watching Verity accept the gift with a bland smile. "This'll be over soon."

"Now," Father announces, raising his voice for the room, "let's celebrate with some cake!"

The doors in the back of the room open at the same time as everyone's excited applause. I glance around the crowd with thunder in my ears, soaking in everyone's tepid expressions. Through the whooshing waves of my pulse, I realize that not one of them wants to be here. We're figurines, stuffed into Father's toy dollhouse.

"Wick?" Lex says, and I can feel he's gripping my shoulder, shaking me. "Go easy on that bottle. You look like you're going to hurl."

I don't look at him because I'm too busy staring at the cake being rolled in. Trudie Stein would *weep* with envy. It's square, decorated in a drab blue, and all five tiers are covered with delicately piped lattice around the sides. It probably took a whole team of poor schmucks days to pull it off, their wrists cramping as they painstakingly created the lacework. The edges are adorned with cascading cream-colored roses, the tips of each petal brushed with glittering gold leaf.

I take it all in with a single glance because the moment I see the top tier, that trickle of anger in my veins goes supernova.

It's topped with a crown, which has already been monogrammed with initials.

MAR.

"What the *fuck*." Pace's words emerge raw and frayed, and I can practically hear his stomach dropping like a lead balloon. Lex probably has something to say about it too. As frozen as he is, he's put it together as quickly as we have. But Verity looks lost—so fucking confused—like she's trying to understand how there are already initials on her baby's goddamn cake, and why they're *these*.

As if Father could welcome his own blood and not call the squalling little shit Michael.

Part of me expects to feel Lex's hand on my arm again, dragging me back, but it's not there. None of them stop me or stand in my way as I stride up to the monstrosity.

In one swift, violent motion, I shove the top tier from the cake.

It lands on the parquet floor with a sickening sound that's accompanied by a sea of gasps.

"Michael Rufus Ashby?" I hurl the words directly into my father's rapidly hardening face. "Not *fucking* happening!"

"Whitaker!" he roars, snatching my wrist in a bruising grip. "Get a hold of him!" He says that last part to his security, Thad marching up with one of his toy soldiers to drag me from the wreckage. It's unnecessary, I'm whirling away from the scene before they can spin me, all too happy to disappear into the ceremonial room. I think if I caught one glimpse of the look on my brothers' faces—on *hers*—I wouldn't be able to stop at desserts.

I'd have to raze the whole goddamn room to the ground.

Behind me, I hear Father ordering the caterers to salvage the cake and serve what's left. "Please, enjoy the rest of the evening," he tells the guests, his voice growing closer.

I know when I hear the door slam behind me that we're alone.

"You have lost your godforsaken mind!" he hisses, stiff with fury when I turn to him. "Explain yourself!"

"Over my dead fucking body," I roar, thrusting a finger toward the door, "are they going to name that kid Michael Rufus Ashby!"

"You think that can't be arranged?" he roars back, the temple in his forehead bulging grotesquely. "Don't pretend like you give a shit about my grandson. You've made your position about fatherhood infinitely clear."

The hatred flows through me like lava, because he's right but so fucking wrong. This isn't about the baby. It's barely even about the thought it could be mine—my blood, my legacy. A Kayes heir with the name Michael Rufus Ashby? It's *profane*.

But I can't even spare the energy to be appropriately repulsed by that. Not when it's all reserved for one simple fact.

"It's not your baby to name," I say, thinking of me and my brothers.

Whitaker, Pace, Lagan, even Verity...

This is an aspect of our identity that Father never had a claim to. It's the only thing our biological parents gave us that still remains. A couple of hours ago, the thought wouldn't have even occurred to me, but now that he's trying to take it away, I understand.

It's fucking sacred.

"She's the mother," I say, fuming, "and she's going to name him just like our mothers named us. I'm not going to let you—"

"*Let* me?" He advances on me, eyes narrowing. "You seem to be under the absurd misapprehension that being a father means anything in this house, so allow me to clear that up for you." He grabs a fistful of my jacket, yanking me close enough to see the veins in his eyes. "There's only one title that matters in Forsyth, and that's *King*." He flinches when my wad of saliva hits his nose.

"That's what I think of both titles," I sneer.

There's a moment when I think he might kill me, his breath shuddering, and then he shoves me back, sending me stumbling. "Clearly, this insolence of yours has gone too far," he grinds out, yanking out his pocket square. He wipes my spit from his nose with short, tense movements. "First, you stomp around here for weeks like a child throwing a tantrum. Then you stand up Trudie Stein for the Mother's Day tea. You *humiliated* her, Whitaker, and a woman like Trudie does not stand for public humiliation." His voice rises to a booming bark. "And now you humiliate me—yet again!"

"I stood her up to be with the mother of my child on Mother's Day." I square my shoulders, lip curling. "Or is that not what a Prince does?"

"A Prince does as he's fucking told!" His face has turned a shade of red I've never seen before. There's no doubt in my mind punishment is coming, more vicious than I've ever known.

That's how much of a fuck I don't give when I say, "That's too bad, because I've decided I'm not going to be your whore anymore."

He jerks back, releasing a sharp laugh. "I think we both know that's not your decision to make." He's never said it before, not so clearly. It's been implied with punishments and leverage. Lex has the scars to prove it. Pace, the days down in the dungeon. What I have is this inability to breathe, not even for a second.

Angrily stuffing his handkerchief into his pocket, he declares, "You—no, *we*—owe Trudie a debt. I've kept you out of her bed out of concern for the health of my grandson, but that's no longer possible. You're going to give her what she wants."

I stand stiffly, fists clenched, as I meet the challenge in his glare. "And if I say no?"

Because I'm going to. It hits me like a train. I'm saying no. I'm Whitaker Kayes. Heir to the Barons. I have options. I hold my own deck of cards.

"If you say no?" He straightens his cufflinks, shrugging. "Then I'll bind you down in the dungeon, naked and cold, and invite every pervert I know to do with you what they will." He dips his chin, stressing, "That's a lot of people."

My response is instant. "I don't care." I know I should, but there's a part of me that feels certain it won't be the same. Better for them to take it than for me to give it.

His eyes flare. "I'll take Lex into my office for a special appointment, and I'll whip him until there's no skin left."

This response is even easier. "Lex won't care."

Father shifts rigidly. "I'll take Pace—"

I laugh. "If you think Lex and I don't care, then just wait until you hear about Pace! He's been trying to take my punishments since the night you sold off my virginity." Leaning in, I pitch my voice low and cutting. "Face it. Your leverage is as useless as your cock."

A small evil smile curves on his mouth, and what he means strikes me as sharply as his whip. "Then I'll do it to her."

Blinking, I almost laugh again. "Verity? Your precious vessel?"

"You think I won't?" he asks, tilting his head. "Just because she's carrying my grandson?"

"I know you wouldn't," I say, ready to call his bluff.

But now it's his turn to laugh, the tenor of it sending a chill up my spine. "Oh, I would. And I have. Two decades' worth of princesses have come through this house during my reign. Each and every one required correction at some point. I know a woman's limits. Even those carrying a child."

"Bullshit," I say, scoffing. "You'd never put your heir in danger."

He nods, contemplating. "And I won't. Not if I do it right. And trust me, *son*, I'm very good at what I do."

It's a lie. It has to be. There's simply no way he'd put his own daughter on the market, take that whip to her back, or throw her into the dungeon for days on end.

There's no fucking way.

But if there is—even one fucking iota...

They'd never forgive me.

Lex looks at Verity's belly like it's become his whole purpose. Pace can hardly focus on anything that isn't keeping her safe. If the two of them knew I put her and the baby in danger, that'd be it for us as brothers.

And like that, the cards come tumbling, every last one, fluttering down to my feet.

Father nods, watching me carefully. "There it is." I'm numb as he cups my cheek. "My beautiful boy. Those people out there think I took you in to make you my son. But you know how wrong they are, don't you?" He offers me a cold, dead smile. "This is what I took you for. This is what I *made* you for. Without this pretty face, you're nothing." Stepping away, he straightens his tie. "Now, I need to see to my guests. Get yourself together. I expect you back in there before the last piece of cake is served, looking like an ecstatic father-to-be."

21

erity

I'M PARALYZED as I stare at the cake on the floor, the crown shattered and mangled in equal parts. The golden 'A' from the monogram gleams in the light, and one of the guests—a middle-aged brunette woman—places her hand on my arm, offering a sad, sympathetic smile.

"These things never go how you imagine they'll be," she says, nodding at the destroyed cake. "Creation is a messy business. Don't let it get you down, dear." She offers my arm a little pat before sweeping toward the cake.

Someone knocks into me, sending me stumbling off-balance, and I hear a small, "Excuse me," as a group of people closes in on the cake with her. I watch, confused and extremely grossed out, as they crouch down, each taking a messy handful of cake and bringing it to their mouths.

"My goodness," the brunette woman moans. "This is divine!"

"Uh..." I wring my hands, pulling a face. "I'm sure there's some plates around here if you'll just—"

But four more people crowd in behind them, expressions eager and curious, as if they're trying to find a place to squeeze in.

"What the hell..." I turn to phrase the question to Pace, but suddenly, he's not there. "Pace?" I call, turning, straining up on my toes to scan the room. He's tall—taller than Lex even—and I should be able to catch a glimpse of him, but I don't. All I see are the guests, each of them dressed in their finest formalwear.

And they keep getting closer.

My pulse ratchets up as I try to see over the crowd, calling out once more, "Pace? Lex? *Wicker*?"

All I get is shoved aside by Coach Reed. "Save some for me!" he says, licking his lips as he lunges for the cake. Turning to gape at them, I'm taken aback by the grotesqueness of it, smears of white and blue down everyone's chin. They're like zombies, kneeling on the floor as they shovel the wreckage into their greedy mouths.

I back away from them slowly, but then Rory Livingston's father pauses, his gaze rising to me.

"There's not enough," he says, squeezing frosting through his clenched fist.

"I-I'm sorry," I stammer, looking frantically for a familiar face. Stella, Danner, anyone. "Maybe there's more in the back."

"No," he says, reaching out to clutch my ankle. "Give us more."

I kick frantically, releasing a panicked wail. "Let me go!"

But then the brunette woman joins him, latching onto my calf. "Give us the creation!" she demands, pulling me down.

I land hard, the breath knocked from my lungs as their hands grab and seek, dragging me to the center. "Wait!" I cry, thrashing against the slippery, frosting-covered floor. "Stop, please!"

But there are too many, their hands all over me, ripping my dress away. Their feral, hungry faces twist into excited grins as they crouch over me, immune to my pleas. I can do nothing but scream as they open their jaws, jagged teeth gleaming, and bite down into my thigh.

Sharp, excruciating pain seizes my lower body, and I thrash, finally making contact with something solid.

There's a series of thumps, and then a bright explosion. More fireworks?

Only, as soon as I have the thought, it's melting away into the realization that I'm waking up. Which doesn't necessarily help. "Ahhh!" I scream, the cramp like a vise grip, seizing my muscle. I grab frantically for my leg, but I'm twisted in both the sheets and Wicker's arms. "Make it stop! Make it stop!"

Bodies scramble around me, Pace leaping clumsily out of the bed, a pistol clutched in his hand.

"What is it?" Lex asks, yanking the sheets off. "Where does it hurt?"

"My leg!" The piercing pain is unrelenting, and my fingers claw at the bedsheets. I try to straighten my limbs, and another sharp jolt shoots through me. I curl onto my side, gasping, "Oh my god!"

"Hold her," Lex commands a startled Wicker, who grabs onto me, pulling my body against his chest. My leg feels like a pretzel, twisted unnaturally. Thrashing, I turn to release a ragged cry into Wicker's warm skin.

"Holy fuck," Wicker says. "Why does her leg look like that?"

Grunting, Lex orders, "Don't let her move."

I feel Lex's big hands wrap around my calf, kneading the muscle in slow, steady motions. "It's just a cramp," he tells me in his soothingly clinical voice. "Hurts like fuck, but it's normal. Breathe, Verity. Relax."

Sweat coats my body, the pain worse than anything I've ever experienced. Inch by inch, the tension eases, and I'm able to ease my leg into something resembling straight. Relief washes over me, and I clutch Wicker's arm like a lifeline, the sticky fever abating.

"Oh," I say, panting. "Oh, fuck. That's—that's better." The pain lingers, as if it could draw up again at any moment, but Lex continues to rub slow circles up and down my leg. "That was horrible."

It's only then that I take stock of the scene, Lex kneeling between my legs with an expression that still manages to be painfully serious, even though he's clearly half asleep. His hair is wild and unfettered, hanging about his face in these crazy tendrils. Biceps shifting, he keeps up the massage, flicking his bleary gaze up to mine. "Stay calm. This is normal for the second trimester. Probably just need to get more potassium into you."

"Sweet ass-fucking Christ," Pace mutters, and I realize he's at the foot of the bed, shirtless, just like Lex, and Wicker behind me. Deflating, a tremor runs through his body when he finally lowers the gun, dark eyes falling closed. "Are you trying to give me a heart attack?"

"It's not her fault," Lex snaps at him. "It's just a pregnancy side effect." He looks at me. "Are you okay?"

I nod, melting back into Wicker. "Yeah, it just... took me by surprise. Sorry if I scared you."

Wicker snorts, and it hits me that he's stroking my hair. "Who among us hasn't woken up to the shrill, panicked shrieks of the person sleeping beside us?"

Pace sets the gun on the dresser, still looking rattled as he steps into his jeans. "Maybe for you two, but it's a first for me."

"Where are you going?" I ask, some of the panic returning. Rationally, I know it's just the dream—the memory of how hard I looked for him, to no avail. But irrationally, I can't shake this feeling that I need Pace here.

I need all of them here.

It's Lex who answers. "Adrenaline. He needs to check the monitors." To Pace, he says, "Bring her back a bottle of water, would you?"

"Wait!" I call just as Pace reaches the door. "Just come back to bed, okay? Everything's fine."

Lex disagrees, "You clearly need to hydrate. That was one bitch of a charley horse. Your calf was visibly spasming."

Wicker groggily agrees, "Yeah, it looked really gross."

"Then, I'll take the bottle of water. Just..." I'm crossing a line here, asking for him to stay. Giving myself to him for comfort, the same way I give it to Wicker. But it's not just about providing them comfort. It's more. "Please just come back to bed. There's nothing dangerous out there. That was all just my body acting crazy."

Pace has braced his hand against the door, his dark eyes watching me carefully, closely. They always are. Maybe that's why I find the thought of having him inside me so weirdly comforting.

The difference between being watched over and hunted.

"I'll stay." His throat shifts with a swallow, and then he jerks his chin at Lex. "Go get her a glass of water."

"Sure," Lex says, fingertips dragging as they leave my leg.

When I came up for bed a few hours ago, I found all three of them already in here. None of them were actually in the bed yet, but they were sort of orbiting it like they wanted to be. We were all wrung out from the party, Ashby's display and Wicker's outburst still fresh. There weren't many words spoken. I just went about getting ready for bed and never got around to picking one to sleep with me.

Maybe I couldn't.

As soon as Lex leaves, Pace stalks over to the window under the guise of checking on Effie, but it's obvious he's doing one last sweep. "You want it? Tonight?" he says, glancing at me, and then Wicker, and then the other side of the bed, where Lex was sleeping.

There's a wariness there that surprises me. He'd slid inside me the night the alarms went off, even though Wicker was in bed with us.

"I thought..." I flick my eyes to a confused Wicker. "You said you couldn't sleep in the same bed with me without... uh, doing that." At the time, it seemed like a threat, only now I realize a part of me had heard it like a promise. Earlier, when they all slid into bed after me, I was secretly expecting it.

But it never came.

Wicker catches on, his chest vibrating with a groan. "I'm about to lose my cuddle privileges so you can soak your cock, aren't I? Man, this is just like that time you tried to play center." Sighing, he begins to extricate himself from me.

"Wait." I grab his arm, alarmed. "You don't have to leave."

Wicker gives me an odd look, his hair all mussed. "I'm just

making room." But then he pinches my chin between his forefinger and thumb, searching my eyes. "Ah, I know that look. You had a bad dream, didn't you?" he asks, voice gruff. "You scared the hell out of us."

Exhaling, I nod. "Like you wouldn't believe. I think I scared the hell out of myself." I shiver as his thumb strokes the edge of my jaw. "Thank God you were all here. I think I'd still be twisted up."

In my periphery, I can see Pace slowly shucking his jeans, but it doesn't register. Not when Wicker has me pinned under the weight of his blue eyes. His lashes are fascinating, long and blonde, and they fan out over his pink cheek when he dips down to brush a kiss against my lips.

It's gentle, lacking that hungry antagonism that usually throbs between us. I've learned the reason he's so good at kissing is that it's the one time he allows all of his emotions to pour out. Anger, annoyance, lust, even the few occasions he's having fun. I know what Wicker's feeling because he shows me with his kiss.

But this one is stilted and new, the kiss soft and jarringly cautious, like he's testing out some unspoken boundary. His or mine? I never know.

When we pull apart, Pace is standing at the foot of the bed, boxers gone. "*Shit.* The two of you look..." He clamps down on the descriptor. It's not often Pace lets me do the looking, putting his finely sculpted body, miles of warm brown skin, on welcome display for me. Right now, he's gripping his cock, the muscles in his abs flexing with a slow, indulgent stroke.

Wicker follows my gaze because he lets loose a deep, lazy chuckle. "Yeah, my boy's got a nice piece, doesn't he? Not as nice as mine, granted. But we've had some good times."

I squirm at the sight—not to mention the thought—and wait for Pace to crawl into bed, to pull me flush against his body and fill me.

But he just lifts his chin, his dark eyes holding mine. "Wick," he says, "get her ready for me."

I stiffen, eyes snapping to Wicker. The two of us have been at a sexual standoff for months. Other than the one night we shared in this bed with Pace and our weirdly vicious nighttime cuddles, we've been firmly in the no-sex zone.

But there's no denying Pace's command makes my belly flutter, warmth building between my legs.

Wicker looks at his brother, then back at me. Quickly, he says, "I didn't put him up to that."

"You didn't have to," Pace says, running his hand over his shaft. "You haven't busted a nut in weeks, have you?"

Shifting, Wicker frowns, the crease in his brow oddly annoyed. "Okay, so I'm building some character."

"You're starving it," Pace replies. "Your wet dreams are back, and every time she touches you, you look like you're taking a hit of Scratch." Pace and I exchange a look, but mine must be utterly stunned. The thought of Wicker not even jerking off in weeks? No wonder his brother is worried. "Rosi?" he asks.

"Yeah," I reply, my tongue feeling too thick.

"You don't have to let him fuck you," he says, dipping his chin. "He can touch you. Or," he pauses, likely noticing the way my eyes drop to the tent in Wicker's boxers, "you can touch him. Use your mouth, even."

Wicker sucks in a quiet, sharp breath, the muscles in his core tightening.

"Is that what you want?" I ask Wick, feeling this need to allow him a decision, even though it's an absurd question. For a moment, I feel like Lex. I can see the skin across his jugular thrumming. Pupils dilated. Mouth slackening.

I know he wants it.

"Do I want to see your mouth on my cock?" He thumbs my bottom lip, eyes darkening when my mouth parts. "Goddamn, Red, I'd probably sell my soul for your hand."

Immediately, I turn, throwing a leg over his.

"That's right," Pace breathes, the cordy muscle in his forearm shifting with another indulgent stroke. "Show me your ass while you go down on him."

Wicker's chest expands with eager breaths, body shifting as I settle between his legs. His thighs are thick, the hair scattered over them golden, just like his feathery lashes. Without hesitation, he grabs for my gown, eyes hungry as he lifts it over my head. This leaves me kneeling before him in nothing but the white lace panties he bought for me.

"Fuck." He falls back against the headboard, blue eyes drinking me in as I do the same. "Not that your tits weren't great before, but they've really become something else."

He touches them like he can't bear to take them in all at once, fingertips caressing them in a teasing, downward stroke. I think I know the feeling. Sometimes it hurts to look at him, like staring into the sun too long. Nothing this perfect could possibly be appreciated all at once. From the ladder of his abs to the flawless skin, Wicker is just what I told him before.

A work of beauty.

Reaching for him, I run my fingers over the taut muscles of his lower abdomen. His stomach caves, fingers curling in the sheets. I finally understand what Pace was saying before—the thing about my touch being like a hit of Scratch—because Wicker's whole face collapses in rapture, breath quickening.

I fight a smile, barely believing that I can affect him this much.

But still, he watches me through a heavy-lidded stare, allowing me to take the lead. It's how I discover he's ticklish, his hips twisting as my fingers hook into the elastic of his boxers. When I pull them down, exposing his long length, I'm shocked to find that my mouth actually waters.

The only other time I did this was when he forced me to in the car, getting him ready to make a hasty deposit on the way to school. This time, I want it to be different. A pleasure we've both chosen.

The first touch elicits a sound that startles me. It's deep and rumbling, nearly a growl, but there's a plea in it too. I get the feeling I could ask him to beg for more, and he would.

Instead, I pump him in my hand, watching the skin thicken and turn a darker shade. His hips rise, and I bend, darting my tongue over the salty tip.

"Holy shit, Red." When I glance up, he's raking aggressive fingers through his hair, the line of his jaw taut. "This really isn't going to take much."

"Take him, Rosi," Pace says, approaching the side of the bed. He reaches out to slide a palm down my backside, fingers running beneath my panties. I moan when he brushes over my pussy. "You're not ready. Not yet."

I'm not sure how because I feel the way his fingers slide into the slick heat. But maybe Pace just wants this for his brother, and to be honest, I want it, too.

Fisting Wicker's cock in my hand, I lick down the side, flattening my tongue over the ridged underside. The move drives him to thrust his hand into my hair, cupping the back of my head with his massive palm.

"Careful," Pace says, the words obviously meant for Wicker.

In a mindless, awed whisper, he says, "Her mouth is so fucking warm."

Spurred on by his encouragement, I go back to the tip, swirling my tongue around the head before taking him all the way. Wicker's hips thrust, and he *keens*, fingers curling against my scalp. "It's been a long time, Red. You keep teasing me, and I'll come faster than a—*fuck me*," he pants as I cup his balls, the grip in my hair tightening. "Jesus Christ, it's so hard not to fuck your mouth right now."

"I found one of those hydration packets in the pantry. It has everything in it for you to boost your electro—" Freezing, I glance over to see Lex moseying into the room, a sports bottle in his hand. He takes in the scene slowly, gaze jumping from Pace, to Wicker, and then to me, the tip of Wicker's cock poised between my lips. I wait for the outburst, but he just sighs. "Guys, this is *not* what I meant about keeping the Princess hydrated."

"Why not? It's salty, right?" Wick gently guides me back down. "I'm just helping her get ready for Pace."

Pace asks, "Or do you have a problem with that?" Maybe he's

expecting just that since he's let go of his cock, arms folding over his chest.

But Lex says, "Nope, not at all," and sets the water bottle on the bedside table. He watches me, eyes darkening as my mouth drags up his brother's cock. "Assuming either of you actually gets her off, it'll help her relax, especially after waking up like that. Her cortisol levels are probably through the roof."

Wicker groans. "Please don't turn the first blowjob I've had in months into a science lesson."

Snorting, Lex walks around the bed. I'm more surprised than I should be when his hand dips down to cup my belly, voice quiet and warm in my ear. "He okay?"

I nod.

Lex's hand slides over my ass and pushes my panties down, no reservations as his fingers find my swollen, slick folds. Inhaling, I rut shamelessly against his touch, basking in his low curse. "Come on, she's ready. Get her off and get some sleep."

"Not yet," Pace says, behind me now.

Wicker touches my chin, keeping my focus on him. It's not hard with his incredible body and hot gaze pinning me as I draw him closer to the edge. He really does seem to be struggling, his breathing coming in these tight, short pants.

For curiosity's sake, I sink down—way down—until he hits the back of my throat.

"Oh, fuck," he hisses, urgency spilling from his words. "I'm gonna come, Red. You ready for me?"

I barely nod when he explodes, shooting into my mouth in a thick, hot spurt. Below the hands I'm bracing on his thighs, his muscles seize, body jolting. The fingers in my hair tighten and release in a senseless rhythm, and when I dart my gaze up, he looks *wrecked*, his pupils blown wide as he watches his cock throb between my lips.

The second he shudders the last of his release, he's pulling me up to straddle his hips, capturing my mouth in a slick, salty kiss. Finally, he takes my breasts in both palms, thumbs sliding over my sensitive nipples. I rock into him, wanting friction, wondering what's taking Pace so long.

I want him inside.

Need him.

"Pace," I gasp into Wicker's mouth.

"I don't know," Pace says, and when I tear myself away from Wicker to look at him over my shoulder, he's thrusting his hand in his hair, looking conflicted. "Maybe we should just go to bed. Lex can get you off. Right, Lex?"

My stomach sinks. "Why?"

"Jesus, you don't need to look so worried," Lex says, close enough that I can see the tent in his boxers, too. "It was a charley horse. I used to get them during training. It's not a big deal."

Pace drags a palm down his face. "I know, it's just..."

"You're worried about her," Lex says. It's not a question, and when Pace's eyes drop down to my belly, I think we all come to a realization. "Oh," Lex says, rubbing his chin, "you're worried about the baby."

"No." Pace scoffs, but his erection is clearly flagging. "That's dumb."

Lex watches him closely. "It's understandable to have worries, but I promise you, he's safe."

"It was fine before," I point out, reminding him of the night he broke into Royal Ink.

With an agonized gaze, he explains, "I couldn't really see him before. He was there, but... not really. Tiny. A lima bean. A kumquat. A plum." He waves his hand toward me. "But now it's this, like, *thing* —a real, 'right there in our faces' *thing*—our son—and what if I hurt him?" His eyes widen, hands gripping his hair. "Guys, you've seen how much I jizz with her. I could fucking drown the baby."

Wicker bursts out laughing while Lex palms his forehead.

"Jesus, Pace, you're not going to—" Lex appears to disallow himself from repeating something so ridiculous. "There's membranes and fluids and—trust me, he's protected."

"Remember?" Wicker asks. "From the book?"

I frown. "The book?"

Pace argues, "Yeah, but—"

"Pace," Lex snaps, "you know protecting and keeping this baby healthy is my singular goal in life. I wouldn't do anything to hurt him." He shoves Pace out of the way, hooking his thumbs into his boxers. "Want me to prove how much she can handle?"

I perk up, bracing my hands on Wicker's shoulders.

His eyebrow hikes up. "Seems like she's down with that."

Warmth climbs my cheeks. "Just... hurry."

If I have any fear of my arousal fading, Wicker stokes it back to full force when his touch wanders to my backside, spreading my cheeks for his brother, who I feel nudging in behind me. I'm more than ready when Lex pushes inside, gripping my hips as he hauls me back into his thrust.

I gasp, fingers digging divots into Wicker's shoulder. "Oh god," I breathe, shuddering at the fullness.

Wicker watches, enraptured as I take him in. "His cock feels good, doesn't it?"

I nod, swallowing back a cry as Lex pulls back, only to punch forward again. I feel his hand glide up my spine until it tangles with a handful of hair.

A soft grunt spills from him. "Fuck, Wick, you really got her soaked."

Wicker's eyes flash at the knowledge, and he bends to suck a mark into my throat. I throw my head back for him—for Lex, who's unrelenting as he fucks into me. It's not as rough as he's ever been, but there's still that same edge to it. Lagan, Lex; right now, they bleed together, his hips snapping into mine while his mouth skates gently against the apex of my shoulder. I feel caught between a storm and still waters, Wicker's tongue gliding slowly, decadently, against the cut of my collarbone as Lex takes his pleasure from me.

It's only when my center brushes against Wicker's cock—*Jesus,* already hard again—that Wicker meets my gaze. He looks half drunk as he reaches between us, angling his cock so that the tip nudges my clit with each thrust from Lex.

"Oh," I gasp, winding my arm around his neck.

That wicked smirk curls his mouth. "*Yeah*. Ride it, Red. Want to feel you come on our dicks."

"Fuck," Lex grits, his cock swelling inside. "Whatever the fuck you're doing to her—don't stop." His hand shoots out to clamp over the forearm I have slung around Wicker's shoulder, as if he's holding us together. Each of Lex's sharp, jolting thrusts brings me closer, Wicker's cock rubbing perfectly against my heat.

My breath hitches when I look into Wicker's blue eyes. "I-I-I'm going to..."

The orgasm pierces through me with an agonized cry, and Wicker reacts by touching my lips with his. It's not a kiss. It's as if he's trying to steal my gasps—to take the pleasure for himself—only to give me new air to breathe. It feels equal parts generous and greedy.

After, Wicker folds me into his arms, soothing me through the aftershocks as Lex releases a pained sound, shoving in deep.

His cum feels hot—hotter than I'm expecting—and I squirm helplessly as he fills me with it, his breaths like fire against my shoulder. "See?" he says, wedging a hand between Wicker and me to feel my belly. "Nothing to worry about."

As we extricate ourselves and go through the motions of cleaning up, I try not to think too hard about the fact Lex hasn't looked me in the eye while fucking me, not once, ever since...

But it's getting difficult, and as we all settle into bed, Pace finally spooning up behind me, I find my eyes fixed on his brother, wondering if that's all I am to him. A vessel for his own creation. A way to scratch an itch.

"Ready?" Pace whispers, just as Lex falls back into his pillow.

Reaching over, I finger a long lock of Lex's hair, tucking it gently behind an ear. He turns to look at me, half startled, half questioning. As soon as those amber eyes lock with mine, I allow myself to relax.

"I'm ready."

Pace enters me with a shuddering exhale, sliding in easily after his brother loosened me up. Wick turns off the light, and under the shroud of darkness, I'm struck by the oddest, most startling thought.

For the first time in months, I feel like I'm home.

"FUUUUUCK." Wicker's groan is followed by the sound of a controller hitting the coffee table. "I fucking hate this game."

"Got shut out by Saros again, huh?" Pace cackles from his desk chair.

"Fucking bastard."

It's one of the rare evenings when the house is quiet, other than the sound of Wicker's complaining. No one has told me why exactly, but King Ashby has ordered the two of them to stay in for the night. "We're on call for a job," is all Pace said when I asked. I didn't ask what the job was, because everyone knows better than to inquire about the business of Royals. The less one knows, the better.

But a whole evening with nothing to do has made it clear that Wicker isn't used to so much downtime. He seems restless, categorically unsure of what to do with himself.

"When does Lex get back?" he asks, fidgeting with the remote to Pace's TV.

"I think he said his group is over around eight," I reply, not looking up from my assignment. Although I'm fully expecting everyone to somehow find their way to my room in a few hours, Pace needs to do some security work on his main computer, which for some reason, meant Wicker and I had to come, too. His paranoia has only increased since he broke into Royal Ink and slept over.

Wicker stands, stretching his arms over his head. His shirt rises up, giving me a peek of his cut lower abdomen and the fine trail of hair leading below the waistband of his shorts. "I can't sit around anymore. I'm losing my mind."

He strides into the other room and comes back with his beat-up sneakers.

Pace turns to glare at him. "Where the hell do you think you're going?"

"For a run," he announces. "I'll take my phone with me, chill." In the middle of tying his shoes, Wicker glances at me, only to dart his eyes immediately away.

Things have been weird between us since last night. It took me a while to suss it out, but I don't think it's bad. Our performance on campus today was less showy and more cautious. Even when he took my hand in the courtyard, he seemed to waver a bit, like he was trying to find what's real and what isn't.

Or maybe that's just me, projecting.

Because I sure as hell am struggling to find what's real.

Before leaving, he pauses, looking back at me with an oddly wary expression. "You, uh, do have my number, right?"

I frown. "Yeah, of course."

"Good." He glances at Pace, and then back at me. "He can get a little fugued when he's like this, so hit me up if anything happens."

Without looking away from the screen, Pace flips him off. Wicker offers one in return before leaving. But I'm left blinking in his wake, because either I'm reading that whole exchange wrong, or Wicker Ashby just showed concern. About me. Specifically.

Unable to process that, I sigh, standing to stretch my back. "What are you working on, anyway?" I ask, leaning over Pace's shoulder. I catch a whiff of his clean, spicy scent, reminded of the way we woke up this morning, Wicker and Lex both already in the bathroom, getting ready for the day.

Pace had slipped from me with a low, gritty sound before palming my belly, his morning kiss unbearably sweet.

Now, he reaches out, looping an arm around my waist and hauling me close. "Just digging into the palace files," he says, idly stroking my stomach. I'm only in my eighteenth week, but when it comes to Pace and Lex, I'm already beginning to feel like one of those statues people rub for good luck, the patina worn down through the ages.

"For... Odette?" I ask, saying it out loud for the first time. I'd given him back the paper he dropped in my room the next time I saw him on campus. I didn't have to ask who Odette was. I just knew.

"Yeah," he sighs, slowly pulling his arm back. He uses it to type something. "So far, there's nothing. It's like she never existed, except I know she did. Adeline has a picture."

"Can I see?" I ask.

Finally, he looks at me, searching for something in my stare. "Are you sure? Because I think this is someone none of us are supposed to know about."

Frowning, I reply, "I'm sure."

He taps a few keys, and the image of a beautiful woman pops up. I lean close to inspect it, noting the white coronation gown. She's young, and I intimately recognize the mixture of excitement and fear in her eyes. She's been through the throning, I realize. She's taken her deposits. In this photo, she's pregnant. Successful. Coronated.

None of that is what keeps my eyes glued to her face. It's the similarity between her and Pace. There's no doubt they're related.

"She looks just like you," I say, voice full of awe. "Do you think she's your mo—"

"I don't know who she is," he cuts me off and closes out the image, shoulders shifting uncomfortably. "But yeah, I'm pretty sure we're related."

I want to ask him how that makes him feel, but I'm not sure I have the right. I grew up with a mother, and never had a clue who my father was until Ashby made the announcement. But Pace is so closed off emotionally, and we've only just made advances in trusting one another. I don't want to risk him shutting down entirely.

"Have you asked your father?"

"Fuck no." He scoffs, opening another file. "Any discussions about our birth parents happened eleven years ago. We were taken into his office, one at a time, given the paltry information he offered, and told that under no circumstances were we to bring it up again."

My heart clenches at the thought of a little eight-year-old Pace sitting in Ashby's office, lost and confused. "What did he say?" Only, as soon as the question leaves my mouth, I wince. "Sorry, that's probably super personal."

But Pace just shrugs. "I was told my mother was black and my father was white. They're both dead, just like Lex and Wick's parents."

"Could he..." The question sticks in my throat, but when Pace turns to meet my gaze, I rally the courage. "Could he have been lying?"

Pace gives me a look that says this answer is obvious. "Of course he could have been lying. That's why the three of us did our research. Wicker's parents... well, you know about his dad."

I wince again. "He was Clive Kayes' son, right?"

"In other words, obviously dead," Pace confirms. The light from his screen cuts the angles of his face in sharp relief as he turns back. "And Lex's parents—their deaths were... let's just say, incredibly public. Nothing to hide there."

Part of me is screaming to know what that means. *Incredibly public*? But a bigger part of me is noticing, "You didn't find anything on yours?"

Pace shakes his head, clicking around. "He didn't really give me anything to go on. No names. No ages. I don't even know if they lived in Forsyth. Lex's parents didn't." Shrugging, he drags a hand over his face, looking tired. "When Father doesn't want you to know something, you don't. End of story."

"What about computers?" I ask, going rigid as I assess all the security components in the room. "Will he be able to see you're searching for information?"

Pace's lips form a lazy grin. "He would if I wasn't so good at covering my tracks." He pulls up a new page, this one a series of numbers and codes, and points at the screen. "I can see everyone who accesses the Palace feeds, and erase my own, as well."

Some of the tension in my spine unwinds. It's strange to think that a couple of months ago, the thought of seeing one of these men punished by Ashby might have felt satisfying. Now it just makes me vaguely ill.

"Wait." Pace's low voice brings all of the alarm rushing back, and the way he snaps straight doesn't help. "Wait a fucking—what the hell is this?"

"What?" I ask, looking between his stony frown and the screen. It looks like gibberish to me.

"This IP," he says, copying the series of numbers. "This isn't one of ours."

"Ashby?" I watch as he pastes the number into a text bar, a page flashing up.

But Pace shakes his head. "This isn't even a domestic IP. This is some flimsy VPN relay. Father wouldn't bother."

"So someone's been hacking into your system," I deduce.

"Only once," he corrects, jaw hardening. "This was a month ago." He glances at me, eyes pitch black. "The night of April twentieth."

I'd never paid much attention to the calendar. Like, if the police called me in and asked me what I was doing on a specific date and time three weeks prior, I'd have no idea. Until I got pregnant, and my life got slotted into something charted in days and weeks. Until I started swapping my life between East and West.

The night of April twentieth is seared into my mind for a completely different reason.

That was the night of the break-in.

"What are you saying?" I ask.

"I'm not sure," he admits, his fingers flying over the keys as he digs deeper. "But someone got past our security, and I haven't been able to figure out how. Because our system was flawless—except someone got past the exterior wall without triggering my sensors."

"Can you trace it?"

"No." He leans back in his seat, eyes focused on the computer screen, but they're not focused. He's deep in thought, thumb making lazy strokes up and down my leg. With a burst of energy, he bends back over the keyboard, typing in a string of numbers. A new screen pops up, and he mutters, "Son of a bitch."

"Did you find them?" I lean over, but nothing on the screen makes sense.

"No, but I don't think I need to." He looks up at me and grins. "They left something better."

"They did?" I'm so confused, and it only continues when he stands and grabs one of his hoodies. He walks over and stands in front of me, pulling the heavy fabric over my head. It smells like him, but it does nothing to answer my questions. "Pace," I say, working my arms into the sleeves, "what's happening right now?"

"There's only one person who could breach my system." He opens his desk drawer and pulls out a gun. "And I'm going to find out who hired him."

22

Pace

IT'S BEEN BOTHERING me this whole time.

How the intruder got through palace security.

I know it's not impenetrable. Every lock can be picked. Every wall scaled. Every fortress breached. But there is always evidence of how. Tools. Fingerprints. *Something.*

But there'd been nothing.

Except now, I see it. It'd been in front of me this whole time.

And that stupid slimy dumbass thought he was going to get away with it.

I pull the Lamborghini up in front of the shitty building, leaning over Verity to open the glove compartment. She sucks in a breath when she sees the gun I stowed in there.

"Pace," she says, "are you sure—"

"Wait here for me." I slide the chamber, the sound loud in the small space. "This should only take a minute."

"Maybe I should come with you," she says, eyeing the gun.

I turn to her, regretting having to bring her along to begin with. She's wearing the prettiest little cream-colored dress, all flowy and delicate, peeking out from beneath my hoodie. Her hands are wringing in her lap, the worry clear in her eyes. She doesn't belong here, but the thought of leaving her alone in the Palace was a complete non-starter.

"Rosi," I say, reaching over to rest my palm on the small swell of her stomach, "there is no fucking universe where Lex would forgive me if I took you into that shithole. Not when I'm handling business." I also don't trust her to be alone. *Anywhere.* Not without my eyes on her all the time, and right now, this is the best I can do. Holding her stare, I command, "Stay here. Keep the doors locked." Handing her my phone, I add, "If something happens, go to the text marked 'W/L' and send the numbers *237*. They'll understand."

"Mayhem?" Her face falls, eyes pinging toward the building. Everyone in Forsyth knows those numbers and what it means. "Are... are you going to hurt someone?"

Yes.

But I can't exactly say that, not with the flash of fear in her eyes. If I did, I might have to find out she's more afraid *of* me than *for* me. "Not if I don't need to," I say instead.

Her throat jumps with a swallow. "Just... be careful."

The words burn like a brand into my chest. I've gone into a lot of stupid situations half-cocked and ready to set the world on fire. This may be the only time I've really felt like I've had something to come back to.

That's why I lunge forward, taking her mouth in a long, self-indulgent kiss. I've had brothers for fourteen years, and the way I feel about them is absolute—never a question. But this tightly wound *thing* in my chest is breathtakingly intense in a way I'm not used to.

I'd kill for my brothers.

But I'd die for her and our son.

When I drag myself away, her eyes have become glazed and dark, reflecting the headlights of a car passing in the distance. "I'll be careful," I promise.

I lock her in and step away from the car, tucking my gun into the back of my pants. There's no doubt he's already seen me out here. There's no location, other than the palace and the Gentlemen's Chamber, with as many security measures in Forsyth. This is why I'm unsurprised when the door opens before I even have a chance to knock.

"Pace," Charlie says, eyes bloodshot, hair matted and flat, "brother, what are you doing here—"

Using both hands, I drive Charlie across the entry and slam him with both hands into the opposite wall. "I'm not your fucking brother." Twisting my fists in his t-shirt, I lift him off the ground.

"Hey!" Charlie's eyes dart around, looking for an out as he squirms against the wall. His foot kicks at my shin. "Pace, whatever this is about, I'm sure it's a misunderstanding."

My nostrils flare as I seethe, "I know what you did."

"Know what?" But I see the flicker of panic in his eyes.

My fists tighten. "I thought a bullet through the hand would be proof enough that I'm not interested in playing games." I grab his wrist and force his hand open, showing the knotted and gnarled spot. The new skin is pink, and still healing. Too bad this motherfucker won't get to see it finish. "Who are you working for? Is it the Dukes?"

"I only work for your dad!" Charlie insists.

"Bullshit!" I yank him forward only to slam him back, his head cracking against the wall. "You penetrated my system on April twentieth. Tell me why!"

He barks, "I don't know what you're talking about!" But when I pull my gun out, shoving it into the meaty part of his shoulder, all the blood drains from his face. "Okay, okay, I got in! But I was just testing security—"

My move is quick. Precise. I slip the six-inch blade out of the sheath and press the gleaming metal against his throat "No one told you to test security."

"Whoa!" Facing down both a blade and a barrel, his eyes are eyes wide, full of fear. "Calm down, man. I admit it, okay? I-I-I was in the system, but it's just a side hustle."

"A side hustle, that coincides with the date someone broke into the Palace. Those odds don't happen." I let the tip of the blade press into his skin. He winces, and I ignore the dribble of blood sliding down his neck. "You better start getting very clear, very fast, or the Barons will have to dispose of your body in two pieces."

"Fuck man, you know how much that kind of footage goes for on the market?" When all I do is stare, he grits through gnashed teeth, "I blurred your faces!"

"What the fuck are you talking about?" I ask, trying to connect the date of the break-in to what he's saying. Then it clicks. "What the hell have you done, Chuck?"

"Pregnancy porn," he huffs, face pale. "I just wanted into your system to find some juicy vids, alright? It had nothing to do with that other thing. If you want a cut, I get it. Twenty percent?"

I've got to give the Bruins their due.

There's hardly any recoil when I press the trigger.

The shot rings loud, and almost instantly, Charlie begins wailing, his face all twisted up. When I let him go, he folds into a sad heap on the floor.

"You shot me!" he screams, clutching his bloody shoulder. "Again!"

"Wonder which limb I'll go for next time?" I rack the slide, pointing the barrel downward. "Kneecap?"

Charlie winces as he struggles to his feet, a sluggish trickle of blood streaming down his ridiculous Hawaiian shirt. Behind him, the bullet is embedded in the wall. A clean pierce. "You *shot* me over selling a few videos of your pregnant bitch?!" His voice is high-pitched, unbelieving. "Videos I know for fucking sure you beat off to on the regular." Then the fucker smirks. "Want to see a video of it? I'm sure I've got one somewhere."

I raise the gun, ready to end this.

"Oh my god."

On the list of voices I don't want to hear while holding this fucker at gunpoint, that one's definitely near the top. I only take a quickfire glance, equal parts pissed and horrified to see Verity standing in front of the lobby door, her wide green eyes fixed on Charlie. "You're selling videos of me?"

"What the hell are you doing?" I hiss, putting myself between them. "I told you to stay in the car." The hoodie is gone, so she's standing there in that pretty dress, gawking at the blood.

Her hand brushes my back. "I heard a gunshot."

Charlie doubles over, pushing his fist into his wound. "Look, I'll delete them, okay?"

"No, you won't," I snap. "Because you're lying. Verity was barely showing on April twentieth, and the only fucking she was doing was done in pitch fucking black."

"I don't make up the rules for what people kink on, man." He squints at me. "You should know that better than anyone."

Jesus Christ, I raise the gun again, but her fist twists into my t-shirt. I glance back to see her face, all drawn and sickly.

"Pace, I can't..." Her throat clicks with a swallow. "I can't have another video of me out there. The cleansing is bad enough. I can't... *I can't.*"

Spitting a curse, I look back at Charlie, jerking my chin. "Let's go into the back. We'll look for ourselves."

"Okay," Charlie says, sucking in these long, hissed breaths. "After you?"

"Like hell." I wave the gun, waiting for him to take the long, painful trek down the hallway.

Verity sticks close, her grip on my shirt never easing as I lead her to the main security room. It certainly smells the same, my nose scrunching up as we enter. But when Charlie goes for the monitor, I make a sharp sound.

"Not you," I bark, motioning with the gun. "*You* go to the corner. Verity can verify for herself."

Charlie moans in pain, staring longingly at the chair. "She doesn't know the root password."

"Then I guess you're gonna tell her," I say, jerking the gun toward the back of the room. "Charlie here has never been the best or brightest," I tell Verity as she moves warily to the seat. "He's Ashby blood, but only tangentially. Some cousin, however-many-times removed. Less of a creation than a shruggable mistake, I'd wager."

Before she sits, she turns to him, grimacing. "Does that mean... you're my family?"

Charlie slumps against the wall, groaning, "I'm a lot of peoples' family."

She probably doesn't understand what he means, but I do. He's also no one's family. The bond my brothers and I share is something Charlie could never conceive of. He skates by in East End on a flimsy technicality. Never Royal, only useful.

Until he becomes a liability.

"Pace? What do I do?" she asks, staring at the screen. There's a wallpaper illustration of a pin-up boy, his ass hanging out as his hand flutters over a shocked mouth.

"Click the folder icon on the taskbar," I begin, hearing the little clicks as she navigates obediently to each directory.

After a couple of minutes, I hear her shift. "This one wants a password."

I arch an eyebrow at Charlie, who squirms.

"Look, do we really need to—" I aim at his kneecap, and he sucks in a sharp gasp. "Okay, no, fine. This is fine. Listen carefully." He then proceeds to grit out a long string of random letters, numbers, and symbols. The password is at least sixteen characters long, making my eyebrows hike up higher and higher as he goes on.

This is his fucking vault.

"I'm in," she says, the mouse clicking a few more times.

Impatiently, I ask, "What do you see?"

There's a small huff, and then, "There's a lot of stuff here. Give me a second."

Scowling at Charlie, I say, "A lot of stuff, huh?"

He tips his head back, eyes fluttering. "I think I'm bleeding out."

It makes my eyes roll. "I hit muscle, not artery. You'll be fine in a week or two."

"West End..." Verity whispers, trailing off as the mouse clicks some more. "There's so much footage of West End. Especially *him*." She turns, tapping at the screen. "I know this guy. Why are you watching him?"

Charlie shakes his head. "That's not important. Go to the directory labeled—" Here, he flicks his eyes toward me, wincing. "Ashbrats."

I sneer. "Nice."

"I see it," Verity announces. As she's looking, my phone goes off inside her pocket, but I don't trust taking my eyes off Charlie for a second. And for good reason. "The cleansing is in here," she says, voice thick with emotion.

"Delete it." The command comes instantly, and I wait for the sound of the keystroke before shaking my head at Charlie. "Guess shredding all your drives wasn't quite enough."

Now, it's his turn to sneer. "You really think you're the only one with back-ups?"

When I hear nothing else, I snap, "What else?"

"These are videos of me," she adds in a low, shocked tone. "In *Royal Ink*."

Charlie laughs. "She doesn't know, does she?" His beady eyes move over my shoulder, toward her. "He's been watching you, sunshine."

"I *know* he's been watching me," she says, "but that doesn't explain why you've got them all saved."

I can't help but smirk at Charlie for thinking my girl is as stupid as he is. "What *else*?"

There's a stretch of stunned silence, and then, "I-I don't know. There's a video of you at some building. Looks like... North Side?" More clicking. "This one looks like Lex, standing on a street corner. The Avenue?"

I file that away for later. "And?" When nothing greets me but tense silence, I urge, "Is there anything from April?"

I just want the face of the fucker I shot.

"Not yet..." her voice trails off.

"If you don't want her digging through your trash, you could just tell us," I remind him.

"I think the blood loss is making my memory worse," he complains. "Nothing about April rings a bell."

"There's a video here called Mayfield," she whispers, the words sounding trapped in her throat. "But it's dated eleven years ago."

Mayfield.

Wicker would have been ten.

It's like my stomach is being yanked out by a bungee cord, my grip against the gun tightening. "Open it."

Charlie sends me a listless grin. "Oh, brother, you don't want to do that." For the first time tonight, he's right about something.

Behind me, the mouse click reverberates more sharply than my own gunfire had.

Jaw clenched, I call out, "Verity? Is it him?"

There was a time Wicker used to talk about Mayfield—the night Father sold off his virginity—with a cocky grin plastered on his face. But there was never a time I bought it. As the years went on, it stopped being something he tried to brag about and became something he wanted to bury. Which is easy when you're talking about one of Forsyth's darkest, most disgusting secrets.

When I get no answer, I snap, "Rosi! What's the fucking video?"

"It's Wicker," she says, confirming the churn of disgust in my gut. Worse than that is the way it emerges from her lips, equal parts dread and conviction. I realize why when she adds, "Pace, this video is five hours long. I can't—I *won't* watch it."

My head whips around to look at the screen, blood turning to ice. There's only one reason that would be so long. Somehow Charlie has the whole fucking thing on video: Wicker being auctioned, Wicker being sold, and Wicker being *used.*

"You sick piece of—"

I hear him moving too late, my vision filled with the image of a stone-faced, ten-year-old Wicker on the screen, his chin held high. In the end, I think that's what gets me so unbalanced in the moment;

this new knowledge that Wicker had been trying so hard to be a man, when in his eyes, all I can see is a scared, lost boy.

That's when Charlie makes his move, barreling toward me with a snarl on his face. Before I can get the gun raised, he's shoving me into the cabinet of servers, and then lunging for his desk. In a few stumbling moves, he's yanking a knife from a sheath hidden below the desktop.

It's like slow motion the second he touches her, his fist wrapping around her silky hair as he hauls her from the seat. My vision zeroes in on that, even though it's stupid. She's crying out, folding in on herself as he places her in front of his scrawny body. The knife he's pressing to her throat is far worse than the fist in her hair.

But it's that first touch that does it.

"You Princes really are drunk on the smell of your own cum, aren't you?" Charlie says, laughing. A moment ago, he looked half dead, but now, aside from the slump of his shoulder, he looks perfectly fucking fine. Verity squeaks as he yanks her head back, blade pushing into her throat. "After your last visit, I took some precautions."

Staring into her panicked eyes, my next command is automatic. "If you don't let her go, the next bullet I put into you will be the last."

"Can't do that, brother." Charlie edges toward the door, dragging her with him. "What you're after, it's bigger than both of us, and we'll all be smart to step away."

I barely hear him over the rush of blood in my ears. "April, asshole. Who and why?"

"It's not your fault. The foreign IP was sloppy, I admit," he rambles. "I was rushed that night; didn't get to cover my tracks as well as I should have, which is a shame. I could have cleaned it up if you hadn't gone so fucking overkill on security after-the-fact." He grunts as they get closer to the door, wincing with every pull. "Now, I'm just gonna need a little leverage to clear this whole thing up. So cut it with the murder eyes; you'll get her back."

The whole time he's talking, I'm assessing every movement, each limb, any hope of a target. But still, the reason we came here is starting to make sense. "What's there to clear up? The night of the twentieth, you lowered the security and let someone onto the property. Someone who knew right where the Princess was sleeping. *You* betrayed your kingdom —and you threatened my family. That's the minute you fucked up, Charlie. Tell us who you're working for, and maybe we'll let you live."

But he shakes his head, almost at the doorway now. "Can't do that. See, my boss is scarier than you and the Dukes combined, and he can—"

Verity lifts her foot and slams it down on Charlie's, the burst of strength and agility leaving me reeling. She doesn't seize the element of surprise so much as she snatches it, wedging a fist behind his forearm and punching it—and the knife—away from her throat. Then she brings her elbow back, slamming it into his stomach so hard that I can hear the breath leaving his lungs.

I don't even have time to contemplate the fear gripped around my heart like a fist. The second I find a target, I pull the trigger, the bullet piercing his upper thigh.

He screams, but I barely hear it past the roar in my ears. I dive forward for Verity, dragging her into my chest. Even when I do, her breath shaky but so fucking *real* against my neck, I can't feel anything but this sinking, numb dread.

"Holy shit," I choke, the words as mangled as barbed wire. "He almost fucking—" I can't even say the words—not until I touch the red mark on her neck, and then the swell of her belly. Not until I know she's whole.

"I'm fine," she says, even though she looks three shades paler. In the hallway, Charlie is writhing in agony, his screams piercing, but it barely registers. She stands there as I struggle to breathe, allowing me to check her over. "I *am* West End, you know." She turns, assessing him. "I was taught how to get out of simple holds from guys who are built stronger than a pencil."

It doesn't ease the doom that's settled into my chest.

If anything, as I walk up to Charlie, watching him flop around on the floor, it just gets more intense. "Who are you working for?"

He screams through gnashed teeth. “You fucking shot me.”

“This is becoming a routine with us,” I say, racking the slide. “Wanna try again?”

“Shoot me all you fucking want,” he grinds out, glaring up at me. “Your father knows what I’m worth. He’d never let you kill me.”

“You still don’t get it, do you?” That look on Wicker’s face flashes through my mind. The gleam of the knife against Verity’s throat. The way it felt that night of April twentieth, shooting blindly into the night. But in the end, it all comes down to one simple fact, and when I point the barrel of the gun at his head, I’ve never felt more sure of anything in my life. “You were dead the second you touched her.”

23

erity

THE AIR inside the car is thick and warm, sweat building on the back of my neck. Summer's going to be here in a month, but it already feels sweltering. Suffocating.

Or maybe that's just the tension between us.

Pace fluidly shifts the car, passing a small hatchback, and I glance at his face. The line of his jaw is taut and sharp, dark eyes fixed on the road, and there's a drop of blood right there on his neck that hypnotizes me.

He killed a man.

We killed a man.

Pace cuts a quick glance toward me, shifting uneasily when he notices me watching him. "You can turn on the air," he gruffly offers.

I shake my head, and we ride in silence for a while. I can feel him taking more glances at me. Once, his mouth parts, the inhale loud in the silence, but he doesn't say anything.

"I'm not going to freak out." Looking down, I pick at my cuticle, feeling strangely devoid of emotion. "He deserved to die. It might have been different if the videos had just been me. In a messed up way, I've become used to being watched." Quieter, I confess, "No moment ever feels like my own anymore."

So yeah, if it'd just been about me, I'd be sitting here lost in a maze of horror over taking a life for something so *trivial*. But anyone who'd seen that video of Wicker and decided to keep it, or profit from it—or God... well they deserve worse than what Charlie got.

It was all I could do not to spit on his body as Pace was rushing about the room, tearing hard drives from the servers, gathering phones and memory cards, and scribbling that ridiculous password down before we both forgot it.

"Look," he begins, "about Royal Ink..."

My laugh is tired and humorless. "I knew you were watching me, Pace. I just didn't know how. Here I was tearing up pillows when all I needed to do was close the fucking curtains." Maybe it's a product of months of surveillance, but the fact that I simply forgot the most basic of things doesn't even surprise me.

There's a moment of silence, and then his deep voice admits, "I would have found another way."

"I know."

Pace releases a sigh, shifting his hand on the wheel. "Is he okay?" he asks, abandoning the shifter knob to reach over, brushing his knuckles against my belly.

There's blood on my dress.

"Yes," I answer, pretty sure Lex would disagree, and then, "What's going to happen to his body?"

He gives me another careful glance, and for a second, I wonder if he'll lie to me. "When the others get home, we'll put a call in to the Barons. They'll take care of it."

It strikes me that he seems more bothered about my reaction—or lack thereof—than there being a body to begin with. "Is this what you and your brothers do for King Ashby?" I ask. "Kill people?"

I'm not exactly naive. I know the Dukes kill people. Sy had to kill

Saul to even wear the Bruin ring, and Perez's sudden disappearance is widely known to be Nick's doing, although there's no evidence. The North Side Count had crossed enough Royals that it was seen as more of a necessity than a brutality.

And I know the Princes *have* killed people. The memory of Bruce's finger is still fresh in my memory. But in West End, that sort of business is tucked away, kept hidden from girls like me. Stupidly, I didn't realize East End was the same as the West when it comes to such things. Part of me figured Bruce was a one-off. A price to pay to my home kingdom. Because that's what death is in Forsyth. Currency.

But Pace stares ahead at the road, his fist flexing around the steering wheel. "We do something a lot worse than that, Verity."

"What's worse than killing people?"

He gives me a quickfire glance. "Keeping them alive."

Activated by sensors, the gate opens before we hit the driveway. On the way over the bridge, Pace rolls down his window, and in an easy toss, throws the gun out into the darkness. The sound of the splash as it lands in the water is faint as he continues to drive up to the front of the house.

"What's going to happen when he finds out?"

There's no need to confirm who 'he' is.

Pace cuts the ignition, frown creased in thought as he turns to me. "If tonight proved anything, it's that Charlie was a liability. He's supposed to work for us, not against us. He disrespected you and the heir." He rests a wide, heavy palm on my stomach, an increasingly familiar and comforting touch. "And even though we didn't find it —*yet*—he had something to do with that break-in. I know it."

Nodding, I agree, "You're probably right." I haven't really allowed myself to worry about the intruder from last month. The only time it really hit home that someone might be out to get me, specifically, was when I came out of the shower at Royal Ink to find a strange man standing beside my bed. It only lasted a moment before Pace revealed himself, but though the panic bled away, the possibilities never did.

Snagging the hoodie I'd tossed into the backseat, Pace says, "Here. Put this on over your dress." I don't look down at the blood. My nausea is better, but I never know what's going to bring it on. He helps me into it, lifting my hair and straightening the collar. I look up at him just before his mouth meets mine, claiming and assured. When he pulls away, he's smirking. "You were a real badass tonight, you know? Remind me to send Perilini a bottle of whiskey for teaching you those moves." His fingers trail down my jaw. "If I had any doubts you'd be a fucking amazing mother, consider them obliterated."

With one last caress of my belly, he opens my door and holds my hand as we enter the house. It's not unexpected for Danner to be waiting, but Thad's presence makes both of our steps falter. Despite his large frame, he's usually clinging to the shadows like a bit of smoke following the King around.

"Danner," Pace says, fingers tightening against mine. "Thad."

"The King is waiting in his office," Danner says.

Pace rocks back on his heels, sliding me a glance. "Let me get the Princess settled in her room, and I'll be right back down."

But Danner shakes his head. "Both of you are required."

There's a pause where Pace and Danner just stare at one another. This, plus Pace's warning not to trust him, brings up questions that I'd rather not have about the elderly man.

"Then lead the way," Pace says, but it's not Danner who starts down the hall toward Ashby's office. It's Thad. The whole way, I watch his back, unable to remember seeing him in the halls before. He feels awkward and out of place, too large for even the enormous door we approach.

It's strange walking into Ashby's office. I have no real connection to the setting, but I've seen the video of Lex. I know what can happen here when the King is displeased. It doesn't help that I sense the change in Pace immediately. Every muscle in his body stiffens. His jaw tightens, eyes focusing on his father sitting behind the desk.

It's then that he drops my hand, moving his own to clasp behind his back.

I take a quick scan of the room. His father—my father—*our* father is waiting behind his desk, a glass of dark amber liquor sweating on the table beside the armchair.

"You get one chance to tell me where you've been," Ashby says, eyes never lifting from his ledger. "And before you answer, keep in mind that even if you turned off every security measure in East End, your flashy black sports car is impossible to ignore."

"I've nothing to hide," Pace replies, voice devoid of emotion in a way that sends chills up my spine. "I found the source of the security breach and went to follow up. That's when I discovered that not only was Charlie involved on the night of April twentieth, but he'd compiled a large cache of exploitative videos of all of us."

Ashby looks up, face blank. "So you killed him."

He knows already.

Pace shot Charlie in the head less than an hour ago.

I expect Pace to feel as stunned as I am, but he shoots off a reply as if he'd never expected any less. "I eliminated a liability and threat to the Kingdom, and to the Princess in particular."

Ashby leans back in his seat, the silence in the room growing more claustrophobic than it'd felt in the car. If Pace feels it, he doesn't show it. He's a soldier standing in front of a general. But I feel it. My skin prickles in awareness of a predator, sitting just out of view. I have no choice but to stand here frozen, hoping it doesn't catch my scent.

"Charles was my asset," Ashby says, voice low and cutting, "working on important, confidential projects for the Kingdom." His hand splays over the top of the desk, his gold crown ring, larger and gaudier than the one on my finger, on display. "By killing him, you've effectively destroyed that work. *Years of it.*"

Pace begins, "I'm sure it's recoverable, I'll just need some time—"

"Killing one of my operatives without approval is unacceptable." His gaze is chilling. "I don't know what's worse: the act of defiance or the sheer impulsivity of it. Of my three sons, you're the rock. You don't have Whitaker's flare for the dramatic, or Lex's susceptibility to weakness. You're hardened. Patient. Diligent. But ever since..." His icy eyes dart to my midsection. "Well, I thought your time cooling off in

Forsyth pen taught you about falling prey to your lesser emotions." His eyes narrow into dangerous slits. "Apparently not."

"Father," Pace says, "this was not an act of defiance. This was me doing what I had to do to protect—"

The desperation in his voice turns my stomach, but not nearly so badly as Ashby's roar.

"Silence!" he shouts, his volume at a level I've never heard before. His face turns a shade of red that makes me swallow in fear. "This is exactly what I mean," he rants, face contorted with anger. "Tantrum after tantrum. Throwing cakes. Avoiding responsibility. Sneaking off to fill a void. Playing idiotic games. One thing after the other!" He stands, circling the desk, and stops in front of Pace. "I'm tired of the insolence, and I have no other option than to teach you a lesson."

Pace has no reaction to this other than lowering his chin, as though he's ready for whatever may come his way. Inside, I'm roaring just as loudly as Ashby did, but on the outside, I try to make myself small and invisible.

Without moving his gaze from his son, Ashby says, "Thad, go into the Princess' room and get the bird."

Pace's head snaps up. "What?" he asks, the panic clear in his voice. "Why?"

Eyes hardening, Ashby pulls something from his pocket. "You were on call for me, Pace. All of you. And yet when I called, I got no answer." It's only then that I realize he has a knife. "If eighteen months in prison isn't enough to convince you how destructive these attachments of yours are becoming, then I'll just have to start getting rid of them." He nods to Thad. "Go ahead. I'll wait."'

My breath gets trapped in my throat.

The second Thad moves, Pace darts in front of him, blocking his way. "That's bullshit! Effie has nothing to do with this! Punish *me*."

Ashby's grin in the face of such utter anguish makes my blood boil. "Oh, I've been informed that none of you care about my usual punishments anymore. I could drag Lex in here and whip him senseless, but that didn't work the last time, did it?"

Unable to stand it anymore, I step forward. "Pace wasn't the one who pulled the trigger." I raise my chin. "I did."

"Verity..." Pace starts, eyes shifting to mine. He looks different. Scared.

"We got caught, okay?" I say. "Don't lie for me. I don't need your protection."

"You expect me to believe that?" Ashby laughs. "We have surveillance of him going in with the weapon."

"Then you have evidence of me following him in," I continue to bluff. There's no backing out now. "Charlie was hoarding videos of me to sell online. Like he said, exploitative videos of my pregnancy that he planned on selling to perverts all over Forsyth and probably beyond. Pace kept trying to get intel out of him, but it was obvious he wasn't going to hand it over." I let my voice crack, willing to show my humiliation and upset. "So I took the gun and ended it. *Against* his orders."

"And you're telling me this, why? To protect Pace? To curry sympathy? To seek my approval?" I can't tell if he's genuinely asking or if it's rhetorical, but in for a pound and all that.

"I'm telling you this because it's the truth. Charlie was a lying scumbag who is an embarrassment to East End, and I put a bullet through his head."

"I guess you really are one of my children." Ashby stares at me for a long moment. "Fine. If you want to take the punishment for your brother, then there's only one thing left to do." He tilts his head at Pace. "Go get the box."

Pace blinks. "Excuse me?"

"Go get the box," Ashby repeats. "If your sister wants the punishment, then I'll give it to her."

"She's pregnant!" he shouts. "You can't—"

"I've already told your brother that I have no problem issuing punishments to a Princess, pregnant or not." He unbuttons his crisp shirt cuff, slowly rolling up the sleeve. "She'll neither be the first nor last that I'll have to discipline."

Pace snaps into movement, stepping between me and his father.

"You'll have to kill me before I let you lay a hand on her or our son." He towers in the small space, shoulders wide and fully imposing. This is the man who beat Remy in the Fury—with a knife, not a fist. Seeing the blade glint as he pulls it from thin air isn't a surprise to either of us, but I still gasp.

Ashby doesn't blink.

"Thad." The name is barely off his tongue when the security guard lunges for Pace, knocking him and the knife to the ground. The fight is dirty, Pace scrambling, his elbow connecting with Thad's jaw in a sharp jab. Loose, he dives for the knife, but the bodyguard is as quick as he is large, grabbing for his ankles and yanking him back across the hardwoods. Using his entire body, Thad jams a knee into Pace's back, pinning him to the floor.

Ashby picks up the knife and levels it at his son. "I suggest you comply," Ashby says, as if this is all an inconvenience, "or I'll skip the whip and use the blade."

With the threat shifted to me, Pace gives, body stiff but no longer fighting. His father continues, crossing over to the cabinet at the back of the room. He removes a wooden box and carries it back to his desk.

"She's carrying your grandchild, you sick motherfucker!" Pace shouts while Thad hoists him off the floor, both arms around his upper body, holding him in place. The objective is clear. Ashby isn't going to kill Pace.

He's going to make him watch.

I stand, frozen in my spot, watching as he methodically rolls up the other sleeve and then pulls out a pair of leather gloves.

"Verity," Pace pleads in a raw, ragged voice. "Tell him the truth. Tell him it was me. Don't do this."

"At this point, it doesn't matter," Ashby says, flipping open the box. Inside is the coiled whip that I saw in the recording. "You, her; you're both spoiled brats who need to learn your place." He points to the fireplace. "Remove the sweater and dress."

It's as if I'm outside my body as I step to the fireplace, letting Pace's hoodie fall to the floor. He won't *really* hurt me, I reason. This is probably all a show to get a rise out of Pace. Still, I'll play the charade for what it is and act appropriately admonished. Reaching behind my back, I lower the zipper. The horror I'd felt earlier at Charlie's returns —the feeling of being exposed and exploited—but it slowly fades into the oddest numbness. Once I'm in nothing but a bra and panties, my stomach on full display, his voice rings out.

"On your knees."

"Don't—" Pace shouts, and behind me, I hear the sound of a struggle; a clatter and crash, something fragile shattering on the floor. His next words are muffled growls.

Ashby steps in front of me, reaching for my chin. He tilts my face upward with his gloved hand. "You aren't the first Princess to lie and defy me, but you are the only one who shares my blood. My sons will tell you I derive pleasure from punishing them, but there's no joy here—just necessity. I am your King. Your father. I *will* be obeyed. And you will suffer for your defiance."

His thumb strokes along my jaw, and he gives me a tight, wistful smile before moving behind me.

I can't help but recall Lex being in this position—the sweat beaded on his forehead and chest. I just feel cold. From fear. From regret. From knowing what it's like to kneel like this, having the man who's supposed to protect you turn his ire on you instead.

I have no idea what to expect, but it's not the cutting whistle of air, followed by a sharp, deafening *crack*.

It's certainly not the pain.

The gasp I suck in feels like it never ends. I'd expected a bruise maybe, something hard enough to make a mark, but not break skin.

I was wrong.

The end of the whip feels like I've been branded, the tip hot as fire. Teeth gouging into my bottom lip, I fall forward, one hand outstretched in support, the other cradling my stomach. The pain takes my breath away, and for an infinite second, I think this might be how I die.

"Straighten up," Ashby barks.

It's then that I feel a pulsing sting, the heat transforming into something that goes deeper. I push back, my skin screaming. I'm barely upright before I hear the hiss of air, and my body seizes, preparing for the second strike. I cry out, deep, like a groan, this time clutching both hands around my stomach.

"Are you sure this is what you want, daughter?" His voice is mangled with something too breathless to be anger. *Pleasure*. He absolutely gets pleasure from this. "To muddy yourself with the lies and deceit of your brothers?"

Hot tears roll down my face, the pain too much—fucking *searing*, like he tore through to the bone. "Screw you," I hiss, willing to stand between this monster and Pace. The man who killed for me. The man who, I know, will kill for our son. "No wonder my mother never wanted you to know about me."

The response I get is the sound of the whip slicing through the air, the third lash both lesser and worse. The pain of it blends with the others into an inferno that tears a gnashed cry from my throat. My cheeks must be wet, but I can't feel it. I can't feel anything that isn't the pain and sting.

"Your mother was a whore," he barks.

My body quakes when I scream, the sound wet and twisted. "And my father was a pathetic rapist!"

I brace for the fourth strike—surely the worst to come—but instead hear a resounding bang. My mind rushes to the thought of Pace escaping Thad's restraints, and when I hear the whip meet a target, I flinch instinctively.

But it doesn't land on me.

The grunt that follows is deep and familiar.

Turning my head, I see a flash of auburn hair, and then a hand wrapped around the handle of the whip, battling his father for control. His amber eyes are murderous pits of black, lips pulled back in an animalistic snarl, and when he raises his fist at Ashby, some part of me recognizes it as protection.

The next crack isn't the whip at all.

It's Lex's knuckles, connecting with Ashby's jaw.

24

Lex

It's been a while since I punched someone.

No one with my ambitions would risk their hands—an instrument of the finest precision—but the sight of the whip slicing into her flesh wipes all logic from my mind.

I see red as I rush across the room, my vision zeroed in on his shadowed face. I've been in that same position she is now, doubled over, body swelling with a sound I refuse to make, only now that I find myself outside of it, everything comes as naturally as breathing.

I barrel at him like a frenzied, wild thing.

There's a *crack*, and then the shock of fire as my metacarpals absorb the force. Pain radiates up my forearm, rattling my ulna, but I don't really feel it.

Father's head snaps to the side, which has to be why he loosens his grip on the whip. I rip it away, tossing it aside and raising my fist again. I slam it right into his nose, not even allowing him to regain his footing. Behind me, there's a scuffle, but I don't pay it much mind. With an arm shoved into his chest, I sweep Father in my furious momentum until I have him pressed up against the fireplace, his head smashed into the mantle.

"What the fuck are you doing?!" I roar.

He clutches my wrist, and through a hot, belligerent glare, growls, "Hit me again, and I'll take this hand off."

"She's pregnant!" I snap, grinding my arm into his chest. "Have you lost your goddamn mind?"

"Have you?" he roars back.

In all my life, I've never seen Father so unhinged as he is right now. His hair, always immaculately combed, looks tattered and limp. His eyes are bulging like a maniac, the tendons in his throat strung taut. It doesn't bother me to know I look the same.

Except for one detail.

In one swift move, I have a knife pressed into his throat. "I haven't lost my mind. Actually, I think I just found it." The laughter that slips from his mouth is ragged and full of menace. "Something funny?" I sneer.

A trail of blood trickles from his nose. "Look at you, all puffed up like a lion. I've been trying to inspire this in you since you were a child, but you just kept taking it, and taking it, and taking it..." His lips curl, the blood dripping over them. "Bit of a waste, wasn't it? All the social workers swore you were wrong. Empty. *Evil*. Imagine my disappointment." Casually, he reaches up to wipe the blood away, a vicious smear over his cheek. "In the end, you're just a man. A slave to your prick."

"Boss?" Thad's voice rings out sharply, but Father flicks his gaze to him, shaking his head.

"This is a family matter."

"Verity," I call, not taking my eyes off Father's bruising face. "Are you okay?"

Her breaths sound ragged, but carefully measured. "It—it stings."

Stomach turning, I adjust my grip on the knife. "I know."

Despite having a knife to his throat, Father reaches up to

straighten my collar, looking nonplussed. "Truth be told, I hadn't realized you'd made her one of you so quickly. But look at her, already taking your punishments for you. All this little outburst of yours has accomplished is confirming my suspicions." He gives me a blood-stained grin. "She's the new precious thing, isn't she?"

Behind me, I hear the unmistakable sound of Thad's gun being cocked. I fix my eyes on Father's throat, the blade so close to cutting, and for a moment, there's a distinct possibility I'd take a bullet if it meant slicing through the skin.

"Let him go."

Only it's not Thad's voice, and a quick glance reveals that it's not Thad's gun, either.

Wicker is standing in the doorway, his pistol raised as he stares Thad down. His hair is damp, and he's wearing nothing but a pair of shorts, but he looks menacing as hell. Pace's arms are still locked behind him, his face twisted in rage as he stares at Verity. Thad's eyes snap to Father's, and when his chin dips in a nod, Thad almost looks relieved.

Pace springs from his arms instantly, lunging for Verity. It's a good thing, too. Somewhere in the back of my mind, I know I have a role to play in this. She's injured, bleeding, the curve of her shoulders tense and trembling as Pace sweeps her carefully into his arms.

"I'm sorry," he's saying, stroking over her hair as he tucks her face into his neck.

"Thaddius," Father says, "leave us."

"Yeah, Thaddius," I parrot mockingly. "Leave us."

He raises his hands defensively, eyes trained on Wick as he backs out of the room.

Wicker slams the door behind him, face hardening. "Someone want to fill me in here?"

"Father was just about to find out what it's like," I say, pushing the blade harder, "to be under my knife."

But Father just snorts. "Is that what you think this is, son?"

"I'm not your fucking son." Saying the words is like plucking a two-decade-old splinter from a finger. Once they're out there, my skin feels looser, as if I've just made some unimaginable new space in my body.

"Which is exactly why you aren't going to kill me."

"Do it," comes Wicker's quiet, tense voice. I'd try to find Pace's opinion on the matter, except he's too busy pushing these little, agonized whispers into Verity's temple, his hands splayed over her stomach between them.

"Do it," Father says, his eyes holding mine, "and you'll have East End to answer to. All those men you've spent your entire Princeship humiliating and disparaging?" He tsks. "I may have adopted you, but none of you carry the bloodline. It'll have to come to a vote, and they don't like you very much. Not nearly enough to accept you, and they certainly won't accept a Princess who's made their lives miserable. They'd have to find a *new* King—one who won't suffer the existence of a competing heir." All the snideness fades from his eyes, replaced with the same evil he'd hoped to find in me. "Ask me what they'd do about the child."

Nostrils flaring, I push until the skin breaks, blood beading to the surface. "Then we'll kill them."

He doesn't flinch. "That might work—for a while. Until the Barons come in to clean up. You see, they owe me a debt." Father's eyes flick to Wicker. "They'd never let him wield Royal power. Even adjacently."

"I don't give a fuck," I bark, heart thudding, "about the Barons!"

But Father just gives me a patient smile. "Of course, you do," he says, gently pushing my arm away. "You're not a fighter, Lagan. You're a strategist. You were made to see strengths and weaknesses, and right now, you're seeing what we both know to be true." In his eyes, I see the same man who took me down to the dungeon for the first time, a mark strapped into that same old chair. "If you walk away, you'll have started a war with me. But if you don't, you'll be starting a war with Forsyth." He speaks more like he's giving a lesson than bargaining for his life. "Think, Lagan. What have I taught you? Which foe are you more likely to overpower?"

"It doesn't—"

"Think!" he snaps, and in his eyes, I see the oddest spark of panic. "What's the priority? It's not me, and it's certainly not you."

I swallow, flicking my gaze to Verity. "The baby."

"Yes," he says, brow smoothing in relief. "Precisely. How do you protect him?" When I don't answer, he grabs my face, pressing, "How do you ensure his safety, Lagan?!"

When it hits me, the knife falls to the floor with a clatter, my shoes stuttering against the floor as I shuffle back.

Father inhales, yanking a handkerchief from his pocket. He dabs the blood from his face as he assesses us. "Now that this nonsense is settled, we can proceed with my daughter's punishment."

"Hit her again," Wicker growls, "and it's not just going to be us that you have a problem with. If the West End finds out about those marks..." He raises a daring eyebrow. "We may not be the only ones you've started a war with."

Lavinia Lucia already blew one kingdom off the map, and something tells me that the Duchess would have no problem doing it again. No matter the collateral damage.

"The Princess *asked* to stand in for Pace," he gives my brother a withering look, "but I can see the thought of her taking more lashes is aggravating an already tense situation, so I'll compromise."

Even now, with a gun and a knife at his throat, he manages to command the room, but he's right. I'm a strategist, and everything he said is true. We don't have the power here. We never wanted this position. We didn't play politics with PNZ. The whole plan, all along, was to run.

"What compromise?" Wick asks.

"Take her to the dungeon." He waves his hand like the matter is already settled. "She can complete her punishment there."

Pace's eyes widen, I see the argument on his face, but I give him a warning look.

Making a deal with the devil himself, I nod at Wick. "Take her down."

~

PACE RETURNS from the dungeon looking more drawn and exhausted than I've ever seen him, and that includes the day he was sent to prison.

"How is she?" Wick asks, stopping his pacing.

"Asleep—finally," he says, exhaling. Yet again, he looks at me, jaw tight. "I don't like leaving her in there, Lex."

The frustration threatens to rise. No one likes it less than me, but there are factors to consider. "The dungeon is awful, but it's our domain," I explain. "She'll be protected down there while we sort this out. Pace," I dip my chin at him, "you know how to endure it. You can coach her through it."

We're in the solarium, tucked back in the corner near the nettles and thorny bramble. It's the one place Father doesn't have cameras, out of respect for Miranda's garden and Michael's grave.

It took both Wick and Pace to help her downstairs, while I'd run to get my kit. Once she was in the cell, I did a preliminary exam to make sure neither she nor the baby were in a life-threatening situation, and then the three of us worked to get her back cleaned.

It wasn't until it was over that she finally, truly cried, and Pace asked us to give them a moment.

"Jesus fucking Christ," Wick says, running his hand through his hair, still damp from his shower. He'd run upstairs and dressed before coming in here. "What the hell happened up there?"

We'd both walked into a horror show—a literal nightmare. The image of Verity on her knees, her split and torn up back, is burned into my mind. Never in my life did I think he would go this far, but as Pace describes the night—discovering Charlie's security breach, the fact he'd been selling videos of Verity, the hoard of exploitative content he had at his fingertips...

It was a perfect storm.

"I tried to stop her," Pace says, voice thick with regret. "I know she thought he'd back down, but the second she stepped up, I saw it in his eye. He was excited."

She took the punishment for him—for us. To think, at one point,

I'd accused her of being disloyal. Time and time again, Verity Sinclaire has proved she's the most loyal of us all.

"He told me he would do it," Wicker says, sitting on the stone wall. His shoulders cut a sad, defeated curve. "At the gender reveal, he said she wasn't the first pregnant Princess to get punished. I should have told you." He looks down at his hands. "God, I let you walk right into his fucking trap."

That's what this is. A trap. We all feel it. We know it. We've lived it. Even Verity has called East End a prison, and she's only been here for six months.

That's why I say, "It's time to enact the plan."

My brothers look up at me.

"Which plan?" Pace's forehead creases.

"Wicker's right. He's *been* right. We have to leave." I swallow, feeling insane for saying it aloud, but even more so for taking so long to see it. "And we're taking her with us."

"Fucking *finally*!" Wick shoots to his feet, relief clear on his face. "When do we go?"

But Pace raises a hand. "Look, not to piss in anyone's protein shake, but the plan was for the three of us."

To my surprise, Wicker's the one to narrow his eyes. "There's no fucking way we're leaving here without her."

"Obviously," Pace says, forehead creased like the implication alone is irritating. "The leverage we've been building all these years might be enough to buy our freedom in a pinch, but his daughter's? His grandchild's? His *heir's*?" Pace looks at me, deflated. "Guys, it's not enough."

"Then we have to make it enough." I look between them, knowing there's no other way. "We can't leave until Verity is healed and ready, so there's time to be smart about this."

Pace inhales deeply, dragging a palm down his face. "Okay. Right. I'll have to do a full backup of all the servers and make sure we're not being tracked." He rubs his chin. "I'll have to get Effie out. Maybe a special cage for travel..."

Wick and I look at one another. It's probably because of the lifetime of upheaval, foster homes, boarding schools, and prison, but Pace is the most attached to his belongings. To this house.

I rest my hand on his shoulder, announcing, "Graduation, okay? We'll leave after the ceremony. That'll give us a little over a week. Father will want everything to look perfect, so he'll want to pretend none of this ever happened."

Wicker straightens, face hardening. "We'll have to make him believe he's won."

"Exactly."

He nods, and I can practically see him shifting himself, turning into what we need him to be. Wicker's always been the best at that, and losing to Father is familiar enough. He'll need to be a brat. Depressed. Drunk and disorderly.

"Nothing too extreme," I caution, nodding toward the house. "He has a new weapon against us."

"We'll leave right after." A little energy springs to Pace's eyes. He's good at projects. "Everyone will be celebrating, including the other houses. Perilini and Payne, Kings of two houses, are both graduating, so you know West and South will have huge blowouts. It'll be easy to slip away with so much commotion."

"I like it," Wick says, warming to the idea, but then frowns. "Do you think she will?"

I grimace. We're not just asking Verity to run with us, the men who put her through so much misery, but agreements have been made. Contracts have been signed.

"We'd be asking her to leave West End," Pace says what we're all thinking. "Her family, her friends."

"What if she says no?" Wicker asks, the doubt clear in his eyes.

Sometimes being the oldest means making the hard decisions. "What if we don't give her a chance to?" I toss it out there like a grenade, watching as my brothers take it in. We won't have the luxury of convincing her.

Slowly, Pace nods. "She's *our* Princess," he agrees. "Not Father's. Not the Dukes'."

Wicker ducks his head, kicking a stone. "Better to ask forgiveness than ask permission?"

Just like that, it's sealed.

In nine days, we'll take Verity away from East End.

Away from West End

Away from Forsyth.

~

EVEN IN LATE MAY, the dungeon is cold. It rankles that I need to clear the supplies in my arms with Father, seeing him frown at the freshly laundered blanket and pillow. It's supposed to be uncomfortable. Luckily, he waves his approval without a word, which is funny.

He thinks he's icing us out.

No doubt he's planning something, but I don't have time to worry about it. Nine days. That's how long we have to endure.

When I reach the bottom of the narrow staircase, Thad almost bumps into me. I just have to steel myself before turning down the corridor to the cell. Verity mentioned once that she sees me as two different personalities. She hadn't exactly expanded on the thought, but I suspect I already know. And when my eyes land on her curled up on the cot in the dark, I turn into the other guy.

The one who wants to hurt.

The one who wants to feel.

But right now, that's not what she needs. She needs *Lex*, the cool, clinical strategist who gets her out of this palace safe and whole. When Thad shoves the key into the lock, I imagine how easy it'd be to kill him. To carry her out of here. To go somewhere until my brothers meet us.

But that would never happen.

Father would kill either of them if it meant getting her back.

She stirs, the sound of her hiss as she pushes up cleaving through the silence.

I give Thad a look. "Some privacy for her exam?" He falters, glancing between me and the cell door, and it might be dark, but not dark enough to notice she's in nothing but a pair of panties, clutching an old, scratchy wool blanket to her breasts. I shift my weight. "Do you really think you're stopping anything here?"

He relents, trudging back down the corridor toward the staircase.

Only when he's gone do I enter the room, setting my supplies on the floor. Among them is a large bottle of water, and I quickly uncap it. Kneeling by the cot, I cradle the back of her head, gently instructing, "Drink."

Her eyes are red, and her hair matted, and while she takes the bottle, tipping it up to her lips, I tug the blanket away.

I'm not sure how long I crouch there, framing her belly with my hands. My thumbs sweep back and forth, as if I could soothe him through the skin, and maybe I could make this seem like something necessary—an examination—but I don't bother.

Wordlessly, I tip forward, resting my ear against the bump.

It should be enough to calm the raging storm in my chest, but it isn't.

Not until her fingers begin fluttering through my hair.

"Lex," she says, her voice a thin rasp. "He's okay, right?"

Inhaling, I lean back, grabbing my notepad from the floor. "Let's see."

Verity is a good patient. She has her mouth open before I even have the thermometer out, arm extended for the blood pressure cuff before I can ask. She waits as I jot it down, and then remains still as I clamp the pulse oximeter to her finger.

When I pull out the stethoscope, she lifts her chin, exposing her chest to me, and she knows the exact moments to breathe in and out. The first time she shows any emotion is when I produce a small, at-home fetal Doppler.

She scrambles to lay back, but immediately winces. "Shit!"

I wince with her, steadying her neck. "Just rest back on your hands."

Her eyes begin welling again, but it's not the same as last time, all miserable and full of agony. Now, she just looks ripe with anger. "How many times?" she asks, voice cracking. "How many times did he do this to you?"

I consider lying as I start the small machine, the crackle of the Doppler loud in the room. "Honestly?" I meet her gaze. "I lost count at twenty. It just stopped mattering."

Her expression crumbles. "God, Lex..."

Shrugging, I begin the search for the heartbeat. "I'm good at handling pain. Some of the nerves back there are dead now anyway."

A tear falls, and she lets it, looking at me like she's feeling more than her own pain. "That's awful. All these years living with him, he's been..." Sniffing, she looks away. "And I just showed it to everyone that night like a petty, vindictive bitch."

My shoulders shift, the skin on my back suddenly feeling much too tight. "I know why you did it, Verity. I held it against you for a while, but now?" The sound of the baby's rapid heartbeat fills the room, and I glance up, catching her watery gaze. "Now, there are more important things."

As soon as she hears his heartbeat, some of the tension in her body melts away. It makes the pulsing rhythm slow, just a smidge. It's another reminder that taking care of this fetus means taking care of her.

"It was because of something they did, wasn't it?" she asks. Her hair is wild and knotted, and when I flick off the device, she looks disappointed. "Like when Pace was put down here after Wicker's fight on the ice. That was meant to hurt Wicker, wasn't it? He punishes you, but it's meant for them."

"Usually," I say, pulling out a fresh pack of gauze. "But not on that particular occasion. Turn around."

She obeys gingerly, sweeping her hair over a shoulder. It's not as bad as it could be. The cuts are a bit more shallow than I'm used to enduring, and there are only three of them. The urtica is a problem though, the skin around the wounds mottled and irritated, and as I dab the cuts with antiseptic, I hope it drowns out the other sting.

"What was it for," she asks. "In the video, when you were being whipped?" There's a thread of urgency to her voice, as if she's trying to distract herself.

That must be why I answer truthfully. "I wasn't making enough deposits."

Her back stills with a held breath, and then, "He whipped you like that because you weren't *fucking me* enough?"

"Yes." I begin tearing little strips of medical tape from the roll. "He was tracking all of us, comparing, rewarding, turning it into a competition." I press a piece of gauze over one of the cuts and adhere it with the tape. "Punishing. It's what he does. It's how he controls us."

It took me too fucking long to realize that. I stare down at the wounds. Almost too late.

"That's crazy." She exhales, but it's followed by a little bout of bitter laughter. "This is all so crazy, Lex."

"For us," I muse, "it's just the way it's always been."

"That makes it even more sick and twisted."

"Yes," I cover another wound. "Which is why we can't let our son live in this place."

She turns her neck, nose wrinkling from the pain, but she catches my eye. "There are other options. You must know that. You're Princes; you can—"

"We're not blood, Verity. None of us are entitled to the throne."

"West End—"

With a glance up at the camera in the corner, I cut that thought off before she can finish it. "Will never accept us."

"What are you saying?"

"*I'm saying* I'm going to do whatever it takes to keep you and this baby safe." I cover the last wound, making sure the tape is secure. The last thing she needs is an infection. "And in order for you to trust that, I'm going to need to be honest with you."

"Wait." Her movements are slow, and she has to grab onto my arm for leverage, but Verity adjusts to a sitting position. "Okay, tell me."

She's making this so much worse, forcing me to look her in the eye. What I have to admit is harder than I thought. Father is right. I'm weak. But I don't want to be. Not for her, and not for our son.

I push the words out like I'm drawing poison from my lungs. "I've relapsed."

"Scratch?" She frowns. "I mean, I know you were on it the night of the cleansing—"

"Yes, but..." I swallow, shame burrowing under my skin. "Not just then. After, too."

She's frozen, her brow creasing. "When?"

"When things get too hard." I look down at my hands. "When the pressure is too much, and I'm too weak to not accept an easy way out." I take a deep breath, knowing Pace will watch this later. "April twentieth, for one."

"That's where you were during the break-in?" Her lips form a grim line, and then she wonders, "That's where you've been all this time when you haven't been around?" When I nod, she grows quiet, until her green eyes widen. "Are you high right now?"

"No!" I insist, taking her hand in mine. I press it to my chest, allowing her to feel the steadiness of the heart beating beneath it. "No, I promise. Not that it means anything, but I was at a meeting. For real. You can ask Maddox, he was there."

"Why? I thought that," she reaches up, brushing my hair back behind my ear, "when we were together, you didn't have those urges anymore. I thought I was enough."

The urge to get defensive is strong. To make excuses about my workload, about Father, about obligations, and being buried under the weight of it all, but the truth is, it's all bullshit. I know that.

"It was never about you, Verity. It wasn't even about Father or the baby. I thought it made me better—able to do everything that needed to be done. But I think..." I try to find the right words. "I think that was just a lie I was telling myself. I know now it doesn't make me better. It makes me weaker. It makes me... absent."

She's quiet, and in the cold stone of her cell, it seems like we've fallen into a deep, numb void.

"Do the guys know?"

I nod at the camera. "They do now."

She takes my hand, small and cold, but comforting. "Why are you telling me this?"

"Because I know my father, and he'll use my failures to turn you against me." I face her, wanting to make sure that she hears what I have to say. "And because I need you to know that after last night, I'm done. This child, our family, it's more important than anything. I know that."

I knew it the second I stepped between Verity and my father. There's no high in this world that's worth being unable to protect them. Maybe there was a time when this woman and the life growing inside of her were yet another duty piled on top of a mountain, but it's different now. They're not an obligation.

They're a purpose.

She assesses me for a long moment, her green eyes searching. Whatever she finds, it makes her nod. "Okay."

I arch an eyebrow. "Okay?"

"You're not like Wicker," she says, watching me closely. "You want to be a father, don't you?"

"Yes."

"Even if..." She worries her bottom lip between her teeth. "Well, what if you find out it's not yours?"

"Verity," I whisper, mouth forming a tired grin. "Family isn't DNA. There's no circumstance in this world that would make Wicker and Pace anything less than my brothers, and there's no universe where I'd see this baby as anything less than mine." I stroke her cheek, the awe so big in my chest that it's almost more than I can contain. "We created him, didn't we?"

Her eyes glisten. "We did."

"All of us."

She nods, and for a moment, I think two people will never be as connected as we are now, contemplating the absolute fucking enormity of what we've made. She takes in a long, shuddering breath. "I want you to drug test—"

"Absolutely."

"And you're going to talk to your brothers about this," she stresses, glancing up in the corner. "No more secrets."

"I will," I assure.

"We'll help you stay accountable." Her hand rests on her stomach. "We need you. Not just me and the baby, but them, too. Especially after what we just went through." When she pauses, I hear the unspoken words.

Especially for what we'll have to go through.

I want to tell her about leaving, that we have a plan, and that I'd never abandon her in this wretched fucking basement a minute more than absolutely necessary. But Father's eyes and ears are everywhere, and he can't know. The plan is too fragile.

Feeling somehow both heavier and lighter, I begin gathering my things. "I need to head back up soon. Is there anything else you need?"

Her eyes track my movements. "Can I keep the Doppler? So I can listen to the baby's heartbeat while I'm down here?"

My heart sinks at the hope in her eyes. "He never allows electronics down here," I say, hating to snuff out the light in her eyes. But then, "Oh, wait. You can have this." I reach into the supplies and grab the stethoscope. Carefully lifting her hair, I loop it around her neck. "It might take some time to find it with that."

She glances around the cell, her grin bleak. "I have time." Another pang shoots through my chest, and I shake out the blanket. "This is yours," she notes as I tuck it around her.

"It's clean." The truth is, something in my chest unwinds at the sight of her wrapped up in it. "I'll send Pace down as often as I can." Sighing, I rub a temple. The withdrawal will start soon. "That is, if I can pull him away from Effie. He's been obsessive—well, *extra* obsessive—since you got sent down here."

She pulls the blanket up tight around her neck. "I guess that makes sense."

Distractedly, I ask, "Why's that?"

"Ashby—Father," her face sours at the word, "he wanted Effie to punish Pace for killing Charlie."

"He was going to take Effie away?" Slowly, it starts to connect. "He was going to kill her." I look at her. "That's why you stepped in. To save Effie."

"Pace killed Charlie to protect me," she says, the expression on her face somber yet knowing. "And she's more than just a bird to him, isn't she? She's... she's his heart." Holding my eyes, her head tilts pensively. "It's like he was afraid of having a soul, so he gave it to her to keep safe. Something untainted that would love him back."

I crouch in front of her, stunned speechless. No one has ever understood that about Pace. In fact, I'm not even sure I fully did. Not until Verity gave it flesh. Springing forward, I press my mouth to hers. Not because of the wild, scratching need in my chest, but because she sees him, and how?

How can I not fall for someone who sees my brothers for what they really are?

Part of me wants to tell her that she's right, but only partially. Whatever paltry thing Pace has granted to Effie, it pales in comparison to what he's imparted to her.

But I have work to do. Pulling back, I mutter a curse. I realize now why Pace is so worried about Effie's safety when we need to focus on getting ourselves out of East End in one piece. I can't have him distracted right now. There are too many balls in the air.

Verity's eyes flutter open, so soft and sad. "What?"

"You're right," I say, thumbing at her bottom lip as I pull away. "We're going to have to find somewhere to keep her safe."

"Actually..." Her green eyes blink, and suddenly, an arm appears from her blanket cocoon. "Can I see your notebook and pen?"

Confused, I hand them over, watching as she crosses her legs and starts writing. When she finishes, she tears out the page and folds it in half. "Coordinate a meeting with West End," she says, voice low and quick with intensity, "but not with the Dukes. Take Effie, and this note, to my mother."

"Your mother," I ask, eyebrow arching.

Her eyes blaze into mine. "Trust me."

I owe her that and so much more, so that's what I do. I stick it in my pocket, and against every instinct in my body, I leave her there on the cot, curled up in the only warmth I can provide her. I don't read the note until I'm upstairs, already wondering if Simon Perilini will take my call.

EVEN BIRDS CAN USE a mama bear sometimes. Please see that this one is loved until we've made a safer den for her. Show her some kindness and a window with some sunshine, and she'll be a fast friend.

Love,

VerBear

25

Verity

I WISH I could say I awoke to the feeling of another presence, but it's the smell of food that rouses me. Before I can even lift my eyelids, a warm palm is brushing the hair off my forehead, lips capturing mine in a gentle kiss.

When my eyes open, it's to the sight of Pace's shadowed face. "Hey," he whispers, tucking my hair back. "Sorry to wake you up, but it's better when it's warm."

The skin on my back is still tender and itchy as I struggle to a sitting position, the wounds tight and hot. Pace helps me, cradling my elbow as I lower my feet to the cold floor. "What time is it?" I ask in a rusty voice.

"Noon," he answers, shuffling around the small space. "Wednesday afternoon."

I don't need to wonder why his answer is so specific. Down here, there's no light, no way to tell if a day has passed. Or worse, if any time has passed at all. I get this ridiculous idea to scratch tallies on the wall, but then I remember *his* tallies, etched into his arm, and my stomach clenches.

The smell of food doesn't help.

"What's that?" I nod to the covered tray just as my stomach releases a loud, unseemly growl.

Pace balances the tray on his lap. "Lunch, prepared by Lex himself." He lifts the lid, revealing a bowl of soup, a hard-boiled egg, and two bread rolls. "Lentil soup." Pulling out a bottle of water, he adds, "And for dessert..." He reaches into his other pocket, producing a plastic-wrapped snack cake.

My mouth waters, but when I reach instantly for the bread, Pace inhales sharply, as if he's about to interject. When he clamps his mouth closed, I ask, "What?" eyeing the rolls dubiously.

"Nothing," he says, pushing the tray towards me. At my skeptical look, he sighs. "I've been down here a lot, so I know the ropes. Soup will get cold, but the egg can stay shelled for a couple of hours, and the bread can get you through the night, in case—" He stops, frowning at the spread of food. "Well, I doubt he'd keep dinner from *you*, right? You're pregnant. You need to eat. Things between him and Lex are nuclear enough, and he'd never stand for it. But just... just in case. You never know."

I stare at him in horror for a long moment. It's like every time I talk to one of them now, they reveal some new, terrifying facet of their childhood. But when he looks at me, all I can see is the tension in his eyes. The worry.

He's afraid, I realize, that I could go hungry.

I touch the curve of his cheek—the mottling bruise from his scuffle with Thad—and swallow past the lump in my throat as I lean over to brush a kiss there. I hear his breath stop, feeling the way he turns into the touch. His hand cradles my jaw as he holds me there, close and warm, for a long second.

When I lean back, he jerks forward, almost like he wants to stop me.

Reaching for the bowl, I nod. "Good plan." It isn't a good plan. In fact, it's a fucking awful plan, and the fact that I'm rationing food inside a fucking dungeon is beginning to hit home. "Do you know how long..."

He doesn't make me finish. "Five days."

"Jesus." My stomach drops. "What am I going to do down here for five days?" And then, "What did you do down here?"

His brow furls in a way that tells me he's taking this question painfully seriously. "Some people aren't good at being left alone with their thoughts, but I think I am. When I was little, I'd make up stories to tell Lex and Wicker when I went back up. Sometimes, I'd make friends, which—"

"Friends?"

He pulls a face, reaching up to rub his neck in an oddly bashful gesture. "Like, with bugs or mice."

I snatch my feet up off the floor. "There are *mice*?"

The vibration of his deep laugh is a stark contrast to the setting. "That's what you took away from that? Relax, that was like a decade ago. I'm pretty sure they've all skedaddled by now without me giving them cracker crumbs all the time."

I stir my soup, stomach in knots. "So you're saying I should think."

He leans back against the wall, humming. "Or *not* think, even. Sometimes being down here felt like a vacation. No school work. No jobs. No events. Just the silence."

I allow it to envelop us as I eat, feeling his fingers stroke through the knots in my hair. I wonder how Pace can look so comfortable here, kicked out on the cot as he stares into the distance, thoughts whirring, perhaps. But I know silence isn't something I'm willing to take for long.

"How's Whitaker?" I ask, still trying to process the way he came into the office, gun raised as if defying his father was something he did every day.

He shrugs. "Okay."

I wait for more, but I guess that's all I'm going to get.

Placing the empty bowl on the floor, I unwind the stethoscope from my neck, plugging it into my ears. The metal end isn't even cold as I tuck it into the blanket, pressing it to my belly. I've been doing this off and on since Lex left it, filling the oppressive quiet with the thrum of life. I've gotten pretty good at finding the little drumbeat that blends in a rhythm with my own body.

Pace sits forward, pulling me into his side. "Is that...? Can you hear him?"

Shivering, I nod. "Do you want to hear? Take the earpieces."

He gently plucks each side from my ears, plugging them into his own. I watch, fascinated, as his eyes widen, flicking up to meet mine with a crooked smile. "It's fast."

"It can be hard to find," I whisper, holding the metal end in place for him.

Pace's eyes drift to where the blanket is open, and he spits a soft curse, face falling. "I didn't think to bring you clothes." I shrug, but he's already yanking the stethoscope from his ears and pushing to his feet. In one swift motion, he has his dark t-shirt pulled off.

I don't make a fuss when he ducks down to push it over my head, guiding it gently over my back. He follows it down, though, pressing a long kiss to the swell of my stomach.

That's where he is when footsteps approach. "Pace," comes Thad's voice. "Your thirty minutes are up."

He groans quietly, lips skating upward as he straightens, tugging me into a kiss. He tastes like heat and flesh, the slightest edge of mint, and I'm beyond disappointed when Thad's voice grows closer.

"Pace?"

Stiffly, he pulls back and reaches for the tray. "I'll try to be back tonight," he says.

"Sorry," he says when I hiss, easing the brush through the knot in my hair.

Spinning the pasta around my fork, I tonelessly assure, "It's fine."

It's not fine. I'm on the floor, the tray in my lap as I eat dinner. True to his word, Pace was able to make it down at precisely seven with more food, which is good because the quiet down here is somehow worse than the cold. It settles into me like an infection, even my thoughts numbing off to a hum.

"I'd never actually let you starve," he says from his perch on the cot. There's a tickle in my scalp that suggests he's worked the knot free. On either side of my shoulders, his knees are spread, bracketing me. "Not unless something crazy happened. Like, what if there's a zombie apocalypse."

I snort. "Seriously?"

He runs the brush through in a long, victorious stroke. "Okay, or a societal collapse, or nuclear fallout, or a plague—"

"You really did think a lot down here, didn't you?"

I can practically hear the grin in his voice. "Oh, you have no idea how many scenarios I've dreamed up for potential catastrophe. Toxic chemicals destroying the population. The whole palace getting carbon monoxide poisoning. An airborne virus that spontaneously removes hands."

I dig my bread through the sauce. "Because they can't unlock the door without hands."

"Fucking exactly." I shiver when Pace's knuckles graze the back of my neck. "Lex thought I was crazy."

"That's obviously a very reasonable worry." I pause, feeling my hair tug in different directions. "Are you... braiding my hair?"

"It'll get all knotted up after five days on this bed, and I can't leave the brush." Desolation settles heavily in the silence that follows, but Pace is quick to shatter it. "You know, Lex never lets me? Drives me fucking nuts."

My lips twitch, the smile small and foreign. "That's a shame. He'd be really cute in pigtails." Pace's soft bout of laughter is a balm to the hidden pang in my chest. My smile plummets as quickly as it comes. "The last person to braid my hair was my mama. She used to love playing with it."

There's a stretch of silence where I lean back, letting him work. He's so good at this, distracting—*entertaining*—me. Before he showed up, I was getting itchy and anxious, trying to acclimate to the idea of being down here for five days.

I've spent all day on the edge of a panic attack, and I don't know if he can sense it, but he just started talking, filling the void. It's surprising because he's usually so quiet, watching while I wait for the next shoe to drop.

Even now, he doesn't let the quiet last long. Eventually, he asks, "What's your mother like? *Really* like?"

I rest my hand on my belly, my smile growing. "A real hardass, but you already know that. Protective, too. More patient than a lot of people give her credit for." But I know he's really asking for other reasons. Choosing my words carefully, I offer, "She wears all these metal bangles around her wrist, so basically, you can hear her coming from a mile away. Kind of like an alley cat with a bell around its neck, to warn the birds." The pressure against my scalp abruptly stills, and I sigh into the silence. It's going to be a long night. "She'll be fine, Pace."

THE NEXT MORNING, it's porridge and a bowl of fruit. "Is this part of the punishment?" I wonder, watching the gloop fall from the spoon.

"Lex isn't on his game."

"I can see that," I say, inspecting the chocolate bar that was sent down with it.

Beside me, Pace looks exhausted. His bloodshot eyes never grant me a reprieve, but the thoughts behind them seem miles away. "He's going through withdrawal."

I try my best to get a spoonful of the porridge down. "Is it bad?" I remember how Remy looked after he kicked it, all sallow and sickly, but I can't even begin to superimpose such an image over Lex's shrewd eyes and perfect posture.

Pace shrugs. "Wick says last time was worse."

Feeling a little more secure in my meal deliveries, I rip open the chocolate bar and take a bite. "Is it bad *up there*?"

In a soft, tired voice, he answers, "Isn't it always?"

~

I KNOW it must be dire when Pace comes down in the evening with dinner, also bearing Lex's examination kit. "He's in the thick of it now," he says, trying to work out the blood pressure cuff. "Puking and cold chills and—" Frustrated, he rips the velcro away once more, snapping, "The fuck is this thing?"

"Here." I show him how Lex does it, and together we manage to record my vitals. There's no fetal Doppler this time, and when Pace takes off my shirt to change my bandages, I can see the responsibility weighing on him. "Have you gotten any sleep?" I ask, wondering if the bags under my eyes look as bad as the ones under his.

My sleep comes in fits, filled with dark dreams that linger with the lack of sunlight. I have nothing to do but rest, although I feel lethargic and gross. It's as if I'm wasting away like all those dead flowers in the solarium.

He counters, "Have you?"

Well, that answers that, and when I flick my gaze up at the camera in the corner, I wonder if there's anyone on the other side, watching as Pace gently applies ointment to each wound.

"They aren't hot," he mutters, relief clear in his tone. "No signs of infection."

This, it seems, he has ample experience with.

~

"WHAT ARE YOU DOING?" Pace pauses at the door, Thad retreating down the hall behind him. There's the ever-present tray in his hands, but also a gym bag.

I think it's Friday morning.

"Just sprucing up a bit," I answer, flipping the thin mattress on the cot. There's not really much to spruce, nor is there anything to spruce *with*, but despite the sting in my back, I just...

Fuck, I need to *move*.

The skin feels too tight, like if I stay in one place too long, it's going to heal like a straitjacket. "What's in the bag?"

He dumps it on the floor, lowering the tray to the newly-turned mattress. "Change of clothes. And Danner's made you—"

I don't really hear what the meal will be, because I'm too busy tearing through the bag, my back screaming as I attempt to bend.

Clean underwear, *yes*. Clean bra, *no*. Sweatpants, *jackpot*.

He watches this with a stunned expression before shaking out of it, taking the clothing from me. "Wait. I was going to clean you up first."

"Even better," I mutter, pulling my—*his*—shirt off.

Or, I try to.

The second I raise my arms, a sharp, pained sound punches from my chest.

He's there in a flash, saying, "Wait, wait. Jesus, what is with you today? You're going to open them up again, just let me..." As he eases the shirt over my head, I get a better look at him, relieved to see he looks a little more rested. The bruise on his cheek is nearly healed, and the cut on his lip is barely a scab. Still, his brow is creased with concern. "You have a lot of energy."

Sharply, I explain, "I'm bored." But that's not the whole truth of it. I can't really explain it, this buzzing need in my body to *do something*. Get up, get moving, get clean. It's driving me crazy, because, "Pace, there's nothing to do. I want to walk," I insist, voice thick with the tears springing to my eyes. "I want to go outside. I want to water my stupid fucking flowers and talk to Stella and Ballsy, and I want to tell Lex his porridge is a crime against humanity, and tell Wicker off for being an ass." My lip wobbles, but I push the sob back. I can't be losing it already. I *can't*. "I want to go home."

Pace watches me rant with an expression that turns more and more bleak, and then he's tugging me forward, whispering, "Yeah, I know." But how could he? It's been almost two months since I stood in the parking lot of the Gilded Rose and asked Pace where home was.

I still haven't found it.

We stand like that his whole visit, my nose pushed into Pace's shoulder as he strokes my hair.

And then his time is up.

~

I'M STILL restless when he returns that evening, determined this time to wash me. I suspect if Pace brought me down a broom and a mop, I'd have this place spotless by morning.

That's the feeling that's been driving me all day, only when Pace gets me out of my panties and begins running the wet cloth over my body, another feeling sweeps me up in its wake. The soap smells like Lex. Maybe that's why a white-hot spike of lust shoots right to my core, even though he hasn't even gotten to the good stuff yet. He runs the washcloth down each arm, and then my neck, lifting my chin to lock gazes with him.

Holding my stare, he slides the cloth down my breast, cupping it in his wide palm as he gives it a gentle scrubbing. He does the other, and then crouches down, paying special attention to our son as he washes my belly. He presses a small, almost absentminded kiss to it, before moving lower to wash each of my legs.

It's only when he pushes the cloth between my thighs that I finally break, releasing a hitched breath.

His hair is lush between my fingers as they thread through his twists. "Verity," he whispers, drawing my gaze down. I wonder what I must look like, my mouth parted with heavy breaths as I rock into the heel of his palm. Suddenly, this is all I want.

No.

Not want.

Need.

"Please?" I ask, not even having half the mind to feel ashamed of it. I know he must feel my slickness—the way my body is preparing to take him in. The thought of his thick cock filling me was once a point of dread, but I can't remember it. I can only remember those long nights in our bed and the way it felt to be so full and... what was it?

Cherished.

That's it.

Pace is never buried inside me casually. Every time I hold him inside, he responds with such utter ecstasy, always soothing and coveting in equal measure.

Right now, his eyes are pools of complete darkness, shadowed by the cell. "We can't."

I spread my thighs, willing him to understand how much we can. It's greedy and selfish, but it's all I can think about. "We did it that other time," I say, reminding him of the time he was locked down here.

His throat shifts with a swallow, and even though he's protesting, I don't miss the way his thumb glides idly over my clit, forefinger teasing my entrance. "That was to make a deposit. It was a part of the covenant." His jaw goes tight, voice gruff as he glances up at the camera. "If he sees me fucking you, I won't be allowed down here anymore." The words seem to bolster his resolve, and without another word, he springs to his feet, wringing the cloth. "Let's get you into these clothes before you freeze to death."

The disappointment isn't unexpected, but the depth of it is.

Pace's fingertip makes a mindless, idle path over my belly. "It's not as fast as before," he whispers, breath tickling my belly button. "Do you think he's sleeping?" He's sitting on the floor, his arm folded on the cot. His cheek is resting there, each end of the stethoscope plugged into an ear. "Or just really calm?"

I'm on my side, uninterested in the dinner he brought. My back aches, and I can't get comfortable in any position; sitting, standing, sleeping. I don't know if it's the cot or the way the baby sits low.

"I don't know." Whatever energy I'd felt yesterday is long gone. I'm hoping if I lay here long enough, time will blink away.

"I used to want to see you like this," he muses more to my belly than to me. "Locked up."

"Because you blamed me for going to prison," I ask emotionlessly, "or because you just wanted me for yourself?"

"At the beginning, the first one." Sighing, he shifts the stethoscope upward. "But eventually, I just wanted to keep you contained. Safe. It's hard seeing you out there in the world, knowing anything could happen to you."

I blink, feeling tired. Irritated. "Then shouldn't you be happy?"

"I should," he answers, glancing up to catch my eye. "Instead, I'm fucking miserable."

I look away. "Because it's your father's cage instead of yours?"

There's a long pause where I can feel his eyes burning into me. "Because maybe you'd be happy in mine."

I give a quiet scoff. "Like Effie is?"

He lifts his head, tugging the stethoscope from his ears. "Effie is miles away right now," he says, voice a touch crisp. "I did that to protect her, even though she's with people who'd really enjoy seeing me dead. Do you have any fucking idea how hard that is?" After a pause, he laughs, the sound hollow and grim. "You know, I've gotten pretty used to you being pissed at me, but I usually know why."

"I'm not pissed at you," I say, rolling to my back. The wounds are scabby and itchy and easily irritated, but at least it's *something*. "I can't fucking breathe down here," I gasp, pulling at the neck of my shirt. Which is ridiculous. It's not even my shirt. It's probably Pace's since it's three sizes too large.

"Only a day and a half," he says, following my movement with the stethoscope. "You can handle that, right?"

I squirm when his elbow brushes my inner thigh. "I don't know, Pace."

He watches me closely, eyes dipping down to where my thighs meet. "I know what you need." Shifting, he takes out the earpieces, levering up to put them into my ears. I adjust them, and he settles back in front of my stomach, putting his lips up against the metal. "Be ready for me tonight."

Pace's thighs flex when I settle into his lap, his arms winding around my waist.

My dinner is on the floor—something with a lot of garlic—but I couldn't care less about it. He feels so warm beneath me, which is only amplified when he drapes the blanket over my own lap, cocooning us.

His cheek grazes my ear as he leans in, clearing his throat. "So Lex said we should read this chapter." Fanning open the book he's brought, I scan the title, realizing this is one of the pregnancy books I'd read months ago.

Pace's cock is rock hard against my backside.

"Week nineteen is a point in the pregnancy journey where the anticipation and excitement continue to grow," he begins, hand stroking the curve of my belly. I lean back into him, fighting the urge to glance up at the camera as his hand disappears beneath the blanket. "It's a time for expectant parents to start making preparations for the arrival of their little one," his fingers dip beneath the large shirt, skating up my thigh, "and to savor the unique experiences that come with each passing week of this incredible nine-month adventure."

Blood humming in anticipation, I turn the page, pretending to study an illustration. "This says," I swallow back a gasp as his thumb brushes my clit. "It says that the baby is the size of an h-heirloom tomato."

I feel his grin against my cheek, a finger sliding through my folds. "Finally, a fruit that's not a type of pie. Wicker will be happy."

I inch my thighs wider for him, belly twisting up when he finds my entrance already slick and ready. "Physically," I continue, trying to keep my voice steady, "the expectant mother may notice that her abdomen is becoming more pronounced."

He slides his finger inside, voice like silk against my ear. "Her hair and nails may still be growing at a rapid pace, and her skin may have a healthy, radiant glow due to the increased blood flow and hormonal changes."

This is the unsexiest book I've ever read.

So why is my pussy gushing?

It might have something to do with how he pulls his hand away, only to tuck it between us, shifting against my lower back. Lowering his sweats, I realize. I pretend like I'm shifting to get comfortable, just to afford him the room necessary, and when I feel the smooth, hard tip of him against me, it's all I can do to stop the whine building in the back of my throat.

His lips graze my earlobe at the same moment his cock nudges my entrance. "Nutritional needs may also shift," he says, gently guiding me upward.

I only rise a couple of inches, just enough to get the angle right, and then I'm sinking down. "Maintaining a balanced diet and staying hydrated is... it's important," I try, picking out any random sentence on the page. I could be reading about anything. It's random words and sounds, all drowned out by the enormity of him filling me.

Even after all this time, my body still needs to adjust to the size of him, and when his hand squeezes my hip hard enough to leave a mark, I know he's feeling the same thing I am.

Ecstasy.

Warm and bright.

Nestled close.

We're not animalistic—not like Lex can be—but we're still animals here. Coiled up tight around each other, seeking heat, taking comfort.

I settle on him with a shuddering sigh, his cock buried deep. "Additionally, regular exercise and relaxation techniques can help manage the physical and emotional changes..."

Pace takes a beat too long to continue, his chest billowing with an inhale against my tender back. Deep inside, his cock twitches. "One of the most delightful aspects of this stage is that by week nineteen, expectant mothers can often feel their baby's movements, commonly referred to as quickening." He pushes a kiss into the sensitive spot below my ear. "Have you?"

I disguise my rock into him as a shrug. "I don't think so." He disguises his grunt as a mere acknowledgment.

We read like that for a while, mindless and too blissed out to care if any of it makes sense. Beneath the blanket, he keeps a hand between my thighs, thumb stroking my clit in a maddening, slow circuit. When he takes the lead, his voice stoking fire in my ear, I lean back and breathe in the scent of him, masculine and crisp. When his pause lingers too long, I take over, only to feel the hot, slick glide of his tongue along my neck.

I wish we had more time, but when he whispers, "Ready?" I'm oddly relieved.

At least I'll get that.

When I nod, going on about prenatal care providers, he buries his face in my neck and inhales, quiet but sharp, and then his thighs tense. He swells inside me first, and then the first pulse comes, the heat flooding into me with each twitch. His breath grows ragged against my skin, and the finger dipping into my folds must catch whatever drips out, because when he returns to my clit, it's sticky and warm, the perfect friction.

My breath hitches against my will, and I struggle to concentrate on the words, which are swimming in and out of focus, a muddy blur. It's impossible with the way he's driving me closer, his cock surging with more and more cum, until I'm so full that I feel like I could burst.

The moment he raises his head and begins taking over the passage, I tip my head back and finally let it take me, biting down on my lip as his fingers coax the orgasm right out of me.

It's sharp and too intense, exploding behind my eyes like hot static, and when I clamp down on his thigh, I feel his cock give one last twitch.

The sound I make can't possibly be called anything other than a cry.

He hums, reaching up to tuck my hair away. "Sorry, did I get your back?"

I nod stiffly, still seizing, and then it's nothing but silence and the sound of my own breath.

~

I SLEEP LIKE THE DEAD.

~

DESPITE HOW I felt my first day, I try not to care about the passage of time too much. I know it's my last day, but I don't know how long it'll be until Pace—or someone else—comes down to... collect me.

So I spend the fifth day walking.

From one end of the cell to the other, I stalk aimlessly back and forth, my feet numb against the chilled stone. Pace came with breakfast, seeming reluctant to leave me when Thad called him away, so it didn't happen then. There's no reason to believe it'll happen during lunch, which Pace rarely brings down anyway. Usually, it's Thad or Danner. So I don't expect to see Pace, and I don't expect to leave.

I don't.

Only, the second I hear footsteps in the distance, I'm plastered right up against the door, hands clutching the bars. "Pace?"

When I get no answer, my stomach sinks.

I slink back toward the cot, but freeze when the sound grows closer. I've been deprived of sound down here long enough to have memorized Thad's heavy footfalls and Pace's long strides. These footsteps are quiet and slow—stilted like someone is trying to find their way.

"Hello?" I call out again.

There's a pause, and then the footsteps grow quicker. "Princess?"

I'm back at the door in a flash. "Stella?!"

When she appears, she's like an angel in dark pigtails, making a beeline for my cell. "Oh my gosh! Princess!" She's beaming, radiant with relief, and when she lifts a hand, I realize she's grasping a key. "The King said I could be the one to get you since Pace had a meeting and Lex had a lecture. Are you okay? We've all been so worried, and Pace kept saying you were alright, but—"

The moment she has the door unlocked, I'm charging through it, gulping in these long, pained breaths.

Ridiculous.

That's what it is.

Five days, that's all. I can't handle five days in a cell. Pace was in one for eighteen months. Probably in this one for longer, cumulatively. And I'm standing here trembling in relief about getting out after only five fucking days.

"Princess?" Stella touches my shoulder, and I turn, so happy to see her face. But whatever she sees in mine drains any trace of excitement from her. "Oh, Verity," she breathes, face falling.

Flying forward, her arms come around me. She hugs me like a Duke, the hold stronger than anyone would expect from someone so small and sweet-looking. I wrap my arms around her and do the same.

And as I'm crying into her shoulder, I can swear I feel her tears on mine.

~

THE WORST PART of being in the dungeon was the cold. It settled in on the first day, bone-deep, and never really left. There's part of me that knows it's psychological. The lack of comfort, clothing, or a real bed. No shower or bath. No sunlight.

Rufus Ashby is the master of torture.

It's this chill I can't shake, even though Stella has the bathroom heaters on full blast after an equally hot shower. I'm clad in only my panties, arms wrapped around my bare chest, standing in front of the sink. Stella slowly dabs my back with a washcloth and warm, soapy water like Lex instructed.

"Does that hurt?" she asks, hand pausing.

"It's fine." I hold back the wince. The wounds are close to being healed, but they're still raw scabs.

"I can be gentler, or maybe we just leave it for now and—"

"For fuck's sake." My gaze jerks up to the mirror, seeing the reflection of Wicker standing in the doorway, his eyes glued to my back. I haven't seen him in five days. Not since he held Ashby and his bodyguard at gunpoint in the library, threatening to kill them all if they didn't let me go. Now he's here, bristling and angry, jaw unshaven, staring at me and my handmaiden like he may murder us both. "The trick is to be quick and decisive. Tip-toeing around it just makes it hurt worse." He sighs, nostrils flaring. "You know what? Just let me do it."

Stella looks at his outstretched hand and then back to me. "Princess?"

"It's fine." Truthfully, I was one second away from taking the rag away from her myself. I give her an encouraging smile. "But I'd love some tea if you could make a pot."

"Of course." She exhales in relief. "I'll be right back."

Taking her spot, he dunks the rag into the water, and pulls it back out, wringing the cloth between his fingers. His eyes won't meet mine. I don't blame him. Wicker is a beautiful man who likes beautiful things. I've seen my back. It's grotesque.

During my five days down in the dungeon, Pace had brought me food. Ashby didn't deprive me, or really his *heir*, of nourishment. But tucked in with every meal, there were little treats—snack cakes, small pieces of chocolate, or a cookie from the bakery just off campus. Even though Wicker never came to see me—not once—I know he was behind that tiny rush of comfort.

Which is why his detached anger makes no sense.

His touch is much firmer than Stella's, and the process is easier to take. I watch his reflection, his unkempt hair, the thick stubble across his jaw, before finally asking, "Are you mad at me?"

He doesn't even blink. "What would I be mad about, Red?"

"Well, you didn't come down to the dungeon all week." I make a face. "And now you're being all..."

"All helpful?" He dunks the rag again and swirls it around before pulling it out. "I've been busy."

I brace my hands on the counter. "That's not what Pace said."

He huffs, the heavy curl of hair on his forehead blowing out. "For all his stalking, Pace doesn't actually know everything, you know that, right?"

I turn, forcing him to look me in the eye. He looks, but not at my face. His eyes dip down to where my breasts are smashed down by my arms. It's a full beat before they lift back up, and his gaze is still slightly off.

"Where were you?" I ask, needing to know. I'd come to Wicker's rescue before, never expecting anything in return, but he'd shown up once, threatening to blow up our entire lives to keep me safe. "What if I needed you down there?"

He moves the cloth, scrubbing it over the ball of my shoulder, letting the warm water run down my arm. His eyes follow the movement of his hands. "What could I do that Pace couldn't?"

"You could have..." I struggle to find the words, remembering that day on the roof of the marina. "You could have been there."

Sharp enough to make me flinch, he snaps, "To *what*? Watch you bleed? To watch you cry? Maybe I didn't want to see you!"

A week's worth of anger churns in my gut. "Because I was weak? Trapped?" I swallow, hating how his eyes go right to the marks on my back. "Ugly?"

He tosses the rag into the sink behind me with a splash, dragging his fingers through his hair. "Is that what you really think? That I'm that shallow?"

"That's the whole point!" I say. "I don't know what to think!"

He spins, and I think he's going to walk away, but after two prowling strides, he ricochets back. There's resolve set in his angular jaw. "I've spent the last five days hanging on by a very thin thread, wavering between killing my father for locking you up, and going down there and stealing you myself. But..." His eyes bear down on me, and I shiver at the mixture of agony and tenderness there. "If I'd seen you down there, with no way to get you out, I would have lost my shit and done something very, very stupid."

Over the months, there's been a lot of emotion between us. Hate. Loathing. Bitter rage. Sympathy. Even pity. But this feels different.

"What are you saying?"

"This thing between us is too fucking much." His hand flattens on his chest, over his heart, fingers curling into his shirt. "I spent all those years not letting those people inside. I kept myself safe," he pounds his fist, "in here. But you showed up in a fancy ballgown, guns blazing, West End wild, taking every fucking thing I threw at you. You were supposed to cry. To run. To make it easy for me to break you. But you didn't break. You just kept fucking going. And then..."

My stomach clenches. "Then what?"

His eyes dart to my belly, then back up, making his hair flop in his eyes. "You rescued me." His jaw tics. "Twice."

"I did what any Princess would do," I say carefully.

"No. No one has ever done something like that for me before." He looks at me with red-rimmed eyes. "Not when I was ten, or fifteen, or twenty." He inhales, eyes searching. "So why, Verity? Why do you do it, knowing damn well I can't rescue you back?"

I lift my hand and cup his cheek, knowing the answer. "Because, Whitaker Kayes, despite how hard your father tried, this isn't a transaction for me. I showed up because I see what you don't." With a sad smile, I stroke his cheek. "That you're worth saving."

26

icker

I TOLD Verity once that I wasn't built for attachments.

I was built to be used, groomed to be a product. Over the years, the thought of caring about anyone—of being cared for *by* them—has become such an impossible, foreign concept that I never allowed myself to pay potential attachments much mind.

Then one day, my father decided to force me into one.

But I'm not like Pace. Where he saw an opportunity, all I saw was something twisted and corrupted, and to accept it—to accept *her*—would be settling for the rotten scraps Father was throwing to us, and *fuck that.*

But her words, just like the warmth of her touch, go off like a bomb in my chest, taking down the walls so carefully built around my heart. It's not so much what she says, but what the words mean.

Even through all the bullshit, Verity Sinclaire *sees* me.

And it's both terrifying and thrilling.

To everyone outside my brothers, I've been a prop. A player. An athlete. A showpiece. A Prince. *A whore.*

But this woman has asked nothing of me but civility, and I've barely been able to muster it.

We're so close our bodies are touching, her swollen belly reaching out to meet the hard line of my abdomen. She's still in nothing but a thin pair of panties. At some point, while living in this palace, she's lost all sense of modesty. I understand this more than anyone; she was conditioned out of it by all of us, giving in to our demands at a moment's notice, spreading her legs, and taking our seed. But I was the worst. Belittling and abusive. Mean.

All because she scares the fucking hell out of me.

When I reach for her now, my touch is gentle. Fingers cupping around the back of her head.

"You should hate me," I tell her, almost hoping she'll admit to it. Give me what I need to rebuild those walls. Stop touching me and soothing this buzzing need beneath my skin.

"I should," she agrees.

"But?" I ask. *Fearful.*

"But I don't." Her face lifts upward. Bracing her hip with my hand, I draw her closer, feeling those bare tits press against my chest. "That's what makes you so confounding. You're so fucking hard to hate."

Tilting her head with my hand, I drop my mouth to hers. Her lips are warm, eager, and needy, meeting my tongue with her own. Deepening the kiss, the sharp press of her nails punctures into my shoulders. The move spurs me on, my cock thickening, and I glide my hands along her ribs.

She arches away, hissing low.

"Shit, your back." I drop my forehead to hers, shuddering at how she feels against me. "I'm sorry." It's been almost a week since she last touched me. I'm fucking losing it.

She shakes her head, exhaling slowly. "Don't stop." Her hot tongue darts out, licking my throat. "Unless you want to."

"Fuck, no, I don't want to." I've never wanted anything—or

anyone—more. I've wanted her since the day I saw her after winning my Fury, so timid and gorgeous in that back hallway. When I saw her in the dressing room for the masquerade. When I took her virginity, already bleeding from the throne. I've never *not* wanted her.

It's just the reason that's changed.

Seeing her on her knees, taking my father's abuse in Pace's place, made it clear that she didn't just save me. She saved him—or, as I found out later, his goddamn bird, but it's one and the same. And how many times has she been the reason Lex wasn't out on the streets, looking for another hit of Scratch? It doesn't matter that he relapsed. What matters is this:

No one's rescued me before, and they sure as hell have never rescued my brothers.

Not until her.

I drop my hands under her backside and lift her into my arms. She immediately curls around me, arms and legs, and it's all I can do to not slam her up against the door.

I carry her into the bedroom instead.

At the foot of the massive bed, I sit, positioning her on my lap, and then I just... look at her. Her hair is still wet from her shower, bleeding these tiny, cold droplets that do nothing to cool the fire beneath my skin. I sweep the heavy strands away from the swell of her tits. They're bigger, a new marvel every time I get to see them, and I palm them in my hands, feeling her nipples pebble and tighten.

My touch is met with a pained hiss.

"Sorry." Flinching, I move to draw my hands away. I've never had to be careful with a woman before. Obedient, yes. Generous, sure. But mindful of hurting them?

"No," she grabs my hands, tugging them back. "They're just so fucking sensitive. It hurts, but it also..."

I skate my lips across her jaw. "Feels good? Yeah, I get that." I ease up on the pressure, the motions softer but no less stimulating. With a shivery exhale, she grinds against me, short-circuiting the connectors in my brain.

Carefully squeezing her tits together, I dip my head to suck one into my mouth, barely distracted when the door opens.

I hear a high-pitched, "Oops!"

"Leave the tray, Stella," Verity gasps, hands grappling at my shirt. She pushes me back so her eyes can take in my body, and I feel a rush at the way she looks at me, heavy-lidded and hungry.

"Hey, Stella," I call, licking my lips. "Why don't you take the day off? You've earned it."

Verity nods. "Weren't you just saying before how long it's been since you've seen your sister?"

Stella squeaks, "Yes?"

"You can take my car," Verity offers, two spots of color rising on each cheek. "Keys on the dresser."

My stomach caves at her touch. "Definitely take her car."

She had Ballsack drive it here after her last stint in West End. It's old and hideous, probably held together with duct tape and Bruin spit, and it's been an unspoken goal between my brothers and me to never give her the chance to use it.

We kiss as Stella snags them, the jingle sounding distant and muddled. "Sure thing, Princess." Her smirk is as audible as her giggle. "You have fun!"

The girl scurries out, and by the time the door shuts, the rest of my stomach and chest are exposed. Verity runs her hands over my torso, and I grab my shirt by the collar, taking it the rest of the way off.

She pushes me back, and I sprawl on the bed, watching her as she rises up to her knees to take off her panties. She's a vision of wild red hair, pale skin, and swollen curves, and I rest a hand on her hip to help her stay balanced. The way her pussy peeks out from under the bump, teasing and almost out of reach, makes my cock stab painfully into my jeans. Impatiently, I unzip, giving myself some relief.

"I like this," she says of my muscles, bending to press kisses across my pecs. Feeling the sharp points of her tits graze over my skin sends a tremor down my spine that only intensifies when her mouth latches on, her tongue laving over my nipple.

"Fuck," I gasp, bucking up. Tired of the barriers between us, I squirm around to shuck off my jeans, kicking them away and drawing her down until my cock meets the hot, wet warmth of her pussy. Groaning, I admit, "Goddamn, I missed this."

Pussy. Sex. Fucking.

It's been *months*.

"Are you okay doing it this way?" she asks, fingers toying with the hair below my belly button.

My stomach jumps, the tickle almost too much to bear. "What way?"

She gives a slow, heavy blink. "Looking at me."

My breath lodges in my throat.

Misreading my pause, her eyes shutter. "Because it's okay if you don't want to." She starts to climb off my lap. "I know it bothers you."

I clutch her by the hips and haul her back. "It was easier not to look at you," I admit, already close to panting. "To not... make you real. Not just you, but anyone. It kept you in the same place as I kept them; just a way to get off. To meet an urge. To pretend like it was my choice, like I had a tiny sliver of control, only giving them what I wanted and getting the same back."

"I'm sorry." Her eyes brim with tears, one sliding down her cheek.

I lunge up to kiss it away. "Don't be." Dragging a hand down her side, I graze my thumb over the side of her growing belly. "With you," I continue, struggling to find the words, "it's different. It *should* be different. I want to be completely at your mercy." I kiss her jaw, dropping my hand to the place where our bodies meet. "You want that, right?" I press my fingers into the slick heat between her legs. "You won't take more than I can give. I know you won't."

She shudders. "Never."

So here's a secret. I give it to her right in her ear. "I want to give you all of me," my lips brush the shell of her ear, "and I want all of you in return."

Her chest hitches with a gasp, pussy sliding over my cock. "Oh, god."

"For the first time in my goddamn life, I don't just want to get off,

Red." I trail my kiss to her warm cheek, watching her green eyes flutter. "I want you to be mine."

The confession spurs her on, her hips rocking, letting my cock glide over her folds. My body reacts, remembering how good it was to feel her orgasm tremble over me last time, in this same bed. But I want more this time. I want to be inside her. To feel her warmth surround me as she tightens up and falls apart.

So I nudge her up, gripping the base of my cock to guide it to her entrance. She's more slick than I ever remember her being, and I know it's a product of her hormones, but *fuck me.*

That's all I can think about as I push up, sliding my cock into her tight hole. *Fuck me* for having this, but squandering it. *Fuck me* for all those times I buried my cock into this perfect hole and let it be anything less than blissful. *Fuck me* for taking her body, but never appreciating the flush of her cheeks, or the fan of her lashes, or the way her jaw goes slack when she takes me in.

She's wet and warm, and the urge to thrust is overwhelming, but I want this to last. With my eyes open, I watch everything. The deep breath she takes as her body adjusts to my size. How her nose wrinkles at the sharp tug of her nipples. The way her tongue darts out when I reach behind her, grip her ass and push myself all the way in.

"Oh God," she exhales, pressing her body against mine. "Fuck me, Wick, please. It's been so long."

Long for us, I wonder? Or long because she's been in the dungeon? Doesn't matter, because it's been way too long for me, and my balls are about to explode. I push up so we're not just looking at one another, but face to face, and thrust in.

Her cry is like music, fingers digging divots into my shoulders as she rocks against me. Immediately, I know I won't regret doing it like this, seeing every hint of reaction on her face as I fuck up into her. I can't get enough of her eyes like this—the way she looks at me, all transfixed and intense, even when the rock of her hips has an edge of frantic desperation.

Sex has always fallen into two categories: good for them, or good for me. The first is strictly a performance because I'm skilled at showing women what they want to see. The second is purely human necessity—all about me.

This is somehow both and neither.

Because when I kiss her, reaching between us to feel her swollen clit, I do it to feel the way she clenches around me. To taste the hitch of her breath. To watch the way her brow screws up in ecstasy. But I want to feel these things because it makes it that much sweeter to buck my hips, indulging in her slick heat.

How stupid that I once saw sex like this as a loss of power.

I hold her every twitch at the mercy of my fingertips.

"Wick," she gasps, arms wound around my neck. She presses her forehead to mine and rolls her hips. "Please..."

I don't need the plea, though. Not with the way she's biting her lip and grinding down, chasing the pressure of my hand, nor how wet she is, her pussy gushing around me. I know exactly what she's searching for, and I know exactly how to give it to her.

I push my thumb against her clit, my other reaching up to graze her nipple.

And then, gently, I pluck the pebbled peak.

Her mouth falls open on a cry that I swallow with a kiss, feeling her clench and flutter around me. Verity orgasms so sweetly, never scratching or bruising, only sobbing these clipped, agonized breaths as she rocks her hips. I feel her body tense and twitch, the way her shoulders jolt in surprise at the sensation, and it's enough to send me right along with her.

I grip her hips and hold her tight, giving her no reprieve as I slam up into her body one last time. It flows through me like liquid warmth, and when I bury my face in her neck, it's not even because I want to hide.

I just need to taste her skin as I fill her up.

I can't even count how many times I've emptied my balls into this girl. I'm sure somewhere in this house, there's a ledger with a tally, and even it wouldn't be accurate. Thirty? Forty? Fifty?

None of them hold a candle to this one.

I come like a rumble of thunder, clouds crashing to release a ray of white-hot light behind my eyelids. Through it all, I feel her fingers in my hair and her lips on my ear, her soft whisper leading me back.

"You feel so good," she says. "Perfect..."

Something in my chest tangles up at the words, though I don't know why it should. Plenty of women have told me that. So why is it that, when she does, her voice released on the cusp of a sigh, it brings a lump to my throat?

I think I understand when I roll us to our sides, finally catching a glimpse of her flushed, blissed-out face. Verity isn't looking at me like she wants to consume me. There are no teeth or sharp edges here. They weren't just words someone says for the sake of the moment.

It was praise.

It takes a long moment for my throat to unlock, and I have plans, however vague, to tell her how fucking amazing she looks right now, all fucked out and euphoric.

Instead, I blurt, "I ate your banana pudding."

She pauses, blinking. "You *what*?"

"You were in the dungeon," I explain, a touch defensive. "It was going to go bad. I ate it."

Her jaw drops, but the outrage is all artifice. "I can't believe you!" Her eyes narrow. "Did you like it?"

I make a face. "Of course not. It was disgusting." Tapping her hip, I add, "So the next time you get some, you should give it to me. Save yourself the trouble."

She snorts. "Oh, really."

Smirking, I push a kiss into her collarbone. "Absolutely. I'm falling on grenades for you left and right here."

She hums, tipping her head to the side. "You can fall on one for me now by taking a nap with me."

"Can't," I say, idly lapping up her sweat. "Have to get dressed so we can go downstairs. I need to show you something." I can practically feel her heart rate kick up a notch, so I'm quick to assure, "Something good."

Looking skeptical but so fucking soft, she agrees, "Okay."

I TAKE her down via the passageway in the wall, holding her hand as I lead her down a narrow, dusty staircase.

"You always take me to the best dark and dank places," she mutters. But her hand squeezes mine, and when we pass the turn that leads to the basement, her palm grows clammy.

"I learned a long time ago it's easier not to run into Father or Danner in the house."

I take her straight instead, pushing open a panel to reveal....

"The solarium," she whispers, a smile lighting up her face.

It's a glass room full of weeds and dirt, so personally, I don't see the appeal. Or I didn't. Not until she came in here and started growing things, making it green and lush. There are new plants popping up from each planter and urn, and the old, wiry vines are almost gone from the stone floor. Up above, the recent rain has washed the ancient panes of glass, amplifying the late May sun, brightening every corner.

Pace would never admit it, but I found him down here a couple of times while she was locked away, standing in the middle of it all with a drawn, broody expression.

"Oh," she gasps, darting to a pot by the door. "My begonias are blooming!"

Basically, over her time in West End and down in the dungeon, the solarium has exploded with color. Flowers and ornamentals are springing up all over the place. "That's not all that's bloomed," I say, cramming my fists into my pockets. At her confused glance, I nod toward a planter in the back, watching as she shuffles her way across the distance.

She freezes when she sees it, a hand coming up to cover her mouth. "Oh my god, Wicker."

I smirk, having seen the flowers bloom four days ago. When I got the seeds, I didn't know what color they'd turn out to be. Annoyingly, they're a creamy white, a lot like the roses around here. "Surprised?"

"You gave me dahlia seeds?" She spins to fix me with a disbelieving stare. "Ashby is going to flip."

Seeing the alarm in her eyes, I wave a hand. "I doubt he'll even notice, but don't worry. He'll know it was me." I slide up to sit on the low stone wall behind them, pulling her between my legs. "I'm the only one with the balls to bring the Barons' flower into his precious garden."

She sighs, winding her arms around my waist. "They're beautiful."

Pressing my nose into her hair, I pull in her scent. "Better than roses?" When she doesn't answer, I duck my head down to look at her face, realizing her eyes are fixed elsewhere. Following her gaze, my face hardens. "Better than those, at least."

She's staring at the big bed of nettles in the corner, her jaw going taut. "I should cut them down."

"It doesn't matter." I don't tell her that in four days, nothing about this place will matter.

We'll all be gone.

Sparing the dahlias a glance, I don't let myself feel any sort of way about it. It was a joke to grow them here. A way to get a jab in with Father. A taste of irony, knowing that Clive Kayes' favorite flower is growing in this cursed place, just like I did.

One day, these flowers will wilt and die.

But the five of us won't.

Lex still looks like shit.

I watch him as he hands over a folder, the tremor in his hand obvious before I take it. "You good?" Most likely, he can barely hear me over the music blaring from Pace's speakers, but the three of us are leaning in close.

He shakes his hand out, scowling at his wrist. "I'm fine. So we're solid on the embezzlement, but we need more for the wire fraud."

Pace's knee is bouncing, jaw tense as he surveys what Lex has obtained over the afternoon. "They had enough for my conviction," he mutters.

"That's the problem," Lex says, palming his clammy forehead. "A lot of it leads back to you, so we can't use it. Just like Wick and the solicitation, or me and the maiming. There's no proof he made us."

Nodding, I muse, "We need to keep it to direct involvement. The stuff he hides from us." There's plenty that happens behind closed doors in this palace—shit that even we're not privy to.

"That's going to be the best leverage," Lex agrees, looking between us. He hasn't bothered to put his hair up today, and it keeps falling into his eyes.

I watch as he rakes it back, offering, "I can get into his office."

Pace groans, flopping back onto his couch. "We'll have to save that for last. No way to obscure any surveillance trickery for more than a day or so."

Lex takes this in, brow creased. "Okay. Morning of?"

With that super risky plan, we start gathering up all the folders, documents, and memory cards we've been collecting. It's late, and I can tell that we're all run ragged, even more than usual. Lex has been at it all day, and Pace hasn't had more than fleeting moments of respite since we decided to enact a plan to leave.

"Are you coming with us tonight?" I ask Lex, already knowing the answer.

He shrugs. "I'm still sick sometimes."

It's a lie, and I know it. Last night was Verity's first night out of the dungeon, and he didn't come to bed with us. He says it's because of the withdrawal symptoms, but I know it's about making our escape. He feels responsible for the plan because he's the one who made it, back when we were in high school.

He won't get any real rest until he knows all of us are safe.

"She asked about you," I say, pinning him with a glare. "Don't make me lie to her again."

His face falls, which is when the doorknob begins rattling. We freeze, eyes flying wide, before we all begin to frantically stuff the evidence beneath the couch.

Over the music, I hear a muffled, "Pace? Are you guys in there?" It's followed by five loud bangs.

We all deflate, Pace standing to turn down the music, and when he opens the door, it's to the sight of Verity and Ballsack. She pushes into the room, and the expression on her face makes me lurch upright.

"What's wrong?" I ask.

Her eyes are brimming with tears.

Pace is already grabbing her, hands framing her face. "Hey, hey—what happened?"

"It's Stella," she says, clutching his wrists. "She's gone."

I glance at Ballsack. "Gone where?"

The Dukeling looks as ragged as Lex. "Gone missing," he grinds out.

Lex stands, holding up his hands. "Wait, slow down. What do you mean, missing?"

Verity takes a deep breath, her face lined with panic. "Wicker and I... we gave her the day off yesterday. She never came back."

Pace frowns. "Well, maybe she went home—"

"No," Ballsack snaps, and from one glance at him, I can tell he's far past panic. "I spoke to Mercer, who spoke to her sister. She hasn't seen Stella in weeks."

"Something's wrong," Verity agrees, glancing between me and my brothers. "Wrong, like Rory's sister. Wrong, like all the other missing girls." She meets my gaze, her voice sharp with conviction. "Stella wouldn't leave me and Ballsy."

"Red," I start, sharing a look with Lex, "I'm sure it's fine. It's only been—what, not even two days?"

Lex frowns, but assures, "I'm sure she'll show up."

Ballsack releases a clipped, angry laugh. "See?" he tells her. "Stella's South Side. I fucking told you they wouldn't care."

"Of course, they care!" She glances between us, voice fervent. "Stella has been a fixture since I got here. She's the closest thing I have here to a friend. She takes care of me, and we'll take care of her." She fixes me with a hard gaze. "Right?"

Sighing, I meet Pace's agitated gaze. "I guess... we can check the footage, right?"

I don't even need to look at Lex to know he's pulling a face. We're days out from graduation—and escaping this hellhole. Investigating the disappearance of Verity's handmaiden is going to be a real dildo in our ass. There's no way to do it quickly and without attracting attention.

Pace seems to mull this over before landing heavily in his desk chair. "Fine, let's check the feeds."

Something in Ballsack's expression roars to life, and suddenly, he's right up against Pace's side, tattooed fists resting on the desktop. "She left at about noon."

Lex and I wait on the couch as Pace leads Ballsack and Verity through the footage. They see her leaving the Princess' room right after she caught us pre-fuck. In the video, she's grinning from ear to ear, all but skipping down the hallway as she leaves. Her being all happy and buoyant? Not a good sign. People don't run away because they're happy. If anyone knows that, it's us.

"You said she took your shitty car?" Pace asks, pulling up the footage from the garage.

Verity's mouth goes pinched. "It's not shitty."

"It's a piece of crap, Red," I confirm. "Do us all a favor and let it go where all things that should never see the light of day again go to die." I wink at her. "The moat."

She frowns at my joke, clearly not in the mood for humor, shifting her gaze back toward Pace, whose fingers are flying over the keys.

"Okay, here she is getting into it." On the screen, she drives away, and Pace switches to the camera covering the bridge, watching her leave the palace grounds. He glances at us over his shoulder, lifting an eyebrow. "This could take a while."

And so it begins.

It takes an hour just to track one tiny, vaguely Asian ball of energy around Forsyth. From the palace to a place off Sixteenth Avenue, Pace manages to jump from camera to camera. Some of them are broken, others aren't attached to a recording device whatsoever, but he makes it work.

"Is that a tailor?" Lex asks when we finally catch her getting out of the car. She walks into the dress shop, and then a few minutes later, returns in the frame, carrying a garment bag. She hangs the bag in the back of the car and drives off.

Verity wrings her hands, looking distressed. "She must have been picking up my dress for Lex and Sy's graduation. I told her to take the day off, not run my errands."

"Anywhere else she might have gone?" Pace asks, glancing at her. "Could help us narrow it down."

Her forehead creases pensively. "Maybe the bakery?" She flicks her eyes at Lex. "I, uh, wanted a cake designed for the graduation afterparty."

Lex looks up, stunned. "For me?"

"Yeah, well," she rolls her eyes, "your father doesn't have the best track record."

Pace nods, and the monitors hop across town, giving various angles from gas stations and light posts to the front of businesses and government property.

"Are these all your cameras?" Ballsack asks, leaning over the desk.

"Some are mine. Others I've hacked into." He leans forward. "Wait, is that your girl?"

We all peer at the black-and-white footage of a girl pulling up to a bakery. I've never been, but I recognize the name. It's the same one that did Trudie's absurd petit fours. We watch her go in, and ten minutes later, she comes back out empty-handed.

When the shitty car leaves the parking lot, Pace spits a curse. "She's in North Side," he explains. "I have a lot of dead spots out there."

He tries to trace her, Ballsack hovering right up against his side, but none of us spot the car in any of the shots. The longer it goes without sight of her, Verity grows more and more upset, pacing in front of the couch with a drawn face.

They're at it for two hours before Pace slumps back in his seat, groaning. "Guys, this is a needle in a haystack."

"Keep looking," Verity demands.

But Pace is gassed, rubbing his thumbs into his eyes. "I'm not going to be much help on no sleep. Maybe we can pick back up tomorrow."

"But..." Verity's eyes begin welling again, jumping from the empty monitors to Ballsack's dejected gaze. "I can stay! I'll look through everything myself. You can trust me."

"You need rest even more than we do," Lex argues, pushing to his feet. "Stella wouldn't want you putting the baby in—"

His words clip off when Ballsack suddenly storms from the room, not even offering us a dirty look in his wake. Lex glances at me, shrugging helplessly, because he knows just like I do that kicking up a fuss about this is a bad idea.

Verity looks at us—all of us—the desperation clear in her eyes. "We have to find her! She didn't just fall off the face of the earth. She's out there somewhere!"

Pace and Lex both stand there, limp as the tears spill over, rolling down her wan cheeks.

Sometimes I hate being the one who has to say the truth aloud. "Verity, he has a point. Stella *is* South Side. The minute she walked out of the palace, she stopped being our problem."

Her gaze snaps to me, flashing in such utter fucking shock that I almost want to take it back. "You're saying you don't care about Stella," she hisses, "because she just so happens to have grown up in another fucking territory?"

Calmly, I reply, "No, I'm saying she has the Lords on her side, which is good because they keep what's theirs. Out of any of the houses, the Lords are the least likely to let something like this slide."

"If something happened to Stella, they'll find her," Pace explains, reaching out to touch the curve of her belly. "But we have you and the baby to think about. We have to let them do their thing, so we can do ours."

She searches his eyes, the anger in her face only growing. "Stella *is* ours!"

"Verity," Pace starts when she follows Ballsack's lead, bursting from the room in a flurry of vicious tears. "Goddamn it," he sighs, dragging a palm down his face. "Just what we need."

Lex stares at him, jaw tight. "Are you thinking what I'm thinking?"

"That another girl has gone missing again, only this one drove out of here in the Princess' car?" Pace glances at me, eyes darkening. "Yeah, I'd say we're all thinking it."

Someone out there is targeting the women of Forsyth, and this one just hit way too fucking close to home.

"All the more reason to stay focused," I reason. "Whatever happened to Stella, if it was meant to be Verity, then chances are, they'll try again."

"We've got two days until we get out of here. We'll just have to keep a closer eye on her than normal," Lex says. "Which will be easier said than done, if she's pissed."

Time and time again, there have been obstacles to us pulling the trigger on the plan, but we don't have to say it out loud to know that nothing is going to stop us this time. Not Father, prison, Scratch, or obligations. Definitely not some psycho snatching women off the street.

Two more days, and we'll no longer be the Princes of Forsyth.

We'll be ghosts.

27

erity

Lex wears his hair down for the ceremony.

On the drive up in the limo, I kept catching his gaze only to see him snap back toward the front of the car. It's like he wants me to want him—as if he hadn't ripped a little piece of my heart out by going to bed instead of searching for Stella a couple of nights ago.

Some part of me understands that's not fair. The next morning, Pace had been right back at it, sifting through feed after feed in search of my car. He even called Ballsy in himself to help, and they spent the whole day like that, curved over the desk until they were haggard and defeated.

But we should be *out there*, looking.

Instead, all of us are in the Forsyth Amphitheater as some old guy drones on and on about prestige and a hopeful future. Lex is, of course, down on the ground, somewhere in the sea of gold, black, and purple. Throughout the whole commencement address, Rufus Ashby is next to Pace, Wicker, and I. He keeps his head held high like he's absorbing Lex's success as his very own.

The suffocating monotony of the event makes my chest ache. I'd been so excited to see Lex walk across the stage. To see his hands take the degree, all the while knowing they're the same hands that touch me so expertly, keeping me healthy and whole. Instead, I spend the whole thing sick with this frantic need to get out there and start looking.

The Lords are down there somewhere too, and the thought just makes me angrier. Maybe it's unfair, but I don't give a damn. They should be on the streets, asking questions. Showing her picture. Turning over every stone until they find what's theirs. Isn't that their thing?

By the time Lex's name is finally called—Lagan Juniper Ashby—I feel half-present, only jumping to clap because the men surrounding me do. I try to take it in, to commit to memory the way he looks sweeping up the steps. The sure strides. The way his hair billows around his shoulders. The handshake with the dean that looks unnecessarily aggressive.

It's more than I can muster for Sy.

Of course, by the sudden roar of rowdy cheering, I'm guessing DKS makes up for it.

I think it's nearly over when the university president has them take their tassel and shift it from one side of their cap to the other, officially proclaiming them graduates and giving them permission to toss them in the air, but it's not.

We still have to take pictures.

The only genuine smile comes from Rufus, grinning as though we're truly one big, happy family. His adopted sons and his recently announced secret daughter, the heir no longer able to be hidden under loose clothing.

"Well," Ashby says after the dean walks away, promising to share cigars at the Gentlemen's Chamber in a few weeks, "top honors, top two percent of the class, and an acceptance to three of the finest med schools in the country. Even I'll concede you deserve a night of celebration." He claps Lex on the shoulder, ignoring the icy look it elicits. "The club is yours and PNZ's for the evening. Food, drinks, women," he waves his hand, "have at it. I'll be down at the marina with the other parents. If there's any trouble, call Danner, not me."

My three Princes look distracted and particularly wooden, but I don't expect them to be excited about it. Things have changed dramatically in the past few weeks. I trust that they'll be faithful, even if it's just out of respect for the baby's health. But I sense the strain in their acceptance of their Father's gift—a rare night off.

"I'm not going to a party in this monkey suit," Wick says, already removing his tie.

"Yeah, I need to change," Lex says, looking distinctly uncomfortable. The only perk of sitting with Ashby was the fact that we had a shady spot up top. The graduates, however, sat in the sun for hours. He's already unzipped his gown and has his cap tucked under his arm. "We'll go home and change before heading to the party."

Lex and Wicker start toward the parking lot, but Pace falls back next to me, hands shoved deep in his pockets. I know he wants to touch me. Put his arm around my shoulder, or rest his hand on my stomach, but I'm still pissed. I'm not exactly freezing them out but... well, they've made their position about Stella clear, and so have I.

He glances back over to where I know Ballsack is standing. "You should go party with your King," Pace says, mouth pressed into a tense line. "We can handle the Princess."

I balk at the obvious directive, but Ballsy just shrugs. "I'm good," he says, adjusting his own tie, which somehow makes him look twelve instead of nineteen. "I'll keep out of the way."

"Give us a minute," I say to Pace. He doesn't look happy about it, but I'm not particularly worried about his feelings right now. Stepping away from my Prince, I approach Ballsack. *Eugene*. "He's right," I tell him, heart heavy. "Go celebrate with Sy and the guys. I'll be surrounded by three obsessive Princes and a whole frat, deep in East End territory."

He shakes his head. "It's fine. They'll all be shitfaced by the time I get to the tower, and Remy will just force all of us to get some stupid tattoo to commemorate the event." He lifts his sleeve, revealing his wrist. "Here's the one he insisted we all get for the waxing moon three months ago."

I know he's trying to be lighthearted, but I see the deep groove creasing his forehead. He looks tired, his arms crossed over his chest like he's holding himself together.

I reach out to touch his arm. "Look, even if you don't go to the party, maybe you can talk to the cutsluts. See if anyone has heard anything. They may loosen up if they've had a few drinks."

Eugene nods, finally relenting, but looks back at Pace, who I've sensed behind me, large and looming this whole time. When he speaks, there's no disguising the threat. "You keep her safe." His Adam's apple bobs under a thick swallow. "Two of my girls have already gone missing. I sure as hell can't take a third."

ON THE RIDE back to the palace, the sun is on the verge of setting, painting the sky a vivid pink. I get this involuntary notion that Stella would love it. She'd probably fill the tense silence with her bubbly voice and happy exclamations. In the end, I think that's what makes me so sick. That she was such a bright light in a dark world, and somehow, Forsyth is trying to snuff it out.

I'll be damned if I let it.

"I'll give you tonight," I tell them, looking out the window at the passing scenery, "but tomorrow, I'm calling the Duchess, and she'll call the Lady. One of them must have a way to contact Regina. Then, we're going to work together to find Stella." I take a deep breath, the idea having come together during the ceremony. Watching the five factions of Forsyth co-exist for a moment in time just bolsters my resolve. "Together, the Royal women will organize a search. Each house will dispatch its members, and we'll comb every inch of Forsyth for Stella and any other girl who's gone missing."

"Jesus, Red, just give it a fucking rest," Wicker says from the back.

I spin around, the rage in my chest combusting. "Did you just tell me to give it a rest?" When he stares blankly back at me, I add, "You and I were the ones who told her to go! To use my car! And why? Because we were too busy fucking to be interrupted." I swallow back the bitter taste of guilt. "I don't know why this is okay with you. Any of you! Are you all seriously okay with someone snatching girls off the street?"

"Look, I'm not saying it isn't fucked," he snaps, running a hand through his blonde hair. "But we can't just—"

"The reason we can't look for Stella is because we're leaving." Lex's toneless words barely penetrate before he adds, "And you're coming with us."

"What?" I look at Pace, who's sitting in the driver's seat next to me, his knuckles tight on the steering wheel. "What are you talking about?"

Pace's jaw tics as he presses the accelerator. "Once we get to the palace, you have thirty minutes to pack," he says, matter-of-factly. "One bag. Nothing frivolous. We'll buy what we need once we get settled."

I look between them, my heart plummeting when it sinks in. "What the hell do you mean we're leaving? Like running away? From Ashby?" Panic rushes up my throat, and without thinking, I reach for the door, pulling at the locked handle.

"What the fuck, Ver!" Pace grabs at my hands, jerking the wheel and making the car swerve. "Stop trying to jump out of the *moving* car!"

Urgency grips my lungs like a fist, making it hard to breathe. "We're going to grab a bag, take one of his cars, his money, not to mention his fucking grandchild, and just... run?" I shake my head, gawking at them. "You've lost your goddamn minds!"

"This isn't some impulsive move we're making!" Wick snaps, eyes flaring. "Everything has been set to go for years. Money, transportation, safe houses. You have no fucking idea how much time and effort has gone into this. The *only* thing that's changed is that you're coming with us!"

Slowly, I shake my head, knowing they can't be this stupid. "And you think the Dukes will be okay with that? My *mother*?" Lord, she'll lose her mind and burn down the entire city looking for me. Then, it hits me. "Son of a—*that's* why you had me send Effie away? So we could run?"

The car pulls up to the house, and I don't miss the anxious looks they're giving one another. There's a reason they told me about this in the car. It must have been swept of bugs.

Pace shifts the car into park, breathing long and measured. "You're going to have to trust us."

"What if I say no?" I ask, suspecting I already know the answer.

"It's simple, Rosi." Pace finally turns, meeting my gaze. I feel a chill at what I see in them. "You can go willingly, or we can take you. Either way, you're coming with us."

I glance back at Lex and Wicker, seeing the same determination in the set of their faces. In all the time we've been together, I'm not sure I've ever seen them so united.

"You'd force me." Blood turning to ice, I try to inhale, but it hurts. "You'd kidnap me. Just like the other girls. Just like Stella."

Through the sound of me hyperventilating, Pace snatches up my hand, thumb running over the ring. "Hey, hey—it's not like that." I haven't tried to take the ring off again, not since experiencing the excruciating pain the first time. These men may care for me—they may have feelings for me and this baby—but they're still Royals.

They possess.

And I belong to them.

Suddenly, Lex is behind me, palm pressed to my cheek. "Remember what I said to you before?" he asks, forcing me to face him. His eyes aren't like Pace's—dark and empty. They're alight with a fire I'm not used to seeing there. It's fervent, bright with conviction, willing me to follow his words. "Our son can't live here. *We* can't follow him to West End. No kingdom will have us."

Leaning close, Pace explains, "Lex can go to med school, and become a surgeon. I'll go into IT. Wicker can still apply for law school."

Wicker meets my gaze next. "We're going to make a nice life for you."

"Both of you," Lex adds, and it isn't until his thumb sweeps across my cheek that I realize I'm crying.

God, I'm so tired of crying. "This is it, isn't it?" I look at Pace, remembering his words from that day in the dungeon. "You're putting me into *your* cage."

Whatever desperation might have been in Pace's eyes, they shutter completely. He cuts the ignition, his jaw hardening. "Thirty minutes," he says, not even having the guts to look at me. "You say a fucking word about this to Danner—to *anyone*—and we're all dead." His eyes dart down to my stomach. "And you'll never see this baby alive."

That's the last thing he says to me as they all begin climbing out of the car.

I TURN, taking in the big, opulent room I've been calling my own for the past six months.

The first time I walked through the doors, I was hurt. Full of nerves, but too numb to properly feel them. Alone, exhausted, and humiliated.

Tonight is much the same.

The big, creepy bed, which once seemed so sterile and overwhelming, now calls to me in the strangest way. It's been witness to so much. Painful things, for sure, but also gentle, safe, secret things. I wonder how many Princesses have found tenderness in it, and how impossible such a thing must be. Was the shine of being a Princess always a lie? Could anything so pure as love ever be created in the midst of something so wretched?

There are clothes strewn about the room. Wicker's socks on the floor. Pace's hoodie slung around a bedpost. Lex's hair ties on the nightstand. A half-empty cup of tea is spoiling on the dresser from where Stella left it.

Her absence throbs inside my chest like a slowly failing organ.

Did they get rid of her so there wouldn't be a witness?

No. *No*. That's fucking crazy.

Pace told me himself. They aren't killers by nature. They're torturers. This couldn't have *all* been a lie. Some of it, yes. Most of it, maybe.

But not that.

What I need is air, time to think, and the flutter of butterfly wings. Luckily, the three of them are off in Pace's room, gathering his equipment, so I don't think twice about going to my dresser and finding the burner phone buried inside a box of tampons.

A plan forming, I walk over to the bed, struggling to recall the gemstones I watched Wicker press before smashing them. A moment later, the wall parts, revealing the small, musty panic room. I step inside, close the door, and turn on my phone's flashlight. It takes a minute to find the tiny lever that slides the wall away, but I do it quickly, silently, with only the pounding of my heart in my ears.

I have less than twenty minutes.

I'm shocked at how well I know my way through the inner maze, noticing landmarks that identify different exits back into the house. Ignoring them all, I march to the one that's most familiar: the stairway down to the solarium.

The cicadas are singing when I step out, the sun barely a glow of memory in the sky. Crouching in the one spot where I know I can't be seen or heard, I take out my phone, pressing the number programmed under *Instar*.

It rings. And rings. And rings.

I'm about to hang up when a voice answers, loud, pulsing music in the background.

"Verity?"

"Lav, oh my God." I jolt in surprise. "I thought you weren't going to answer."

"I'm at the tower. Are you coming?"

"No. I need to talk to you—"

"Hold on," she says, and then more muffled, "Nick, *Jesus*, give me a minute, okay?"

I pace, treading back and forth in front of the twisted vines, one eye on the door that leads upstairs.

Over the phone, the background quiets. "Okay, Ver, what's going on? Have you heard something about Stella?"

My heart twists at the hope in her voice. "No, it's the Princes. They're planning on running away—leaving Forsyth—and taking me with them."

"Slow down," she hisses. "They're running? Why would they do that?"

I didn't ask that question myself, but I know in my bones. The dungeon. That was the last straw. It was one thing for Ashby to take out his twisted rage on them, but something else for him to take it out on me—and our son.

"It's complicated," I say, eyes jerking toward the windows, "and I think they're trying to do the right thing, but you and I both know Sy won't see it that way. Neither will Killian." I take a deep breath, trying to calm the raging wildfire within. "The point is, I need somewhere to go until we figure this out."

There's her soft curse, and then a beat of silence. "Do you remember the plan we came up with after the cleansing?"

Frowning, I answer, "Yes." They'd set it up in the winter, a solid plan to get me out of this place. But once the pregnancy test came back with two blue lines, I'd refused. I look toward the tree line, nodding. "There's a path that leads from the woods down to the river."

Lavinia's voice is crisp. "We'll meet you there and get you somewhere safe."

"Okay," I say. "But Lav, don't tell the Dukes. Not yet. The guys...." I bite my lip, stomach clenching at the thought of them up there, ready to flee. "They're trying to protect me, I just... I have things to do in Forsyth."

I have to find Stella, I don't say.

Lavinia knows. "We'll need twenty minutes."

I grimace, estimating that I'll only have ten before the guys come looking. "I'm on my way."

The back garden is dark in the dusk, the hem of my dress catching on thorny rose vines as I make my way toward the tree line. I'm not wearing the dress I originally intended to, and the thought has sat sourly in my gut all day, but right now, I'm almost grateful. It was chosen by Stella herself for me to wear at Lex's side, dark and painfully delicate.

The thorns would have torn it to shreds.

I pass the tombs on my way, only sparing them a quick glance before disappearing into the woods. The dense canopy of ancient trees blocks out most of the fading light, leaving the forest floor shrouded in twilight. I can't count how many spiderwebs I almost run into, having to divert my course because of undergrowth that's too thick, or fallen limbs, the branches brittle beneath my shoes. The ground is soft with old, damp, musty leaves, and my heels constantly sink into the forest bed, forcing me to jerk a knee upward to free my feet. Above me, the limbs rattle their leaves in a passing breeze, the glow of the rising moon creeping through the canopy like thin fingers, casting ominous shadows everywhere.

The woods are alive with unsettling sounds—the rustle of hidden creatures, the mournful cry of the wind through the leaves, the echo of my own uncertain footsteps. The distant hoot of an owl startles me, but once it's gone, I pause, breathing heavily.

For a hair-raising moment, all the sounds are gone.

No cicadas.

No birds.

No breeze.

It's as if the forest is holding its breath and I'm suspended inside its chattering inhale, peering around me through the trees.

Trees that suddenly seem twisted and grotesque, their limbs spreading outward like skeletal arms. My heart races with each slow, wary step, and I can't explain why. From the mossy undergrowth to the gnarled branches, something about this place just feels... sick.

Diseased.

That's when I hear it.

Somewhere to my right, a branch snaps.

I gasp, whirling toward the sound, but all I can see is an inky abyss. It'd be just like Pace to follow me out here, his eyes watching me as I push further toward the river. Because that's exactly how it feels—like I'm being watched.

Turning back to the east, I push onward, determined not to let it get to me. That's what months of being Princess has instilled in me. Paranoia. Fear. Anxiety. The men I've come to care for are the same men I'm scared of finding me. Suddenly, I feel like a mouse caught in a trap. Prey for a predator.

The unsettling feeling ratchets up when a gust of wind shakes the branches, and I whirl at the sound, half expecting to see Pace behind me.

But there's nothing there.

"Jesus," I breathe, hand pressed to my thudding chest. "Get a hold of yourself." The creeping unease dissipates with the ridiculousness of it all, and I turn back to the river.

But there's a dark figure right in front of me.

I gasp, stumbling back so hard that I nearly lose my balance, catching my heel on a rotten, downed branch. None of that registers, though. My eyes are glued to the form twelve feet ahead.

He's wearing a black ski mask.

Not Pace.

I can't make his eyes out, but I can feel them on me as his head tips to the side. Worse than his presence is the deep, raspy sound of his voice.

"Do you believe in fate, Sinclaire?"

My blood runs cold, and unthinkingly, I press a palm to my belly, taking two steps back. "M-my Princes are coming for me," I stutter, panicking as the man follows me, two steps forward for each of my two steps backward.

"No, they aren't." His voice is like sandpaper, low and rough. "I think it's fate that you came out here," he says, advancing on me slowly enough that I get a glimpse of his hands—one curled into a loose fist, the other clutching a knife. "I've been waiting for the right moment to come to you, but I didn't need to. Here you are, like a pretty little gift." There's a twist to his voice as if he's smirking beneath the mask. "I'm glad it's happening here. Fitting, isn't it? So much better than trying to get into your bedroom again." He breathes deep, as if he's trying to catch a scent.

I quicken my pace, backing away from him with a shuddering inhale. "That was you," I realize, dread settling into my stomach like a brick. "You tried to break in that night."

"Almost did, too." He stalks forward like a cat, his movements as fluid as smoke. "God, we would have had so much fun. Just you, me, and hours of uninterrupted depravity." He sighs, reaching across his chest to rub his shoulder. "I would've been back sooner if your boyfriend hadn't hit me, but in the end, it worked out. Gave me more opportunity to watch and understand you. Far more effectively than your scared little Princes."

Abruptly, I stop, watching as he freezes in place with me. "You took Stella." It covers me like a cold veil, the knowledge that this man did something to her, and for a heartstopping moment, I think I'll rush him. Attack him. *Fight* him.

To the victor go the spoils.

But the hand on my belly says otherwise.

It says to *run*.

So that's what I do.

Fear clenched in my throat, I whirl around and dash toward the palace, my feet pushing frantically against the soft ground. I duck around a thick patch of brambled undergrowth, barely hissing when a thorn slashes against my cheek. It's all adrenaline now—that, and the instinct to survive. To escape. To run to the safety of my Princes.

Because here, at the end of it all, that's what they are to me.

Protection.

Salvation.

Home.

Behind me, the malevolent presence draws nearer, his heavy footsteps echoing ominously through the trees. The fading light plays tricks on my vision, making the forest a disorienting labyrinth of twisted trees and elongated shadows. I know I'm slow—he could probably catch me easily. But it's almost like he's toying with me, letting me dodge around fallen limbs and weave through the thick trunks.

My instincts urge me to run faster, but my legs feel like lead. It doesn't help that the roots and branches seem to conspire against me, snagging at my clothes and scratching my skin. My lungs are on fire, but all I can think about is the faint glow of the Purple Palace through the trees, its windows glowing with life. It feels so close that I chance a peek over my shoulder, immediately regretting it.

The man is springing toward me with a speed that makes me cry out in shock.

But when I turn back, I'm breaking through the tree line, desperation fueling the beat of my feet as I fly toward the house. I'm so close that I wonder if I have the voice to scream—to alert them.

As soon as the thought arrives, my foot catches on a vine, sending me hurtling forward.

I slam into something hard and solid, the collision making my vision swim with pinpricks of stars. Worse than that is the way my breath is knocked violently from my lungs.

And worst of all is the way I land, stomach first onto Michael's hard marble tomb.

If the fall hadn't taken the breath out of me already, then this pain would've. It's immediate and intense, shooting through my abdomen like lightning. The sound that's ripped from my chest is ragged and sharp, and when I try to push myself up, tears welling in my eyes, my limbs refuse to cooperate.

It takes everything in me to roll to my back.

When I do, he's standing above me.

"P-please," I sob, clutching my stomach. I can hardly make out the shape of him, my vision blurred by the tears.

But I still see him crouch above me, brandishing the knife. "Is this what it's like?" His voice is quiet and winded, and when he ducks down to smell me, I shrink away. "Seconds from death, and you're begging. For what? Your life? Your baby's?"

Choking on a sob, I turn away, eyes clenched shut. "Yes."

I feel the blade on my chest, just below my throat, dragging downward, and then the hiss of his breath, hot against my cheek. "Fuck, you'd be so pretty, all opened up. Spilling out. That's why I took this job, you know? Because you're so ripe, Verity Sinclaire. A creator, like me." His words are rough with desire. "I just want to pop you like a fucking balloon."

I whimper, the tears coming in hot streams.

There's a long, torturous sigh, and then the heat of him is gone. "Too bad I can't take you back with me," he rumbles, sounding frustrated, "tie you up and watch you squirm, see just how much pain you can take. But that's not why I'm here." When I peek out from behind fluttering eyelashes, he's touching himself. Bile rises in my throat as I watch him, one gloved hand grasping the bulge between his legs. "I'm here to show you that creation and destruction are two sides of the same coin." He releases himself, and my eyes follow as he spins the knife around his forefinger. He saunters backward—just as the sounds of commotion begin coming from the direction of the solarium. "Do you really want to keep flipping it?"

In a blink, he's gone, nothing but the dark sky hanging overhead.

Clutching my stomach, I roll to my side, trying to gain the strength to push to my feet. It's useless though, pain lancing through me with each attempt.

"Verity!" Pace's voice sounds distant, far past the roar of my pulse in my ears, but then suddenly, it's terrifyingly close. "She's here!"

I feel him before I see him, hands wedging beneath my shoulders.

"What were you thinking?" he rants, voice tight. "You were seriously running away from—" My sharp cry makes him freeze, his face finally coming into focus. He's raking his hair back, watching me with a shocked expression, and then he's shouting, "Lex! Get over here!"

"H-he was in the woods," I say, pushing the words through a wet sob. "He was... he was waiting for me."

Pace spins. "Lex!"

But suddenly Lex is here, shoving him aside to kneel over me. "Verity?" His face is stone, even though the panic in his eyes is obvious when he sees the way I'm clutching my belly. "Hey, look at me. I need you to tell me what happened. Did you fall?"

"Tripped." With a jagged inhale, I point to the tree line. "He ran when he heard you."

Immediately, Pace is shooting to his feet, pulling a gun from the small of his back.

"No," Lex barks, yanking him back by the shirt. "I need you to stay here and cover us!" Lex begins shrugging out of his button-down shirt, draping it around me. The instant I move, my midsection contracts, a cramp shooting across my belly.

"Ahh!" I grab my stomach with both hands.

Heavy footsteps follow, and Wicker appears over us, eyes wild. "What's happening?" His gaze darts to mine. "Red?"

"Go get the car," Lex rushes out, throwing his brother the keys. "Drive straight through the garden—hurry." When Wick runs off, Lex turns back to me, resting his hand over mine. "It's going to be okay. I need you to take a deep breath." He's pushing up the hem of my dress when another cramp spears downward.

I shove my hands between my legs, crying out at the sudden clench, and when I pull them back, my eyes dart to Lex's.

My fingers are slick and warm, red with blood.

"Lex..." I hear my voice, but blood rushes through my ears. I see his mouth move, and Pace's terrified expression. There's only one thing I want, and when I grab Lex's wrist, my fingers sliding against his skin, I make sure he's listening. "Promise me..." Darkness seeps into the edges of my vision, but I whisper through the pain, "Promise me that you'll save the baby."

28

Pace

"Just hold on," I repeat the words over and over into her hair, Verity's limp body clutched against my chest in the back seat. Lex is shoved up against the passenger side, staring blankly between her legs. That's at least half of my panic; the total loss of any expression from him. He's wooden and efficiently mechanical.

When he drags the back of his wrist across his forehead, it leaves a smear of blood.

To Wicker, I snap, "Drive faster!"

"I fucking am!" he snaps back, eyes flicking to our reflection in the rearview.

To his credit, I hardly remember how we get to the hospital. It's like one second we're driving over the bridge, and the next, the black SUV is screeching to a stop in front of the doors.

Even getting to the car was a blur. Lex, carrying an unmoving Verity toward the headlights, blood dripping down her calves. Wicker's pale face and panicked expression as he drove over Father's prized roses.

I just remember dragging her into me the second we got inside, trying desperately not to freak out.

If we lose her...

If we lose him...

"Pace!"

I blink, looking up at my brother. The glare of the emergency room lights burns behind him, turning his long, auburn locks into a fiery halo.

"Let go of her, brother." He leans over her body, prying my arm from around her chest. "It's okay. They're going to put her on the gurney and take her in."

Another blink, and she's gone, the three of us following blindly, breathless and trembling as she's carted away by the hospital staff.

We only get as far as the waiting room before she disappears behind some bullshit, official-looking double doors. I barely have time to inhale before Wick spins around, hurling his words at me.

"How did you let this happen?! It's your job to keep track of her!

"Me?" My jaw locks, and I spring forward, jabbing a finger into his chest. "You're the one who showed her all those passageways! You know they're not monitored."

His face twists murderously. "Because keeping her locked up was killing her! She needed some freedom. Some air!" His hands slam into my chest. I rock back, avoiding his next hit, but preparing to make one of my own.

"*Fuck you*!"

"Hey!" Lex's roar carries over our fight. "Knock it off!"

He appears between us, hands shoving at both of our chests. But even though the sudden emergence of emotion on his face is like a bucket of cold water poured over me, it's not his intervention that keeps me and Wick from pummeling each other.

I feel a strong hand curl into the back of my shirt at the same time I watch Wicker lurch abruptly backward.

"You heard him," a deep, rumbling voice says in my ear. "Knock it the fuck off."

Simon Perilini's face is an inch from mine, his hand perilously close to my neck. I took Maddox in the ring, but only with my knife. Based on pure physicality alone, Perilini could snap my spine in half.

"Fine," I say, shrugging him off, but I direct my glare at Wicker, who I now realize is being held back by a stone-faced Nick Bruin. "But keep him away from me."

I turn around and—

Crack!

A fist slams into my mouth.

"You had one fucking job!" Ballsack stands a foot away, vibrating with rage. "I told you to keep her safe! *You*—specifically."

I spit blood on the floor, wanting nothing more than to release all this helpless, frenetic anger building in my chest. But no one here deserves it less than Ballsack. "Look," I begin, trying so hard to keep my fury in check that there might as well be electricity arcing from my skin, "she freaked out and ran. This wasn't us."

"Wasn't it?" he barks, fist balled again. "She called the Duchess and said she was running away from *you*."

"What did you do to her?" Remy Maddox says, suddenly marching up into the mix. Behind him, I see the Lucia girl, who looks angrier than any of them. What the fuck did Verity say to her?

"Hold the fuck up," Lex says, voice level and calm. "There's a lot of misunderstanding here because I know everyone wants Verity to be safe."

"She was scared," Lavinia Lucia says, eyes burning into me. "She said she was out in the garden and wanted me to meet her."

"Meet you where?" Nick asks.

Lucia's mouth clamps shut. Her Dukes eye her, obviously wondering themselves, but she doesn't crack. "It doesn't matter. All I know is that she was alone when I spoke with her."

"But she wasn't," I say, the events of the night rushing back. "She said... *he was waiting for me*." My eyes meet Ballsack's. "She said someone was in the woods."

"Stop." Lex sounds tired and deathly serious. "None of this shit matters. Not right now. Verity suffered a significant injury from the fall. She's bleeding. Vaginally." The last word makes Lucia pull in a shocked gasp, a hand fluttering to her mouth. Lex takes the moment of grim silence to look between the Dukes. "*Why* she ran away, *who* attacked her, *all* of that has to wait until we know she and the baby are stable."

If anyone wants to argue, they keep it to themselves.

Lex looks at Wicker, then me, the blood still stark on his face. "I have to get in there."

I'm about to ask about Father—what to tell him, if we even should—when the aggressive clack of heels in the distance grows closer.

The dread forms a pit in my gut because I don't even have to look to know.

I can hear the jangle of her metal bracelets.

Fucking hell. As if this could get any worse.

Mama B strides into the middle of the group with fists clenched, like she's wondering who to hit and what to hit them with. Worse than that, however, is the look on her face.

Pure, naked terror.

"Where the hell is my daughter?"

IT FEELS like it takes hours for Lex to return.

All of us had been moved to another waiting room lobby, off the women's care ward. I keep waiting for the Dukes to leave, but they're planted firmly in place, sprawled around the room like sentinels. It's an indicator of how protective they feel about Verity. I'm not sure I like it. Jealous over the fact other men hold importance in her life? Or should I be glad to know she's not alone in her own territory?

Not the way my brothers and I are.

"Sir, I am sorry you weren't notified about her arrival." The receptionist's voice carries over from the admissions counter. "There is nothing on her paperwork indicating that you should have been given a call. Her mother is listed as—" Her next words are a stutter, "Y-y-y-yes, sir."

Father.

Wicker and I share a dark, tense look. If he comes in here right now, while things are bordering on explosive, the consequences will be unavoidable.

I stand, crossing the room to where Perilini sits, watching the door. Like Lex, he's still dressed in the suit he wore for graduation, but the blazer is draped around his Queen's shoulders.

Steeling myself, I say, "I need a favor."

He scoffs. "You're the last people I want to do any favors for tonight."

This is all so easy for him. He's a King now. He answers to no one. When he challenged Saul Cartwright, it sealed his fate. But we're not Dukes. We're Princes, which means we're trapped inside a web that only seems to get stickier the harder we try to get out of it.

"Listen," I try in vain to keep the irritation out of my voice, "whatever happens here tonight, or tomorrow, or twenty fucking weeks from now..." I press my fingers into my temple, "Don't let him near her."

"That's the first smart thing I've heard any of you say yet," Mama B chimes in three seats away. She casts her gaze on Perillini. "He's right, Simon. Ashby comes in here, and we're all fucked."

"I'll handle it," Nick says, pushing off the wall where he's been standing for the last hour.

"No." Sy shakes his head at his brother. "You said there was an intruder at the palace?"

My jaw tics. "Yeah." It rankles to admit it. All my equipment was being packed away. I didn't even have a screen up when it all went down.

Sy nods, then looks across the seating area to where Maddox is curled over Lucia's arm, doodling on her with a marker. "Remy."

"Yeah?" Glancing up, he pauses his artwork.

"Your cousin still working the night beat?" A flicker of communication passes between them before Remy stands, capping the pen.

He sticks it behind his ear. “I’m on it.”

“Who’s his cousin?” Wicker asks, watching Maddox pull out his phone and exit the room.

“Someone who can keep Ashby busy handling a reported break-in at home for a while.”

“Thank you.” I exhale, knowing it won’t matter in the long term, but we need a minute with Verity to figure out exactly what happened—and what we’re going to do next.

Maddox is gone for ten minutes, and in that space of time, I notice their Duchess watching me, her eyes hard and penetrating. “She said you were trying to do the right thing.” Her stare wanders over my face like she’s searching for some truth. “You were running from him, weren’t you?”

If they find out about the dungeon, we’ll lose her for good. “That’s family business,” I say, glaring.

Nick Bruin stares me down. “The family business of taking people?”

“You know,” Maddox drawls as he returns, loping casually back to the group, “this is all really interesting, actually. A lot of girls are going missing lately.”

“A couple on your territory,” Mama B unhelpfully adds. She won’t even look at us.

Maddox pulls the marker out from behind his ear and twirls it between his fingers. “The three of you wouldn't happen to know anything about that, would you?”

The accusation is crystal clear, and it makes Wicker straighten, the line of his jaw hardening. “What are you implying?”

Mama B finally looks at him, her expression turning to ice. “He’s not implying anything. He’s saying it outright.”

“You tried to kidnap a girl tonight,” Maddox says, pointing the tip of his marker at us. “From where I'm standing, that makes you the most obvious suspects yet.”

It’s a shame we had to dump all our weapons before being allowed entry into the ward because I’d like nothing more than to put a knife to this fucker’s throat. “Then stand somewhere else,” I grit out, "because we didn't try to kidnap a girl tonight. We tried to save our own."

"It wasn't them," Ballsack suddenly says. He's sitting between Wicker and Perilini—his King—the separation of our houses and his position caught between them more obvious than ever. "I don't know what happened to Stella, but I know the Princes had nothing to do with it."

Perilini sighs, cutting him a sympathetic glance. Something tells me this isn't the first time they've had this discussion. "You can't be sure."

"Yes, I can." Ballsack pulls something from his pocket, holding it out to Simon. "In fact, I'll stake my Bruin pin on it."

Wicker and I share a look at the reaction. All the Dukes straighten, looking at their recruit like he basically just said he's a lizard in a meat suit. It's a long beat before Perilini reaches out, but he doesn't take Ballsack's frat pin.

He pushes his hand down instead. "If you say it's not them, I'll believe you." He slides me a narrow-eyed sneer. "Or try to."

I'm not entirely sure why Ballsack would bother vouching for us. Stella was good to Verity, and she was good at her job. She never kicked up a fuss. In a way that none of us were used to, the two of them blew into the palace like a tornado and filled it with life. The twenty hours he and I spent pouring over footage hardly makes up for one simple fact.

We could have tried harder to find her.

"Ballsack," I call, knowing how I'd feel if it'd been Verity. I wait for his tired eyes to meet mine before nodding. "I'm sorry."

His mouth presses into a tense, joyless grin. "Funny, isn't it? How easily you'll say it to me, but it's taken you months to say it to her?"

It's loaded, but isn't everything tonight? It's like we're walking on the edge of a knife. Thank Christ, I'm saved from replying when Lex walks into the room. It takes me a moment to realize it's even him because he's in a pair of scrubs now, his hair pulled back into a sloppy ponytail.

Everyone shoots to their feet.

"How is she?" Mama B asks first.

My brother looks like he's been put through a grinder, his expression drawn and shuttered. "The Princess is conscious and alert," he says to Mama B more than anyone else. "Both she and the baby are stable." He turns to me and Wick, lowering his voice. This news is meant for us. "She has a mild placental abruption, but the baby looks good. Strong."

"What is that?" Lavinia asks. "A placental whatever?"

He lands heavily in a seat, propping his elbows on his knees. "When she fell, the impact separated part of the placenta from her uterus. That means..." I tune him out, unable to focus on anything that isn't a flood of relief. My ears throb with it, the sound of my pulse deafening.

The relief on Mama B's face is short-lived. "I want to talk to her doctor."

Lex blinks. "You *are* talking to her doctor."

"Like hell I am," she snaps. "I'm talking to a boy whose Daddy lets him play dress-up to circumvent real standards."

I expect Lex to argue with her—start listing his credentials, maybe—but he just looks resigned, dragged down by exhaustion. "Doctor Munson is the OB on call," he mutters, staring at his hands. "You can speak to her when you go in."

This brings Mama B up short, her gaze flicking to Perilini. "I can see Verity?"

"Room seventeen." He nods to the door, then adds, "She wants to see the Duchess, too."

Wicker and I share a look that's so much more complicated than disappointment. It says *it should be us going in there*. We're her Princes. This hospital—the best in Forsyth—is in *our* territory.

But we've spent all day—all week—laboring to get free of those titles.

It's a specific invitation that only means one thing.

Verity doesn't want to see us.

Once Mama B and Lavinia are behind the double doors, Wick turns to Lex, asking, "Did you see her?"

"Not for very long." Lex rubs the back of his neck, grimacing. "She's... upset."

"Did you get to check on the baby," I ask, scooting closer. "Like a scan, or sonogram or something?"

"Jesus Christ," Nick mutters, the disdain rolling off him in waves. "That's really all you fuckers care about, isn't it? Your precious heir?"

Lex comes alive, every ounce of exhaustion fading as he turns on Bruin. "Her last words to me were to save our son!" Leaping from his seat, he takes a prowling step closer. "So yeah, I care about it, and if you don't, then you can fucking leave."

"We're not going anywhere," Sy says, pushing Nick aside and going toe to toe with Lex. "You tried to break our contract tonight when you attempted to leave Forsyth."

There's a long, tense silence. Because once we reveal the reason behind us leaving, we're opening the door to parts of our lives in the palace we can't shut again. I'm still trying to figure out how much to say, and how to say it when Wicker jumps in.

"Verity and the baby aren't safe in the palace right now." He looks up at the Dukes, and I can see how much it costs him to put that knowledge out there. Wicker has been trained to keep up appearances, to never show cracks. Right now, this crack looks like a goddamn fault line. "We know that. She knows that. But despite what happened earlier tonight, they're our responsibility. *Ours* to take care of. Not yours."

"If you can't keep her safe from threats, external *or* internal," Nick fixes him with a look, those big, tattooed arms crossing over his chest, "then she needs to be with people who are up to the job. That's why she's coming back with us."

I bolt forward. "Verity and our son will leave with you dirtbags over my dead body."

"Stop!" Ballsack steps between us, his expression tight with disbelief. "You're not fighting over a goddamn doll here. Verity is a person, and you broke the terms of the contract. That means she gets to decide where she goes." He gives us a warning look. "Don't make me call Killian Payne in to mediate your dick-measuring contest."

I pause.

The last thing this situation needs is another Royal house interfering.

Everyone else must agree because we all wander stiffly, resentfully, back to our respective corners of the waiting room, taking a seat to wait a little more.

I watch the next thirty minutes pass on the clock across the room, its second hand spinning relentlessly. Beside me, Lex's eyelids are slumping, but never closing. Every twitch, every sound, has his eyes jerking to the double doors.

The tension I feel is less about the Dukes or Father, or anything else.

What's the point of any of it if we lose her?

29

erity

"DOES IT HURT?" Lavinia asks. She's hovering on my right, almost like she's afraid to touch me.

My mother does not share those reservations. "We can call the nurse," she says, clutching my hand. She touches my chin next, getting a good, long look at the scratch there. Just what I need—another grisly wound.

Her eyes are beyond murderous.

I offer an assurance that I don't feel. "It's fine."

"It's not fine!" she snaps, but even though the words are sharp, the look on her face is anything but. Her eyes shine with unshed tears. "I should have never let you go back to that place."

"Mama, please," I try, squeezing her hand. "This isn't your fault."

Her voice trembles when she whispers, low and fierce, "I should have killed him that day he showed up on my porch."

I don't need to ask who, or what day she's even talking about.

"Well, he did bring a dick to a gunfight."

I've never been in the hospital before. In all my life, I've never had any injuries that couldn't be taken care of at home. There was the one time I got a sprain from practicing round-offs on the gym mat, and Mama sent me in to see Pauly, the gym's trainer, and asked him to take a look. He wrapped it in a long, beige ACE bandage and gave me a stick of gum before sending me on my way. Until tonight—with the exception of Rufus Ashby's whip—it's been the most extensive injury I can recall.

Now I'm in a hospital bed, the IV attached to my arm dripping some clear fluid while monitors flash red and green. Nothing drowns out the sound of angry, loud male voices carrying down the hall.

"Jesus," Mama says, flicking a glare toward the door. "Leave it to men to turn your crisis into being about them."

Lavina snorts, but I rub my forehead, trying to ease the building pressure. "Will you just go get them?"

Mama's eyes narrow. "Which ones?"

I give her an exasperated look. "The Princes. They're not going to stop until they lay eyes on me," I rest my hands on my belly, "and him, directly."

"Good," is her answer, the metal bangles on her wrist clattering as she flicks a hand. "Let them carry on. They should get to feel a fraction of the panic I felt when I got that goddamn call. None of this would have happened if they'd—"

"Mama." My voice is firm, brooking no argument, and I almost regret it when her face falls.

"You don't belong to them," she says.

Quietly, Lavinia agrees, "They broke the agreement, Ver. You'd be well within your rights to tell them to fuck off."

I look at Lavinia, and then my mother, allowing them to see the determination in my eyes. "I know," I say. And then, "Let them in."

"Fine," Mama says, snatching up her purse, "but if they start up with more of that nonsense, I'm kicking their spoiled little asses out of here."

Lavinia doesn't follow her, instead moving closer to the bed. It's the first time we've been alone all night—in weeks, really.

Once we're alone, she asks, "Do you want to tell me what really happened?"

Taking a deep breath, I wonder where to even start. The roller coaster of the past few months? The way Lex seeks me out, looking to fill a gaping hole with my body and soul? How Pace soothes me in ways I never knew possible? How Whitaker Ashby is a man so lost, so abused, that it took a lifeline to drag him back?

Or do I tell her about the dungeon? The reason I took the punishment? How terrible living under Ashby's rule is? Do I dare tell her the only thing that kept me alive was the hope of getting back to the men upstairs?

Or maybe I should tell her about Stella, and how her going missing seemed to trigger something in all of us.

Fear.

"Things have become... tense," I begin, "with Ashby. He's gotten more controlling. Demanding. Especially with the baby." Swallowing, I still remember the unhinged look on his face as Lex held that knife to his throat. "I understand why they wanted to go, and I believe them when they say it's been planned for a long time, but..." I blink, feeling fresh, hot tears form. "When Stella went missing, I knew I had to stay and find her. That's when I called you."

"Verity," her tone is cautious, "this person who was chasing you in the woods? Are you sure it wasn't... you know. One of them?"

I reach out to grab her wrist. "No! I promise. I saw him, Lav." The masked man's image is seared into my mind. The way he touched himself and the way he spoke, his cadence clear and precise. The threats he made were depraved but intentional, like he was conflicted between desire and duty.

He sounded Royal.

Shadows move outside the door, and I take Lavinia's hand and squeeze it. "Tell the Dukes I'm going to be okay, and that I don't need them out there protecting me." I hold her stare, willing her to believe me. "The Princes may have done something stupid, but they aren't going to hurt me."

After searching my eyes, she relents with a heavy nod, stepping back just as the doors open. Lex peeks his head inside first, eyes landing on me immediately, but then he moves aside to let Lavinia through before holding the door open for the others.

Pace stalks in first, eyes sweeping the room, but it's Wicker who approaches me. His blue eyes fix right onto the scratch on my face, and when he reaches up to touch me, there's a deep frown etched into his forehead.

I shrink back, shaking my head. "Don't."

Wicker pulls his hand back like he's been burned.

Lex is in a pair of scrubs, and it's such an odd thing. In situations like this, I'm used to seeing him in a lab coat. Right now, he looks ragged and lost, his amber eyes taking in the equipment. "Munson thinks you're going to heal up fine," he says, voice uncomfortably bland. "With a little downtime to heal the abruption, and a lot of close care, your pregnancy should progress normally."

My tongue feels fused to the roof of my mouth. "She... she said you worked fast."

Lex makes an odd face, as if he's smelling something unpleasant. "Wicker, mostly."

Pace crosses the end of my bed, a hand coming out to brush the lump of my feet over the blanket. "I'm sorry," he says, the words sounding foreign but sure, just like the remorse in his eyes. "We—" he flicks his eyes to Wick. "No, *I* fucked this up."

"A lot of crazy shit went down tonight," Lex interrupts, shooting me a quick glance, "but the only thing that matters is that you're okay."

"But I'm not okay," I say, unable to put it off any longer. I meet their gazes, one by one. "You were going to take me away. From my family. From my friends. From my responsibilities. You were going to keep me from looking for her."

Wicker groans. "We were doing it to keep you—"

"Safe. I know that." I take a steadying breath, aware that I need to keep my heart rate down. Even Lex sends a worried glance to the monitor. "You could have told me what was happening, and I would have told you there were other options."

"Red," Wicker starts, mouth pinched, "I know you've gotten a crash course in Ashby'ing these past few months, but there are no three people more qualified to know what getting away from it is going to entail. Fast and under the radar was the only option."

"I know it was shitty for us to not include you, but we couldn't afford resistance," Pace adds. "Not when there was so much on the line."

That's the crux of it, though. When it came right down to it, they didn't care about my opinion. It held no value to them. It doesn't matter that their intentions were pure.

Their actions weren't.

But mostly, there's this: "How am I ever going to trust you with our son?"

Lex's forehead knits up. "What are you talking about?"

I've seen what it's like to belong to a Royal who hates me. Spites me. Resents me. That was awful in its own right, but our child is going to see a side of them that's possibly even scarier.

Because they're going to love him.

"You'll take him away," I say.

All of them rear back, like they've been slapped in the face. I don't understand why—not at first. Not even when Pace promises, voice low and intense, "Not from you."

But the fear is fresh, nagging at the back of my mind. "If I become a big enough obstacle, you will."

Wicker's eyes darken, that same thread of bizarre disgust pulsing from within them. "You're wrong," he says. "We're not in the business of taking babies. We're not *him*."

The realization is galling, churning in my gut like a sickness. "I-I-I didn't mean..." But I suppose, in some way, that's exactly what I mean. Stealing things, ferreting them away, controlling and imprisoning...

This is all they know.

Breathing deeply, I decide, "It doesn't matter. The fact is, I'm not trading one cage for another, and I'm definitely not subjecting my child to one."

This next part should be easy to say, but it isn't. The sad truth is that somewhere, deep down, I want so badly for these men to have the chance at becoming something more than what their father has made them into.

But not at the expense of the small, fragile life growing inside of me.

...creation and destruction are two sides of the same coin...

"When I leave here," I announce, "I'm going back to West End with my family."

There's a tense moment where I see it sink in. Wicker looks away, fists flexing, but he doesn't even look surprised. Pace's nostrils flare like he wants to argue, but in the end, he releases a sharp breath without bothering.

It's Lex whose stare pins me, the quiet fury obvious in his eyes. "Let me get this straight," he says, eyes narrowing into slits. "We can't take our son away from you, but you can take him away from us?"

That voice, smooth and venomous, makes a chill run up my spine. "Right now?" I don't back down. "Yes."

Marching over to the bed, he rips the metal chart from the foot of it, holding it up. "Like there's anyone in West End who's going to give this baby a fraction of the care I would?" He runs his finger down the first page, fuming. "Who's going to monitor his heart, Verity? Perilini? Maddox? Bruin? Who's going to watch over you while you're on bed rest for two weeks, or—"

He flips over to the next page, but suddenly, his words clip off. The gnarled anger on his face blinks to slack confusion.

"What the..." he flips another page, and then another, eyes zeroing in on something that makes him deflate entirely.

"Lex?" Pace says, frowning at his brother, whose eyes are glued to the chart.

Wicker pushes past Pace. "What is it? What's wrong?"

"Nothing, just..." His eyes drag up, darting from Pace to Wicker, then over to me. "These records are more extensive than the ones I have back home."

"What does that mean?" I ask, dread curdling in my gut. I've gone through so many exams tonight—so many blood tests. Maybe one finally came back that wasn't what we wanted to hear. Urgently, I demand, "Tell me, Lex."

His gaze meets mine, and all that fiery rage from before is gone. "Father must have updated your and the baby's records with paternal medical history," he explains, eyes wide with awe. "It has the paternity results."

Pace shifts, the sound of his shoes shuffling nervously against the floor acting as an anchor. "Who?" he asks.

Lex looks at me, the question clear in his eyes.

Am I ready to know?

That's an easy question for me to answer. "The last thing we need between us is another secret."

Mechanically, he slots the chart back into place, glancing at his brother. "It's you," he says, and if someone had told me five seconds ago that I'd ever see light in Lex's eyes again, I wouldn't have believed it.

But it shines like the fucking sun.

"It says Wicker is the father."

MAMA SLEEPS in my room that first night.

I'm not sure how because the sound of the monitors is maddening, not to mention the nurse coming in to check my and the baby's vitals all the time. I watch her for a while, curled on my side as I struggle to find a comfortable position. She looks older than she did in January, when I left home, although I can't really explain it. Her hair and skin are as flawless as ever. There's just this tightness around her eyes that never really goes away.

Maybe this is what it's like to be a mother to a Royal.

And maybe also the father to one.

I can't get the memory of Wicker's shell-shocked expression out of my mind. The way he stared at Lex like he wasn't hearing him right. How his stunned gaze pinged between us before shuttering, offering me and his brothers only a single, limp response.

"I guess practice really does make perfect."

Not exactly confetti and cigars. I try not to be hurt by the memory of him slowly detaching from the rest of us, easing back against the wall. It was no surprise he was reeling from the news, but at that moment, I was too exhausted to fight for him.

At some point, Whitaker Kayes has to learn to fight for himself.

Pace, for his part, just seemed happy to know at all. "One less thing to wonder about," he said, eyeing my belly with that same, possessive glint. "Security is going to be a bitch. God knows how the Barons are going to take it when they find out."

"They won't," Wicker said from his spot by the wall. "They can't."

Learning about the baby's paternity didn't change my mind about going home. If anything, like Pace said, being a Kayes will add more complications.

I didn't throw them out. My mother did that for me. And now I cradle the swell of my stomach and close my eyes, as if I can speak to him.

Hello, baby Kayes.

Will he be blonde, like his father? Even through all the torment and uncertainty, the fear and the sorrow, I feel a soft smile spring to my lips at having this new little nugget of knowledge of who my son will be.

He'll be so beautiful.

Just then, I feel him move, my mouth parting with a gasp.

"I remember that look." Mama's voice startles me, and when I open my eyes, she's watching me, a soft smile on her own lips. "When I was pregnant with you, I used to lay with you for hours, just feeling you flip around in there. It's hard, isn't it? Clinging to the parts that bring you joy, all the while knowing there's so much pain that lingers just outside of the cocoon."

Slowly, my grin fades. "Yeah, it is."

Hers doesn't. "Don't let it. You'll need that joy, Ver Bear. Don't let one second of it go by, and never, *ever* feel guilty for it."

Long after she's fallen back asleep—or, at least, pretends to—I stroke the curve of my stomach and do just that. I feel him as he moves and finally remember what Pace called it that day down in the dungeon.

The quickening.

The next morning, West End begins filing into my room.

The Dukes and Lavinia come first, each bearing a little gift. A stuffed bear from Lav. A donut from Remy. From Nick, a knife.

"Put that away," Mama snaps, although when she takes it, I notice she crams it into her purse.

Next comes Ballsack, who doesn't bother with gifts. He just sits with me as we watch some mindless daytime talk show on the TV.

Eventually, I gather the courage to ask, "Have they found anything yet?"

I think he must sense that it's killing me to be in this hospital bed when my friend needs me because he gives me a smile that's probably meant to be comforting. Instead, it looks like a grimace. "Something will turn up soon."

I'm not sure either of us believes it.

Other DKS roll in after him, and I begin wondering if my mama or the Dukes have some kind of chain organized.

That is until the most surprising visitor yet appears. Rory Livingston comes shuffling into the room with a vase of roses. Mama finally went downstairs to get herself something for lunch, so for an awkward moment, it's just the two of us staring owlishly at one another.

He puts the vase on the stand below the TV, clearing his throat. "I was sorry to hear about what happened. Not just with," he gestures vaguely to my stomach, "but I mean, Stella, too. She's a really nice girl."

Rory might be the first person to refer to her in the present tense.

I have no idea what to say to him.

This guy jacked off into my lap a few months ago.

"Thanks," I say, eyeing him warily.

He rocks back on his heels, looking twice as awkward as me. "Can I get you anything? Or do anything?" When I shake my head he adds, "The guys and I... we've been handing out flyers on the Avenue."

"For your sister?"

He nods. "Yeah, I can make some for Stella."

My eyes begin welling. "Would you?" I ask, knowing I don't have the right. PNZ is supposed to be at my beck and call, but I've never really harnessed or claimed them.

"Of course." He gives me a sad smile. "This is bigger than territory lines. If someone in another kingdom did it for my sister, Kelsey, well... I know I'd really appreciate that."

He doesn't stay long, the two of us having nothing but tragedy and remorse to fill the silence with. But when he leaves, I look at the flowers and think it might be the first time since I became Princess that seeing roses hasn't made me nauseous.

Which is a good thing, because that afternoon, more of them start rolling in.

I get a delivery from Adeline and the staff at the Gilded Rose, and bouquets from a couple of other guys in the frat. Professor Winston sends a whole bundle, as well as Coach Reed.

But every time there's a knock on the door, I feel a lance of panic. I can't hide from Rufus Ashby forever. Whatever string Remy pulled to keep him out of here must have its limits. Which is why I'm antsy for Doctor Munson to release me from Forsyth General and get back to Royal Ink.

I've been here five days when Kaz knocks, peeking his head through the door.

"Yo, you have visitors." He pulls a face. "I can tell them to make like a tree and fuck off?"

"Not a chance," a voice says, and then the small figure it belongs to pushes past him. "I got like seven layers of Royal approval to be here." Story's eyes widen when she sees me, sweeping over my belly, which seems bigger and bigger every day. "Wow, you're, like... definitely pregnant."

My lips twitch. It's been almost two months since our last boiler room rendezvous. "That's what they tell me."

She's followed in by Tristian Mercer, who's carrying a brown bag. "Killian sends his best wishes," he says, placing it on the tray next to my bed. His eyes scan the room without a trace of shame, even bending to peek under the hospital bed. I'm starting to learn that paranoia is a trait every Royal must possess.

"He told me to get flowers," Story says, setting her purse on the chair. She's wearing a light summer dress, and I can see the straps of a bikini peeking out from her neckline. "But I figured your house would have that covered, so we brought you lunch instead." She turns her head away from her Lord, mouthing, "Sorry."

I peer inside, idly hoping for something greasy and delicious. "Oh," I say, inspecting the container of salmon, steamed broccoli, and wild rice. "You have one, too?"

"One what?" Tristian says. He's in a soft-looking leather jacket and dark jeans. Everyone knows his family is one of the wealthiest in the city, and it oozes off of him in the same way it does Remy.

"A health food guy." His eyebrow raises, and I explain further, "Lex manages my meals and nutrition. *Closely*."

Or, at least, he did.

"Good," he says with an impressed tilt of the head. "You're carrying their kid. You shouldn't poison it with the shitty food they serve here."

"That's very thoughtful." I set the food down, already knowing I won't eat it. "How's Augustine?" I ask, cutting right to the chase. "Has she heard anything?"

"She's worried," Story admits, hands wringing nervously. "It's not like Stella to stay out of contact." Every shred of hope I've had diminishes every day, and it's impossible to miss the guilt and regret in Story's eyes. She was the one to recruit Stella to stay with me and keep them updated.

Stella was the second Monarch operative.

"Killian's got our men looking," Tristian says, tapping the nose of a stuffed bear. "And your boy and I have linked up some of our security feeds to double our coverage."

"My boy?" I ask.

"Pace." He turns away from the bear. "It was his idea, actually. The coverage of his network is insane, but my father's company has some North Side surveillance that can help rule some things out."

"Oh, right." I give him a tight smile, a little bewildered. "Thank you."

He shrugs, as if fraternizing with the enemy is completely common. "She's one of ours. We take the abduction of a Lords' asset seriously."

I frown at the term—*asset*—and Story catches his attention.

"Babe?" Sliding up against him, she tucks her hands under his jacket, wrapping her arms around his waist. "Can I get a minute with the Princess?" His hand curls around her neck, eyes tracking the sweep of his thumb down the elegant column of it. She bats her eyelashes. "Girly stuff."

"Don't think I don't see how diabolical you are." He lifts her chin and brushes his lips over hers. "I'll be right outside."

She waits until the door closes to turn to me, expression collapsing. "Ver, I am so fucking sorry, about all of this."

The force of her grief is like a stab to my heart. "None of this is your fault."

She paces in the small space, fists pressed to her stomach. "No, but everything is out of control. You getting hurt. The girls going missing. Stella. This isn't what Lavinia and I had in mind when we encouraged you to go to the masquerade, but I should have known better. What happens in Royal households is never what it seems."

I pick at the tab on the hospital bed sheets. "Do you remember that day in the library bathroom when I asked you how you love them?" She nods, sitting on the edge of the bed. "I understand it better now."

Her jaw slacks, eyebrows hiking up her forehead. "You love them?"

Shrugging, I confess, "I don't know. Maybe? Everything is so twisted and confusing, and trust me, the hormones don't make it any better. I just know that they aren't what they seemed. They're complicated, and confusing, and angry, and traumatized, and—"

"They're Royals," she says, lips pressed into a grim, understanding smile. "They're fucked up."

I rest my hand on my stomach. "Yeah, and I'm about to add another one to the mix."

A double legacy.

Her eyebrows furrow. "So what are you going to do?"

"Go home with my family where it's safe and easy?" Exhaling in defeat, I shake my head. "But it's like you said. They're Royals. They're not going to give up on their own child, and honestly, isn't that a good thing? It's part of the reason I feel this way about them." I swallow, lowering my voice. "They're giving me space, I guess, which is more than I expected."

"I've been in this position, you know." She twists the cuff on her wrist, the motion idle but significant. "Not the hospital and definitely not pregnant, but at a crossroads, where my Lords gave me the option to leave." She scoffs. "At least, in theory—not that I believe for a minute they'd really let me go. It was a gesture that meant something to me, though."

"What did you choose?" I ask, eyes darting down to the scarred initials carved into her chest. She never hides them. Instead, she wears them like a badge of honor.

"I chose to stay." Her eyes flick to the door, where Tristian waits outside. "But I chose to do it on my terms, not theirs."

I arch an eyebrow. "And they just accepted that?"

She laughs. "Not all at once, but as much as they could."

I think about everything that's happened before drawing in a deep breath. "If I tell you something, Princess to Lady, do you promise not to tell anyone?" I hold her eye. "Especially not Lavinia."

Story frowns. "Why don't you want to tell Lavinia? I thought you two were really close."

"Too close," I say. "Not just us, but our houses. The Dukes are my family. If they knew..." I shake my head. "Let's just say there'd be a war that I'm not sure any of us would survive."

Story's gaze turns serious, sensing the gravity of the moment. "I understand, Verity. Whatever you want to tell me, I won't tell anyone. I promise."

So I tell her.

Everything.

From the masquerade to the throning, to the months of deposits, to the cumulation of the Royal Cleansing. I look away when tears fill her eyes at my description of the Coronation, and then more recently, what I experienced in the dungeon.

"You're right," she says, voice thick. "You can never tell Lavinia about this. If she knew they locked you up—"

"Not *they*, just him," I correct. "King Ashby."

"Even worse," Story says, eyes shining with sympathy. "She wouldn't be able to be objective. Christ, it's her dad all over again."

I nod knowingly, feeling an enormous weight lifted off my shoulders. Someone else needed to know the truth. "It's why they wanted to run with me," I explain, frustrated. "So when I tell people they were doing it to keep me safe—"

"They don't understand how true that is," she guesses. At my nod, she takes my hand, inhaling shakily. "You and Lav are so much stronger than I could ever be. I had no business asking you or Stella to go in there. I was so attached to the idea of a sisterhood that I—"

"Was right," I say, knowing this in my bones. "If it hadn't been Stella, it would have been someone else. Someone like Kelsey Livingston or Laura Walker." When her eyes blank, I nod. "Yeah, you don't know them. But you will. Everyone will—because of Stella." I stress, "Because of the Monarchs."

"Is that what you want?" she asks, watching me curiously. "To go back to West End and work with Lavinia on the Monarchs?"

"My gut is telling me it's the smart thing to do, but," I rest a hand on my belly, "other parts of me aren't so sure." Feeling the baby move once again, I confess my worst fear. "Story, maybe I'm too weak to change things."

Her gaze follows mine, taking in the way I'm stroking my belly. "This has to be your decision, Verity. Not your mom's, or the Dukes, or your Princes—certainly not mine. But before you make it, I need you to understand something." She places her hand on mine, eyes soft but no less piercing. "No matter what you choose, you'll have three of the Royal houses on your side. Take a moment to let that sink in because it might be more power than anyone has ever had in Forsyth." Her thumb strokes over my hand, lips curling into a tender smile. "You've already changed so much. Don't ever think of yourself as weak."

Long after she's gone, I turn it over in my head, shocked at the weight of the thought.

Three Royal houses.

SUMMER IN FORSYTH has this smell to it.

It's a warm scent, a little musty with every breeze carrying a tinge of the river algae. Even though I can never handle it, always burning pretty much instantly, I've missed the sun. Tipping my face up, I let it warm the bridge of my nose, already knowing my freckles are going to come out in full force.

"*You little fucker.*" Beside me, Effie walks the length of the shovel I've set up for her as a perch, her head jerking with each syllable. "*Little fucker.*"

I give her a stern look. "I see Mama taught you some new words."

She trills before squawking, "*Cute little fucker.*"

Laughing, I realize, "Thawed her heart, huh?" Which I already figured out, considering the frown Mama gave me when I went into her office to snag the cage.

I give her head a gentle pet. "It's just too nice of a day to be cooped up inside, isn't it, Effie?"

"Effie is a pretty bird," she agrees, her mimicry of Pace's voice the best out of all of us.

I'm careful not to exert myself, sitting on a pillow as I use the pruning shears to lop off a thick stem. The whole concept of bed rest is torture, even if it's only for two weeks. I spent six days in a hospital bed, and not long before that, five days in the dungeon. The last thing I want to do is waste away in another small room.

Not when there are important things to do.

"Verity?" The voice doesn't surprise me, nor does the long, charged silence that follows it. But what surprises me least of all is his next words, delivered with a long-suffering sigh. "You're supposed to be in bed."

Glancing over my shoulder, I see Lex putting his phone away.

Something tells me his brothers won't be far behind.

"I'm taking it easy," I explain.

Helpfully, Effie adds, *"You little fucker."*

Lex's eyes cut to the shovel, a touch accusatory considering it doesn't even have dirt on it. He sighs, descending the steps slowly, his footfalls heavy. "Why didn't you tell us you were coming?"

"Honestly?" I look around at the solarium. The dahlias Wicker gave me are looking bigger than ever, their petals fanned out dramatically. "I thought Pace would have seen me."

Effie jolts at his name, zipping down the length of the shovel. *"Pretty bird?"*

Lex approaches me, bending to carefully take the shears from my hand. "He hasn't bothered setting his equipment back up, seeing as how..." He waves vaguely, inspecting the bed of nettles. I can see the question on his face before he even gets it out. "How is he?" he asks, eyes dropping to my belly.

Humming, I reply, "Are we going to pretend like you haven't been looking at my records?" I hope the sly look I give him lessens the sting of the accusation.

His mouth twists wryly. "I know the vitals and prognosis, but not... not how he *feels*."

The statement, spoken so stiltedly, but so earnestly, makes my chest clench. Softly, I say, "He's been moving."

Lex's head snaps up, eyes flashing in shock. "Really?" Then, his face falls. "I missed it."

I'm just about to tell him how new it is when another voice sounds from the doorway.

"What are you doing here?" Pace asks, voice deep and tinged with fear. But as soon as he says it, Effie is flapping her wings wildly, clumsily flying to his shoulder.

"*Pretty bird,*" she squawks, the words rushing out so fast, they're barely intelligible. "*Good girl.*"

If there was any ice around my heart, it melts at the way he greets her, a painfully tender smile on his face as he touches her. "Hey, hey, girl," he coos. "Miss me, huh?"

She jerks her head. "*Cute little fucker.*"

Pace freezes, cutting me a look, but ultimately mutters, "I'll allow it on grounds of accuracy."

On the crest of my laugh, I see movement near the back, realizing Wicker's taken the secret passage down. He stops beside the begonias, hands stuffed in his pockets, and the hard expression on his face makes my stomach swoop unhappily. "The Dicks seriously let you come here?" he asks, jaw ticking as he glances upward. "We're not alone."

"I know," I assure, acknowledging that Ashby is up in his office. "But I have something to say to you. All of you." It's one of the reasons there's a van full of DKS members parked right up the bridge, itching for a reason.

It's also why I take another stab at the bed of stinging nettles.

Wicker darts forward, snatching the shovel from me. "This bed rest deal looks suspiciously like manual fucking labor." Pushing up his sleeves, he adds, "If anyone's going to gut this thing, it's going to be me."

"Here," Lex says, helping me up from the pillow. I don't argue as he leads me over to an ornate bench.

"Say what you came to say," Pace says, glancing nervously at the door as if Ashby could walk through it at any moment.

He won't, though.

Someone's keeping him busy on the phone.

The first stab of the shovel into the dirt spurs me on, and I take a breath. "I've made a lot of compromises since becoming Princess. First, my idea of sex, and then my concept of motherhood. I settled for something that wasn't love, and then I gained the world's worst father." I follow Pace's anxious stare. "I settled for what I was given because I was never in a position to ask for anything more." Looking at Lex, I say, "I've decided I'm done settling."

He frowns, shifting uneasily. "What does that mean?"

I slide my phone from my pocket. "It means that Simon and Killian are standing by for my call." Wicker flicks his eyes at me, confused. "When they receive it, they're prepared to join you at the old courthouse for a meeting."

"About what?" Pace asks, guiding Effie to the pot hanging beside him.

The knowing tension in his voice isn't enough to stop me from putting it out there. "About our father, and what they can do to bind his power." The moment he spins, I reach for him, snagging his shirt hem. "Pace, stop."

Miraculously he does, reaching up to push his fingers through his hair. "Goddamn it."

"I understand why you wanted to run," I begin, looking at Lex. He's as rigid as the statues in the distance. "You were all raised in a cage, and then taught to keep it a secret. It never even occurred to you to look outward instead of inward, because you can't trust them." Holding his stare, I add, "But you can trust me."

After a strained pause, Lex asks, "What did you do?"

I look down at my hands—at the ring I'm now realizing can't be removed. Not without cutting a piece of myself away. It's demented, but in some ways, symbolic. "I realized I'm more than just a Princess. I'm a Royal, and for once, I'm going to be selfish because... because I want it all." I look up, catching Wicker's glare. "I want my family—

East and West—and I want my baby to grow up with fathers who love and protect him. The kind of father his parents never had."

Lex rubs his forehead, nostrils flaring with a deep inhale. "Father can't be ousted, Verity." When he meets my gaze, there's a rueful sort of resignation in them. "PNZ won't back a claim from us."

Wicker slams the shovel into the dirt. "And our son will have two targets on his head instead of one!"

"Not yet," I admit, keeping my voice steady. "But with the power of three Kings behind us, we can buy our safety and stay in Forsyth." I try to imagine what raising a son will even look like. This is Forsyth, so there aren't really many good examples out there.

Sy and Nick's mom did it, though.

But she didn't do it alone.

Pace spins once again, only to snap right back. "So they're going to... what? Politically neuter him?"

At least he doesn't sound completely unhinged about the idea.

"For lack of a better word." Shrugging, I watch Lex carefully, because I get the feeling they'll follow him. "But they're going to need more. I know you've been hoarding leverage—"

Pace bursts, "We're not handing everything we've spent our whole lives building over to three rival houses."

"Who's the third King?" Wicker's voice oozes with quiet fury. "The man who killed my father?" he asks, pinning me with his blue eyes. "The murderer who gave me to Rufus fucking Ashby? That's who you're asking us to trust?"

My heart sinks. I knew some part of them would see even the suggestion as a betrayal, but I couldn't have begun to expect the severity of it.

Wicker looks destroyed.

"I'd never ask that of you," I reply, imbuing the promise with as much intensity as I feel. "Which is why I made the Dukes give me his identity." I glance between the brothers. "Mutually assured destruction."

"They know?" His grip goes slack on the shovel, mouth parting on an aborted inhale. "Who..."

"Timothy Maddox." My lips press into a tight line. "The King of the Barons is Remy's father."

I watch as it hits him, seeing his tormented gaze drift into the distance. "Fucking *Maddox*?"

It's dangerous to give this information to him—I know that. I don't even like knowing it myself. Timothy Maddox destroyed his own son, but long before that, he sentenced Whitaker Kayes to a life of abuse and degradation.

I can only think of one man more vile.

But if they're going to trust me, then I need to trust them.

I take a deep breath. "I know you don't like it, but if we're going to raise this baby together," I nod at Lex, "these are my terms."

Like Pace and Wicker, he's still reeling from the identity of the Baron King, but I watch as he regains focus, eyeing my belly with a skeptical frown. "What if we have terms of our own?"

I thought they might say as much, and the smile I offer him is sour and so, so tired. "This isn't a negotiation, Lex. This is... it's a relationship." I glance at Pace. "No more contracts. No more secrets. No more plans made behind my back—"

"Or plans made behind ours," Pace cuts in, eyebrow raised.

"The plan hasn't been made," I remind him, waving my phone. "That's why I'm here. Because I want you to listen to me. I know I'm not always right, but I promise, I'll always try to understand." Eyes pleading, I add, "I just want you to do the same."

Lex is the one to straighten, turning to me. "This is what it's going to take to keep you? To keep our son?" He flicks his gaze to Wicker. "An alliance with the other houses to control our father?"

It sounds bigger when he says it like that. Enormous. Punching above my weight class. That's what the Dukes would call it.

I take my swing. "Yes."

But he and Pace don't look at me. They turn their gaze toward their brother, something painful and significant passing between them. Another mistake on my part, thinking they'd follow Lex.

They follow each other.

Wicker dips his chin before turning back to the garden bed and slamming the shovel into the dirt.

Lex turns to me, sucking in a bracing inhale. "Make the call."

But just as my finger hovers over the screen, Wicker makes a sharp, startled sound. "Uh, guys? We might wanna hold off on doing that."

Pace glances at his brother. "Why?"

"Well..." Bending, Wicker pulls a stick from the dirt, holding it up to inspect it. "You were saying we need more leverage?"

That's when I realize it's not a stick.

It's a bone.

Lex marches toward him, eyes jumping between the bone and the garden bed. "What the fuck?" He snatches it right out of Wicker's hand, inspecting it. "This is a human femur," he reveals, gaze moving to the dirt. My heart sticks in my throat as he jams a hand into the soil, digging out something else.

A skull.

"Oh my god, is that—" I gasp, clutching at Pace's arm as I stand. "The missing girls?" I stumble back. "Stella?"

Lex looks at me, the confusion on his face turning to urgency. "Hey, no, these are... these are too old to be Stella or any of the other girls. Look." He gestures to the pile of cut nettle bushes. "This place hasn't been disturbed in years."

Beside me, Pace's throat clicks with a swallow. "How old are they?"

"I don't know," Lex admits, forehead creasing as he turns the skull over in his wide palms. "I've taken my share of human anatomy classes, so I might be able to identify the age, sex, and race of a skeleton, but I'll need to find other pieces to—"

Wicker stops digging to say, "Other pieces?" Glancing at Lex, he reaches into the soil and pulls something else free.

A second skull.

"That might take a while."

I look around the solarium, the revelation hitting me like a sledgehammer. "He told me to stay away from that corner of the garden."

Pace spits a low curse, tucking me into his side. "This is why cameras have never been allowed down here."

But it's Wicker who says what we're all thinking, his expression a twisted, gnarled thing. "This is his fucking trophy case, isn't it?"

Lex drops the skull back into the dirt, the line of his jaw tense. "Verity, make the call."

"What are you going to do?" I blink at him, sensing the ominous danger in his voice.

He dusts off his hands, looking between his brothers. "What we do best."

30

Lex

"SECOND THOUGHTS?" Pace asks, wrapping his knuckles. Neither of us looks away from the sight in front of us. It's not the first time I've been on this side of the glass, looking at a mark with his arms strapped to the chair.

It is the first time the mark is my father.

"No," I answer.

It'd been easy enough. The first question he asked Father after we'd barged into his office, lips pulled back in a snarl, was, "Did you bury her there? Did you even let her see me before you killed her?"

I now know he was referring to his mother.

Father's biggest mistake was answering with a smirk. Pace didn't waste muscle on him. He just brought him down with the sharp zap of a Taser. We'd secured Danner up in his quarters, and Thad...

Well, he's off having fun with some hungry DKS attack dogs.

Despite the annoyed expression, Father looks small in the dungeon. Less threatening in our domain than up in his own.

"Do you think he'll talk?" Wicker asks, standing to my left. Pace is on my right. Verity is somewhere upstairs, coordinating with the Lady on this meeting we're supposed to attend in a few hours.

But not before we have a small token of our seriousness to take them.

"Not without a little motivation," Pace says, handing me a pair of gloves and a wooden box.

The one with the whip.

Ever since this became my role in the family, I've made a promise to myself to never gain enjoyment from it. All those people when I was small—the ones who said I was empty and evil—knew then what I know now.

It's in my DNA.

It's the reason Ashby took me away that night, in the midst of blood and flashing lights. He didn't want a son. He wanted his own little purebred psychopath. Someone who could cut and hurt and maim, and feel nothing while doing it.

Just like my *real* father.

With one last glance at one another, Wicker opens the door, the three of us filing through. I haven't been down here in a couple of weeks. Our last mark was some bookie who's been threatening the son of a bureaucrat.

He'd cried.

And I'd felt nothing.

"Oh, you're all so cute," Father says, watching as I set the box and gloves on the worktable next to the other tools Pace has already prepped. His hair is flopped to the side, a fine sheen of sweat covering his brow, but other than that, he looks so pristine. Whole. His smile is sharp enough to cut. "Little boys, tromping around in Daddy's shoes."

I open the box with a slow, mechanical reverence. "Who are the bodies in the garden?"

His eyes track Pace, who's stalking around him in a slow, predatory circle. "Your mother. Is that what you want to hear?" He tips his head back as Pace moves behind him. "She was a bitch, you know. Not in the personality sense, granted. She was actually a rather sweet thing. I kept her chained up in the same room I used to throw you in." Pace doesn't react, continuing his slow path. Father twists to catch his gaze. "Are you listening?" he hisses. "I fucked her, so I had to wait for her to give birth. I had to see if you were mine." He barks a low, menacing laugh. "You weren't, so I slit her throat. Cut her up. Buried her in the solarium."

Pace replies in a toneless voice. "You're lying."

"Naturally," Father sneers. "You'll never really know the truth, because you can't handle it." He looks at Wicker, spitting, "Creation was never something you were made for."

"But I did, didn't I?" Wicker says, tilting his head. "It must have just fucking killed you to get those paternity results."

"Is that what you think?" Father stares at him, unblinking. "Because I'm glad it was you. The only things that make you special are your pretty face and your Baron blood." He leans forward, grinning. "My heir will inherit them both. It's the perfect combination, is it not? Light and dark. Creation and death."

"Two sides of the same coin?"

I stiffen, but am careful not to turn. The last person I want to see me like this is her. "Verity," I warn, "you're supposed to be upstairs, in bed."

But she saunters forward, her chin held high as she takes in the sight of him. "He's not bleeding yet."

She sounds disappointed.

It's the only reason I allow myself to touch her chin, turning her to me. "You don't need to see this part."

Her green eyes bore into mine, and when she surges up to brush a kiss to my mouth, my blood rushes hot and frantic. I take her face in my hands and kiss her back, tasting the sweet edge of approval on her tongue.

"I'm not scared," she whispers, breaking free. "I understand now. It was him."

I follow her like a man possessed. "What was?"

"He told me he came for me because he took a job," Verity says, turning to look at Pace. "To show me that there are two sides of a coin, creation and destruction."

Pace stops, glancing down at Father. "The man in the woods?"

She nods, hand running over her stomach. She should be upstairs, in bed, not down here, stressed and being witness to this.

But something about what she says tugs at a notion flickering at the edge of my mind. "It was a test," I say, cutting my eyes to Wicker. "You hired that bastard to break in, didn't you? You sent the intruder. It was a test to see how we would react under pressure." The reality of the idea hits home.

The crimes this man has committed grow by the second.

"And you failed," Father says, eyes gleaming at Verity in the fickle lamplight. "They can't keep you safe, Daughter. That's what I've been trying to show you." He squirms like he's trying to get closer. "It should be you and me, Verity. We should raise him together. My boys don't understand the coin, but you do."

"He almost killed me," Verity says, bearing down on him. I step forward, never wanting her close to something so toxic again. "He almost killed our son!" Her face twists and she gasps, touching her belly.

"Lagan," Father hisses. "The heir!"

But I don't need his direction. In an instant, I'm in front of her, pushing her back as the blood drains from my face. "You need to be in bed, you're going to—"

"No, no," she says, grasping my arms. The look on her face when she meets my gaze takes my fucking breath away.

She's *smiling*.

"Lex, he's—he's moving. He's *kicking*." Grabbing my hand, she jerks it down to her stomach, flattening my palm to the swell. Her eyes are wide and expectant, but I touch her, and my stomach drops.

I don't feel it.

I don't feel anything.

"Wait," she whispers, and I hold my breath.

Then, it happens.

The tiniest little thump against my palm.

"Holy shit," I breathe, turning to call, "Pace, come feel it."

He's there in a blink, letting Verity and I position his palm. He waits just like I did, his dark eyes pinging back and forth between us. I don't feel it when he does since our hands are too big to find the same small movement, but I still see it in Pace's expression when it happens.

His mouth parts in shock. "I feel him." Glancing at me, he releases a deep, breathless laugh. "Fuck, he's strong." He glances over his shoulder. "Wick, come here. He's a power forward. I feel it."

Wicker doesn't move, standing at the back of the small room with both hands shoved in his pockets.

Gradually, her face falls, eyes swimming with too many emotions to track. "It's okay if you're not ready," she tells him. "This is one more thing you didn't get to make a decision about. I get that."

I don't miss the searing glare she sends Father's way.

"It's not that," he says, taking a halting step closer. "It's..." His eyes are cast down, shoulders sinking with a defeated sigh. "I don't know how to do this, Red. Be a good dad. Take care of a kid." He looks up at Verity from beneath the thick weight of his hair. "I don't know how to take care of you."

"None of us have a fucking clue," Pace says, "but we'll figure it out. We sure as fuck can't be as bad as him."

He grabs Wick by the arm and drags him close. I think he may refuse, and I think we'll have to let him, but my brother slowly places his hand on Verity's stomach, expression tight. I know he feels the baby kick when he snatches his hand back, eyes flying wide. "Jesus, he's really moving in there." After a couple of shocked blinks, he places his palm right back on the spot, exhaling slowly. "That's so fucking weird."

"Right?" Verity says with a nose-scrunching smile. "It feels even crazier from the inside. Like something's fluttering around in there."

She looks happy but pale, and I know it's time for her to get back upstairs. "You need to get into bed." I take her hand and press a kiss against her knuckles. "We've got work to do."

It's a shock when she doesn't argue.

It's not a shock when Pace drags her close, drawing her into a long kiss. Watching her with them used to be strange, but it isn't anymore. They touch her differently than me. Pace holds her belly with one hand and grabs the back of her with the other, and when she pulls away, Wicker is there to tuck her hair behind an ear, making her eyes go glassy with the slow, sensual kiss he gives her.

Maybe a better man would feel jealous that they can give her something I can't.

But I just feel grateful.

"You're staying, right?" I whisper the question just as she meets my own kiss, her palm solid and sure on my chest.

"I'm staying," she assures, "just do me a favor?"

"Anything."

Flicking her eyes behind me, she demands, "Make it hurt."

At least this is a promise I know I can keep.

Once she's gone, we turn to him, and maybe it's petty, but it feels good to know he's seen what we're like without him.

Better.

Stronger.

A family.

Especially given the hard set of his jaw. "Are you really going to withhold my daughter from me?" Father asks. "Refuse me the miracle of my grandson?"

"You don't get it, do you?" I turn back to the worktable, pulling on one glove and then the next. Looking down at the coiled whip nestled inside the box, I say, "You're never going to see either of them again."

Emotion flickers in his eyes, but whatever it means is covered by a dark grin. "You think I can't take whatever it is you're about to hand out? That I don't know what it's like to be on the other side of that whip?" He lifts his chin and in that moment, biology or not, I see a flicker of myself in his defiant gaze. "That child belongs to me. The only way you can stop me is to kill me and throw East End into chaos."

Pace runs his finger down the long, sharp edge of a knife. "Oh, we're not going to kill you, old man."

"That's not what Princes do, is it?" I grip the handle tight, giving the floor a testing lash.

"Practice," Wicker says, closing the door, "makes perfect."

AFTERWORD

Princes of Legacy, book 9 of the Royals of Forsyth U series, will be available in 2024 and is currently available on Amazon.

ALSO BY ANGEL LAWSON

Welcome to the World of Forsyth U—five interconnected series that follow the dark underworld of the Forsyth Greek System. Men, Sex, Guns, Torture, Death, and Drugs have ruled the houses for generations. That is, until the Monarchs change everything.

ACKNOWLEDGMENTS

Queens,

Thank you so much for reading Princes of Ash. As many of you know the last six months have been especially hard on the Angel Lawson Family. Mr. Lawson has been fighting and in treatment for cancer for the last two years and recently had a reoccurrence that has taken up a considerable amount of time. You all are the best group of readers and supporters an author can have. And Sam is the best co-author in the world, putting up with my scatter-brained, in and out, chaotic life while helping make sure this book was released as quickly as possible.

Sinking into the world of Forsyth is one of the things that makes life a little easier right now and I appreciate the love you give this series every day on Facebook, Discord, Instagram and TikTok. It's such a motivator.

There are many others that help this Samgel village run. Christina has stepped into the role of Alpha/Therapist for the two of us and things are running more smoothly than ever. Lisa and Nadia keep the Monarch's group running when we're both too swamped to get in there and answer questions and provide updates. There are so many others that are constant connections, Sara and Megan at the Bookover podcast, the ladies in my Bada$$ author group, and Emma St. Clare who writes the total opposite genre than I do, but provides amazing insight.

Anyway, know that you all are appreciated and help this crazy train stay on the tracks!

Angel

~

Phew. I've really missed hanging out with all you Monarchs in the group and on the discord while I was locked away in my attic writing this bundle of trauma bonding! I'm so excited to get back to you all! It's honestly one the best part of releasing a book for me, getting down in the dirty trenches with you, having fun, and finding out what to create next. So thank you for reading and participating when you can, and for always welcoming me back to the land of the living when I'm done absolutely fucking your soul up. Besties!

They say it takes a village, but Princes of Ash took a small, very neurotic city, without whom I would still be rocking in a corner somewhere eating my hair. Christina deserves at least 5k words of thanks for keeping us sane and steady, but we wrote her 166k words of this book instead, so I hope she feels the love. C, you are a rock who rocks, and I can frankly and very dramatically say that I don't want to write another book without you by my virtual side. So I was serious about rolling you in bubble wrap.

Massive thanks to Nadia as well for not only keeping me company in the night hours when things can get lonely, but also for picking up the slack for me while I was social-media-suspended and keeping me connected to the wonderful Monarchs of the world. A massive thanks to both Lisa and Nikki for doing the same!

Also a big thanks to our audio narrators, Bridget and Jake, for crushing it so completely on Chaos, and I just know they'll do the same for Ash! And much gratitude to Edgar and Crowley, and my husband for wrangling them while I was writing about a bird dropping F bombs because my life is so weird.

Sam